I0760923

THE

FATED BORN SERIES

BOOK TWO

FATED REIGN

Kristin L. Hamblin

This book is a work of fiction. The names, characters, and events in this book are the products of the author's imagination or are used fictitiously. Any similarity to real persons living or dead is coincidental and not intended by the author.

FATED REIGN

Kristin L Hamblin – kristinlhamblin.com

Editing by Kelley Lynn of Cookie Lynn Publishing Services

Map by Angel Perez

Library of Congress Control Number: 2023902687

ISBN: 978-1-959230-04-5

For Jonathan, I loved you even before we were born.

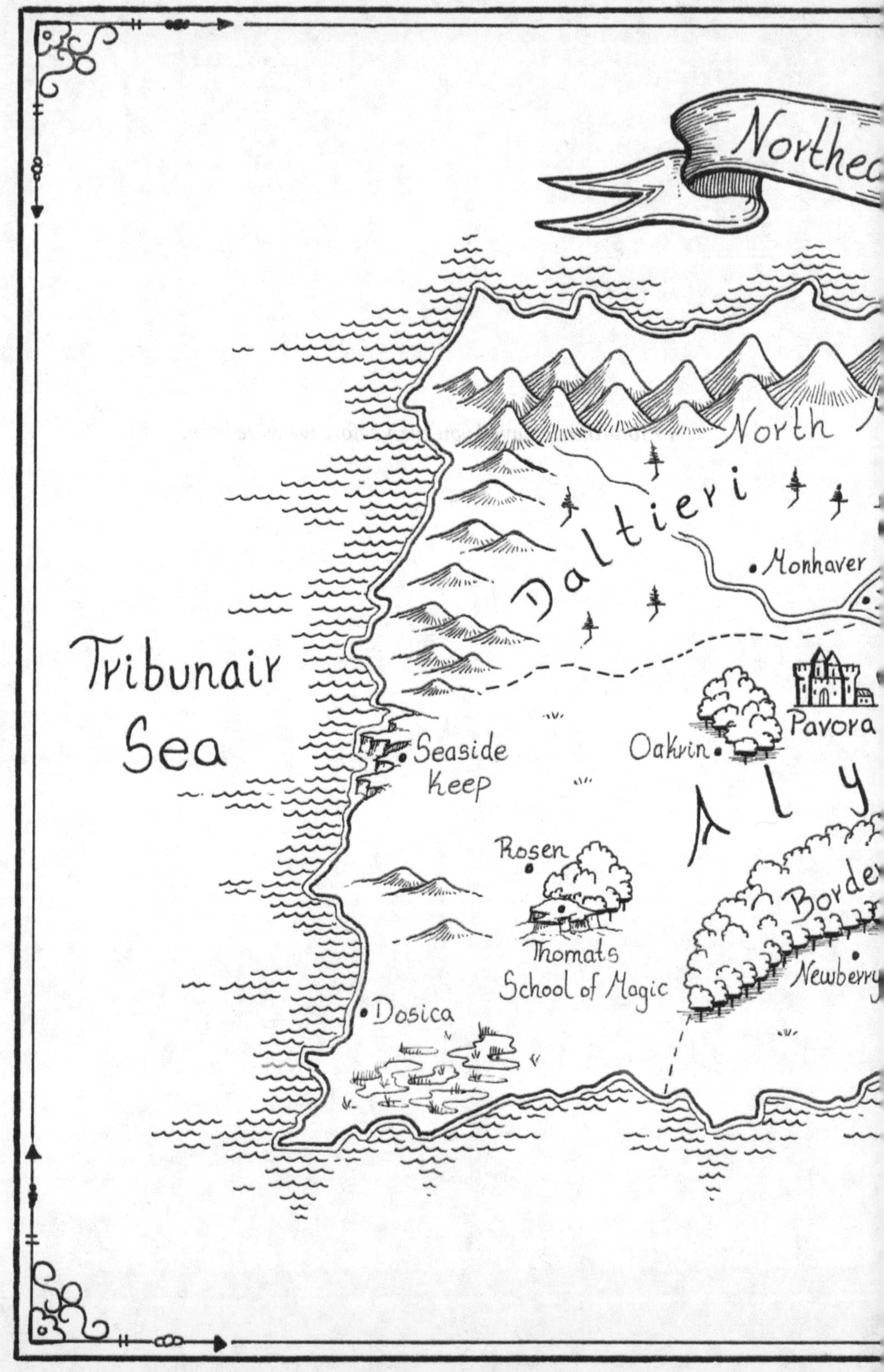

Northea
North
Daltieri
Monhaver
Tribunair Sea
Pavora
Oakrin
Seaside Keep
Rosen
Thomats School of Magic
Borde
Newberry
Dosica

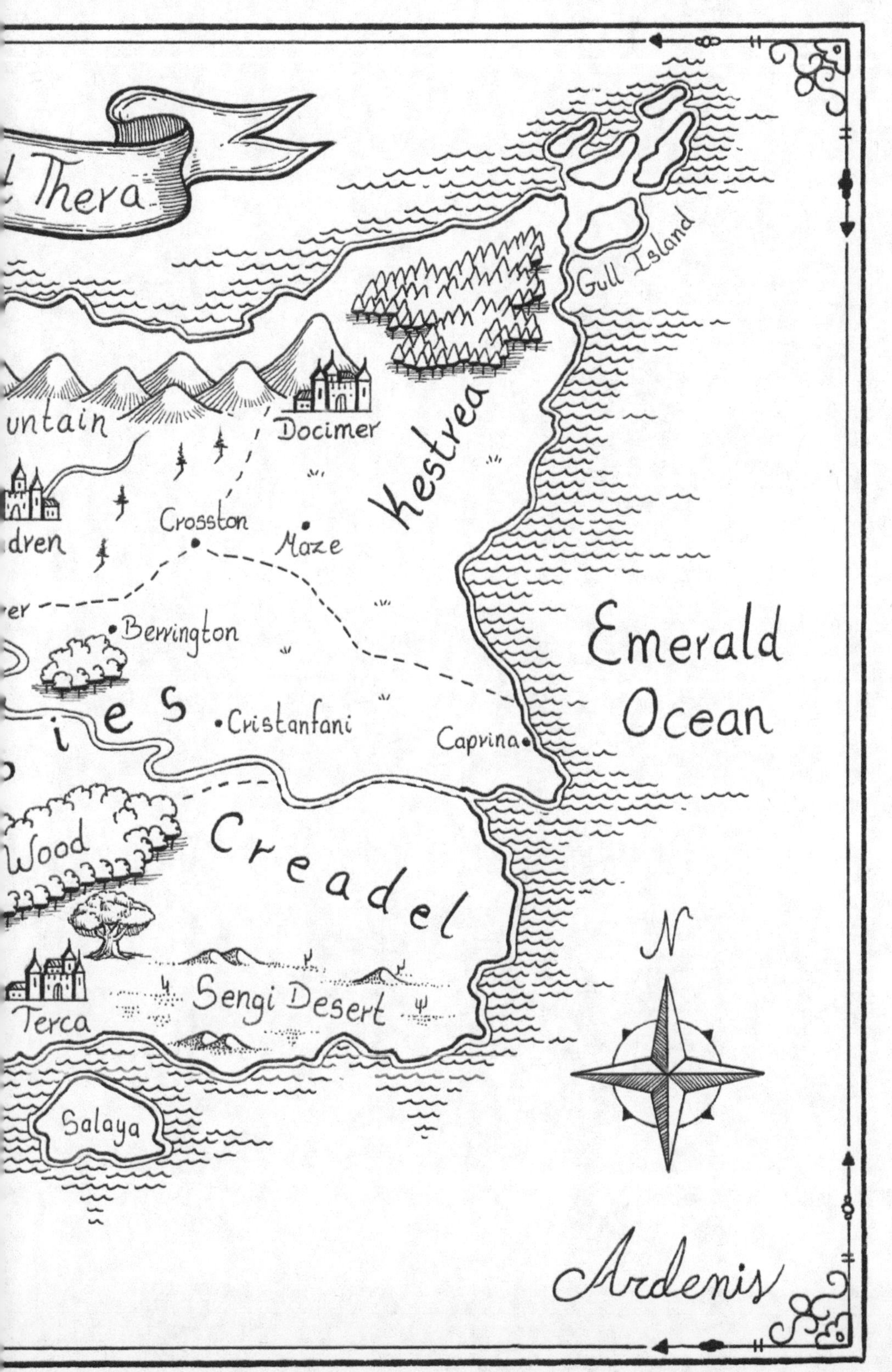
Thera
Gull Island
Docimer
untain
Kestrea
Crosston
Maze
dren
Berrington
Emerald
Ocean
ies
Cristanfani
Caprina
Wood
Creadel
N
Sengi Desert
Terca
Salaya
Ardenis

PROLOGUE

On soft footsteps, Faelyn Eva Rylandor dragged the pilfered sword down the hall of the castle in Pavora. Though tall for an eight-year-old, it was nearly as big as she was. A pleased smile formed on her lips. *Father will be proud.*

The practice leathers she'd taken from the armory hung low over her knees. The straps were a tangle of twists and knots, but held the armor in place well enough. Her blue silk dress peeked out underneath.

Faelyn tightened her grip on the leather pommel and approached the side door to the training yard. Peering around the splintered wood, she looked left and right.

She held her breath and focused her hearing. From the corridor behind her came the muted steps of castle servants and guards walking to their duties. The heavy steps of her nanny, Mary, thumped from her bedroom in an even gait. Faelyn's absence had not been discovered. Mary would be cross when she found Faelyn missing—she was supposed to be practicing her embroidery.

Faelyn frowned and eased back into the shadows. If she went back now, she'd avoid seeing Mary look at her with disappointed eyes and the sad feeling it put in her stomach. Faelyn always tried her best to keep Mary happy, even if she often failed. Her nanny was the only one who truly loved her.

The clack of swords echoed from the training yard. The boys—minor lords' sons lucky enough to be in her father's good graces—practiced their lesson. They laughed at each other's expense while Benton, the swordmaster, barked them into order.

Faelyn seethed, tensing her muscles. Why shouldn't she be allowed to learn swordfighting? Her age shouldn't matter. It shouldn't matter if she was a girl or a shunned princess—she was ready. And so what if some of the boys were older? She could still win. Maybe—if her magic would listen and not interfere.

She gripped the too-large hilt and marched across the dusty yard toward the boys lined in a row. She raised her chin and didn't slow her stride, taking a place next to Patrick at the end. Nearly all seven boys stared with disbelieving smirks. Their gazes flickered from her ears—which she'd forgotten to conceal—to her outfit. She faced Swordmaster Benton, and he lifted an eyebrow.

"Can I help you, Lady Faelyn?" Benton rested a hand on the pommel of his sword, exasperation barely concealed on his weathered face.

"I'm here to learn, Swordmaster Benton." Her melodic voice carried across the training yard. Several heads turned her way.

Patrick sniggered, his red shaggy hair shaking. The rest of the boys joined in. She fought the urge to stick her tongue out at them.

"You're too young for swordfighting, My Lady." He glanced from side to side, probably trying to figure out whose care she'd escaped.

She raised her sword, though she needed two hands and a good amount of strength to do it. "I'll prove to you I'm able. I can do it."

He held his hands up in a placating gesture. His voice remained calm. "Put that away, My Lady. I don't want you to get hurt."

"Give her a chance, Swordmaster Benton," Calem said, then ducked under Patrick's glare. Calem Kinsman was a quiet boy who enjoyed chess more than swordplay. He was son to one of King

Isaac's top advisors, Lord Richard, and he'd never been mean to her like the rest.

"Yeah, give her a chance." Patrick smirked and glanced at his friends. "How about a test? Let me duel her, and if she wins, she can stay." The other boys shared conspiratorial grins.

Faelyn seethed. They deserved what they got if they thought her an easy target.

Benton pointed a finger in warning, but that was as far as it went. Patrick was the son of the king's righthand man, and you didn't cross the king's righthand man.

"Sounds good to me." Faelyn made a sweeping arc with her large sword, impressing herself.

Patrick's smile faltered. "The practice swords are over there." He jerked his head toward the fence.

Faelyn followed his gaze to a rack of wooden swords. She hesitated, then stomped to the fence, traded her iron sword for a wooden one, and turned to face Patrick. He stood, practice sword at the ready. The other boys fanned out behind him. They used their fingers to mime elongated ears. Faelyn's blood boiled, and she clenched her teeth.

Doing her best to push the anger away, she nodded to Benton. He crossed his arms. Patrick circled her like she was prey. She stayed in place, sword raised, pivoting to keep him in front of her. Her eyes followed his movement. She'd studied him and the other boys from her window, practicing the commands only her ears could hear from such a distance.

She prodded her sword forward, and he jerked back. His hair stuck to the sweat breaking out on his forehead. She sensed fear beneath the bravado. Fearful people did stupid things. Like the time she was five, in town with Mary. The townspeople threw rocks at her, and she accidentally burned the nearby fruit stand. Mary said people are always afraid of what they don't understand. Her ears and uncontrolled magic instilled much fear.

The boys said she wasn't even human. Fae, they called her.

She frowned at the distracting memory. Patrick lunged, almost connecting, but she blinked and raised her sword to block. She'd seen the swordmaster teach the boys how to hold a sword and balance their weight, and she mimicked each move, though her leather armor threw her off. Patrick was taller, but she was faster.

She sensed his intention before he struck. She struck first. Her blow landed on his upper arm. The sharp whack as wood met muscle took her by surprise.

Patrick jumped back, his fighting stance forgotten as he examined his arm. His self-doubt coated the air between them. Hate flared in his eyes, promising future punishment, but it was worth it if she won, just this once.

She'd never liked Patrick. He picked on her and called her the worst names when the adults weren't listening; freak, pointy, unwanted. That last one stung the worst. Because it was true.

Patrick sprung, wild swipes seeking a solid hit. Swinging just as wildly, Faelyn blocked every one of them. Her chest swelled with pride. She might actually win.

His slashes became more coordinated. He reared back for another blow. She flicked her sword and hit him right in the side. A winning torso hit. Patrick gaped.

She withheld her celebration and raised her sword to tap out, as the boys did in practice, touching swords together to show the match was over.

Benton stepped forward. "Tap out, Lord Patrick." His tone held a warning.

Patrick shuffled forward and slammed her sword with his. The boys, who had been cheering for him, went silent. Standing behind them, Calem looked both pleased and relieved.

Faelyn gave a thin smile that she couldn't contain as she walked toward Benton. Rather than seeming proud of her victory, his face was set in anger above crossed arms.

"Look out!" Calem said.

She ducked at the whoosh of Patrick's sword as he threw it. Not fast enough. The weapon slammed into the back of her head. The world blurred as it pitched her forward. She landed hard, scraping her palms and knees.

The boys burst into laughter.

Patrick leaned over, casting her into shadow. "You don't belong here, fae freak."

"That's enough, Lord Patrick," Benton said. There wasn't much he could do. If he laid hands on the son of the kingdom's prized lord, they would do more than just exile him from the castle.

Faelyn examined her bleeding palms, tears burning her eyes. Her hands stung with the gritty dirt of the training yard.

Benton kneeled next to her. "Let's go, Lady Faelyn. I'll help you find Mary."

Lady Faelyn. It was so unfair. She should be *Princess* Faelyn, but no one had ever called her that. Groping for her practice sword, she gripped the hilt hard, ignoring the pain from her scraped palms. Her wounds were healing already, anyway. She hopped to her feet and glared at Patrick through watering eyes.

"I do belong here." She raised her sword and ignored Benton's sudden panic. "This is my home. I won that duel, and you cheated." Her voice turned icy.

Benton and Calem both took a step forward.

Patrick snatched his sword off the ground. "How can this be your home if your father doesn't want you?"

The boy's laughter and Benton's protests faded into the sound of her breathing and her tears splattering the oversized armor.

Don't do it, don't do it, don't do it. She squeezed her eyes shut.

Patrick shifted his stance. "Who'd want someone who killed their own mother?"

Faelyn's eyes snapped open. Water funneled from the nearby troughs, draining them, and a sphere of water erupted above her. Perfectly round and as big as she, the water churned within. The boys screamed. Her breath huffed at the magnitude of the magic, and the effort drained her. She struggled to hold the water together, shaking with effort.

Patrick went rigid. He would pay for his words. She pushed it toward him—or tried to. The sphere didn't budge. The shape broke apart, and water cascaded down, soaking her from head to toe.

Patrick chortled, then laughter burst from his lips.

"Lady Faelyn." Benton stormed toward her. "Go inside now before you do something you'll regret."

Face burning with embarrassment and anger, Faelyn concentrated with all her might to reform the water. Her skin tingled as the water lifted, and she gasped. The magic actually listened. The water coalesced, the shape moving toward Patrick. His laughter ceased, and he stumbled backward, falling hard. The water shot forward, engulfing him in a liquid sphere.

People shouted her name, but the sound barely registered. Her pain and fury deafened her. She wasn't unwanted. She wasn't unloved. Patrick thrashed, reaching and fighting for breath. The more he struggled, the faster the water currents churned, tossing him around the sphere.

Benton slapped her across the face, but she didn't flinch away from the boy who'd hurt her time and time again. Patrick's movements slowed.

"Stop her!" Her father's commanding voice cut from across the training yard.

Faelyn snapped back to reality.

She blinked and dropped the magic, sagging nearly to her knees. The sphere crashed to the ground, turning the dust to mud and releasing Patrick from his watery prison. He coughed and heaved water while his friends rushed to his side.

Her eyelids drooped. Heavy exhaustion sent her swaying on her feet. Screaming panic subsided as everyone who'd gathered bowed to their king with gaping mouths. Benton watched her with a mixture of horror and awe.

She hadn't realized how many had gathered in the training yard.

They pointed and whispered. "Lady Faelyn, she nearly killed Lord Patrick."

"Abomination."

"I told you those ears foretold trouble."

"Did you see what she did? She used magic without a mage crystal!"

"The king came out of the castle!"

They didn't know she heard every word.

Mary stepped through a side door of the castle and put a hand over her mouth.

Faelyn's father, King Isaac, didn't look at her. He glared at the crowd for a few more seconds before turning and marching back inside. His guards followed.

Faelyn hung her head. She'd made a mess of things again. She could have really hurt Patrick. All she wanted was to prove she could be a good fighter like her father. Instead, she had shown him her magic side, the side people feared. He couldn't even look at her. Her breathing hitched. He would never love her.

Mary's comforting arms wrapped around her wet form. Faelyn leaned into her, grateful for the body to cushion the blow and shield her from the crowd. Their whispers turned to shouts of outrage. She avoided looking at Patrick. Her face burned with shame. The hate and anger let her magic take control... again.

"Come, Lady Faelyn. Let's get you cleaned up. I'll tell Professor Hadden there'll be no lessons this morning." Mary rubbed Faelyn's arms and led her into the castle, supporting most of her weight. Mary's eyes were sad again.

The hot air turned cool in the shade of the stone walls, sending chills across Faelyn's wet skin. She was usually glad to miss lessons, but she'd attend them night and day to erase what she'd just done.

By the time they arrived at her well-appointed room, Faelyn felt less sleepy. Her room comforted her. She may not be a declared princess, but she still lived in luxury as a young lady of the court. Shaking away from Mary, she rushed to her planter box by the large window. After yanking the curtains closed against the sight of the training yard, she pulled up a chair and stroked the petals of her lily.

Mary sighed and knelt down to work at the knots in the armor straps. Faelyn had tied them several times to keep it in place on her small frame.

“Why doesn’t Father love me?” Faelyn's lower lip jutted out. Sadness flowed through her, and the flower petal beneath her finger turned brown.

Mary's eyes turned sad. “Oh, my sweet girl. He loves you, in his own way. But you know you aren’t allowed to call him that. He’s King Isaac to you, me, and everyone in between.” After hoisting the armor off with a huff, she swept Faelyn’s long golden hair back, exposing her pointed ears. “I wish it wasn't so, but it's best you learn the way of things while you're young."

Mary took a deep breath, as she always did before trying to explain something difficult. "Your mother loved you so much. And King Isaac loved your mother. Her death is not your fault, but it makes him unhappy. Do you understand?”

Faelyn shook her head.

Mary smiled. “One day you will. I pray every day for the Fates to bless you with a brighter future.” She pulled her in close, stroking Faelyn's hair as she knew she liked. “You are destined for great things, Faelyn. But you must control yourself. Walk the path of the future you wish to obtain.”

Faelyn didn’t completely understand everything Mary said, but felt peace nonetheless. She smiled and concentrated, turning the brown petal back to vibrant white.

Mary began to undo the buttons on Faelyn's dress, but a knock at the door stopped her. Professor Hadden—Faelyn recognized him by the clink of the long medallion he always wore over his silk shirt. Mary shot her a warning look, then went into the hall, closing the door behind her.

Faelyn pushed off the chair and settled at her writing desk, dragging a yellow quilt from her bed and wrapping it around her. She hoped there wouldn't be lessons after all. She didn't like it when Professor Hadden gave her extra arithmetic or history work just because she was a "quick study."

"Did you witness what she did to Lord Patrick?" Professor Hadden asked.

Faelyn frowned.

"Shhh. Be quiet," Mary said.

"She almost killed that boy!" His voice rose in volume.

"She'll hear you," Mary pleaded.

"That door is at least two inches thick of solid wood. She cannot hear us all the way out here." But he lowered his voice.

Faelyn opened a drawer in the desk and clicked the latch to the secret compartment in the back. From it, she took a delicate wooden hair comb inlaid with a blue stone. It had been her mother's most prized possession, Mary once said, and like her mother, Faelyn loved looking at it when she felt sad.

"Her magic is out of control. How many more people must get hurt before she's finally sent to Thomats?" This was not the first time Professor Hadden had presented this argument.

"King Isaac forbids it. He wants her to live as normal a life as possible. You know this." Mary sounded exasperated.

Faelyn smiled. So long as her father wanted her close, this was right where she'd be. Her magic served her well enough when she needed it, and without any fancy school.

Mary cleared her throat. "I'll keep her away from the other children. It's the only way. Now if you'll excuse me, I need to get back."

Professor Hadden didn't reply, but Faelyn could imagine his exasperated look, the same one he wore when Faelyn complained about their lessons.

Faelyn slipped the comb back into its hiding place as Mary entered. "Who was that?"

Mary closed the door behind her. She pulled a pink dress from the wardrobe and shook it out. "Professor Hadden, coming to check on you. Now, let's get you dressed. It's almost time for lunch."

Faelyn longed for a nap, but she'd never tell Mary that. She'd think she was a baby. While Mary stripped off her favorite blue dress, still dripping wet, Faelyn stood with her arms hanging limp, only moving when Mary tsked and asked her to pay attention and help.

The sleepiness from using her magic bothered her. Mary had once explained the first time Faelyn used a practice sword and her muscles hurt the next day that she'd only get stronger and less sore with practice. It must be the same with magic. She'd get better at swordfighting and learn to control her magic. Then people would see they needn't fear her. Father would see she was worth loving.

CHAPTER ONE

Ardenis pushed back from the watch window, resisting the urge to scrub his face. *Love her!* he wanted to shout to King Isaac's soul. Isaac was a fool.

The death of Faelyn's mother, Eva, had been a great loss. Ardenis would never forget the horror of that day nearly eighteen years ago, especially Isaac's behavior afterward.

Eva had fallen in love with Damien, and together they taught Ardenis what it means to love. After Damien died, Eva married King Isaac. Ardenis had hoped Eva would be happy with him, but she fell ill and died giving birth to Faelyn.

If it wasn't for Faelyn, Ardenis might have broken down the same way Isaac had—crying, shutting out the world. The Fates and Eva had taught Ardenis of love, in a world where it didn't exist. He had no doubt the object of his own love, Laida, had been born in Thera as Faelyn, the first of her kind—an elf.

Ardenis had watched her every day since, sharing information with his friend Amalia so he had eyes he trusted looking out for her. It helped him through his melancholy over missing Laida.

Mary, Eva's former handmaiden, raised Faelyn ever since her

mother died. Isaac, whose reign should have been so promising, would have nothing to do with his daughter. 'An abomination who killed my true love,' Ardenis heard him say to Mary once, after one of her many failed attempts to reunite father and daughter. Thank the Fates Faelyn had not witnessed that conversation.

Isaac was a fool.

Ardenis stood and left the tower. Mealtimes were kind to Faelyn because the cooks and servants she preferred to dine with mostly treated her like a person, instead of an outcast. She didn't need him watching over her for the moment.

The warm golden sunshine hit his dark blue robe, reminding him of Laida. It took him a long time to stop looking for her golden hair in the sea of black.

He started along the path between the rose bushes, away from the tall, stacked-stone tower, but stopped when the door opened behind him.

"Ardenis," Amalia said, closing the door behind her.

He smiled. Amalia was the only friend he had left in Acantha. His closest friends, Vinia, Bram, and Laida had all been born. He'd tried to make new friends, but their lack of emotional awareness always left him feeling tired. He spent the duration of their conversations pretending his emotions were as muted as everyone else's. The things they discussed, like the evening concerts or the latest council bulletin, didn't interest him. It felt fake and forced. It *was* fake and forced. So even though it wasn't wise—together they had no need to disguise their emotional awareness—he spent his free time with Amalia. Things were easy between them, and he enjoyed her company.

"Are you ready to heckle Hector?" Amalia asked.

"After you." Ardenis grinned and gestured ahead of him toward the dining hall. When they arrived, the open-air building revealed several empty long, rectangular tables.

They went down the line, filling their plates with meats, cheeses, and bread, then sat alone at the bench along one of the tables.

"I still say Faelyn needs formal training," Amalia said between bites. "She may be able to use her magic instinctively, but even after all these years, she can't control it. Not when it really matters. Thomats could help her. And maybe there's more power there she could access with the right knowledge." She waved her sandwich for emphasis.

Ardenis frowned and stared at his plate. Magic was scarcer than ever in Thera, but Faelyn was unique in more ways than one. Thomats *could* help her, but that was not what she needed most.

Amalia sighed. "Look, I know you're still hoping Isaac will come around, but it's not going to happen."

He looked up at her. "She deserves to be loved, Amalia." He shifted his eyes around the room, then lowered his voice. "It kills me that Isaac won't give her what she needs so badly."

"It doesn't help she looks so much like Eva."

He nodded. "Except for—"

"Her hair. I know. And her ears." Amalia resumed eating, so he did too.

Faelyn's hair was one reason Ardenis knew she was Laida. Of all the people in Acantha, Laida had been the only one without black hair. It had been a beautiful pale golden color, the exact shade of Faelyn's.

Ardenis knew he'd exhausted this topic of conversation. Amalia was near the point where she'd tell him to get over it and move on, that this was part of Faelyn's trials on Thera and nothing more. But it always weighed heavily on his mind. It helped to voice his concerns and vent his emotions before delivering a detached report of Theran happenings to the council.

"Hey!" Amalia exclaimed. "You ate all your food."

Ardenis looked down at his empty plate and grinned sheepishly. "Sorry."

She harrumphed. "Here." She scraped some of her food on his plate. They mixed it around with water from their cups until it was a gooey mess, both smiling the entire time.

"It's the little things," she said as they carried their dirty dishes to the wash bin.

They dumped their plates in the bin and were rewarded with Hector's seething glare as he grabbed the dishes for washing. He wore the same blue robes as them, with short black hair and a pointy nose. Hector had once been the great rule enforcer everyone feared to cross wills with, but the council had demoted him for his crimes.

Ardenis felt eyes on his back as he left the dining hall with Amalia, sharing discreet chuckles.

"That never gets old," Ardenis said.

"Never," Amalia agreed with a smile.

"Any news of the elf?" Hector's sharp voice cut through their revelry.

Ardenis drew up short and turned. Hector stood with his hands forming fists in the doorway.

"Why does an ex-enforcer care about an elf?" Ardenis's words came out harsher than he intended. Hector had never hidden his hatred toward the idea that an elf would be born among humans. He thought it went against the natural order of things and had done everything he could to stop it from happening as soon as Ardenis had fated Faelyn's birth.

Amalia placed a hand on Ardenis's arm, and he relaxed his coiled muscles.

"You'll have to check the bulletin like everyone else," Amalia said, with a practiced calm that irritated Ardenis at the moment.

"Ardenis Watcher Fater," a strong voice said from behind, making Ardenis jump. He turned to see one of the new rule enforcers watching him impassively. "Head Councilman Averick requests your presence at the council hall immediately." He looked between him and Amalia and left without waiting for a reply.

Ardenis's heart skipped an entire beat. Was the council truly watching him and Amalia? They'd been entirely too silly and hyper to pass for unaffected Acanthians.

"Better hurry. Maybe they will finally force you to be born like they should have when the freak elf left." Hector smirked and went back under the cover of the dining hall.

Ardenis curled his lip and stomped off toward the council hall, trying to bury his fury. "What do you think Averick wants?" He looked over his shoulder, half expecting an enforcer to be lurking in the shadows. A summoning was a rare thing.

"I don't know. Probably nothing. But you shouldn't allow Hector to affect you that way," Amalia said, following him. "You know what Rhea will do if you prove too emotionally influenced."

"Amalia, he burned down half the transfer hall! He tried to prevent Laida from being born. Why can't anyone seem to remember that?" He spoke too loudly, but didn't care. He still had trouble controlling himself when he got angry. His lips lifted in a slight smile as he realized he had that in common with Faelyn. "Besides, Rhea trusts me."

Head High Councilwoman Rhea had warned Ardenis she'd be watching to make sure he didn't fall further under the influence of his emotions. She didn't know just how far he'd already fallen; she knew nothing of his love for Laida. He had to maintain the outward appearance of being emotionally uninvolved with Thera, or Rhea could force him to be born before his fated time.

Maybe they were about to.

Amalia glanced around. They neared the council courtyard. The expansive stone space was known for echoing words you didn't want others to hear. "No one remembers that because no one else knows about it." She sighed. "I mean it, Arden. Stop letting him upset you. If for no other reason, do it because it will anger him more to see you unaffected."

Ardenis looked to see if she was serious. Her black hair fell in a braid down her back, and her blue eyes held no mirth. Just the normal 'do I have to explain everything to you?' look he had come to know so well.

"Really?" He grinned. He was still new to his emotions, but the thought he could feign neutrality to anger Hector cheered him. It was the only revenge he could safely enact for all Hector had done.

Ardenis approached the council doors flanked by a pair of smooth columns. He swallowed thickly. "Thanks, Amalia. Helpful as always."

Amalia rolled her eyes. "I live to serve." She hesitated. "It probably is nothing, but be careful. I'll be watching out for you." She turned and walked back toward the tower.

Her speech did nothing to alleviate his vibrating nerves. And did she realize what she had just done with her eyes?

It had been nice, more than nice, to have her company and support, but together they were more relaxed. Theran influences seeped into their demeanor and conversations, almost as if they were mortal. What if the enforcer had reported that to Averick?

Ardenis loved not being on guard with her like he was with others, which might have proved dangerous. It was past time to gain some distance from his one remaining friend, and that thought left him hollow inside.

Ardenis entered the council hall with a pounding heart. He hadn't felt this kind of dread in years, not since Hector and Gharum were no longer part of the council. Though he had much to hide, this new council had never suspected him before.

Mina scribbled behind the foyer desk, black hair tucked behind her ear. She smiled as he entered. She'd replaced Hector as the main enforcer and possessed a much more pleasant disposition.

"Ardenis Watcher Fater, how can I help you?" She set down the quill and gave him her full attention.

He appreciated it when people used his full title. It showed respect. "I was summoned to the council."

"Oh? Well, Cadence Watcher is in session, but she should be done shortly." Mina picked up her quill and resumed scribbling in the record book. His breathing ratcheted to panic, and the sound seemed to fill the quiet space.

A short time that felt like a long time later, Cadence exited the council room. She nodded to Ardenis, but did not speak as she left the building. She used to share information with Ardenis in between watching, but it had been a long time since they'd been in each other's confidence. Now she maintained a cool, neutral distance.

He finally entered the council room. Averick, the new head councilman, waved him to the podium atop a small platform on one side of the room. Averick made a fine head councilman since appointed by Rhea after Gharum's horrific corruption. He was strict, but Acantha needed someone close to the rules after nearly the entire council had been replaced. He was one of the few who hadn't given in to Gharum's control and manipulation of the council.

Ardenis took his place in front of the council—twenty men and women seated in tiered rows, their blue robes adorned with a golden embroidery—a map of the northeast region of Thera with a gavel posed above it, the region Ardenis worked and lived in. Their gazes weighed him to the cold floor.

"Let's begin with your report." Averick sat among his council on the front row. He'd adopted Laida's bun hairstyle and made it his own by wearing it low at the back of his head, a fashion replicated by many of the council members.

Reporting on his findings from the watch window was how all Ardenis's sessions began. The regularity of it wasn't comforting this time. He gleaned nothing from Averick's pleasant tone.

"From Daltieri, Queen Vatrice recently welcomed home her heir, Samual, from military training." The woman was more ruthless than her dead husband. Ardenis hated having to spend any time watching that vile kingdom. "They could pose a real threat to the neighboring territories since their gold discovery is serving them so well. They've been slowly altering trade agreements to their favor, especially with Alysies." Daltieri was landlocked by thick coastal mountains, and Alysies held the advantage over them with their multiple seaports and abundant timber. But Isaac's retreat into depression had the vultures circling overhead.

Averick and the council stayed silent, listening, so Ardenis continued. "In Alysies, King Isaac's advisors have petitioned him to name an heir, since he still declines to name Faelyn." *Or talk to her, or look at her, or embrace her and tell her he loves her.* "When that was met with refusal, they suggested he remarry, but Isaac will not. He continues to ignore the needs of his kingdom and people." In fact, Isaac had been so infuriated at the suggestion of replacing Eva, he'd thrown a silver tray full of goblets of wine right at the advisor who'd dared speak up. "Faelyn's coming-of-age ball is very soon."

Averick nodded. The council, most of whom were appointed at the same time as Averick, stared straight ahead. "Faelyn is becoming powerful as she grows, yes?"

Ardenis suppressed a smile as pride rushed through him. Faelyn was very powerful. So far, she had shown earth, fire, wind, and water magic. It roused the council each time Faelyn discovered a new ability because, like her, they were unprecedented.

"She still lacks training, but what she can accomplish even without it is astounding." If only she had someone besides Mary who could show her what she was worth, someone to love her as she should. "That is all I have at this time."

"Thank you for your report, Ardenis." Averick glanced back at his council. "So now we will divulge the reason I've summoned you."

Ardenis held his breath.

"We've come to a consensus as a council and have decided to grant you a rare responsibility." He seemed to gather his words. "We've seen evidence not only through the reports of watchings, but also witnessing the effects those reports have on our population. It seems the repercussions surrounding Faelyn's uniqueness have far-reaching consequences."

Averick spoke so indirectly, Ardenis was ready to rip his hair out. He seemed to expect Ardenis to say something.

"Yes, I agree." He'd seen the ripple Faelyn had made in the world and in Acantha. Even being cast out from society hadn't stopped that. And Ardenis's Fating had set the whole thing in motion.

"While we stress impartiality as one of the utmost rules watchers must follow, there can occasionally be exceptions. We feel the history surrounding Faelyn and what she may do in the future is and will be profound. We also deem you to be particularly strong in your calling, and more able to resist the charms of mortals." Ardenis kept his face blank. "As of today, we are assigning you to watch Faelyn full time, so long as your instincts don't direct you elsewhere."

Ardenis barely kept his mouth from falling open. It took everything in him not to go bounding across the room to hug Averick.

"I'm grateful for this opportunity," Ardenis managed to say, trying to act as indifferent and emotionless as possible. "As always, I'll watch and report."

"Thank you, Watcher Fater. That is all." Averick gave a slight incline of his head, and Ardenis did the same.

He nearly skipped his way back to the tower to tell Amalia. He hadn't been caught for his behavior, in fact, the opposite. Though, why Averick hadn't just given him the assignment without the explanation was odd. It was as if Averick needed to justify his unusual request to Ardenis, a non-council member. Ardenis didn't need a reason to watch Faelyn and nothing else. If the council wanted to give him one, he'd latch onto it with both hands.

Separated by time and distance, there was nothing in Ardenis's power to do for Faelyn, except love her with his whole heart. But maybe his reports about her would encourage more Acanthians to be born, and one of them, one day, would be a help to her.

So he'd watch and report. It was all he could do.

CHAPTER TWO

Faelyn spun in a slow circle in front of her floor mirror. She'd never worn a more form-fitting gown, and she loved it. The bodice squeezed what little breasts she had into perfect cleavage, and the corset made her small waist even tinier, if hard to breathe. The pink rose-colored fabric expanded into a full gown from her hips, and a petticoat finished the look.

"Oh, Mary. I just love it. King Isaac has been most generous." She spun again, earning a scowl from her longtime friend.

"Stand still, will ya? I'm not done with the hemming." On her knees, Mary grabbed at the fabric and continued pinning it to the right length. "To be sure, it will be an event to remember, my dear."

Faelyn beamed. "All the local and foreign courtiers have been invited." And her father would have to acknowledge her as an available, of-age, Lady of the Court. She clasped her hands together with joy.

She'd long given up on the idea of being named heir. Even further back than that, she'd stopped speaking to Mary of such things. It upset Mary, who wasn't so young anymore. Her hair was mostly gray now, and she had more lines on her face each time Faelyn stopped to study her.

"Yes, from the servants' talk, they'll begin to arrive by the end of the week." Mary grunted and pushed herself up off the floor. "There now, let's get this dress off you so I can hem it. You'll be late for your training with Swordmaster Benton."

Faelyn gasped. "Oh!" She glanced out the window where dawn was just lighting up the world. "Hurry, Mary."

She'd been training with the swordmaster for nearly six years now. It was the one thing she looked forward to most in her day.

"Easy now." Together they removed the delicate dress. It had to go over her head in a silky tunnel, and it was a two-person job.

Faelyn threw on her tunic and worn leather armor and rushed from her room.

She ran to the training yard, where servants carrying baskets of laundry or trays of food bustled out of her way. Grabbing a practice sword from the rack, Faelyn slipped down the alley between the castle walls and ran toward the stable. The clearing where she practiced with Swordmaster Benton lay on the other side, just before the first of the perimeter walls. He'd trained her privately since her twelfth birthday.

All the running left her exhilarated. As late as she was, she had no time to stop and listen to the morning birds chirp their beautiful music or give the vegetable garden a caring hand. The song in the wind as it whipped past her would have to do, though it felt foreboding and left her with an uneasiness in her stomach.

She rounded the corner of the extensive wood stable with its scent of fresh hay, and stopped in her tracks.

Benton stood in the clearing swinging his practice sword. Fanned out around him, looking none too pleased about it, were most of the young lords of the castle; what was left of the ones who weren't too old for lessons, minus the new, inexperienced ones. Patrick was there, but she ignored him. He'd gone back to teasing her at every encounter, even after she'd apologized to him. They all wore armor and carried wooden swords, including Calem. The sight of him took her by surprise.

Calem, nearly the same age as her, eyed her with a coy look. They'd become almost friends in the years shared at the castle, if exchanging brief pleasantries and the fact he never picked on her like the other boys counted as friends. Richard, his father, had sent him to Monhaber, the famous preparatory school in Daltieri, owned and run by a single family for generations. Some of the best swordmasters in Thera came from that school, including Swordmaster Benton. Calem must be on holiday.

"Faelyn. Glad you could join us," Benton said.

She inclined her head to him. "What's going on, Swordmaster?" Benton had always trained her separately from the boys. Yet, here they were.

Horses pawed at the ground and whinnied in their stalls, and wind churned the distant trees and stalks of grass.

"The truth of the matter is, I'm tired of being beaten day in and day out. You need a challenge, and since King Isaac won't allow you to leave the castle to train, this is my temporary solution." He swept his sword toward the boys.

Calem had only been studying for a few months, but the school was famed for its tutelage. It would be interesting to see how far he'd come.

Benton caught her looking at Calem. "He is the one who rounded up the others." No surprise there. Before he left, Calem often organized recreational games for the other boys, becoming popular among them. "We will attack you at the same time. Try not to inflict too much damage." He chuckled, then winced.

She flinched at the memory of the day before, when she'd got past Benton's defenses and whacked him hard on the side.

"All at once?" That would be interesting. "No magic, I assume?" She knew the answer, but savored the moment as the boys' eyes went wide.

He pointed his sword at her, glancing once at Patrick. "No magic. Basic kill strikes only."

Oh well. She wasn't very powerful with it anyway.

"Sounds like fun." Faelyn raised her sword, and Benton smiled. Some of the boys looked around uneasily, and some appeared ready to beat on her. Calem met her eyes and nodded. Whatever that meant.

The six of them, including Benton, formed a circle around her.

Faelyn closed her eyes. She breathed in through parted lips. She sensed the woods beyond the castle, and focused her ability closer. She sensed the fear and anger from the boys forced to participate. She felt the eagerness of her swordmaster for her to succeed. She recognized Calem and his intense curiosity and willingness for friendship that had always been there. Faelyn smiled.

"Begin," Benton said.

Her eyes snapped open, and she bent her knees into a ready crouch. Directly in front of her, Benton approached first. He engaged, but she knew his style, his every move before he made it.

Someone rushed her from behind. Without time to spare for style, she charged the swordmaster, locking weapons with him, then shoved with all her might—and okay, fine, maybe just a bit of wind magic, no more than she ever used sparring him. It threw his arms back. She brought her sword down, slowing its descent as it reached his neck.

She didn't have time to take pleasure in his surprise at her quick victory. She spun, sword out, meeting the thrust of her next opponent as he aimed for her back. In the next instant, she ducked as a sword from her left swiped past her head. She jabbed his knees, and he retreated.

The whoosh of a sword came from behind. She raised her arm too late to block. The sword hit her arm, and pain flashed. She stood and glared at the offender—Patrick. His mouth went agape, and she realized she held a ball of flame in her hand. She quickly extinguished it.

Faelyn rushed him, and their swords jarred as they collided. A dull pain throbbed where he hit her arm. She swiped out, and on his retreat, switched hands to her left.

Patrick traded places with another boy so she couldn't attack him head-on. She endured many more injuries to her arms and legs as she fought on—mostly from Calem—but they couldn't land a lethal strike. The boys had changed since she'd stopped training with them from her window. She no longer knew the exact way they moved, though remnants remained. Still, they received more blows than they dealt, and she began to feel the rhythm of the game, despite the many players.

Moving was the key. Constantly moving. They couldn't match her speed and dexterity. She twirled to miss a blow to the side while striking out. Her sword met the armored torso of one of the boys. Patrick! A lethal hit.

She threw her sword behind her, deflecting a blow to her back, then punched Calem in the face. She felt bad about that one. While he nursed his jaw, she took out his three remaining friends with deft movements and sure aim. She breathed, and the air tasted of exultation, sour disappointment, and seething rage.

Panting, she faced Calem, her one remaining opponent. He held his sword up and ready for her attack. His jaw clenched. She'd made him angry with her punch. She caught her breath while he simply waited to see what she'd do next.

It was over, she knew. Calem had never been good at sports, much less swordfighting, though he'd improved vastly during his time away. He must have known it was over, too.

How best to end it? Would the anger in his eyes dissipate if she let him win? Would he still want to be friends if he lost?

"Quit standing around, you two," Benton snapped from the edge of the clearing.

She'd been staring at Calem. Her cheeks warmed.

He approached with caution in his steps, so she met him just as slowly. Their swords met, but merely tapped in a non-aggressive sort of way. It seemed he didn't want to strike the first blow, either.

"What are you doing, Lady Faelyn?" Calem asked in such a low whisper, none of the boys would have heard. The anger had left his eyes. Faelyn wondered for an alarming moment if he knew how well she could hear. She'd tried to keep her best secrets to herself. "Finish it."

What *was* she doing? Her face scrunched in part confusion, part anger, and she swept her sword back to strike. He parried her swing, and the bout was on. Back and forth, their swords clacked together. He left a thousand openings, whether he realized it or not—and she suspected he did—but she didn't take advantage.

"Faelyn!" Her swordmaster reprimanded her.

She narrowed her eyes at the world in general, then feinted left and struck right. Calem's brief training wasn't enough to compensate for the fact she used her left hand, and she landed a blow on his side. The hit would have hurt if not for his armor. He smiled slightly and raised his sword to tap out. She grinned back and whacked his sword in return.

"All right." Benton stepped forward, lifting his sword. "Again."

Yes. Faelyn bounced on her toes. The boys groaned in unison.

They did it twice more before Benton called it quits. Faelyn was bone-tired and sore, despite her quick healing. Never willing to admit she needed a break, she frowned in feigned disappointment while the boys scattered like dandelion seeds in the wind. Calem nodded and grinned before taking off after them.

"You did well." Benton approached her, stopping a sword's length away. He rubbed at his side. "I'm not certain I can convince the young lords to do that again, but I believe the exercise was good for all. You established a good rhythm at the end. Remember that, if we ever train in a group again."

Faelyn smiled. "Yes, Swordmaster."

"I think it's time we branch out and try something different. There's not much more I can teach you." Faelyn looked up, hopeful.

Was he finally going to let her use magic in her training? "How would you like to try knife fighting?"

She frowned. "Sounds good, Swordmaster."

He smiled, pleased with himself.

Training over, her thoughts turned to her coming out ball and Calem's curious behavior.

CHAPTER THREE

Queen Vatrice of Daltieri, in her stiff gown of crinkly silken crimson and jeweled accents, rested on her throne. Once belonging to her deceased husband, King Zachary, the throne had been plain and stripped of ornamentation. Now it represented the crowning achievement of the new Daltieri generation. The entire chair, from foot to crest was adorned in gold, as if dipped in a vat of the melted metal, then molded into filigree patterns before hardening.

From the watch window, Ardenis peered down at the scene with sharp interest. He had read the reports of the vast wealth the country had accumulated since their discovery in the mountains. King Isaac of Alysies, in all his wallowing, had no idea the formidable opponent his neighbor was becoming. His advisors knew, but some were in league with Daltieri, and the others' protests went ignored by a lackadaisical king.

"How much longer will this take, Alister?" Vatrice took a sip of wine from her nearly empty gold goblet.

Alister stood before her, his black mage robes quivering with his shaking arms as he weaved a spell in the air. Dark smoke formed between his hand and his staff, topped with its glowing crystal. He stared into the smoke with deep concentration and didn't answer his queen. Ardenis doubted he'd heard.

An image formed in the smoke. Vatrice sat forward, gold earrings swinging, and passed her drink to a servant. She gazed hard into the spell.

Prince Samual's face glared at her through the image with irritation. "What is it, Mother?" he asked in clipped tones. Behind him, a young woman scrambled for her clothes.

Vatrice smiled—a wicked thing, shaped from years of ruthless tactics and political manipulation. "Apparently summoning you through usual means is insufficient." She narrowed her eyes. "I'll see you in the throne room. Immediately."

Samual stood, exposing his bare chest, muscled with the strength of youth.

"Alister, end it." Vatrice looked away.

Alister released the spell, pulling his staff away from the cloud and opening his fingers wide. He wiped the sweat from his brow.

"That obstinate son of mine will come when I say, or I'll name his eldest sister heir," she said to the room. "Timothy," she called out.

Vatrice's advisor stepped from the shadows wearing a tunic of black with gold thread, and dark grey trousers. He'd aged since Ardenis had last seen him. No longer did he quake with fear, but paced toward her with his nose in the air, confident in his role.

"Yes, Your Majesty." Timothy bowed.

"Leave. And take the servants with you."

Timothy nodded to each servant in the room, and one by one they filed out, leaving Alister and Vatrice alone in the room. The door shut with a bang, its echo absorbed by the new tapestries placed around the stone box of a throne room. Vatrice locked eyes with Alister. He stared at her with such intent, Ardenis wondered if he was casting a spell, but his mage crystal didn't glow.

A slow smile spread on her lips, and her knees slid apart. Alister's gaze flicked to the dress draped over her legs, then to her chest as she trailed her fingers above her low-cut gown. The door opened, and Vatrice closed her legs, sitting up. Alister bowed and stepped to the side of the room.

Samual strode in, wearing an untucked cream-colored silk tunic and disheveled sandy hair. “Yes, Mother?” He carried a simple gold crown, which he plopped on his head.

Ardenis didn't know much about Samual, other than he was the only son of Queen Vatrice, and she'd spent his life molding him to be her mirror image in ruthlessness.

Vatrice eyed him up and down, frowning at his sloppy attire. “You’ve been invited to a coming out ball.”

Samual narrowed his eyes. “You summoned me from my bed to tell me this? Mother, you must be joking.” Anger and disbelief dripped from his words.

“In Alysies.”

Samual threw out his arms. “Okay. And?”

Vatrice smiled, seeming to enjoy drawing it out. Ardenis held his breath, knowing exactly to what she referred. “It’s for Lady Faelyn.”

Samual dropped his arms and studied his mother. “Princess Faelyn? She can’t be almost eighteen already.”

“Make no mistake, Samual. She’s no princess. She has some wealth, to be sure, but otherwise she’s simply an oddity. A fae freak.”

“Then why go?” Samual’s expression turned bored again.

“You’re close in age. She’s only one year your junior. I want you to make friends with her.” Samual grimaced. “Don't make that face. Aside from those freak ears, she's rumored to be very beautiful." Vatrice rubbed her hand down her arm and touched her face. "With flawless skin, smooth golden hair, and eyes as bright as turquoise. Plus all those other features you tend to favor with your... diversions." Samual's grimace remained, and Vatrice frowned. Her voice turned flat. "Find out what you can about her. Find out if there’s any chance she may inherit the throne.” She stood. “Then I want you to kill her father.”

Samual balked. “What? No. Get your assassins to do that. Or

have Alister do it like you did to Father." He punctuated his words with a jerk of his head toward the mage.

Vatrice's face contorted into an angry snarl. She marched up to Samual and slapped him across the face. Samual's head snapped to the side with the force of the blow. He straightened slowly and stared at her with fire in his eyes. She slapped his other cheek. He lunged for her, and she jerked back, but he stopped himself.

Samual smiled, and it was an evil thing to witness from Ardenis's seat in the tower.

"You'll do this, Son, if you want to begin the path of conquest you so desire. I'll not die soon, despite your wishes, and you'll need a kingdom to rule in the meantime, before I kill you myself." Vatrice reached out and stroked Samual's flaming red cheek. "Isaac refuses to name an heir. His most trusted advisors report to me. We're slowly taking over their trade routes." She smirked. "The country is in disarray because of his failure as a king. There is no better time than now."

With impressive restraint, Samual took her wrist and lowered her hand away from his face. "Alright, Mother, since you asked so nicely."

Vatrice smiled up at her son. "Timothy will give you the details and make all the arrangements for your travel. Alister will help you with the poison. Isaac's advisor, Lord Hammond Perring, will help you with your task."

Ardenis gripped the armrests of his chair. This could not be happening. Faelyn had enough trouble without some arrogant prince trying to use her for his own gain.

Samual sneered and turned his back on her. "You may continue your sexual escapades," he said over his shoulder. Vatrice narrowed her eyes as he threw open the double doors to the throne room. "Timothy, I believe you have information for me," he called out into the hall.

Ardenis ended his watch. He locked eyes with Amalia from across the white marble watch window. He jerked his head toward the exit, and she nodded. Together, they stood and left the tower.

Keeping silent, they meandered deeper into the rose garden that never needed tending. The weather was perfect, as it always was in Acantha. The light of day shone down on him, clearing his mind of the poisonous fog that crept in from watching such a disturbed family. The full blooms of the roses filled the air with their fragrant scent, reminding him of Laida and her love of flowers, further distancing him from Thera. The scent reminded him this was home, not the soiled throne room below.

"My instincts have me watching Daltieri as of late," Amalia said, breaking the silence. "I thought you should see what they are planning."

"Thank you." Ardenis sighed. "I warned her of this, before she left."

"Laida?" She raised an eyebrow.

"Yes. I told her to watch out for the heir of Daltieri. I wish she could remember my warning."

Amalia shook her head. "You tempt the Fates too much, Arden. You shouldn't have told her anything."

"She's smart, though. Perhaps she'll see through Samual's scheme."

"And if she doesn't?" Amalia ran her fingertips over a large bloom as they passed.

"We'll watch and see, I suppose." His heart squeezed.

She stopped him with a hand on his arm, but she wouldn't meet his eyes. "Arden... I need to ask you for a favor."

It wasn't like her to be so hesitant. "What kind of favor?"

She glanced around the empty rose garden. Only the chirp of the songbirds sounded in the distance. "Do you remember the kingdom of Lasidia?"

Ardenis thought back through a few centuries of Theran history. Lasidia used to be located southeast of Alysies. It reigned supreme over the land until the final king died without an heir. Ardenis tensed, suddenly aware of what Amalia implied.

"No," he spat, understanding and anger raising his voice. He backed away from Amalia's touch. "That's not going to happen."

Amalia's brow creased in concern. "But it might, Arden."

A rival kingdom overcame Lasidia, killing anyone with even a trace of royal Lasidian blood. His breathing turned ragged. His head shook violently back and forth.

Amalia placed her hands on his shoulders. "Look at me." He lifted his heated gaze to her. "It might, Arden."

"It won't!" he yelled in her face. She flinched back.

His eyes widened. "Amalia, I'm sorry." He reached out and took her hand. "I'm so sorry. The thought of her in danger... I shouldn't have yelled." Amalia had been nothing but kind and patient while he struggled through the constant barrage of newfound Theran emotions. She nodded and squeezed his hand. "Please, what's this favor you ask?"

"I need you to promise me you'll seriously consider that we could be witnessing Faelyn's final days on Thera." It was his turn to flinch. If he could have covered his ears and shut out her words, he would. "You must be prepared to react appropriately if it comes to that. Please, Ardenis. You won't be able to excuse away another emotional outburst. Not with Rhea watching."

He stared at her, and she stared back, unwavering, daring him to argue. They warred silently until finally he let loose a gust of air. "I know you're right, but how can you be so calm, so rational about it? Don't you just want to scream with the thought of what might happen?" He ran his hands through his hair.

"No. Not at all," she said with her signature irritatingly calm and matter-of-fact tone of voice.

"What? And why not? That's our friend down there!" He pointed to the ground at his feet.

Amalia sighed. "Those are all our friends down there. Look, I know how you feel. You've already lost her once. But face reality. One way or another, she will die just like everyone else. Whether it's by Daltieri's hand, Fates' design, or the effects of time. You need to prepare yourself for that fact so you can be ready when it comes. Because it will come." She peered into his eyes. "Do your duty, Arden." The same words she'd told him time and again.

Amalia turned and walked back toward the tower, leaving Ardenis alone. He nearly screamed. He hadn't felt this helpless since the day Eva died nearly eighteen years ago.

Of course, Faelyn would die one day. Death was a natural part of existence. He, of all people, understood that. His perspective as a watcher of Thera—seeing Acanthians leave this premortal life, and watching them born and die on Thera—meant he was more intimate with death. More than those who didn't witness it the way a watcher did. But he hadn't considered it could be so near. And not at the hands of her enemy, before she had the chance to experience *life*.

Worst of all, there wasn't anything he could do about it.

CHAPTER FOUR

When Faelyn gave it some thought, she just knew the awkward matter of her coming out ball had been resolved by Mary. A lady's coming out ball was traditionally held at their parents estate. If the king favored them, or their family was high-ranking, it was held at the castle. Though many joyous holidays had gone uncelebrated since her mother's death, coming out balls were a must to maintain a semblance of normality among the king's supporters. Though only in title, Faelyn had been raised a lady of the court, yet with no family to claim her. Regardless of her father's desire in the matter, Faelyn's ball was to be held at the castle.

In light of the pending arrival of the lords and ladies from across Thera, Benton canceled her daily practice. Instead, Faelyn had to endure countless hours of etiquette and dance lessons.

"Mary, I already know which fork to use and how to speak when spoken to. What more could there be?" They sat at a table in the sitting room, drinking tea.

Mary furrowed her brow. "Despite what you think, you've been left out of the social circle far too long. We're going to tighten up your manners and learn who's who among the aristocracy." Mary smiled and steepled her fingers. "Then there's dancing." Her eyes took on a dreamy quality.

"I don't see why I should bother." Faelyn crossed her arms over her chest. Her father would greet her from his throne as she made her traditional pass through the room on the way to dinner. The rest she couldn't care less about.

"Maybe not, but trust me. You'll be glad when the ball takes place and you know what you're doing."

So she endured the dance lessons, which she secretly enjoyed, and the etiquette lessons, which taught her nothing she didn't already know. She even paid attention while Mary drilled her with a book of renderings of the lord and ladies of Alysies and neighboring kingdoms so she'd know them by sight at the ball.

"Where's my picture?" Faelyn asked, trying to be disagreeable. She'd never posed for a painting before. The portrait hall remained empty of any evidence of her existence. When looking for a good reason to cry, she'd visit it and gaze upon her mother next to the empty spot where her picture should have been. It was almost like looking into a mirror, except for her hair. And her pointed ears.

"Is it because I'm Fae?" she asked Mary while pouting from her window. "Because I have no land or property?" She pounded her fist against the wall. "Because I'm the daughter of a king who won't even look at me?" The wood charred beneath her hand. "Why, Mary?" She turned her gaze in time to see Mary drop her hand from covering her mouth in despair.

Faelyn hung her head in shame. She'd vowed never to speak of such things in front of Mary. Mary did her best. None of this was her fault. She didn't have the answers any more than Faelyn did.

"You're sitting for one this afternoon, as a matter of fact." Mary nodded and smiled at Faelyn's wide eyes. "You'll be an eligible Lady after the ball, and a rendering is only proper."

Faelyn mirrored her smile. Her life was finally turning around.

With the ball only days away, when she wasn't busy grumbling about her lessons, she curled up at her window, growing flowers and watching for the arrival of faraway lords and ladies with eager eyes. But too few came—only a fraction of the amount other girls had for their coming out balls. They were given rooms, or even entire halls of the castle to house them and their entourage. The day before the ball, most of the castle reserved for guests remained empty.

Then the heir of Daltieri arrived. She'd studied the history between their kingdoms, how they'd made war against Alysies several times. She even knew of Prince Samual, though the portrait was of him as a child. He was nearly the same age as her.

Faelyn worked out her frustrations with the lack of guests in the training yard. Alone, she threw herself into drills until she sweated and puffed with exertion. Thrust and parry. Pivot and lunge. The straw dummy didn't stand a chance.

"My Lady?" a smooth male tone inquired. His shoes crunched against sand as he approached.

Faelyn continued throwing her weight and anger into each thrust as she worked through the issues in their group duel from before.

The young man cleared his throat. "Lady Faelyn."

He's asking for me? No one ever came looking for her. Except Mary. Faelyn finished a lethal sequence, and then faced him, panting and full of suspicion. His immaculate clothes were the first thing that alerted her to his position. Black satin with gold sleeves billowing at the shoulders. Crisp linen pants without a smudge of dirt or a hint of stitching except where gold thread decorated the hem. The second thing to alert her was the gold on his fingers and around his neck, but she didn't recognize him from Mary's instruction.

"Yes?" Faelyn raised her eyebrows and lowered her sword.

He smiled and swept his dark hair back from his green eyes. "I'm sorry if I'm interrupting."

She glanced at the sword in her hand. "Not at all." She walked to the weapons rack, putting her sword away. While her back was turned, she smoothed the hair that had come loose from her braid off her sweaty face. “How can I be of assistance, Lord…” She still hadn’t a clue who he was.

“*Prince* Samual, actually. Of Daltieri.” He placed an arm over his chest and bowed, flipping his hair as he rose back up.

The prince of Daltieri? Yes, he did resemble the portrait of his younger self. She’d never met someone from outside her kingdom before. Had she been named heir, she likely would have been betrothed to him. As it stood, he ranked much higher than her, but she didn’t bow. She gave a curtsey instead. It didn’t escape her attention when his lips quirked in an amused smile, but he didn’t comment on her lack of propriety.

“Nice to make your acquaintance, Prince Samual. As you’ve guessed, I’m Lady Faelyn.” She watched him carefully, but he did not react to her words. For most, her title proved a source of discomfort. She looked past Samual around the training yard and to the wings of the castle, but no servant seemed to be in attendance to him. “Are you lost?”

Samual grinned. “Actually, yes. I’m afraid I’ve been separated from my attendant.” There was an awkward pause in which Faelyn realized too late, she was supposed to fill. “I’m trying to find my room.”

“Okay, well, there are a lot of servants about. I’ll have one show you the way.” Faelyn looked around the yard, hoping to see someone she recognized who might help. She spotted a laundry maid who’d smiled at her once, and raised her hand to call to her.

“Would you mind showing me the way?” he asked, halting her action.

“Me?” She looked down, taking in her disheveled state. Training yard dust and hay coated her from head to toe, and she didn’t smell all that good. Was it even proper for her to do so without an escort? A flirtatious smile lit up his eyes. She breathed in the air around her, trying to get a better read on him. He was oddly devoid of emotion, even the friendly emotion his demeanor tried to convey.

What was there to lose? She knew a thousand ways to kill him if he tried anything. “Of course.” She thrust her hands into a bucket, cupping water. She splashed her face, washing off sweat and dirt, then patted dry with a towel. That was as good as it was going to get.

“I honestly have no idea where you’re being housed, but I’d guess the west wing. I can show you the way.” She gestured ahead of her.

He nodded. “I would be most appreciative, My Lady.”

Faelyn suppressed a sigh. The west wing was an enormous distance away. “If we cut through the gardens, we can arrive quicker.”

“I’d love to see the gardens.” He stepped forward with his hands clasped behind his back, looking ever the proper gentleman. His smooth gait carried him closer to her. She doubted he’d ever held a sword in his life.

Faelyn loved the gardens even more than she loved the training yard, so at least there was a bright spot to catering toward this foreign prince.

“Follow me.” She forced a smile and tromped ahead of him. He hurried to catch up, matching her brisk pace.

“Let’s slow down, shall we?” he asked.

She looked over at him, just a couple feet separating them now, and was caught off guard by his good looks. His green eyes looked deeper than she'd originally assumed, as if maybe he actually had depth to his soul. His square jaw lent perfectly to his full lips. He smiled as they left the training yard and glanced at her mouth. She was gaping. She pressed her lips together.

“I’m still rather taxed from my journey here,” he added.

“Forgive me, Prince. I’m used to roaming these grounds at my leisure.” She slowed her pace and sensed his relief.

“Nothing to forgive. Please, call me Samual.” He inclined his head. The path changed from training yard dirt to smooth paving stones.

“I don’t think that would be proper. It wouldn’t be respectful.”

“It’s proper if I say it is.” His tone was playful, friendly. “Besides, you’re practically a princess, so it’s more than proper.”

Faelyn's cheeks burned with shame, and she said no more as they rounded a corner and entered the gardens. The sparkling fountains and rows of rose bushes with their baby buds of reds and yellows did not relieve her unease. The west wing loomed in the distance.

Prince Samual stopped her with a hand on her arm. She stared until he removed it. "I'm sorry, Lady Faelyn. Truly. Was it something I said?"

Faelyn looked into his beseeching eyes and felt his real repentance. But how could he not know what had made her uncomfortable? The entire situation was completely bizarre, and she was starting to suspect why. He thought he could woo her and one day be king of Alysies.

"Don't waste your time on me, Prince Samual, if that's what this is. Maybe the rumors never reached Daltieri, though I doubt that. I will never be a princess." She swept her hair back from her ears, revealing them in dramatic fashion.

Prince Samual glanced at them, but made no reaction other than to gaze back into her eyes. "I don't care about that, Faelyn." His gaze became so intense, she couldn't look away. "I want to know you, title or not."

He meant it. Every word. She couldn't breathe. She'd never had a boy be so forward with her before. She'd never had anyone show interest in her at all. Her stomach fluttered.

"Please, call me Samual." He stepped forward and extended his hand until it cupped her cheek. It felt warm and pleasant against her skin.

But also wrong, somehow. He shouldn't have been touching her, and she shouldn't crave his touch.

She jerked out of his reach. "The west wing is over there." She pointed behind him. It was rude, but she didn't care. "A servant can show you the way." She turned and walked away as fast as she could without losing more of her dignity. He didn't try to stop her.

Pompous prince's ass. Thinks he can touch anyone he wants. Faelyn stormed back to the training yard and picked up where she'd left off.

She hadn't realized how good it would feel to have someone want to be with her, to accept her for who she was. And it scared her because it couldn't be trusted.

CHAPTER FIVE

That pompous ass! Ardenis glared at Samual, who smirked and watched Faelyn until she rounded a corner out of sight from the gardens. Samual shoved his hands into the pockets of his fancy tunic and spun on his heel. He cut through the gardens, precisely where Faelyn had pointed, then entered the west wing of the castle through a side entrance. Passing many servants, he went straight upstairs and into a bedchamber.

The space was well-appointed, with rich wood furnishings, thick rugs, and heavy cream curtains. Porcelain vases littered small tables around the room, interspaced with mirrors in silver frames and gilded doors leading off to private chambers.

"Back so soon, Prince Samual?" Timothy asked. He snapped his fingers, and across the room, a servant poured a goblet of wine and carried it to Samual on a silver platter.

Samual sneered and drained the glass, slamming it forcefully back on the tray. "Not to worry," he said with a calm voice that belied his actions. "It's just a matter of time before she's begging me for the privilege of breaking her heart." He pulled down his long sleeves, one by one, then marched out of the room.

Timothy made an obscene gesture at Samual's retreating back. He crossed the hardwood floor and over a thick lush rug with green intricate swirls, to a cabinet next to a window. He pulled the sheer curtains aside and glanced out. Satisfied, he yanked a second set of heavier cream-colored curtains closed, blocking out the light. Opening the cabinet, he displayed a silver decanter.

With shaking hands, he reached out, but then drew his fingers back and shut the cabinet door. He spun, glancing around the room at the other servants, and cleared his throat. Then once more, he reached into the cabinet, grabbed the decanter, and passed it off to a servant.

Ardenis ended his watch and glanced at Amalia on the other side of the watch window. She stared into the marble pool, concentrating on Thera. Her instincts had kept her in Daltieri recently, and she told Ardenis everything, even the things the council didn't share with the people of Acantha—especially those things. An army massed in Daltieri, well trained and well fed off the kingdom's influx of gold from the North Mountains.

Ardenis's fear for Faelyn's safety grew by the day. Queen Vatrice had everything in place. With Isaac's passivity and ignorance of the corruption within his own court, he might not even need to be poisoned first. Daltieri's army could sweep in and be done with it. And now her vile son had taken the liberty of touching Faelyn's soft, innocent cheek.

Ardenis wasn't naive enough to think Faelyn would never fall in love. He wanted her to know happiness and have her love reciprocated by a worthy man. Samual would never be that man.

Ardenis gripped the ledge in front of him. Closing his eyes, he put all his effort into not praying for lightning to strike Samual down. A nudge from his instincts touched upon his awareness. Thera beckoned.

His eyes snapped open, and there Hector stood, hovering behind Amalia. He peered over her into the watch window. Ardenis stood, scraping his chair back. Hector glanced up and smirked.

"You can't be in here." Ardenis remembered to keep his voice down, but still some of the day watchers looked up.

Amalia remained within her watch. It was irrational for Hector to be staring into the watch window. He couldn't see anything without being gifted with the ability to watch, and that could only occur with high council approval, which would never happen.

"I've been promoted, Ardenis." Hector locked unblinking eyes with him.

Ardenis stared in disbelief. "Why would they make you enforcer again?" He wanted to shout Amalia's name and bring her out of Thera. He'd have to speak to the council immediately. Hector could not be an enforcer of Acantha.

Hector frowned. "Actually, Ardenis, I've been made a watcher."

"*What?*" Ardenis's mouth dropped open.

Amalia came out of her watch. She took one look at Ardenis's face, then followed his gaze behind her. She jumped, glaring.

The day watchers smiled at Hector and offered their congratulations. It had been decades since they'd received a new watcher.

Ardenis ignored them. "You are joking. There is no way you're a watcher."

Amalia stared at Ardenis in disbelief.

"Acanthians don't lie, Ardenis." Hector nodded at the smiling faces of the day watchers and took a seat next to Cadence. "Cadence has agreed to help me, but I believe I can handle it all right." His lips twisted into a slow smile. Ardenis shot his gaze to Cadence, and she nodded while staring at her hands. "It will be fascinating to finally see the glorious Thera I've only witnessed through second-rate renderings."

Ardenis clenched his fists, and Amalia shot him a warning look.

"Welcome to the tower, Hector," Amalia said with an overabundance of sweetness. "I'll give you your first lesson. Ardenis is the longest-standing watcher. That's his chair." She pointed to where Ardenis stood. "If he's not here, it remains empty. We defer important dealings to him."

The day watchers nodded their agreement. Ardenis felt a swell of pride, and gratitude toward Amalia. What she said was true, though it was never spoken aloud. Hector scowled through her speech, but did not argue.

"Now, for your second lesson," Amalia said. "Take care not to become emotionally involved with any person or event in Thera. We wouldn't want you emotionally altered and forced to be born before your time." She delivered her unconcealed threat, nodded to Ardenis, and left. Hector's lips curled into a snarl. His spurned love for Amalia had given way to hate.

Ardenis could only watch the scene unfold. He felt horrorstruck. As helpless as he was to alter happenings on Thera, now things were falling apart in Acantha.

Cadence placed a hand on Hector's arm, and his face snapped into neutrality.

What in the Hereafter is going on? Ardenis's emotions pulled him in so many different directions. He wanted to follow Amalia and make sure she was okay. He wanted to go straight to the council and confirm this insanity was all a farce. A tingling at the back of his mind became a hammering when he acknowledged it. Thera still called to him.

'Do your duty,' Amalia always said to him.

'Don't allow yourself to fall further from Acantha,' Rhea Head High Councilwoman had said.

Ardenis ignored Hector, who sat listening to Cadence's whispering, and rushed back into his chair at the watch window. His instincts thundered into him. He plunged into Thera, briefly closing his eyes. His instincts would lead him.

When he opened his eyes, he beheld Isaac in his throne room, surrounded by his long-time advisors and lords. Richard, who'd advised Isaac's dad, was thicker around the middle and graying. He balanced on the edge of the chair on Isaac's right. Hammond, wearing thick gold rings and a stern expression, lounged on his left.

Three more lords formed a circle for their counsel with the king. The table in the middle held trays of meats, cheeses, and pastries. And a silver decanter. Ardenis gripped the folds of his robe in his fists.

Isaac's rigid posture feigned attentiveness, but he stared at the table, not speaking while his advisors shouted in circles around him.

"I know how to read the reports, Hammond." Richard beat his fist against his palm. "There is movement in the kingdom of Daltieri. They've been buying salt from us. Much more than one nation should need, especially one with access to the mountains. Fish, too. And they're paying less money than the supplies are worth."

Hammond shook his head vigorously. "Why do you question what is good for our kingdom's economy?" Some of the others nodded.

"That's not all," Richard said. "I've heard reports from several lords approached by representatives of Daltieri for rights to harvest their trees." He glanced at Isaac, but Isaac remained impassive, as if he wasn't physically present. Richard looked to the others for support. "Wood." He scooted impossibly more forward in his chair. "Tell me, gentlemen, why does Daltieri need so much wood?"

Hammond glared. "Those reports also state Daltieri's population is expanding. They need wood for their houses." Richard opened his mouth to argue, but Hammond cut him off. "King Isaac, are you well? Are you in need of refreshment?"

Ardenis gaped. How brazen.

Isaac blinked and looked up. Hammond nodded to the side of the room, and one of Prince Samual's servants, dressed in castle livery, stepped away from the wall and crossed to their table. He lifted the silver decanter and poured a small amount of the ruby-red liquid into a goblet.

This couldn't be happening. Was this the end of Isaac's reign? He hadn't named Faelyn heir yet. Ardenis wished Amalia was here—wished he could scream.

The servant handed the goblet over to Isaac under the watchful eyes of both Hammond and Richard. Isaac took it in his hand. He stared into the golden goblet and swirled the liquid around.

"Let's move on," Richard said with gruff impatience. He'd grown more assertive under Isaac's rule. He'd had to. "If you don't want to discuss immediate outside threats to Alysies, let's talk about the unrest within our own kingdom." Hammond didn't respond. He watched from the corner of his eye as Isaac contemplated his drink. "The lords worry about what will become of the kingdom without an heir. They've increased taxes to pay for what they consider an inevitable war. More of our people are starving than ever before."

Richard looked around their group, but no one responded. He pounded his fist on the table, causing everyone to jump. Isaac's eyes snapped from his goblet to his advisor.

Richard's eyes went wide. "Forgive my outburst, Your Majesty, but the future of our kingdom depends on the solutions we can formulate right now, and you all," he gestured to the other advisors, "act as if we're discussing the weather!"

"Richard." Isaac finally spoke, his tone almost pitying.

"Fine." Richard pulled a letter from his pocket. His movements were hurried, fidgety, as if he'd lost confidence all of a sudden. "This is dated a week ago, Your Majesty. It was discovered amongst Lord Hammond's personal correspondence." Hammond's hand twitched toward his sword. "A mayor in the village of Berrington—a village within Lord Hammond's own lands!—states they witnessed troops marching on the outskirts of town."

Amalia hadn't said anything about troop movement. She watched Daltieri the closest. If the report was true she would have said something.

Isaac rounded on Hammond.

"Your Majesty." Hammond smiled as he would when humoring a disruptive child. "I sent a rider at once to confirm this report, and it was relayed to me that the pig farmer who made this claim was mistaken, so I did not think it relevant to bring to your attention. As for what Richard was doing nosing around my rooms," he glared at Richard, "I will reserve that inquiry for another time."

Isaac relaxed and turned his gaze to Richard, who sputtered in disbelief. "Richard, you've been my advisor for a long time. And my father's before me." He smiled warmly. "Perhaps it's time for a rest. There's no shame in it." He swirled his cup.

Ardenis groaned inwardly.

Richard's face went deep red, and Hammond coughed to cover a smirk. Isaac looked at the drink in his hand, then brought it to his lips.

Ardenis held his breath.

The throne room door opened, and Swordmaster Benton walked past the guards. Heads swiveled his way.

Isaac removed the goblet from his lips without drinking.

"What are you doing here?" Isaac asked. He stood and held out the perilous goblet, then waved it when a servant didn't immediately take it.

Hammond gave an almost imperceptible nod of his head. Samual's servant took the goblet and the silver decanter and departed the throne room.

Ardenis breathed a sigh of relief.

Benton approached and bowed low. "I'm here with a report."

"Who let you in?" Hammond asked, voice booming. "We're in the middle of a council session. Guards, escort him out."

"Report," Isaac said, as if Hammond hadn't spoken. The others took this time to nibble their pastries.

Benton cleared his throat. "Lady Faelyn is nearing the completion of her training. I'm most impressed with her progress. I'd like permission to send her to Thomats. She's learned all she can from me, and this would help her continue her training."

"The magic school?" Hammond burst out a laugh. "Nonsense."

Isaac stared at Benton for a long time, a bored expression on his face. "That will never happen. And never request it again. Get out."

Benton looked as if he would argue, or maybe explain the need, but he bowed instead, showing himself from the room.

Before ending his watch, Ardenis checked in on Faelyn. She sat at the desk in her room, listening to Professor Hadden lecturing. She scribbled notes on parchment. This would be one of her final lessons, if not *the* final lesson. The world didn't believe in educating women, even ladies, beyond eighteen, which would happen in two days' time.

CHAPTER SIX

A knock on Faelyn's door awoke her from a deep sleep. She blinked against the bright light of full morning streaming between her curtains.

Unbeknownst to Mary, Faelyn had been up late walking the gardens. She didn't need the sun to find her way, and she found herself drawn to the roses. Trailing her hands, she'd turned buds to blooms as she went. She made it as far as the west wing before puzzling out why she was so wound up.

Today she would see her father. She'd bow to him, and he'd be forced to acknowledge her. Then the whole of Thera would recognize her as an eligible lady, even if not a princess. Calem would be there. And Samual. His directness and assumptions irritated her, but for more than one reason. No boy, much less a prince of Daltieri, had ever been interested in her—a fae freak, the people called her. Not even the girls would befriend her. Sure, her body had filled out in the right places, and Mary said her beauty was unparalleled. If only people could see past her ears, is what Mary didn't say. The fact that Samual seemed interested, and the fact she couldn't get a good read on him or his intentions, unnerved her.

The knock sounded again, and Faelyn groaned, shoving her head under her goose-down pillow. "Lady Faelyn, you must rise," Mary called from the hall. She entered without waiting for a response, tsking at Faelyn. "Prince Samual has requested to break his fast with you."

Faelyn shot up from underneath her pillow. "Whatever does he want to dine with me for?" Disbelief colored her tone.

Mary smiled with a twinkle of excitement. "He's here for your coming out ball. Perhaps he seeks to strengthen his kingdom with your friendship." Mary opened the wardrobe and pulled out a slimming, powder-blue day dress. She held it in the light from the window and nodded.

Faelyn rolled her eyes, then rolled over in bed. "If that's his goal, it will only have the opposite effect. Tell him I respectfully decline."

Mary gasped. "You can't decline! He's a prince."

And I'm a princess, she longed to retort.

Mary's lips formed a slight frown as she folded the dress over her arm and leaned on Faelyn's bed. She stroked Faelyn's hair, smoothing it down the length of her back. Faelyn loved when she did this and closed her eyes in contentment.

"You're grown up now, My Lady." Mary sniffled. "That's what we are celebrating today. And with this step comes new responsibilities. But it's good. You deserve the chance to become more than you are. More than you've been allowed to be."

Faelyn caught Mary's hand as she reached to stroke her hair again. She kissed the back of it, sending thoughts of love, health, and strength into her. Mary gave a quick intake of breath, then smiled.

"Alright, Mary. I'll do it for you."

"Thank you, my treasure, but don't do it for me. Do it for yourself."

Faelyn gave her a long hug. Warmth and love filled her up, but all too soon, she had to let go.

Mary stood and wiped her eyes. "Well," she said, fluffing out the blue dress, "let's get you ready."

When Faelyn was bathed and dressed, her hair piled high on her head in an elegant updo, she felt better. The tight dress made it difficult to breathe, but she didn't mind. Gone were the previous day's dirt, sweat, worn trousers and tunic, and bitter feelings. In its place, the mirror revealed someone who looked the part of a princess. A princess with pointy ears. She touched them, then swept her hand over her hair to hide the action.

Mary caught her looking at her reflection. "You're beautiful under all the mud." She winked, and Faelyn laughed. The sound tinkled around the room, and Mary beamed.

"I want to wear my mother's comb." Faelyn felt herself blush. She didn't talk about her mother and avoided mentioning her to Mary, but it seemed right.

Mary's eyes filled with tears. She nodded and fetched the comb from the secret compartment in the desk drawer. "It suits this dress just fine. We'll need to take it off for the ball this evening, though." She slipped the comb into her hair.

Faelyn touched it with light fingers, twisting to see in the mirror. The turquoise stone was a different shade than the blue of the dress, but it didn't matter. She hoped her mother would be proud.

"Okay, Mary." Faelyn took a deep breath and faced her friend. "Where am I meeting his royal highness?"

"In the garden, actually. His servant mentioned something about Prince Samual being promised a tour."

Faelyn groaned and glanced at her bed.

"None of that." Mary opened the door to her room. "This way." She beckoned, and Faelyn followed her through the stone hallways and winding staircases until they exited the back door leading into the gardens. "I won't stand around and eavesdrop on your breakfast. There will be plenty of servants on hand to chaperone and for anything you need." Mary stopped outside the garden near a bubbling fountain. "Have a good time."

Faelyn nodded and licked her lips, then walked into the garden where Mary pointed. It was the same path she'd taken the night before, marked by an obvious trail of fragrant rose blooms bursting open between the tiny buds she'd left untouched. The occasional servant nodded as she made her way into a clearing within the garden. There, a table was set for two beside a buffet overflowing with enough food to feed the Daltieri army.

Samual sat at the garden table the ladies of the court used for afternoon teas on nice days. He hurried to his feet when he saw her, his mouth gaping. She fidgeted with her dress. He'd only seen her in dirty, reeking training clothes.

He did his one-armed bow thing again, and Faelyn found she was smiling. She breathed in the scents around her and sensed his attraction. It set her stomach to fluttering.

"Good morning, Prince Samual." Faelyn avoided bowing or curtseying.

"Lady Faelyn." He cleared his throat. "Won't you be seated?" He gestured toward the other chair, placed next to his instead of across, and a servant pulled it out for her.

A white tablecloth, crystal goblets, a dozen silver forks and spoons, and a porcelain vase of her own rose blooms turned the ordinary setting into an elegant affair.

She wasn't used to such formal dining. Her meals were spent avoiding the courtiers, hidden in the kitchen where the servants took their meals. Running through the list of what she knew of etiquette, she took her seat. Someone tucked it in behind her. Samual sat as well, and the servants began filling their plates. One filled her glass with squeezed orange juice—a rare treat since oranges had to come all the way from Creadel.

Both seemed determined not to open the conversation. Samual watched her, so she stared at her plate heaped with food.

After more awkward silence, Samual set down his glass. "I'm sorry if I was out of line yesterday." She sensed he told the truth. "I haven't had a lot of experience with women, and I'm afraid I've overstepped my bounds. I hope you can forgive me."

She remembered the touch of his hand on her cheek. A part of her wondered what the touch of his lips would feel like. "You're forgiven," she said quickly. "I'd like to apologize as well, for not seeing you to your room. I trust you found your way all right."

Samual laughed, so she smiled. "I think I surprised a couple of your servants, but I managed." He picked up his fork and ate.

"They're not my servants, but I'm glad you managed." She picked up her fork and took a bite from a bowl of cream topped with tiny pieces of colorful fruits. The flavors burst on her tongue, more vibrant and delicious than she could have imagined.

"They should be." The intensity of his words cut through her delight. "They're yours by birth. Why won't your father claim you?"

Caught off guard, she didn't have time to come up with any answer but the truth. "Because I killed my mother." Her eyes filled with mortifying tears, which threatened to overflow.

He placed a warm hand over hers where it rested on her leg. "Despite what you may think, word does travel to Daltieri. You didn't kill your mother. She was sick, and there were complications." He squeezed her hand and let go. "Forgive me for saying so, but your father is making a mistake. You were born to rule." He continued eating, giving her time to recover.

She knew her mother had been sick, but the other children always blamed her for her mother's death. She thought that was what everyone believed. To hear that wasn't so caressed the deepest of her deep wounds.

Faelyn dabbed her eyes with a napkin and smiled at Samual. He'd said exactly what she needed to hear. He was the only one who'd ever claimed her father was wrong. They talked of lighter things for the duration of their meal and their walk through the garden afterward.

Faelyn found herself at ease in Samual's company. She forgot to keep her guard up against the insults her instincts had been honed to expect. By the end of the walk, she held Samual's arm, smiling and laughing as he spoke of his older sisters picking on him back in Daltieri. The more time they spent together, the more unguarded his eyes became—the more she sensed his feelings develop, and the wider her smile grew.

When they reached the training yard, Faelyn let go of his arm and stepped away. "I need to get back, but I had a lovely time." Faelyn meant it. It was one of the best times she'd ever had.

Samual took her hand and raised it to his lips. His mouth on her skin sent shivers up her arm. "Will you save me a dance tonight?"

She beamed, and her face burned. "I will, Prince Samual."

"Just Samual." He nodded, pleased, and let go of her hand.

Faelyn returned to her room, entering with a sigh and a smile. Even if nothing came of it, it was nice to be around someone her own age who treated her with respect.

"Where have you been?" Mary rushed over and placed her hands on her hips. "We are behind schedule to get you ready for tonight." Faelyn opened her mouth to gush over the great time she'd had, but Mary cut her off. "Oh, never mind all that. To the baths with you."

"Another bath?" Faelyn launched into a valid argument about why two baths in one day were completely unnecessary, but then the stern look on Mary's face stopped her. She frowned and marched to the bathing room.

After a warm soak and scrub—which the servants handled for her, much to her embarrassment—her hair, makeup, and dress were redone. Her mother's comb was placed back in the drawer, and instead her hair was styled into elegant curls and then pinned up with pearls. Faelyn's nervousness grew as the time drew near. For a distraction, she ran through sword drills in her head until Mary snapped at her for moving too much.

When she was ready, Mary told her to spin in a slow circle. All the servants who'd helped her exclaimed how beautiful she looked. When she faced Mary, Mary gasped and covered her mouth. "Oh, Faelyn. You look just like your mother."

She walked to the mirror, and there stood the portrait that hung in the castle. If her hair had been dark instead of golden, and her face less narrow, she could be mistaken for her mother's ghost. Her rose-colored dress fit perfectly, narrowing at the waist, with the hem just barely skimming the floor, thanks to Mary's skills as a seamstress. Pearls had been sown into the bodice and matched her hair. The updo subtly crowned her head, then draped to conceal her pointed ears.

Mary beamed and wiped away a tear.

A bell tolled from the courtyard announcing the time. Mary jumped. "Oh my goodness, it's late. Let's get you down to the throne room."

Mary's jitteriness grated Faelyn's nerves. Outside the window, over the rooftops of the castle beyond the training yard, the sun had turned golden orange in the sky, beginning its quick descent into the end of another day. This was her night, and tomorrow she'd be a Lady of the court, a woman of age to marry or be bequeathed the throne.

Holding her dress so as not to trip, she followed Mary at a brisk pace down the hall, gulping down air in a futile effort to calm her racing heart. The throne room was the first stop, where all coming-of-age ladies of the court passed through and bowed to the king before going to a feast in their honor. Today it'd be just her.

Footsteps and conversation echoed out into the hall. Her own footsteps were silent in her soft shoes, a product of years of practice sneaking around the castle. His vision blurred at the edges.

Mary stopped before the closed throne room doors and smoothed over Faelyn's hair, adjusting one of the pearls. "It's time, My Lady." She turned to the two guards flanking the door. "Lady Faelyn is here for her audience with the king."

Faelyn fluffed out her large skirts. She struggled to remember how to breathe.

"The king is not seeing anyone at this time," one of the guards said, attention fixed on the stone wall ahead. "Please continue to the dining hall."

Mary gasped and looked at Faelyn.

The seconds ticked by, marked by a pounding roar in Faelyn's ears.

"What?" cried Mary. "How could that be? Lady Faelyn is coming of age. The king must acknowledge her."

Faelyn latched on to Mary's words. There had to be a mistake. Perhaps the guards forgot what day it was.

The other guard wrinkled his nose. "The king has given his orders, woman. To the dining hall with you."

Faelyn's breath shook. It'd be okay. Mary would sort it out.

Mary bristled. "This is ridiculous. Come, Lady Faelyn. Your guests await. Let's enjoy your feast."

The roar in her ears grew louder. She stared at the throne room doors, chest burning with the crush of emotions. Disappointment, agony, anger, and disbelief—then shame that she didn't consider this as a possibility. Her hammering heart became a stabbing pain that threatened to bring her to her knees. Grief roiled inside, while her outward stillness tried to hide it away. After all, she'd had a lifetime to shove this kind of hurt to a place it couldn't touch her.

He'd denied her everything, and she'd accepted it. She wouldn't accept this. She relaxed into her anger.

The world turned dark.

The braziers flanking the door dimmed to a dull glow. The lanterns lining the stone hallway guttered out. Faelyn extinguished the light until her surroundings were as dark as she felt inside.

The guards unsheathed their swords, backing up into the wall.

Mary grabbed her arm, then hissed and pulled away. The palm of her hand turned bright red.

"Come, Faelyn. We mustn't keep your guests waiting." Mary's voice shook.

The energy from the fire hovered invisible at her fingertips, waiting for her to direct it. Her eyes locked on the throne room doors.

"Lady Faelyn," a male voice called from down the hall.

Faelyn followed the sound. "Samual." The sight of him lifted something inside her, and she released the magic. The torches and lanterns ignited again.

The guards huddled closer together.

Faelyn lunged for Mary's hand, intending to heal her, but the redness was already fading. The pain of hurting Mary pierced one hundred times deeper than her father's rejection. "I'm so sorry," Faelyn said, but Mary didn't reply, too busy bowing at Samual's approach.

"Did I miss it?" Samual asked, seemingly unaware that she'd almost done something regrettable. "Let me escort you to the feast." He offered his arm, and she took it automatically, belatedly realizing she might burn him, but her skin had returned to normal. "You look exquisite this evening."

So did he, in a long coat of black with gold braids and buttons, hair combed back with a part down the middle, and striking eyes that didn't judge her for what had just happened.

Faelyn took a deep breath, shoving her devastation down, down, down. "Thank you, Samual. Yes, I'm done here." She couldn't disguise the bitterness in her voice.

They walked forward, passed a wide-eyed Mary and the wary guards. She leaned into Samual's calm and steady presence, and was glad for it. She might have done something she'd regret if he hadn't appeared.

Her insides squeezed, trying to keep her emotions locked down. The one time she could count on him to be forced to look upon her, and he'd found a way out. She should have known.

They turned through the wide entrance into the dining hall. The expansive room of stone and wood beams featured golden chandeliers hung intermittently around the room, bathing the rectangular tables in gentle light. Food was piled high on each table, though most seats remained empty of guests.

If she'd been named princess, they would have had to double the guards to keep people from breaking down the doors to get in. Her cheeks burned with shame.

Samual did not comment on the lack of attendance. He led her to a chair at the high table where a servant pulled it out for her to be seated.

"I hope you don't mind." He gestured to the chair on her left.

She brushed a strand of hair from her eyes. "I'd be honored. You're the only friend I have here." Besides, the seat was his by rank anyway. As he sat, she hid her shaking hands in the folds of her dress and studied the smattering of guests around the room.

Some of her father's advisors and much of the local court were in attendance. Most of the young lords were there. They sat with their parents, awaiting the gong to begin eating. She caught Lord Calem's eye from across the room. He gave her a sympathetic nod, so she concentrated on him. The familiar sense of friendship and loyalty had her offering a tentative smile.

Samual touched her elbow, his inviting conversation a distraction from her father's rejection and the lack of guests who'd come to honor her.

Ardenis did not know what to make of Samual's behavior. He laughed with Faelyn and leaned to her when she spoke. They shared stolen glances and smiles. It all looked genuine to Ardenis, though he was still learning about love and courtship. He didn't think Samual was faking any of it. Gone was the smirk and manipulative gleam in his eyes. Faelyn looked happy, for once. They sampled all the fare, swapping conversation.

Had Faelyn won him over with her sincere heart and decent soul? Yet, Ardenis's brow creased further and further as he watched them eat and laugh together. Every time she casually touched Samual, Ardenis gritted his teeth.

He refused to look back in on Isaac, the bastard. The wide range of emotions when Faelyn discovered what Isaac had done nearly gutted Ardenis. And she'd leaned a new element—light and energy. Aether.

Isaac had chosen pride and grief over his daughter. And to think, Ardenis had once seen so much potential in him, but he'd turned to ruin. It was almost as bad as Hector becoming a watcher.

"Can you believe this insanity?" Amalia had demanded later that day after Hector's announcement. She stood in his living area with her hands curled into tight fists. "After everything Hector has done, who in their right mind would make him a *watcher*?"

Ardenis had scrubbed his face. "What did you find out?"

"He's telling the truth. For once. Apparently, he's shown an aptitude for the capacity to connect to Thera. Combined with his good behavior at the dining hall all these years, he convinced Averick Head Councilman to promote him."

"That's some promotion." Yes, Hector probably understood Therans more than most watchers, but only because he was emotionally altered. "They can't promote a new watcher without the high council approval. Why would Rhea allow this?"

"The Fates have it in for me." Amalia sighed and dropped into a chair. She'd been plagued by Hector's unrequited love for decades now, a topic Ardenis was not allowed to talk about.

Ardenis's brow furrowed in concern. "Do you think he's changed? Maybe he's ready to move past the mistakes he made under Gharum." The words sounded ridiculous even as he said them.

Amalia rolled her eyes, but then sat up taller and grinned. "On the bright side, he's not talking to me. He doesn't even acknowledge my presence in the room."

Maybe he was trying, then. Ardenis shuddered. The repercussions of the decision to make Hector a watcher were unfathomable. A corrupt Acanthian who lied and manipulated, set loose with the power to watch a world, with no sense of duty or obligation to relay the truth. And no one would ever know if he lied because Hector was the only one who could see what he watched. He could report anything he wanted to the council, and they'd believe him.

Ardenis shook his head clear. One disaster at a time. Before him sat the laughing, carefree girl in the pink dress which matched the flush on her cheeks. Behind her, Samual's servant approached bearing a tray, and on it, a silver decanter.

Ardenis's scream was choked off by terror grabbing his throat.

CHAPTER SEVEN

As the feast continued, Faelyn found she could almost forget her troubles with her father, and became lost in Samual's handsome eyes. The musicians playing sweet notes in the corner covered up the lack of guests. She hardly noticed when each new dish was served. Never had anyone been so kind to her. Well, besides Mary, Calem, and some of the servants. But she found herself staring at Samual's lips, wishing for a kiss. When he wasn't regaling her with funny stories, she caught him looking at her lips in return.

A servant brought a tray to their table, interrupting Samual midsentence. Samual gave a nearly inaudible gasp. His essence changed from flirtatious to nervous, though he barely missed a beat, picking back up where he'd left off in a story about the time he'd caught his eldest sister kissing a boy, and she'd chased him with a broom. He shed his nerves so fast, Faelyn must have imagined it.

The servant gestured to the wine in silent invitation.

"None for me, thank you," Samual said. He swallowed twice. "Would you care for some, Lady Faelyn?"

"No, thank you. Not if you're not having any." She'd never had wine before and wasn't about to take her first taste alone.

"Then we'll both have some," Samual said with enthusiasm.

The servant poured their drinks and walked away. Samual handed her one and licked his lips. "How about a toast to your birthday?" He raised his glass, so she raised hers.

The air felt thick with apprehension. Her eyes darted around the room, meeting several others who quickly looked away. Sweat popped out on Samual's brow.

"What's wrong?" she asked.

Samual leaned forward and kissed her. Her eyes went wide. It was a quick peck on the cheek, but her skin burned. Unease was replaced by warmth fluttering through her body.

"Forgive me. You're just so beautiful I couldn't help myself." He smiled and tilted his glass toward her. "To you, Lady Faelyn."

She touched her warm cheek, then clinked glasses with him. "And to you, Samual, for making this an unforgettable night." She raised the glass to her lips and drank. The first drops of liquid hit her tongue, and she cringed. Wine was horrible nasty stuff with a foul taste and burning bite.

After a swallow, she lowered her glass. Samual watched her, not drinking. The smile had gone from his lips. Awful feelings of horrifying guilt mixed with triumph emanated from him. She set the glass on the table, unease pooling in her stomach.

A searing pain scorched from inside her. She clutched at her chest. "What have you done?" *Acantha above, it burned.*

Samual's face turned pleading, and he took her hand. Her head swam with panic. "Forgive me, Faelyn. I had to."

She shoved him away and pushed back from the table, overturning her chair. All heads snapped up. She doubled over, clutching at her middle.

Stumbling through servants and guests, Faelyn ran out of the dining hall, screaming. "Mary!" Tears streamed down her face. The poison worked its way through her pumping blood. She stuck her finger down her throat and vomited.

Mary sat on a bench nearby, her waiting escort. She jumped up. "Faelyn!"

Faelyn clung to her voice, rushing to her safe haven. She tripped over her large skirts and collapsed at Mary's feet.

"Poison," she croaked, shaking between her tears. She curled onto her side squeezing her middle as hard as she could. She sent every ounce of healing magic she had, flinging what little control she'd learned, toward the source of the pain.

"Fetch a doctor!" Mary's voice was shrill with panic. More words were yelled by Mary and others, but they faded into the background of the pain and vomit.

Faelyn's vision dimmed. She fought the poison with animalistic fury. It was winning. The magic petered out, sapping the strength she needed to fight the poison. Her body hurt like never before. She lost control of her limbs. The last thing she knew was Mary's cool hand on her damp forehead.

No! Ardenis could only watch in horror as servants, courtiers, and old Dr. Romand surrounded Faelyn. He slammed his fists on the watch window's marble ledge when Samual, the very person who'd poisoned her, swooped in and picked her up.

"Which way is her room?"

With a trembling hand, Mary pointed.

"Ardenis." Amalia shook him. "Get a hold of your emotions." Though her voice came to him quietly, the urgency was plain.

He shifted halfway out of Thera. In one layer of his vision, Samual raced through the castle corridors following a sobbing Mary. In the other layer, Amalia leaned and whispered into his ear. "Hector is still here, and he's watching you. All the night watch knows what has happened to Faelyn. Be careful."

Ardenis took a breath and nodded. He moved his hands under the table and pushed himself back into Thera in time to see Samual place Faelyn on her bed.

Samual ran his hand across her forehead and down the length of her face. Ardenis clenched his robes. Samual brushed his fingertips over her pointed ear. Ardenis's mouth dropped open in horror. *Sick bastard!*

Dr. Romand entered, breathless.

“Hurry.” Mary clutched Faelyn’s lifeless hand to her breast. “My Lady said she was poisoned, then collapsed.”

“Did someone notify the captain of the guard?” Dr. Romand asked. “Never mind. Everyone out.” While Mary ushered Samual, the courtiers, and unnecessary servants out of the room, Dr. Romand kneeled over Faelyn’s pale form and checked her pulse. He looked up at Mary and shook his head.

Mary burst into tears, falling into a heap at Faelyn’s side.

That shake of the doctor’s head was punctuated by a profound silence in Ardenis's mind. The span of his many millennia could fit in the hole that one simple movement created within his heart and soul.

After an eternity in which he comprehended the truth of what he was witnessing, while Mary sobbed over Faelyn's prone form, Ardenis left Thera. Hector’s knowing stare bore into him, but he didn’t have room to care. He stood and walked out of the tower into the dark of night. He made it as far as the rose garden before he broke down sobbing.

CHAPTER EIGHT

A warm hand squeezed Faelyn's, waking her up. She squeezed her eyes tight against the ache radiating over her body. *Poisoned.* Mary's breathing hitched beside the bed. Nighttime shrouded the room, only a dim lantern on the bedside table.

"Mary?" Her voice came out a croaked whisper. She'd never felt so thirsty.

Mary jumped and cried out. "Lady Faelyn, you're awake." She bent and wept over Faelyn's hand.

"Water." Her dress was gone, instead she wore a cotton nightgown.

Another servant in the room filled a glass and held it to Faelyn's lips. Faelyn drank deeply. When the glass had drained, her thirst was not quenched. "More." She drank another glass and ate a slice of plain toast before she felt better.

"Mary." Her voice came out clearer this time. "Did Samual get away? Was he captured?"

"Prince Samual?" Confusion and concern crossed her features. "He's been holding vigil outside your door." She sniffled. "I didn't think there was a hope of you living through the night." She squeezed Faelyn's hand tighter, fresh tears spilling. "But you're okay now, my lady?"

Faelyn strained her ears and heard the distinct deep breathing of someone asleep in the hall. She propped up on her elbows, sending her head spinning. "Why is he not locked away? He tried to kill me!"

Mary's eyebrows creased. "I'm so sorry you were put in harm's way, Lady Faelyn. The servant poisoned you, not His Highness. The servant is locked in the dungeon. Prince Samual is worried about you. Indeed, all your guests have asked after your well-being. I think we'll be able to convince the court to hold your ball when you're feeling better."

Faelyn fell back against her pillow, and the spinning subsided. The last thing she cared about was her ball. Why would someone want to kill her? Something had happened just before she drank the poisoned wine. Her eyes drifted closed under the weight of fatigue. What had Samual said?

That he had to do it, that he was sorry.

"Mary, you have to tell someone. It was Samual." Exhaustion overtook her before Mary responded.

She next awoke curled on her side facing the window. Sunlight poured into her room. Gone was the soreness and pain. Gone was the worst of the weariness. In its place beat intense hunger. She breathed deeply and was alerted to a strong presence beside her. Seated stiffly and staring straight at her was her father, King Isaac.

Faelyn sat straight up and rubbed her eyes, but he didn't disappear. He remained in the chair, expressionless. It'd been years since she'd seen him this close. Deep frown lines had formed in his skin, and his eyes were red-rimmed. In the corner of the room, Mary dozed upright in a cushioned chair, head resting at an awkward angle.

"You know, Dr. Romand looked after your mother when she fell ill." Her father's baritone voice washed over her. He looked down at the bed, and a tear ran down his cheek.

She soaked in his words like dry earth gathering a summer rain. It was the first thing he'd ever spoken directly to her. Her mind roved for the right words, but what did you say to a father that had denied you everything you ever wanted for eighteen years? It was her birthday today. Was this his gift to her?

"You look just like her. She was your age when we met." He rubbed his hands on his trousers. "She died eighteen years ago today, you know."

Faelyn flinched. Of course she knew. Her birthday was never anything but a reminder of her mother's death.

"I have something for you." He slid a small wooden box toward her across the down comforter, quickly withdrawing his hand.

Faelyn drew in a breath. She picked up the delicate box and held it in her hands. He'd never given her anything before. She opened it, hinges creaking. Inside was a ring. Diamonds and sapphires decorated the gold band.

"Look on the inside."

She turned the ring over, and underneath the precious stones, etched into the gold was an emblem of the family crest, a coat of arms with waves on one side and a tree on the other, to signify the wealth of their kingdom. Faelyn ran her finger over it, memorizing it. She slipped it on her finger and imagined it was her father's arms, hugging her for the first time.

"It was your mother's wedding ring." His voice was hollow.

Faelyn's eyes burned, and she clutched the ring to her chest. Her father finally looked up, amusement crinkling his careworn eyes. "You mourn her, too. And here I thought I was the only one."

She found her voice, and it was full of ire. "Of course I mourn her. She was my mother, and she loved me."

He shook as if waking from a dream. His eyes widened, and his expression cleared. He squared his shoulders. "I don't pretend to care for you, Faelyn. But I do love you. You're Eva's daughter, how could I not?"

The words slapped across her face, and Faelyn reeled. She suddenly wished she wasn't in bed in nothing but a nightgown, but dressed to endure this pain in something less vulnerable. "I'm your daughter, too, Father."

"That's right." He stood from his chair. "And today I'm going to do something I should have done a long time ago. I'm going to name you heir."

Faelyn gasped.

Then a sword exploded through his chest. His eyes went wide as blood soaked his shirt. He reached for her, then fell. Mary screamed. Behind him, Samual held a bloody sword.

"I can't let that happen." Samual watched her father writhe on the floor.

Faelyn stared in shock. What was happening? Maybe it was a nightmare.

Her father stopped moving, stopped reaching for her. The essence drained out of him. It was all real.

Swords clashed from the hall. Men cried out in pain. Servants ran screaming. The cold numbness of shock locked her limbs in place.

Samual examined the blood on his sword. "I truly am sorry this is how things turned out, Faelyn. I really do care for you. But things were set in motion, and I can't turn back, you see. And I'm afraid I can't let you live."

He stepped forward, sword raised. The numbness vanished, replaced by adrenalin. Faelyn hopped up on her bed. He swiped at her legs, but she jumped over his sword. He growled.

"Mary, the passage. Go!" she shouted.

Mary hesitated. Faelyn leaped, putting the bed between her and Samual. "GO!"

Mary scrambled toward the wall, prying her fingers into the crevice of the door and flinging herself into the passage. Faelyn beheld Mary's terror before she slammed the door. Samual watched her go with a bemused expression. Faelyn threw herself to the ground. She reached under the bed and pulled out one of her old wooden practice swords. She held it ready.

Samual smiled. "Don't be ridiculous, Faelyn. Look at you. A girl in a frilly nightgown. We've dispatched your guards. Your king is dead. My men wait outside your room. It's over."

Fury blazed in her narrowed eyes. With sure and slow steps, she rounded the bed and pointed her sword straight at Samual's heart. Let him see what was coming.

"You're right. It is over." She didn't need magic to take down this pompous ass.

He grinned and brandished his sword, still coated in her father's blood. He swiped at her, an overhanded swipe confident of a sure victory. She twisted out of his path and slammed her wooden sword into his forearm. He cried out, sword clanging to the ground. On a bounce, she caught it with the top of her bare foot and flung it into the air

Samual could only gape as she pivoted, snatched the sword from midair, and stabbed him in the upper torso. She couldn't help but smirk as she moved to strike again.

His wide eyes finally conveyed real fear. He flung himself away from her killing blow and ran out of the room. "Kill her!" he shouted to his men in the hall.

Faelyn slammed the door closed and locked it. She panted, shoving back the rising panic. She had minutes at most to escape. Men crashed against the door. Ignoring her father's body, she threw on a tunic, trousers, and sturdy boots. She grabbed an empty satchel, stuffing it with loose gold and the first spare clothes she touched. The frame gave a loud crack. She spared a precious moment to retrieve her mother's comb. At the last minute, she grabbed the circlet off her father's head, and his ring with the family crest, adding them to the satchel alongside her mother's ring. Then she slipped a silver ring Mary had given her onto her finger.

The wood gave way with a splintering crash. With a last glance at her father, she hurdled through the secret door, barring it from the inside. She made it only a few steps into the dark tunnel before Samual's men hammered against it.

Her steps faltered. She couldn't run. She couldn't allow her kingdom to fall.

Heart racing, she opened her ears, focusing hard to pinpoint where Samual had gone. Pounding boots and shouting rang out around the castle. More soldiers than just Samual's guard must have attacked. From the clang of swords, the twang of bows, and the shouts of men, it had to be an army. And the screaming, the screaming was a horrible thing. People were dying, and their loss took her breath away.

Mary's cry of alarm from the training yard broke through all senses.

"Don't harm her." Hammond, her father's advisor, said. "We can use her if it comes to that."

The filthy traitor. Faelyn was running back to her room before she even realized, her satchel bumping against her hip. She unbarred the door and burst through. Four soldiers in dull metal armor cried out in surprise and attacked. She cut them down in less than a minute. When no one else entered her room, she broke the glass out of her window and jumped onto the ledge.

Daltieri soldiers were scattered across the training yard. The black raven in flight painted on their armor clashed against the guards in Alysian blue. Far in the distance, ranks of their soldiers marched toward the castle. The Alysians were outnumbered and overrun.

Mary stood across the training yard. A soldier held her by the arm, pressing a sword against her side. Mary stared up at Faelyn. Fear radiated out from her, coating the air, coating Faelyn's every thought.

Samual emerged from a doorway below with a contingent of soldiers. He wore a hastily applied bandage around his shoulder. Samual followed Mary's panicked gaze until he stared up at Faelyn through the glare of the sun. Glass crunched beneath Faelyn's readied stance. She had to save Mary.

Samual gave an order, quick and decisive. The soldier grabbed Mary—the woman who'd raised her from a baby, her true friend, and the only one who'd loved her—by her gray hair and pitched her forward. Mary cried out as her old body sprawled across the ground.

Faelyn didn't know who to kill first. She didn't think. She jumped from her second-story window. Her knees popped, and she rolled to absorb the impact.

"Give up, or we'll kill her," Samual yelled across the clearing. The same soldier hauled Mary back to her feet. Blood welled from a scrape on her cheek.

The world went red. Then the world burned.

Fire erupted around the training yard. Samual's closest soldiers were the first to be engulfed. He screamed, backing quickly away.

Faelyn couldn't torch Mary's captor without harming her. She clenched her teeth, focusing harder than she ever had. The magic listened. Instead of flame, she cut off his air. He grabbed at his throat, dropping Mary and his sword. Mary crumpled to her hands and knees. The guard crashed to the ground, clawing at the dirt, fighting for air. None came.

Samual tried to run, but everywhere was cut off by fire or battling soldiers. The flames caught the sides of buildings and stacks of hay, now blazing with little help from her. Movement took effort, but she had enough left to finish what Samual started. She channeled her magic. His eyes went wide, and he raked at his throat. He tried to scream.

She couldn't even feel the satisfaction of hurting him like he'd tried to hurt her. Her mind blocked everything except one reality—Mary had to survive.

Samual sagged to the dusty ground.

A powerful force slammed into Faelyn's back. A dark aftertaste coated her mouth. Her magic slipped its leash, fleeing from her control. Samual gagged, breaths gasping. Faelyn whirled to find a man pacing toward her. He stepped out of the shade of the portico wearing robes of black, which trailed nearly to the ground. He wore no weapon she could see, but carried a staff topped with a glowing crystal. The crystal emitted a potent essence unknown to her, a source of magic belonging distinctly to this dark man.

The man tipped his staff, and another blast of power hit her, stronger than the first. She stumbled backward, tasting blood. Her whole body stung like being slapped by the hand of a giant. Behind her, Samual got to his feet. Mary still kneeled between them.

"Finish it, Alister," Samual said, coughing and sputtering.

Faelyn squared her shoulders, backing slowly up to Mary. She'd heard of Daltieri's mage, their infamous beck-and-call assassin. But he didn't know what she was capable of. She focused her remaining strength, calling the magic to her. She directed it to steal his air.

He tensed, then his staff quivered in the air, mage crystal blazing bright. He took a deep breath despite Faelyn's continued efforts. She stared in disbelief. He'd counteracted her magic. Fear sent her heart racing.

"Mary, run now!" Faelyn screamed, not daring to take her eyes off the mage.

Mary gave a pleading whimper. Samual stood above her with his boot planted on her back, sword raised. *No!* Faelyn shoved her magic ahead. He stabbed down, straight through Mary's heart.

Faelyn screamed and threw her magic into healing Mary as she hurtled across the clearing. Mary's body lay still, blood pooling around arms that had once held Faelyn so tight. There was no hint of life, no essence to cling to.

"You can't be gone." Faelyn fell to her knees, ignoring the knife Samual pointed at her. Soldiers rushed into the training yard.

Samual shook his head and pulled his sword from Mary's body. "I said finish it."

Magic meant to end her pooled in the air. Alister weaved his spell, but Faelyn didn't care. She didn't get to say goodbye, or thank Mary for always being there, or tell her she loved her. Now she'd never get the chance. She caressed the hair scattered across Mary's face. Mary hated being untidy.

The battle continued around them—the Alysian soldiers outnumbered and fighting in vain. She grabbed Mary's hand, unable to weep. Mary was a mother to her, had loved her when no one else would, and deserved better than this. Faelyn had failed to protect her. Let Alister's spell take her.

"Faelyn!" Benton's voice sounded from the edge of the yard.

Her head raised slowly. Alister's magic rose like an invisible black wave. Benton sprinted toward her. All the trained lords of the castle who hadn't fled or been killed followed behind, including Calem. The soldiers of Daltieri converged, attacking. Benton cut through the first enemy.

"Get up, Faelyn. Fight!" Calem raised his sword against a strike.

Her friends had come to help her. A thread of hope remained. Faelyn unsheathed her sword and stood, looking for Alister in the chaos.

Calem fought his way to her, swinging and blocking through the melee. "You must run, Faelyn. You must hide." He puffed with exertion. "The king is dead. You're Alysies' last hope."

She spotted Alister in the shadow of the portico just as he unleashed his spell. Calem was caught in the middle. With a weak cry, Faelyn raised her arms and poured herself into a shield of water. The bubble surrounded her and Calem. The spell smacked into her shield. A deep purple bled through the water. It burned her mind, and she gritted her teeth against the pain and exhaustion. Her magic gave way, and water splashed around them, staining the dirt.

Alister bared his teeth and immediately set to rebuilding the spell. Samual was nowhere to be seen. Calem pulled her closer as he parried an attack. Faelyn shoved her sword through the Daltieri's unprotected side.

"Let's go, Princess. I know the way." Calem stepped toward the south side of the yard.

That word pried her from her shock, and she blinked. A soldier attacked, and she raised her sword instinctively, killing him. They fought side by side until they made their way out of the training yard, past where Benton and the other lords fought, then they ran. The enemy pursued them into the garden. A pair of soldiers caught up, and Faelyn turned and cut them down without a thought.

"Follow me." Faelyn wiped blood on the grass and then pulled ahead of Calem. She led him through the garden to a door hidden around a cluster of large bushes. Those who didn't know it was there wouldn't be able to find it. It was for royal blood only. Mary had shown it to her because Faelyn was royal to her, she'd say.

They sprinted down a short staircase and entered a dark underground tunnel. She blinked, and Mary's body lying prone upon the earth flashed in her mind. She rubbed viciously at her eyes.

Calem stopped her with a hand on her arm. "Does this tunnel have another way out?"

Faelyn nodded. "There's a door at the very end to the south. It opens to the outskirts of Pavora Woods."

"Good. Get as far away from here as you can. Don't stay in Alysies. Go south to Creadel and lay low there. Here." He thrust a bag at her. "I'm going back."

"Why?" She slung the bag over her shoulder. "There's no hope. If you go back, you'll die."

Calem clenched his fists. "They took my father. And I won't leave Swordmaster Benton to fight by himself."

"Then I'm coming, too."

Calem stepped in her path. "You're our only hope for the kingdom to return to what it once was. This battle is King Isaac's doing. You're the rightful heir to the throne. When you're ready," he squeezed her arm, looking straight into her, "come back and claim it. Those of us who survive will be waiting for your return."

Faelyn clenched her jaw and shook loose of his grip. "They don't care about my claim. They never have! This is wrong, Calem. I shouldn't be running away."

Calem placed a hand on both of her shoulders. "They care, and so do I." He kissed her on the mouth, and she surprised herself by kissing him back. She sensed his real affection for her, nothing like what she'd received from Samual.

Calem held her close, and she leaned into his comforting embrace. "I'm sorry I didn't do that sooner. I'm sorry it took me so long to call you my friend. I'm a fool."

"Come with me," she blurted. She didn't want to be alone, didn't know how to be.

Calem gave a tight smile and tilted her face up by her chin. "Live, Faelyn. Come back for us."

Before she could recover, he turned and ran back up the stairs. He slammed the door behind him, plunging her into darkness.

CHAPTER NINE

She's okay. She's okay. She's okay... for now.

Ardenis had reached the limits of his emotional endurance. He watched Faelyn contemplate the door leading back into the garden, where Calem had just left. Calem, there was something familiar about him. Had he known him in Acantha?

Faelyn panted and leaned over, putting her hands on her knees. She stayed like that as the clanging swords slowed and the enemy won over. Tears lined her eyes, but no drops fell.

Ardenis breathed in relief as Faelyn stood, shaking her head from side to side. It was nothing short of the Fates' design that she'd made it this far. All hell had broken loose, and just as she was about to get everything she'd ever wanted—the start of a relationship with her father, and validation that she truly did belong to this kingdom, that she was the heir. The look on Faelyn's face as she watched her father die would haunt him forever.

Faelyn took a step back toward the door, then ran the opposite direction. Ardenis watched her walk through the dark tunnel with nothing to light her way. He'd seen her explore these tunnels as a child, but it always amazed him how she found her way in the dark, where humans shouldn't be able to see.

The occasional light from a breakaway tunnel or a door accompanied the sound of her tired breathing. The crunch of her boots in the dirt, and the swing of her sword and satchels became a cadence, a rhythm Ardenis used to ensure Faelyn continued on to safety. He had no clue what was in the bag Calem gave her.

He'd never seen her expend so much magic at once. It was a miracle she was still standing. Each horrible scene replayed in his mind. After witnessing her drink the poison, he'd fled the tower. Amalia found him in the garden, sitting on a bench, trying to hold it together. He thought Faelyn had died.

"She's alive." That was all Amalia had to say, and he pulled her to him in a tight embrace.

"Arden," she said, squirming out of his arms. "They've arrested Samual's servant. Go home and rest. She's asleep with guards outside her door. I'll have someone wake you when she does."

He wanted to resist, but nodded and stumbled home. He returned a few hours later when Gunter summoned him, reporting Faelyn had awoken in the middle of the night. That was when the world fell out from under his feet again. Ardenis overheard Cadence speak of an army approaching Pavora. He cursed himself for not seeing them coming. He couldn't be everywhere at once, even with Amalia's help.

Amalia. She must have known Daltieri was coming. She'd been watching them for a long time. Amalia hadn't warned him.

He'd almost roared with the anguish of watching the castle burn and its guards and soldiers decimated. Alysies was a peaceful kingdom, one of the best he'd ever watched.

Ardenis couldn't even attempt to recall the memory of Mary's death. His heart hurt for her loss, as close to physical pain as Acanthians could come. She'd been everything for both Eva and Faelyn.

Ardenis switched his gaze from Faelyn navigating the dark tunnel, to the castle courtyard. Soldiers of Daltieri rounded up wayward servants. Some of the lords had surrendered. They knelt in the dirt with their hands tied behind their backs, enemy swords pointed at them. Calem was among them. His scowling face promised defiance. He bled from a wound in his arm.

Benton's body lay bleeding, discarded and forgotten in the training yard.

Two guards hauled Isaac's loyal advisor and Calem's father, Richard, to the courtyard. He didn't struggle. They brought him before the arrogant Samual who stood casually with his feet apart, his hand on the pommel of the sword sheathed at his side. Ardenis was glad for the wound Faelyn had dealt, that now seeped blood through the bandage.

"Hammond," Samual said, staring at Richard.

"Yes, Your Highness?" Hammond stepped out from a group of Daltieri soldiers and bowed on one knee.

"Is this one of the loyalists?"

"It is." Hammond stared somewhere past Richard, not looking him in the eye.

Richard's jaw rippled as he clenched it. Calem went still as stone.

"Kill him." Samual motioned to his soldiers.

Richard raised his chin.

"No!" Calem shouted. The guards shoved him down.

"Wait!" Hammond lifted his hand in protest. Samual glared. "Forgive me, Your Highness. Richard claims the loyalty of many lords of Alysies as well as the people of his land holdings. You may have an easier time with them if you keep him alive."

Samual studied Hammond, and Richard studied Samual. "Fine," Samual said. "Find the dungeon and lock him up."

Face set with unflinching stoicism, Richard glanced at his son only once before they dragged him from sight. Calem gaped in horror, but didn't make any foolish moves.

Ardenis let his shoulders droop. It was too much. Isaac's inattention and lackadaisical rule had led to Alysies' overthrow. Their only hope lay in an unclaimed heir to the throne with hardly any supporters, who was wisely fleeing to safety.

Kingdoms had fallen under much more dire circumstances, but those were different. They never affected him before. He hadn't been emotionally aware, and suddenly missed the detached way he used to be able to watch. Faelyn made him emotionally invested in the fate of Alysies. So much death and destruction, so much potential for a beautiful future lost in a day. Ardenis pressed a hand into his chest.

He changed his focus back to Faelyn. She neared the end of the underground tunnel, which led to the south side of the palace grounds. The area brightened as she reached a wooden door. Her brow furrowed in pain. She clutched the satchel strap with a white-knuckled grip. Dirt and ash smudged her face and clothes. She reached the door and paused, even halting her breathing. She cocked her ear, then placed her hand against the worn wood and pushed. The door groaned as it scraped against rock. It opened to the afternoon sun filtering through thin cloud cover. Faelyn stepped onto a thick valley of green grass. It stretched to the tree line of the surrounding Pavora Woods.

She took ten steps toward the trees before taking a deep breath and turning back to face the castle. When she did, her eyes widened and mouth fell open. From behind the castle wall, black smoke rose, choking the sky. Screaming filtered through the deceptively beautiful spring day, blending with the birds chirping from the trees. The grass turned brown around her as silent tears fell down her face.

"Oh, Mary," she whispered. "I'm sorry I couldn't save you."

Ardenis's heart broke. His hand twitched to reach for her.

Faelyn turned and ran, a trail of dead grass following her into the forest. Ardenis prayed it wouldn't be discovered.

She ran lithely, hopping over branches and streams flowing with mountain snowmelt, and the animals watched her. The sun descended into evening, and her breathing and pumping legs grew unsteady. Ardenis knew she still headed south, and hoped Faelyn knew it too. Her steps were sure.

When the sun's rays turned golden, Faelyn's body gave in to exhaustion. She collapsed to her hands and knees, panting. Her panting turned to sobs. She backed up against the trunk of a large tree, dragging herself and her possessions through dirt and leaves. Hugging her legs to her chest, she put her face into her knees and cried.

Ardenis lost track of time as the sun set, fighting his own tears. She'd reached the limits of human emotional endurance.

But Faelyn wasn't human. She wiped her face roughly with the back of her sleeve. Trees loomed in every direction, and a steady breeze sent shadows dancing in the fading light.

She pushed to her feet and walked to the next stream. Cupping water in her hands, she drank several handfuls. She cleaned her sword of blood and ash with a rag from her bag, then walked until she found an opening in the middle of a cluster of bushes. The crude shelter hid her from view and would protect her somewhat from the cold of night.

She pulled Calem's satchel from over her shoulder and lifted the flap. Ardenis peered inside. It was stuffed with food—bread, cheese, and apples, along with some meat that Faelyn ate right away, taking huge mouthfuls at a time. When the meat was picked to the bone, night had fallen. The only sounds were the chirp of insects and the whistle of the wind through the trees. Faelyn curled into a ball, using her satchel as a pillow and draping a cape as a blanket. Her sword rested near her head within easy reach.

When sleep claimed her, Ardenis ended his watch. It was dark in the watch room. Amalia, Hector, and the rest of the day watch were gone, leaving the night shift behind. Faelyn was safe for the moment. It was a good time for Ardenis to rest, but the thought of any comfort while Faelyn suffered made his stomach sour.

He reluctantly left the tower behind. When he arrived home, he found Amalia pacing his living area.

She stopped when he entered. "Are you okay?"

He couldn't think past Faelyn and her dire quest. "Faelyn's all right for now. I left her sleeping in the woods so I could rest." He gave Amalia a pointed look, which she ignored.

"I watched the battle at the castle. It was inevitable, you know. Daltieri prepared for this moment for decades."

Ardenis narrowed his eyes and opened his mouth to complain against Amalia's casual dismissal of Faelyn's world coming undone.

Amalia stood and pointed at him. "Don't get upset with me, Arden. I'm simply stating a fact. It's terrible for Faelyn, but she'll be okay. She's resourceful and more powerful than she realizes."

Ardenis closed his mouth. Amalia didn't see the consequence of the battle with the same eyes as him, even if she was as emotionally altered as he was. But she'd reminded him of another point.

He strode to her. "You knew! You knew they were coming. For weeks—months!—you've known. How could you not tell me? How?" He was being unfair, not giving her the benefit of the doubt, but his emotions wouldn't allow him to calm down.

Amalia winced. "I know. I'm sorry, Arden. I didn't tell you when it was just a possibility, thinking you'd find out for yourself. Your instincts are unparalleled. Then they began their march, and I thought it was better you didn't know." She ducked under his accusing gaze. "There's nothing you could have done but worry. I was trying to help."

Anger boiled in him so fast he could only sputter, unable to form cohesive sentences. When he realized his fists were clenched and his nostrils were flaring, there was only one thing he could say.

"Goodnight, Amalia." Ardenis stomped into his bedroom and fell into bed, not bothering to undress. He heard Amalia let herself out as his mind ran wild with the day's disastrous events, and the way Amalia's decision left him with a new feeling.

Betrayal.

CHAPTER TEN

Faelyn awoke to hooves beating against the ground and the quick rustle of underbrush beneath many legs. She jumped to her feet. They'd found her. She grabbed her sword and threw her packed satchels over her shoulder.

Through the dark of deep night, lights bobbed in the direction of the castle. A squad of Daltieri soldiers, some on horseback, some on foot, combed the woods bearing torches. Looking for her.

Faelyn picked her way out of the bushes, careful not to snap any twigs. Once clear of her hiding place, she ran. Her feet ate up the dusty path. Wind rushed in her ears, and tree limbs reached to grab her clothes.

The bellow of bloodhounds pierced the quiet of the woods. They'd found her scent. She could outrun soldiers, even on horseback they'd have trouble navigating the dense woods. Dogs were another matter. She pushed herself even faster, but the speeding gate of at least six dogs thudded ever closer. Their snarls and howls cut through her confidence. The soldiers charged their horses, yelling to encourage the dogs.

Water rushed ahead. She pumped her legs faster. If she reached the river, the dogs wouldn't be able to track her scent. She weaved between bushes and trees and leaped over roots and fallen logs. A thorn bush scraped her legs as she stumbled through. She lost precious time tearing herself loose.

Barking and snapping, the dogs caught up just as she found the river's edge. It was impossibly wide and rushing faster than she anticipated, but there was no choice. She sheathed her sword, sprinted, and jumped as far as she could for the other side. She sailed over the halfway point before splashing into the freezing river. Her body went under. She fought to the surface as the water swept her away. She surfaced, gasping in shock at the cold. The strong current carried her downriver of the dogs howling from the riverbank and the men who followed close behind.

The water pulled at her bags, and her clothes weighed her down. Her sturdy boots became lead weights in her struggle to remain above the water and avoid rocks and tree limbs. She swam with all she had left for the riverbank.

Reaching out, she caught a branch slick with moss. She hauled her heavy body to shore, barely making it to dry land before collapsing, panting and shivering in the dirt. She must have fallen asleep because when she next opened her eyes, the forest was bathed in the blue light of dawn. Still wet and shivering, she crawled quickly behind the cover of a large tree and listened. No signs of her pursuers, but the braying howls of their bloodhounds still haunted her.

She'd never felt so cold. After gathering some nearby kindling, she used her magic to light a small fire. Her magic barely responded, and she ached with thirst, but it was enough. She huddled around its warmth, with a shaking body and chattering teeth, nearly burning her hands until she felt a bit better.

When she could linger no longer, she extinguished the flame and kicked dirt over the remains.

She got her bearings from the rising sun—the river had carried her far—then took off heading south again. The way she figured, it didn't matter where she crossed to the southern kingdom of Creadel, only that she did. And before Daltieri found her. Once out of Pavora Woods, she'd keep off the trails, avoiding the major towns until she entered the Border Wood, separating her from Creadel.

Faelyn couldn't go home. She wasn't prepared to face Samual again. He'd just kill her as he'd killed all those she held dear. A tear leaked down her face, and she roughly wiped it away. There was no time to mourn what was lost, though she'd lost much. As she walked the rough animal trails, the howls of hounds faded away. The sun rose warm on her shoulders, drying her sodden clothes. She didn't know if she'd ever see Alysies again, but she vowed to try. Someday she'd be ready to avenge her kingdom and take her rightful place. Now, she had to get away and honor Mary's memory by surviving.

She stopped around midday behind a cluster of pine trees. After laying her spare clothes and supplies to dry against a large boulder, she opened Calem's satchel to view the remainder of the food. The bread was ruined. Its soggy crumbs coated the fruit and cheese. She carefully lay the items on a flat rock, picking off soaked chunks as she went. When the bag was empty of food, she dumped the remaining contents into her hand. Crumb-coated gold coins overflowed and clanged off the rocks at her feet, along with a mountain of river water.

The last thing to drop out of the bag was a brass key on a chain with a ruby set in the handle. She turned the key over in her hands, examining it. She didn't know what it went to. Why would Calem give this to her? It was certainly valuable for the stone it held. Perhaps she could sell it when her gold ran out.

She sat up. It was Calem's key. These were his possessions, his rations. And he'd given them to her. He didn't think he would make it out alive. She'd left him behind.

She added his sacrifice to her list of failures, put the chain around her neck, and tucked the key underneath her shirt. After laying her satchels to dry next to her clothes, she curled into a ball in a rare patch of sun filtering through the trees, letting the last of the river's cold leak from her body. A rare sense of peace tried to overtake her, but anguish crashed over her. Mary was dead. Faelyn had no right to feel such things.

The forest sounds surrounded her, the sun kissed her brow, and she embraced the pain. The trees seemed aware of her presence, and the birds sang just for her. She opened her eyes, and new flowers had sprouted. Her tears slowed, and she stretched and sighed, falling into a restful sleep.

The weather didn't always remain perfect as she traveled. Some days she trudged through rain and mud. When the storms and lightning raged, she was forced to find cover beneath the roots of larger trees, in small alcoves formed into the sides of hills, or in old abandoned barns. Her ears helped her keep away from people.

Once, she found a warm cave in the side of a cliff and almost considered living there and never leaving. The nearby creek provided water, and the bushes promised summer berries. The animals didn't bother her, not even the wolves she'd heard from a distance.

She spent two nights at the cave, gathering food when Calem's supply ran out and using her spare shirt like a net to catch fish in the stream. Unlike at the castle, here she'd be able to grow anything she liked. The freedom of it empowered her. But she was still in Alysies, still too close to danger and the memories which threatened to overtake her each time she let them in. She missed having conversations with someone other than herself and the birds. She missed Mary.

Cold baths in the creek would only hold their appeal for so long. When dawn broke, she grabbed her bags packed with nuts, berries, and smoked fish, and once again headed south. The Border Wood seemed to have no end, but she knew from Professor Hadden and her study of geography that once she crossed out of the trees, she'd be in the kingdom of Creadel.

There she'd have to adopt a new identity. She'd hide her ears and who she was or risk being turned over to Daltieri.

After nearly three weeks of hard travel, Faelyn saw a brightening in the forest that meant she had finally reached her kingdom's border. Gold light shined through where the trees stopped ahead. This was the edge of the woods. She sunk to her knees in the dirt. Only a little further, and she'd cross out of Alysies and into Creadel, truly leaving her home behind. She didn't know what awaited her on the other side of the tree line.

She combed through her hair with dirty fingers, picking out leaves and dry grass, then smoothed it down to cover her ears and used a strip of leather to tie it in place.

"It will have to do," she said to herself. Gone were the days of hot baths and servants to clean her clothes. She took a deep breath and sent a prayer to Acantha to keep her safe on the other side of the forest. "Goodbye."

She pressed her palm against the nearest oak and then marched ahead. The yellow glow of the midmorning sun grew blindingly bright. Finally, she reached the edge of the trees. She peered around, eyes and ears ready for an attack. What stood before her was a giant never-ending field of golden wheat.

Faelyn smiled at the sharp contrast in scenery, the deep browns and greens of the forest to the bright sunlit field. She ran her hands over the soft stalks. They tickled her palms. This was the outskirts of a farm.

She found a narrow path between the rows of wheat and followed it south. The first signs of life reached her ears, and she ducked within the thick stalks. Someone kicked a ball, bouncing it off something hard like a tree. Straining her hearing ahead brought the sounds of other activity—someone walking over grass, fabric fluttering in the wind.

Carefully, moving only when the wind shifted the wheat to cover her sounds, she found the edge of the field. A woman a couple years older than her hung clothes from a line, occasionally kicking a ball back to a young girl.

"You're getting good at kickball, Ellowen." The mother laughed.

The little girl with hair as dark as her mother's laughed and sent the ball back.

Faelyn smiled. The smell of roasting meat drifted over the breeze and rumbled her stomach. It had been some time since she'd eaten meat other than fish.

Boots crushed wheat behind her. A bowstring twanged. Faelyn swung around in time to see the man loose the arrow. She pushed at the wind, trying to deflect the arrow, but she wasn't fast enough. It struck her. She flew backward, landing in the farmer's yard. The little girl screamed. Blinding pain was all she knew before blacking out.

CHAPTER ELEVEN

He shot her! That ignorant short-sighted farmer shot her right in the chest! Ardenis ran his hands through his hair. Was he witnessing Faelyn die again?

She lay on the ground, body halfway in the wheat field, unconscious, but breathing. Blood welled up and flowed out of the puncture wound just below her collarbone where the arrow stuck up straight to the sky.

The mother grabbed the little girl, Ellowen, and threw her behind her skirts. Ellowen sobbed uncontrollably.

“What have you done, Myrick?” The mother turned to Ellowen, who couldn’t have been older than eight, and shook her by the shoulders. “Ellowen, go get my kit.”

Ellowen gaped and nodded up at her mother through tear-filled eyes, then turned and ran for the small farmhouse. The farmer, Myrick, stepped out of the wheat field. His plain features were set in anger under of mop of chestnut hair.

He shouldered his bow and brandished a knife at Faelyn’s prone body. “I warned you thieves to stay off my land.”

Ardenis nearly cursed Myrick to the fiery Hereafter. He clenched his jaw against the words forming in his mind.

"Put that away," the mother said, running to Faelyn. "How could you shoot a young woman like this?"

"Stay back, Nia," Myrick warned as she knelt next to Faelyn and applied pressure to the wound. Ardenis liked her already. "She's armed."

"She's unconscious." Nia glanced back at the house as Ellowen came out the front door carrying a wooden box. Her little legs pumped as she ran with all her might. "Slow down, Ellowen. We don't want to trip in our haste to be helpful. Those vials are made of glass." Ellowen slowed to a fast walk.

"She was hiding in the field, Nia. She snuck up on you." Myrick did not relax his stance, only moved closer and tightened his grip on the knife.

"Look at her. Dirty and half-starved. That sword hasn't seen any action. It's shiny and perfect. I wouldn't doubt she came here looking for help or food." Nia rummaged around in the box, vials clinking, and pulled out come clean cloths and alcohol. "Probably a runaway by the look of her." She nodded toward the knife. "Put that away and help me clean up this mess you made."

Myrick hesitated, glancing at his daughter who peered up at him with blame in her eyes. "I didn't get a good look at her, but she looks just like the last bunch. Dirty. Desperate." He sighed and put the knife into its sheath. "What do you want me to do?"

Nia ripped Faelyn's tunic, pulling it away from the wound. "The arrow didn't hit anything vital. Hold her shoulders down. The only thing I can do is pull it out and try to control the bleeding. If we can get it under control before she loses too much, she might live. I'll sew it up." Nia dumped some alcohol on her hands, then gingerly touched around the arrow.

Myrick nodded, bracing his hands on Faelyn's shoulders.

"Ell, I want you to watch what I do here," Nia said.

Ellowen sniffled and moved to her mother's side.

Ardenis could barely watch.

Nia wrapped both hands around the shaft of the arrow. She glanced at Myrick who nodded he was ready. "One, two, three!" She pulled the arrow hard. It ripped free of Faelyn's chest with a sickening tearing sound.

Faelyn's eyes shot open, and she screamed. Myrick held her down while Nia pressed new cloths into the bubbling wound. Ellowen ran halfway back to the house before Faelyn passed out again. When the cloths soaked through, Nia swapped them out for new ones, keeping firm pressure on Faelyn's chest.

"The blood loss is slowing. These cloths aren't getting soaked as fast. That's good. Good." She nodded. "We need to move her inside so I can stitch her. Ellowen!"

"Mama?"

"Prepare a pallet by the kitchen. Thick blankets and a basin of water. Take my kit with you." As Ellowen darted for the kit, Nia turned to Myrick. "I need you to carry her inside while I maintain pressure on this wound."

Ardenis exhaled. Nia would take care of her.

Myrick frowned and glanced at the house. He nodded in defeat. "If she pulls through, she's out of here as soon as she's able. And she better not try anything. I promised I wouldn't let anything happen to you again."

Nia nodded. "That's in the past, Myrick. They arrested those thieves. It'll be okay."

At her signal, Myrick lifted Faelyn, and Nia rose with them. Faelyn's eyes fluttered, but she remained unconscious. Slowly and carefully, they carried her into the wooden house.

Ellowen had thrown a few blankets on top of each other in the area by the front window. A small table, a kitchen, and a pair of chairs filled the rest of the space. Myrick set Faelyn gently on the blankets.

"Is that the blanket my mother made us?" Nia asked, then shook her head. "Never mind. Where's my kit, Ell?"

Ellowen set the wooden box down, then rifled around until she found a needle and thread and held it out.

Nia smiled. "Thank you, my dear." She slowly pulled the bloody cloth away from Faelyn. "What..." Then she pulled it back further, lifting it all the way. Though still a mess, the wound had already begun closing.

Ardenis smiled, and relief washed over him. He pried his hands from his knees.

"I suppose it wasn't as bad as I thought." Nia gave a bewildered look to Myrick and Ellowen. "I won't need to stitch it after all. But I need to wrap it tight. Myrick, do you want to step outside? I have to remove her tunic."

Myrick folded his arms over his chest. "Do what you must. I'm staying here."

Nia shook her head and bent over to work.

Out of habit, Ardenis looked away while Nia and Ellowen removed Faelyn's tunic and wrapped the fast-healing wound. Instead, he studied Myrick, currently Faelyn's biggest threat. Myrick had the decency to blush and avert his eyes. The man was young, in his mid-twenties. His muscled arms, calloused hands, and dirt-stained shirt and trousers painted a story of a lifelong farmer who knew hard work and even harder times. He clearly took good care of his wife and child.

"There now," Nia said, a good indication it was okay to look again.

Faelyn lay unconscious on the makeshift pallet wearing a clean brown linen shirt. Nia dipped a rag in a basin of water and wiped dirt off Faelyn's face. When she began smoothing Faelyn's hair, Ardenis gripped the arms of his chair. Nia stopped before pushing Faelyn's hair behind her ears. He sat back and sighed.

"Now she just needs to wake up," Nia said. "And pray she doesn't get an infection."

Faelyn was out of immediate danger, so Ardenis ended his watch and blinked Thera out of his vision. The shock of seeing her harmed yet again wore off, and he studied the room. Hector stared into the watch window. Amalia watched as well, looking out for signs of pursuit from Daltieri.

Though it wasn't in his nature to hold on to anger, he still hadn't forgiven Amalia for withholding information from him. She'd apologized several more times and since given him every detail of her observations, to the point of becoming annoying. He did not need to know how many times a day Samual used the privy at the castle in Alysies.

It hadn't all been useless information. Amalia told him how quickly the Daltieri soldiers spread the news of their overthrow. They set up permanent stations, taking over the collection of taxes directly from the lords. Samual sent parties to search for Faelyn, but they lost her trail once it crossed out of Pavora Woods and into southern Alysies. Ardenis held on to hope she'd made it far enough away not to be caught, and that she could trust the people whose care she now relied on.

CHAPTER TWELVE

Faelyn awoke and grasped for her sword, except it wasn't where she kept it every night. The soreness of a healing wound put tears in her eyes as her hand fumbled in the dark. A stove burned low in the corner, its embers glowing red with a pleasant heat. She tensed, the feel of soft, clean blankets causing panic to set in.

"Looking for this?"

She tensed at the baritone voice. A burly man sat in a chair, pointing Faelyn's own sword at her. He turned up the flame of an oil lamp on the rickety kitchen table. The low light flooded the small room.

Faelyn jumped to her bare feet—they'd removed her boots, her weapons, and she wore a loose-fitting tunic. The counters were bare of anything useful, like knives, offering only worn dishtowels and empty bowls.

Her satchels were gone. If they went through them, they'd know who she was. Magic then. If it would cooperate.

Faelyn concentrated. Skittering and rumbling sounded beneath the floorboards. A soft glow filled the room as pebbles forced their way through the wood, joining to form a crude blade in Faelyn's hand. The pleasant surprise at the magic obeying remained in the back of her mind.

The man jumped out of the chair, brandishing her sword. “Now, hold on. I won’t bring you harm if you don’t mean me harm.”

Faelyn watched him, breathing in the atmosphere. He seemed nervous, scared, angry—all things she felt at the moment. She eyed the front door. He took a casual step in her path.

“You shot me.” Faelyn laid it out like a challenge. Clearly, the man was capable with a bow, probably her sword too.

He adjusted the sword and frowned. “I have to protect my own. Now, who are you?”

She didn’t need this. “Give me my things, and I won’t cause you or your family harm.” Faelyn relaxed her offensive posture and dissipated the blade as proof of her words. The pebbles pinged harmlessly off the floor.

He blinked a few times. “You need to heal and rest.” He dropped the point of the sword to the floor, but his grip did not relax. “Look, I’m sorry I shot you. You don’t seem the type to steal or harm an innocent person. We’ve had bandits in these parts before, and I can’t be too careful.” He scratched the back of his short hair. “My name is Myrick. What’s yours?”

“Myrick. I appreciate what you’ve done for me. I’m sure I gave you quite the shock. Now, I need my things so I can be on my way.” Faelyn touched her hair, ensuring her ears were still covered.

A door to the side of the room creaked open, and the woman she’d seen hanging laundry entered. She wore a warm smile and a plain cotton nightgown that hung to her feet.

“What my husband is trying to say is we owe you a debt. Please stay until you’re rested. We can feed you and make sure you don’t have an infection. Besides, it’s not safe to wander at night. How will you see the way?” The woman stepped to her husband’s side, placing her hand over where he held the sword. “I’ve mended the rip in your tunic, and I've washed your clothes. They are hanging to dry, so at least wait until they are ready."

The husband and wife stared at her. The man, Myrick, wore a displeased frown of resignation. The woman had a kind face, full of understanding—of Faelyn's injury and fear, perhaps. The wheat farmers couldn't know what Daltieri had done to Alysies, not this soon.

Though, Faelyn had traveled for quite some time. Word of the fall of King Isaac could have reached them if they'd been to town. And here was a lone girl, dirty, travel-weary, arriving at the south edge of a conquered kingdom. With the circlet engraved with the Rylandor of Alysies family crest in her confiscated satchel.

They knew.

Faelyn shifted uneasily from foot to foot. She strained her ears but did not hear sounds of men on horseback bearing swords and torches, coming to take her away. Only the crickets and night owls filled the countryside around them, and the soft breathing of a sleeping child.

"I'm Nia." The woman took a step closer. "We want to help you."

Feelings of relief and suspicion, sadness and loss, and bone-tired weariness almost sent her to her knees. She didn't know who to trust. She didn't know what was real or where to go or what to do next. An infuriating tear leaked from her eye.

Nia glanced at her husband, and then rushed to Faelyn, taking her in her arms. Myrick's disapproval radiated as loud as if he'd shouted it. Faelyn tensed for some kind of trick, then relaxed into the embrace, hugging back. The contact filled her up, reminding her of Mary and a better time she could barely recall.

"It's okay, Princess," Nia whispered. "Stay as long as you like."

Faelyn nodded and dropped her arms, too stunned to react. She'd called her Princess. Nia stepped back and smiled.

With a deep breath, Faelyn buried her emotions where they belonged. She didn't know why she trusted this woman, but she felt familiar, as if they'd met before.

"I'm Fae. I'm a traveler making my way across the kingdom. I'm sorry I startled you. A hot meal and a bath would be a good trade for you having shot me." She offered a small smile.

She wanted her sword, but by Myrick's grip, he wouldn't part with it willingly. If they were trying to deceive her—and her instincts said otherwise—it would be easy enough to get it back.

"We'll start with that and go from there," Nia said. "I need to check your bandage. Myrick, out."

Myrick hesitated. At Nia's stern look, he sighed and went into the room Nia had come from, taking the sword with him.

"It's okay. I'm just very tired." And she was.

"Nonsense. I know a thing or two about wounds from living life on the farm away from any doctors. Some of the townsfolk come to me for ailments now and then. That wound will need attention. Now let me see."

Nia reached for her, so Faelyn gave in and let the woman lift the tunic off. She almost expected to see Mary's full face as the fabric slipped over her head. Pain lanced her heart.

The arrow had struck her upper chest. Nia's brow furrowed as she removed the bandage. A pale pink patch of skin surrounded by dried blood. The wound had healed.

Nia quit trying to find a hole in Faelyn's chest and looked up, locking wide eyes with her.

Faelyn shrugged. "I'm a fast healer."

Nia dropped into a kitchen chair, head in her hand. "And here I thought it was my superior skills." She shook her head. "All right, get some sleep. It's almost dawn, and my little one, Ellowen, will be awake. Try not to startle her." She stood and went into the bedroom, closing the door behind her.

How unusual. Faelyn was thirsty and hungry, but hadn't been offered anything. By the subtle increase in the light outside the small windows, dawn did indeed approach. She lay down on the hard floor, slightly cushioned by the thin blankets, and drifted quickly back to sleep.

Two large blue eyes startled Faelyn awake. She gasped.

The little girl ran out the front door, yelling, "Mama! Mama! She's up!"

Faelyn propped herself on her elbows, smacking her dry mouth. A cup of water sat next to her, and she drank it all. She was alone in the house, and the sun appeared high in the sky. Someone walked up the porch steps, and Nia entered, smiling and drying her hands on an apron she wore over her linen dress. Her hair was piled on her head with loose strands framing her face.

Nia flicked her chin toward the kitchen table. A small vase of wilting wildflowers decorated the space. "I expect you're hungry. Have a seat." She took a glass and filled it with milk from a pitcher.

Faelyn's stomach rumbled. She sat at the table, head ducked. Should she have offered to help? Nia set the milk and a large glass bowl covered with a linen cloth in front of her, then lifted the cloth off the bowl. Steam wafted the most delicious smells. Saliva welled in Faelyn's mouth.

"Breakfast was a couple hours ago, but I made sure Myrick saved you some." Nia set down a fork and backed away, giving Faelyn space.

Faelyn grabbed the fork and dug into warm eggs, bacon, and fresh biscuits with butter—a feast after all her time in the forest. Between bites, she drank deep gulps of the thick, creamy milk. It wasn't long before she couldn't eat another bite. She held her full stomach and stared longingly at the last biscuit.

Nia chuckled.

"Thank you, Nia. That was one of the best meals I've had in a long time." Gratitude overwhelmed her.

Nia took the dishes to the kitchen. Faelyn reached her finger out to the wilting flowers and touched them. They turned from brown and dead, to white and yellow again.

"Wow! Mama, Miss Fae has magic!" Ellowen stood in the doorway, pointing.

Faelyn ducked her head, ready for what usually happened when she used magic in front of people—screaming terror.

"Can you do that again, Miss Fae?" Ellowen scooted closer. "I've seen magic from the traveling fair people. Theirs was better, but yours is good too."

Faelyn laughed at the little girl's refreshing honesty. It gave her the courage to peek at Nia.

Nia wore a wavering smile, drying the bowl from Faelyn's breakfast. "That's quite a skill, Fae. I imagine you must be good at growing things as well. Crops and such?"

Faelyn had never tried to grow crops, never even seen a wheat field before yesterday. A small vegetable garden and fancy flower boxes, yes. But crops?

"Maybe. I could give it a try."

Nia set the bowl down. "Ell and I have chores to tend to at the house. Do you feel up to a walk?" Faelyn nodded. "Then why don't you go see Myrick? He's in the cornfield south of the hill behind the house, past the big oak. Maybe you could help him with the crops."

She might be able to help him, but to what end? They'd already made it clear she was to leave when she was healed and there was no sign of infection. Though, Nia had seen that for herself already. Did Nia mean that she could stay longer if she could prove helpful?

Did she want to stay longer?

"Can I show her the way, Mama?" Ell tugged at her mother's apron, a child's hope in her eyes.

"Papa and Miss Fae need to have a grownup conversation, Ellowen." Nia smiled. "Don't worry, she'll be back." Nia winked as Faelyn stood and pushed in her chair. "We still owe her a bath. Your boots are on the front porch, Fae, and your possessions are packed into your satchels just there." Nia pointed to a low shelf by the front door. She bent and picked up a leather bag, holding it out to Faelyn. "Lunch for you and Myrick. It'll soften him up if he eats before any talk of business." Nia took Ell by the hand and led her outside.

Talk of business? So Nia really was trying to pave the way for Faelyn to stay. But she'd have to go through Myrick to do so.

Faelyn shouldered the bag and drank the last swig of milk. It seemed rude to leave it on the table, but she didn't know what else to do with it. After a cursory glance through her satchels, ensuring her mother's comb and father's circlet were intact, she headed out the door. From the edge of the well, Nia pointed behind the house, away from the woods and the wheat field, then smiled and waved. Ell's wave shook her whole body like a puppy wagging its tail.

Faelyn smiled and waved back, then walked around to the other side of the house, where Myrick was undoubtedly waiting with some kind of lecture. She stopped in her tracks. Down a gentle hill, before the edge of a tilled field, grew a massive oak tree. It towered into the sky even from Faelyn's distance. She goggled at it as she descended the hill.

The tree looked so out of place this far away from the forest, but even the forest didn't have trees this big. Underneath, its canopy seemed to stretch forever. Faelyn ran her hand over the rough bark, circling the trunk. She couldn't circle her arms even a quarter of the way around. It had to be ancient. She loved it.

Despite the dread at speaking to Myrick again, the tree cheered her up, as though she'd seen it in a dream of happier times. She walked the rest of the way to Myrick. He buried seeds in the tilled earth. His horse nickered and trotted over to meet her. Myrick squinted up through the sun, adjusting his bag of seeds around his shoulder. Faelyn held her hand to the horse, who sniffed and pawed the ground.

"He'll eat your lunch if you're not careful. Clip Clop's ornery and doesn't like anyone."

"Clip clop?" Faelyn smirked and found it felt foreign. Her horse back home, which wasn't really hers, was named Majesty. Majesty wouldn't allow anyone but Faelyn to ride him. Faelyn missed him.

Myrick frowned. "Ellowen named him."

Faelyn's smirk became an amused smile. "Well, it's your lunch, too. Ready for a break?"

Myrick set down his bag and wiped his brow. "I could eat. What'd you bring?"

Faelyn had no idea. She sat down in a thick patch of grass and unpacked the leather bag. Myrick gave her a wary look and sat down across from her. The bag was filled with sandwich fixings; bread, cheese, and slices of meat, two cups and a flagon of cold water. Two slices of strawberry pie in a bowl at the bottom had Faelyn's mouth watering despite the fact she was still full from her late breakfast.

The simple motions and conversation allowed her to pretend the horrors of her past didn't exist, and she latched on to it with desperate hands. Could she stay here and just leave it all behind?

Myrick dug in, assembling a massive sandwich and eating with substantial bites. Faelyn didn't eat, saving her appetite for dessert. Wind blew through the distant trees, relaxing her further and helping to cover the smacking sounds as he chewed.

Myrick went silent. He watched her hand. She'd been stroking the grass, growing periwinkle without realizing. Faelyn stuck out her chin and didn't attempt to conceal the palm-sized patch of tiny blue flowers.

She'd hidden her abilities her whole life and was tired of it. Tired of being told to keep her magic contained. Tired of not learning how to use it. This was a chance at a new life far from the pain of loss.

"I'll skip the pleasantries, Fae. We've heard the news of Alysies being overthrown by Daltieri and King Isaac's assassination."

Faelyn stared at her flowers, trying to block out his words as he casually described her living horror. Her brief respite dissipated.

He plowed on. "We've guessed who you are." Faelyn's shoulders slumped. They'd reached the moment where he told her it was too dangerous for her to stay. "Fae, look at me." He said it with impatience in his voice. She kept her head down, her mind already preparing for another hard journey. "Princess." He said her title whisper-quiet, and it echoed in the soft spring breeze.

She lifted her face to meet him, chin up, defiance in her eyes. "I'll leave this afternoon. I wouldn't want to bring harm to your family." She repacked the lunch bag without touching the pie, in a hurry to escape Myrick's pitying stare. He was right. Her presence did bring danger upon this family.

"We'd like you to stay. At least for a little while." His words brought her up short. He stared off into the horizon. "I could use some help on the farm. We aren't bothered much this far to the north. I don't know what your plans are, but you are welcome here if you'd like."

"Why would you help me?"

He let out a long breath and ran a hand through his hair. "Honestly? I don't know. You can thank Nia for this. She has her mind set that you need our help. I can see you being trouble for us." He glanced at the blue flowers. "But maybe you can help as well." He was silent for a long time. Faelyn gave him his moment to reflect on all that her presence could wreak upon his simple farm. "You don't have to talk about it, but I appreciate what you've been through."

She'd never talk about it if she had any say. Her secrets were her own. "I appreciate the offer, Myrick. It's been a long time since I've known kindness from strangers. But I can't stay. I can't put your family in danger. You can't be caught harboring me."

He nodded slowly. "That risk is mine to worry about, not yours. We won't be dumb about it, and don't think I haven't already thought this through, else I wouldn't have offered." He dusted his hands and tunic off. "Well." He sat up and clapped his hands once, startling her from her gratitude. "Let's not let a good pie go to waste."

Faelyn offered him a small smile. She could do this, and she'd work hard in exchange for their selfless sacrifice.

At the first bite of the delicious pie, she closed her eyes and nearly moaned. It was the perfect end to such a difficult conversation. The pie and the fact she had a place to stay for a while eased some of the tension from her shoulders. She almost tricked herself into feeling safe.

When she'd packed the empty plates and bowls away and fed an apple to Clip Clop, Myrick handed her a large, heavy bag. She looked inside at the multitude of seeds.

"Let's get started," he said.

They spent the rest of the afternoon planting the cornfield. Myrick was a patient teacher, showing her how deep and how far apart to plant the seeds. Her back ached, but it felt good to get her hands dirty and learn a useful skill. The methodical motions and her connection to the land helped her forget her troubles.

When the work was done and the sun turned a luscious orange low in the sky, Myrick, Faelyn, and Clip Clop returned home. They walked in silence until they passed beneath the big oak. Faelyn smiled up at the sun's glow filtering through the leaves.

"You've a knack for farming, Fae, but a woman with your upbringing... would you rather help Nia oversee the house and little Ell while you're here? I'm sure you've already guessed you'll have to work for your keep."

The thought of being stuck at the house all day cooking and cleaning made Faelyn's lip curl. "I'm not opposed to hard work in the fields. In fact, I'd enjoy it."

Myrick nodded his approval. "Well, alright. Welcome to the farm."

When they returned, Nia had set out a giant metal tub full of steaming water on the front porch. A towel and clean clothes sat beside it, along with a bar of soap. Faelyn eyed it warily. Myrick muttered something about tending to the horse and headed toward the barn with Clip Clop. Nia came out of the house and smiled, followed by Ellowen.

"Don't worry about him. He won't be back for a while. Go ahead and wash up. Supper's almost ready." Nia steered Ellowen back into the house, leaving Faelyn standing with a gaping mouth.

Did they expect her to undress and wash in front of the whole world? There weren't even trees for cover. Just an open field between the house and the wheat field. Faelyn glanced at the barn but saw no signs of Myrick. She trudged to the bath and stuck her hand in the water. The warmth felt so good, and she was dirty and sore.

She gritted her teeth and undressed as quickly as she could, then hopped into the water. She had to bend her knees and arch her back to fit, and the water only came up to her ribs, but it felt delicious. Loosening her braid, she picked up a nearby bucket and dumped water over her head. She had to scrub and rinse with the soap several times before the dirt all washed away.

By the time she was done, the water was brown and cold. She peeked around the yard and, seeing no one, hopped out and dried off with the threadbare towel. Her nerves made her get dressed still dripping, but she used the towel to catch most of it off her hair before it soaked her clothes. After a few tries, she managed to wrap her hair up in the towel on the top of her head as Mary had always done for her.

Poor, sweet Mary. Acantha above, she missed her. The ache pulsed anew.

She knocked on the front door.

"You don't have to knock, Fae," Nia said from inside, then she opened the door and her mouth dropped open. Her eyes went straight to Faelyn's pointed ears. Faelyn hadn't thought to cover them. "Um. What I mean is... You belong here now." Nia took a breath. "I hope you'll consider this your home."

Faelyn ignored Nia's surprise. "Thank you. So much. You don't know what it means to have kindness bestowed on me." She sent her feelings of gratitude and appreciation into Nia, who blushed.

"Have a seat next to Ellowen. It's time to eat."

At a shake of Nia's head, Ellowen closed her mouth and didn't say a word. Faelyn removed the towel, then rebraided her hair tight, keeping her ears exposed.

When Myrick came inside, he traded glances with his wife,

saying nothing. They all sat around the old kitchen table eating the roasted chicken and warm rolls Nia had cooked. Nia had also set up a permanent pallet in Ellowen's already small room, as there were only two bedrooms. Faelyn slept soundly that night, weary in mind and body, but with growing peace in her heart.

CHAPTER THIRTEEN

Before dawn the next morning, Faelyn snuck out to the barn. It didn't take long to find her sword hidden behind a bale of hay. Samual's sword. The sword that had killed her father. She hadn't had time to retrieve her own sword. Benton had given it to her long ago, and she knew it intimately.

Myrick found her running through her favorite drills on the lawn beside the barn. She finished her current pattern and faced him, panting and sweaty.

"Well, that didn't take you long." Myrick crossed his arms, amusement playing on his face. "I thought that thing was just for show. Now I'm kinda glad I shot you before you saw me."

Faelyn couldn't help it; she burst out laughing. It felt good, but with a bitter aftertaste of betrayal to Mary's memory. "I don't want to get rusty. I—"

She cocked her ear. The distant sound of horse hooves pounding into the ground stopped her short. Her heart hammered in her chest.

Myrick raised an eyebrow. "Are you okay?" He shifted his stance. "I'm not upset you took your sword. I was going to give it back to you."

"Shhh. Quiet!" Faelyn squatted, getting lower to the ground to better hear and also hide from view. The hoofbeats grew closer. Myrick raised both eyebrows this time. He didn't hear what she could. "They're coming." Her voice was laced with panic. "A lot of them. On horseback."

Myrick swiveled around. "Who's coming? How do you know?"

"Nobody good. They can't find me here." Faelyn stood and stepped close to Myrick. "Run for the house, hide my things, and hide them like your life depends on it. I can take care of myself, so don't worry about me. Tell Nia and Ell to tread carefully." Myrick gaped at her. "Go now! They'll be here in moments. Run!"

Myrick turned and ran faster than she thought possible back to the house. Faelyn hurried for the cover of the wheat field. She slipped into its comforting embrace just as the first horse came into view on the horizon. She ran halfway back to the cover of the woods leading to Alysies before stopping.

After several panting breaths, her breathing slowed. She strained her ears. The horses reached the house. She wasn't skilled enough to tell by their sound how many had come, but she did hear the clink of armor and weapons. She squeezed the hilt of her sword, immensely glad for its company.

She fully expected the soldiers to comb the wheat fields, but she did not want harm to befall the family that had been so kind to her, so she stayed close and listened.

"By order of Prince Samual of Daltieri, we are here to search the premises and question you about a missing person." The man's voice was clear even from a distance. He sounded stern, yet monotone, as if he'd delivered this speech many times. "You will cooperate, or we will use force."

"We will cooperate, of course." Myrick's voice sounded softer, but hinted at defiance.

Careful, Myrick.

"But, if I may ask, what are soldiers of Daltieri doing in Creadel? Does King Sebastian know of your investigation?"

Faelyn gritted her teeth and bent her knees, tensing for the fight.

"That's none of your concern, peasant." The soldier's voice had exchanged its monotone for venom. "Have you seen this girl? Be honest, or it's your throat."

The rustling of disturbed wheat distracted her from whatever Myrick said next. The soldiers had entered the field. She moved toward the trees, stepping carefully. No wind came to aid the sound of her retreat. The soldier's plodding footsteps approached from multiple directions. They moved quick without the need to tread carefully, quicker than her.

"I heard something!" one of the men to her right shouted. The rest of the men moved faster. They chopped at stalks of wheat as they went, now mere paces away.

She urged the wind to cover her retreat. The magic reacted to her panic, blasting the field with a gale. She ran, catching sight of the soldiers shielding their eyes from the wheat whipping into them. She made a mad leap into the forest and kept running, dodging limbs and thorn bushes. Tucking her sword into her belt, she jumped to the first branch of a tall oak, swinging up, climbing high enough to be concealed by the foliage. Her heart raced, and she gasped for breath.

The sounds of pursuit did not follow her into the forest. Her legs went numb and aching as she squatted in the tree until the cover of nightfall. Still, no noises reached her. With a heavy heart, she climbed down the tree and made her way back to the farm. She stopped every ten feet to look and listen, but the men seemed to have gone. Thick dread weighed her down. What would she find at the house?

She crossed through the woods, surprised at how far she'd come, then across the ruined wheat field lit by the light of the moon. She stopped at the edge. Contents were strewn about on the yard. A lantern lit from within cast shadows with someone's movement. Faelyn raised her sword and crept to the house. She stepped lithely on the porch, avoiding the creaky second step.

“I just hope she’s okay,” Nia whispered from within the house.

Faelyn nearly dropped her sword with relief.

“She’ll be okay,” Myrick said. “Let’s get some sleep, and we can clean up the rest in the morning.”

Faelyn knocked on the door. Gasps rang out. “It’s me.” She kept her voice low.

Nia yanked the door open. “I told you there’s no need to knock.” She pulled Faelyn into a crushing hug.

“Is everyone okay?” Faelyn asked.

“They had your portrait.” Myrick led her to the table while Nia fixed a plate of leftover food. “They scared Ell when they started tearing up the house.” Faelyn surveyed the room. The house looked in order. “We straightened the inside. They ate our food and broke a few of Nia’s heirlooms. Old plates and such. They didn’t find your bags.”

Faelyn sagged with relief. “Where did you hide them?”

Nia smiled and set a plate of biscuits with honey in front of her. “We were expecting another mouth to feed for a few hours this morning.” She patted her flat stomach.

Faelyn grinned. “Brilliant.” She took a big bite of biscuit, nearly swallowing without chewing. “I have gold. I’ll repay what they destroyed.” She met Myrick’s gaze. “I understand if you want me to leave.”

Nia put her hands on her hips. “Of course we don’t want you to leave. And keep your gold. Just help us replace the food by tending the crops with Myrick.”

"I'm sorry about the wheat field, Myrick." She'd repaid their kindness with nothing but trouble. Is that how Mary felt all those times Faelyn acted up? She vowed to do her new friends better.

"I had a feeling that was your doing. You saved me days’ worth of labor having to cut it all down. Now all that's left is to bundle and stack it. We'll thresh and winnow some for the granary, but sell most to the mill."

He was being kind, but Faelyn sensed his sincerity and felt a lot better. She took another bite.

"Anyways, I don't expect them to come back." Myrick clasped his hands at the table. "We denied seeing you. Even Ell kept quiet. Seems like they are combing the border. I'm just a simple farmer, like my father before me, but I hear the talk in town. King Sebastian won't stand for Daltieri foreigners in our kingdom. It could mean a war."

"A war, Papa?"

Faelyn glanced up to see Ellowen standing in her bedroom doorway rubbing her sleepy eyes and clutching a little doll.

Nia stood. "Ell, to bed with you." She ushered the little girl into her room.

"Mama, Fae's back." Her high voice rose in volume before Nia closed the door.

Faelyn turned to Myrick's heavy glare. "I'm truly sorry, Myrick. I don't know what to say. I didn't know whether to leave or stay, fight or flee." She dropped her gaze into her lap, ashamed, her honey biscuits forgotten.

"You did the right thing, Fae," Myrick said. She looked up. "I can see you care for us. We made our choice to take you in, and you protected us. Your warning saved us. Don't beat yourself up about it." He stood as Nia reentered the room. "Let's get some sleep."

Faelyn nodded, hugged Nia, then entered Ell's room and climbed onto the pallet. She placed her sword reassuringly by her head and spent the rest of the night listening for distant hoofbeats.

CHAPTER FOURTEEN

"Sit down, Ardenis. You're making me anxious." Amalia sipped tea at the table beside Ardenis's Tafl board.

Ardenis paused his pacing long enough to glare at her. "That was too close. Faelyn is taking too many risks. They almost caught her!"

"Wearing a path into the floor isn't going to change anything." Amalia moved the Tafl civilians around the board.

Ardenis stomped to his bedroom and removed one of his favorite drawings from beneath the bed. His eyes lingered on Laida's goodbye letter, and his heart wrenched. He crossed back to Amalia and shoved the drawing in her face. She leaned back to look.

"A giant tree in the rain." She looked up with boredom plain on her face. "You're losing it, my friend."

"Amalia." Her name came out a whine. "This is Myrick's farm. Don't you see?" He pointed to the house visible through the rain. "I showed this picture to Laida. She escaped right to a place she'd already known about." His lips almost curved up at the memory of Laida giving him a hard time about drawing rain. "They aren't so far from town. The soldiers could come back."

Amalia rolled her eyes. "If you don't stop being so paranoid, and trust in the Fates' design, I'll throw you in the transfer gateway myself."

Ardenis set the drawing carefully on the table and slumped in the chair next to her. "I know. You're right." He let loose a gust of air. "I can't control these feelings of helplessness. She's there and I'm here and I have to watch her struggle and there's nothing I can do about it."

"You can always choose to be born." Amalia passed him the soldier piece.

Ardenis glared at her again. "I missed my opportunity to be born with her because of my blind obsession with my duty here. I made my choice to follow my Fating and the Fates' design and be born in a more advanced technological edge, so that's what I intend to do. And you know that."

"Then stop questioning what the Fates have in store for Faelyn. You said yourself you can't control it, you can't change it, so let go of your worry before you give yourself away and get caught. I know Hector's been quiet, but he watches us too."

Ardenis toyed with the soldier in his hand. "I love her, Amalia." He looked up into Amalia's knowing eyes. "My love for Laida followed her to Faelyn. I can't help it."

"Of course you do."

A knock at the door broke Ardenis's concentration.

Amalia smiled. "You said we needed some non-watcher friends, so I took the liberty of inviting someone over."

"Who?" Ardenis stood and walked to the door. He raised an eyebrow. Amalia shook her head, so he sighed and opened the door. Night poured into the room.

Idonea Transfer Leader smiled up at him. "Thanks for inviting me, Ardenis."

Ardenis smiled back. He'd always liked Idonea. "Come on in."

"Hi, Idonea," Amalia called out from behind him.

The three of them played a long round of Tafl. Amalia won, but only because Ardenis let her. He found it difficult to turn off his emotions again in the presence of a non-watcher. It was freeing though, to let go of the need to worry for Faelyn out of obligation to protect his secret.

Ardenis watched Faelyn every day from nearly sunup to sundown. Days turned to weeks, and weeks turned to months, but the soldiers did not come back. In the morning, Faelyn practiced her swordfighting. There was an unmistakable fire in her eyes with each swing. It faded when she put the weapon away, but it was clear some part of her was still in there, fighting through the grief and fear. She hadn't forgotten Alysies.

After practice, she followed Myrick around the farm. He showed her everything about planting, growing, harvesting, and rotating crops with the changing of the seasons. He taught her to make repairs on their tools and fences, and to care for their horses, cattle, pigs, and chickens. When a storm damaged the roof, Faelyn was up there replacing boards and making Ardenis worry. She even reluctantly let Nia teach her to cook and clean.

She once asked Myrick why Ellowen never accompanied them to learn about the farm. Ellowen was definitely capable. It started quite the argument when Myrick explained that, in the real world, a woman's place was in the home.

Ardenis left the tower chuckling that day, feeling lighter than he had in years. Laida had indeed taken her promise to promote gender equality in Thera, and Myrick had learned a valuable lesson when it came to Faelyn and her ideas of a woman's place.

Faelyn never complained, and she never spoke of her past or of any plans for the future. Ellowen would ask at times, but Faelyn always found a way to divert her until one day she stopped asking.

Ardenis knew she was hiding from the pain of all that had

happened. Part of him was glad to see her happy and safe and loved. But part of him knew she'd never be truly happy while her past and future hung in the balance. Like the performances he'd witnessed from the traveling troupes Ell loved so much, Faelyn was playing a part she'd convinced herself was real.

Months turned into years and Faelyn grew stronger. The only thing she didn't do was ever leave the farm. She told Myrick she wouldn't take the risk, and he didn't disagree. When they had visitors, Faelyn gathered truffles from the woods, hiding out until it was safe.

On market days, when it was time to sell the surplus crops, Faelyn happily assured them she was fine to stay at home by herself. But Ardenis saw how her shoulders slumped and her face drooped when they'd driven the wagon out of sight. She'd take out her father's circlet and clean it, but she never put it on.

She didn't stay sad for long. It was on these lonely days when she used her magic the most. It always amazed and pleased Ardenis to see her ability. She used it to grow the vegetable garden or help decorate the lawn with a multitude of wildflowers to surprise Ellowen when they returned. She used it to the point of exhaustion on those days, probably just because she could without enduring second glances from the family. Ardenis doubted Faelyn noticed the trees from the forest leaned toward her a little more on these rare days. If she noticed the animals watching, she didn't let it show.

Even though Faelyn no longer resided in Alysies, Ardenis still kept track of the kingdom's happenings. Part of him didn't entirely trust Amalia to inform him of everything, though she did tell him the news when she watched. He also read the bulletins and listened to the scant gossip.

Prince Samual took up residence at the castle in the capital city of Pavora. Queen Vatrice sent a steady stream of gold and troops, and a steady stream of new laws. The day Richard died alone in the dungeon was a sad day for Ardenis. When Lord Calem and the other lords of the former kingdom were released, he returned to Seaside Keep and grieved. The surviving lords were allowed to maintain their lordship status once they swore fealty to the new king.

Calem had pledged with a blade to his throat and hate in his eyes. He'd since married and had a child on the way. His time was divided between struggling to gather the money for Samual's ever-increasing taxes, and plotting a revolution in Faelyn's name. Samual had killed many, and the fear of death kept most far from Calem's efforts.

'Alysies is a lost cause,' Calem's would-be revolutionists said. Even if Samual could be overthrown—doubtful due to more troops piling in from Daltieri, backed by their gold from the mountains—there was no rightful heir to take the throne. They presumed Faelyn to be dead, but only Calem would back her if she wasn't.

The Daltieri soldiers took residence in every major town of Alysies. They seized money, food, and property by force. The Daltieri colors of black and gold hung from every lord's keep and decorated the town. The seaport town of Dosica was overrun with Daltieri soldiers and civilians who took control of the trade routes, sending profit directly into the hands of Daltieri. None of the money went back into the Alysian infrastructure or people.

The next move of Daltieri's overtake shook Ardenis the worst. They raided libraries and schools, made new laws with harsh penalties, and all with one goal in mind: to rip Alysies from living memory. History books, customs, holidays, even the very name 'Alysies' became outlawed.

People starved. Sickness raged. And Faelyn didn't know any of it.

What state would the kingdom be in when she finally decided to return home? She wasn't learning the valuable skills of war she would need to secure her position. She had become a grand farmer, and maybe that was where her place was in the world, safe and secure with a family who loved her, but Ardenis didn't think so. She had much bigger things in store for her.

The worse the situation became for the people of Alysies, the more Ardenis felt she was wasting her life avoiding them.

It was easy to brush his harsh judgment aside the year Faelyn turned twenty-eight and little Ellowen, who wasn't so little anymore, married and moved away.

CHAPTER FIFTEEN

"I'm going to miss this." Ellowen, who'd grown nearly as tall as Faelyn, walked by her side through a path cut between the wheat field. Her dress flowed gently in the light spring breeze, a sharp contrast to Faelyn's dirty trousers and tunic. "You're more than my friend, you know. I consider you my sister."

The sun warmed Faelyn's face, and she closed her eyes, tilting her head back. Her lips formed an easy smile. "I still can't believe you're getting married tomorrow. Promise to come back and visit."

Ell stopped in the middle of the path. "Look, Fae. I know you don't like to talk about it. Mama made me promise when I was little not to say anything." Faelyn studied the trees, knowing what was coming. "Drake's land is far from here, and I won't get another chance to speak my piece." She took Faelyn by the hands. "You're safe here. You've grown complacent. I understand what that means. Do you intend to stay here forever? To never marry or have children?" Faelyn glared at the dirt trail. "Someone has to say it." Ell took a deep breath. "What of your kingdom? What of Alysies?"

Faelyn pulled her hands out of Ell's callused grip. She wanted to run from the words that threatened to tear open her tightly knit wound. But she didn't want to hurt Ell, because she was right.

"Alysies is gone. It was never my kingdom in the first place." She took a step back from Ellowen's pitying gaze. "Yes, it might have been a dream of mine, but at some point I have to put away childish things. Like you."

"I'm sorry, Fae. I didn't mean to upset you. I just want to see you happy, and I don't think you'll find that here." Ell took Faelyn by the arm, and they continued walking back toward the house. "Though I am glad Mama and Papa will have your help on the farm. Papa still thinks he can do it all on his own, but he's getting older too."

"I worry it's because of me they don't hire someone. Because I could be discovered." Faelyn stared at the house as it came into view, glad for the change in subject. Her heartache had nearly surfaced in a blubbering admission of the guilt and fear she'd suppressed all these years. She couldn't go back. Who was she to take on a kingdom? Nobody.

Every word of town gossip concerning Daltieri's movements, every confirmation that their evil kingdom still controlled her homeland, was a blade to her heart. None of the neighboring kingdoms had aided Alysies. None of them were strong enough to take on such a powerful army.

"We get along okay." Ell squeezed Faelyn's arm, then pulled her into a tight embrace. "I'll say goodbye now, or tomorrow I'll spend the whole day crying. I wish you could be at the ceremony."

Faelyn did too. She'd been safe for many years, but even if she hid her ears and wore a disguise, too many questions would be raised by her presence. They'd long-stopped sending soldiers to search for her, but Myrick reported her portrait still posted from time to time, so it was the wisest decision to stay away.

Faelyn pulled the ring off her finger, one of the few precious gifts she'd kept from Mary. Silver leaves framed a sparkling blue stone. "A wedding gift for my sister."

Ellowen cradled the ring, then crushed Faelyn in a fierce hug. "Thank you."

They held each other for a long time. The ceremony would be held at the church in town, which Faelyn had yet to visit.

Faelyn threw herself into her chores while the family spent the day in town, celebrating Ellowen and her new husband. Nia cried for a solid week after Ell was gone. She'd lost her daily helper and companion. Myrick and Faelyn worked on planting corn again, neither saying much. It was only at night Faelyn shed tears for missing her adopted sister. The room felt empty without her.

They sent letters back and forth, but mail was slow-going. Faelyn wrote under the name 'Mama Nia' to distinguish herself from Nia and remain anonymous should the letters be discovered. Faelyn remained on the farm, squashing any urges to leave. It was easy to do—Myrick was noticeably slowing, and Faelyn took over more and more of the farm duties.

Ellowen wrote to say she'd had a baby boy and that he was happy and healthy. They named him Myrick. Faelyn wrote back to report a hard year on the farm because of dry weather. Then Ellowen wrote to say the boy, who'd grown into a toddler had died of a fever. She'd also given birth to a healthy baby girl she'd named Lynn. Five years later Ellowen wrote to say she had two more children, boy and girl twins. Ten years after that, she wrote to say she was the happiest she'd ever been and asked again that Faelyn come visit when she got the chance.

Faelyn didn't visit. Her heart was broken. Myrick had passed away from old age. Before the letter with the news had even reached Ell, Nia followed him to the Hereafter. Faelyn held her hands as she slipped into sleep, a smile waiting for her lost love. Faelyn hadn't known such pain since losing Mary.

She was in her forties when Ellowen finally came back to the farm. She came to bury her parents.

Faelyn sat at the old kitchen table, her head in her hands, and her tears pooled into puddles beneath her. What was she to do now? She'd loved Myrick and Nia like her own parents. She never thought about them dying. The letters she'd written to Ell had been the hardest of her life. Losing them had been as big of a shock as losing Mary, and both memories consumed her in grief. It took a long time for Ellowen to return home. Faelyn continued the farm duties, but she was running low on supplies Nia normally bought in town.

Her head snapped up at the sound of a knock. She barely had time to wipe her nose before the door burst open and in walked Ellowen carrying a bag of provisions. Both women gasped in shock. Faelyn stood and covered her mouth, mirroring Ellowen.

Ellowen had aged since she'd left the farm. Gone was any sweet roundness of youth, leaving wise eyes with the faintest of lines around them. Her body was thicker as well. She looked so much like Nia it hurt. Fresh tears spilled over Faelyn's cheeks.

"I've missed you so much, Ell." Faelyn stepped to embrace her long-lost sister, but Ell took a step back, shaking her head behind the hand still covering her mouth. Faelyn lowered her arms, furrowing her brow. "What's the matter?"

"You..." Ellowen took another step back. "You're the same."

"What?"

"You haven't aged a day since I last... last saw you." Ell stumbled backward into the doorframe, placing a hand on her head. "I don't feel well." Her knees gave out, and she slid down the wall.

Faelyn gasped and rushed forward, catching Ellowen's head before it smacked into the hardwood floor. She lifted Ellowen up and carried her to her parents' bed. It was true she hadn't changed much, but she didn't think it warranted the hysterics. She didn't make a habit of looking at herself in the mirror. Every time she did, she expected to see Mary's gaze over her shoulder.

Neither Myrick nor Nia ever said anything to her. Faelyn glanced in Nia's mirror, the wood worn and chipped on the edges. Her bright green eyes stared back at her, accented by her golden hair. She could use a bath, but there wasn't a wrinkle or a hint of the age Ell showed. She touched her face, her skin still bright and clear, compared to Ell's skin, which had dulled.

She still looked like a woman in her twenties, but that was due to eating well and staying active on the farm, surely.

Or was she truly not aging? Was she staying the same while everyone around her was growing old and dying? She touched her pointed ears. She was alone. Myrick and Nia were gone. Ell would go back to her family. If she wasn't aging, then she couldn't even count on death to wrap her in its comforting embrace.

Faelyn looked at her sister sleeping on her deceased parents' bed. She'd missed her so much. It had taken a week for her to travel. Faelyn had already buried her parents beneath the old oak tree. It had been a lonely week.

She hurried to grab a clean rag. After dipping it in cold water, she patted Ell's face and neck. Ell stirred, and her eyes fluttered open. She looked around the room.

"What's happening to me, Fae? Am I dreaming?" Her face was white as a cloud.

Faelyn placed her hand over Ell's forehead. Closing her eyes, she concentrated, sending strength and peace into Ell. Her palmed glowed, surprising even her.

Ell gasped and scrambled back on the bed.

"It's okay, Ell. You're okay. And you're not dreaming." Faelyn raised her hands to show she meant no harm.

"How do you still look the same?" Ell accused.

"I don't know. But I do have the power to heal. Maybe it's kept me from aging, too."

Ell's eyes filled with tears. "I've never heard of such a thing." She wrung her hands and took a deep breath. "But nothing about you has ever been ordinary. And I do trust you." She crept forward, then gave in and hugged Faelyn hard. She buried her face into Faelyn's hair. "They're really gone, aren't they?"

Fresh tears fell from Faelyn. She nodded, unable to speak. Both women cried together into the night. Faelyn tried not to feel guilty that some of those tears fell for herself.

The next morning, Faelyn took Ell to her parents' graves. She'd made a marker out of wood and carved their names into it.

Ell fell to her knees in the dirt, crying anew. The sight broke Faelyn's heart. A long time passed before she broke the silence.

"I know it's hard, Ell." Faelyn stared at the rustling leaves overhead. She closed her eyes as the cool breeze gave her courage and awoke her senses.

Ell nodded, sniffling, hand outstretched to her parents' grave.

She spoke the only words she could think of to provide comfort. "We live our lives here to the fullest, making mistakes and learning to rise above them. Then we die, and who knows what will happen, but I believe we'll all be together again in the Hereafter. So you don't need to miss them." She wrapped an arm around Ell's trembling shoulders. "It's only for a short while, after all."

Ardenis tore his gaze from the scene beneath the ancient tree. He stared into the white marble watch window. A tear rolled down his cheek. He struggled to master his emotions.

Laida.

She'd said those exact words to him before she left Acantha.

His heart lurched. She'd said those words, and he had thought that was the end. She'd grow old and die and go to the Hereafter, and he'd be in Acantha to watch it all happen.

But now...

Ardenis scooted his chair back and rushed out of the tower. He'd almost made it out of the rose garden before he heard Amalia's hurried steps behind him. She stopped him with a forceful hand on his arm.

"What is going on?" She kept her voice down, but the irritation was plain, making the delivery a hiss in his ear.

He turned to her. "She's not aging, Amalia." He put his hands on her shoulders trying to force her to understand how much this meant to him. He'd suspected for a long time, but seeing her next to Ellowen made it all the more obvious. "She's not aging, and who knows how long it will last? This is the second chance I thought I'd never get to be with her on Thera. I can find her, and then we can be together." He dropped his hands and stepped away.

Amalia furrowed her brow. "Where are you going?"

He smiled. "To the transfers. I'm going to be born."

Amalia reeled her arm back and slapped Ardenis across the face. The sound stilled the singing of the birds in the trees. Both of them wore identical masks of shock. He rubbed his cheek even though it didn't hurt.

Amalia closed her gaping mouth and glared at him. "What did I tell you, idiot? Do your job. There's a reason you're still here." Ardenis's brows rose. "You've fated yourself to be born in the future, remember? It's not your time yet."

Ardenis gritted his teeth, his happiness shattered by Amalia's reminder. "I don't care." He lifted his chin, daring her to argue. "What have the Fates ever done for me? I choose to be born."

"Arden." Amalia's tone softened with a sadness bordering on pity. She paused and absently pulled a hand through her long black hair. "What you do is up to you, but I know what my instincts say." She tossed her hair behind her. "What do yours say?"

Ardenis frowned and walked away, though his steps were less sure. Amalia sighed and followed him. They passed other Acanthians on the stone pathway, ensuring Amalia couldn't further push her point. It allowed Ardenis time to think.

He was so close to seeing Laida. It didn't matter he'd forget everything. He knew he could find her. Once he was on Thera, he'd walk to the ends until they were together again. He breathed, trying to calm his excitement. He needed to push his emotions aside in order to listen to his instincts. It didn't help that Amalia's attention bore holes in his back.

Stay or go? If he waited until his fated time, would Faelyn still be alive that far in the future? A time with technology and large cities with buildings that towered into the sky? The woman from his Fating—all he'd seen was her hand. Was it Faelyn's hand?

And why not be born now? What could be gained by staying? If he stayed, he would fulfill his Fating by waiting until the proper time, and he could continue to provide service to Acantha with his gifts. And something... something else.

His instincts crept up, slowly filling him with an urgent nudge to his middle with each step he took toward the transfer hall. His instincts. They were telling him not to go.

But she was so close. Just a few years of waiting to find her on Thera, enough that he'd be old enough to feel these vast feelings, to love her there as deeply as he loved her now.

His instincts pushed against his chest, like gentle hands shoving him backward from the transfer hall.

Amalia was right. His purpose hadn't been fulfilled in Acantha yet. He needed to stay, and his instincts confirmed it. His shoulders slumped under the pain that weighed him down considerably. Once again, he'd have to make the higher choice over his love.

Ardenis pivoted and trudged back to his house, stomping the last few steps to his door. Inside, he turned to face Amalia's smug smile.

He pointed at her. "You know something, don't you?"

She crossed her arms. "I know what you've undoubtedly felt. We are needed here, for now."

He plopped down in his chair and ran his hand through his hair, pulling at it. "This is an impossible choice, Amalia." He met her eyes. "Would you leave? If you had a chance to be born and grow old with your love, would you take it? Even if your instincts said otherwise?"

"Yes. I'd be gone in a heartbeat. But you're a better person than me." She blew dust off the brown flowers on the windowsill. He refused to get rid of them. Laida had given them to him.

"What? That's not an answer."

"Of course it is. Besides, you've already made up your mind, so quit fighting it."

He growled at her. She was right. He was staying.

It wasn't until later he remembered that Amalia had already made the choice. She had loved someone once, and when he left, she trusted her instincts and remained in Acantha to suffer alone for the unknown greater good. So he would, too.

CHAPTER SIXTEEN

Faelyn brewed a pot of tea and took a hot mug out to Ellowen where she sat in a rocking chair on the front porch. Ell wore a cotton nightgown with a pink trim that swayed with the rhythmic movements of the chair. Faelyn handed her the mug, earning a tired smile in return. She rubbed her arms for warmth against the chilly morning. The sun rose, changing the wheat field into shimmering strands of golden yellow.

"I'm sorry I didn't come back sooner." Ell broke into Faelyn's contemplative silence.

"That's all right. The time seemed to pass so quickly." Faelyn sat on the porch, resting her back against a post.

"What are you going to do now?" Ell blew the rising steam off her tea and took a tentative sip.

"Now? I'll keep working I suppose. I assume you'll go home soon." It was easy enough to insinuate she'd be okay, but the reality was she couldn't continue on alone, not without exposing herself to people.

"Fae." Ell stopped rocking and sat forward. "Have you been to town? I've noticed you're running out of salt and other essentials."

Faelyn gave her a tight-lipped smile and shook her head. She had to remind herself she was speaking to Ell and not Nia. Ell didn't need to know everything. She had enough burdens.

"It's been so long, and you're still... you don't look as old as you should. Do you think anyone would suspect who you are?"

Faelyn tapped her pointed ears. "Probably."

Ell squinted. "You can cover those up with your hair." She set the mug on the small wooden table beside her. "Mama and Papa's land and property go to me, naturally. You know I'd turn it over to you if I could. It's more your land than mine, and I don't need it. But since I can't give it to you, I've made a decision." She took a deep breath. "You can't stay here anymore."

Faelyn laughed. Ell didn't join her. Instead, she wore a pained expression. Faelyn jumped up, mind reeling. "What do you mean I can't stay here? This is my home. That's my wheat field, and in that barn is my horse." Fear and anger pulsed in her veins.

"I'm going to sell off the animals. You can keep your horse. The fields will lay fallow waiting for your return, but you can't stay here now."

Faelyn stepped toward her sister with upraised hands. "Why are you doing this?" Her voice was a plea, but she didn't care. She'd beg if necessary. Why now? Did she misjudge how far apart they'd grown? A betrayal, that was what this was. She'd devoted most of her life to this farm. It was all she had.

Ell dashed tears from her eyes. "This isn't who you are. You've forgotten yourself, Faelyn. Princess Faelyn."

Faelyn recoiled as if slapped. She stepped down the porch stairs in a hasty retreat from the hurtful words.

Ell's voice trailed after her. "You'll never leave on your own, so I'm going to force you. Seeing you so young and healthy has only strengthened my resolve."

Faelyn shook her head, still pacing away. "Stop. I don't want to hear anymore."

"I've heard what's become of Alysies. Things are terrible. King

Samual has taken everything from your former people." Faelyn covered her ears, but she couldn't drown out Ell's sharp words. "Listen to me!" Ell stood at the top of the stairs, yelling. "You've hidden your whole life, but it's time to stop hiding!"

"What can I do?" Faelyn turned and screamed. "Nothing!" She threw her arms out wide, panting. Frost coated the ground in a burst around her. "Nothing! I'm just one girl with no army and no power to do anything!"

Ell reared back her head and laughed. "You have the power. You are capable."

Faelyn clenched her hands to keep from conjuring something else she shouldn't. "How dare you laugh at me? You have no idea what I've been through."

"Whose fault is that?"

Faelyn rose her arms above her in the air and clapped her hands together. A bolt of lightning rippled through the cloudless sky, followed by deafening thunder. Her nostrils flared, and she stomped off toward the wheat field.

"I'm sorry, Fae." Ell spoke quietly, but the words carried to Faelyn anyway. "You're bigger than this, and I won't help you waste your life."

Faelyn stormed halfway into the wheat field before stopping. She grabbed a seed from a stalk of wheat and rubbed it between her fingers, then stuck it in her mouth, chewing. The grain cracked between her teeth, but stayed hard. Almost time for harvest. She spent the rest of the morning tearing weeds without gloves. The pain from the slices healed quickly, but the pain of Ell's words did not.

Where would she go?

At midday, she reluctantly went back to the house to find Ell piling her parents' things into crates. Faelyn stopped inside the front door. She crossed her arms and leaned against the frame.

Ell wiped sweat from her brow and stood, holding her back and wincing. "It's tough getting old. If my kids were here, I'd have them doing this job."

"What are you doing?"

Ell faced Faelyn. "I'm getting the house ready to close up for a while. Someone will be here in three days to collect the animals. I'd suggest leaving before then."

Faelyn nearly fell over. "The wheat is only two weeks away from harvest. You'd let that whole crop go to waste just to prove a point?" Her blood and sweat were in that crop. She couldn't let it go to waste.

"I've sold the crop, minus the cost of laboring the harvest."

Faelyn clenched her fists. "When did you have time to arrange all this?"

"I stopped in town on the way here." Ell crossed her arms.

Faelyn shook her head. "I can't believe you're doing this. Have I not earned my place here? I took care of your parents and your farm. Why, Ell, why?"

"As I said, the land is yours as soon as you give me the okay to put it in your name. Until then, what I say goes."

Faelyn sneered. Ell knew what she was doing. The only way it would ever be okay to transfer the land to her was if she was no longer being pursued. "And where should I go?"

"Well. If you don't know..." Ell eased herself into a chair at the kitchen table. "I'd suggest looking within yourself. Is there anywhere you've always wanted to go, but never have? Anything you wanted to do but never did?"

Faelyn stared coldly across the small space. Of course there were places she wanted to go. Back to Mary's loving arms. Back to her father naming her heir. Back to Samual to end him in a slow and painful death. But none of those things were possible.

"No." She set her jaw, refusing to play Ell's games.

Ell sighed. "You can have the gold Mama and Papa saved, and from the harvest, of course. That should get you far enough to find the answers you're seeking."

"I'm not seeking any answers."

"We all have questions needing answers, Fae. We all have a past that needs faced or laid to rest."

Faelyn didn't reply except to go to her room and shut the door. She heard Ell sigh again, but ignored her. Grabbing her old satchels, she began stuffing them for the inevitable journey and departure from her beloved farm and home. Spare clothes, her father's circlet—kept shiny after all this time—gold coins.

Faelyn became angrier with each shove. She grabbed things at random, tears burning her eyes, trying not to scream. A distant splintering noise drew her up short. She gasped.

"No. Please, no." She looked into the bag. Pieces of her mother's comb lay scattered among the clothes. "Oh, no."

The turquoise stone lay within the rubble, and she picked it up between her shaking thumb and forefinger. Sinking to her knees, she cradled the stone in her hand, feeling ill. She'd loved that comb since she was a little girl, and now it was nothing but splinters. She'd crushed her most sacred possession in anger.

Faelyn trembled under her emotions scraped raw. Her temper had always been her downfall. She hadn't felt like this in so long. Ell was right again. She'd closed herself off from the world, from her past.

She stood, attempting to master herself, and put the stone and small pieces of wood into a leather pouch, placing it tenderly back into her satchel. Like her, it was broken beyond repair, but maybe something new could be forged from the splinters.

Two days later, Faelyn held the reins of her horse, Clip Clop the Third, and bid goodbye to Ellowen for what could possibly be the last time.

"Good luck with the farm. Take good care of her for me." She didn't step close to Ell. The possibility that Ell might change her mind lurked in the forefront of her thoughts, alongside a constant ache in her heart. She'd miss the woods and the connection she felt working the land and growing things. And the blessed safety of the farm.

Ell's eyes crinkled into a sad smile as she stepped forward and embraced her sister. "Don't be angry forever, Faelyn. I believe you'll thank me one day. I love you."

Faelyn clenched her jaw. "I may not understand what you're doing, but I love you too."

That wasn't true. She did understand what Ell was doing. Taking her safe refuge from her and putting her in danger all over again.

Ell released her. "Travel well, sister."

Faelyn nodded and mounted. She walked her horse down the hill past the enormous old oak and fallow cornfield without looking back. Ellowen's gaze weighed heavy, like a lamentation following her as she retreated further into Creadel.

When she reached a fork in the road, she dropped the reins and let Clip Clop choose which way to go. He turned left.

"East it is."

CHAPTER SEVENTEEN

Ardenis walked home from the tower with steps as heavy as Faelyn's sadness. He'd watched her travel all day, and she didn't pay any attention to where she went, letting her dumb horse decide for her. Maybe it was as good a plan as any. Maybe the Fates would come through for her in the end. He didn't have much faith in that after all this time. Not after what he'd seen Faelyn go through and what he'd seen her mother, Eva, endure.

He stared at the ground as he walked, and didn't notice Hector standing in the path until he almost ran into him.

"Watch yourself, Ardenis." Hector jerked to the other side of the path, glaring. He never used Ardenis's full title anymore.

Ardenis's heart was too heavy to fight with Hector today. "Good evening, Hector," he said and kept walking.

"I've been watching Faelyn lately." Hector delivered the words to Ardenis's back with calculated casualness. They rooted him to the spot.

Ardenis watched Faelyn fulltime. No one else needed to watch as well. It was a waste of time and energy when there was so much else to see.

“Things aren’t going so well for the elf.” Hector sounded almost gleeful.

Ardenis spun and stepped closer toward Hector, thankful the paths were clear of people this time of night. He didn't need witnesses to his emotional state. He’d almost been forced to be born before, coming close to violence to save himself. He wasn’t above considering it again. In fact, it sounded appealing at the moment. Just one punch to Hector’s face. And then? The council would force him to be born where he’d run right to Faelyn.

“Why are you watching her? You know she’s my assignment.” Ardenis clenched his fists.

“After viewing Thera all this time, I can see now how watchers become so easily affected. The council already suspects you. You’re being watched, you know. I’ve seen enforcers you didn’t even know were enforcers following you.”

Ardenis remained stone-faced, but his stomach roiled. Rhea had warned him, and he’d been careful. “Are you trying to tell me you’ve been emotionally influenced by Thera? Because we’re way passed that now.”

“Simply making conversation with my fellow watcher.”

Ardenis turned to go. Hector may be a watcher, but he'd never be an equal.

“I knew there was no place for an elf in Thera. Time is doing for me what Gharum failed to do when he was here.”

Ardenis trembled with rage, but kept going. Hector followed.

“You think it’s Laida, don’t you?” Hector forced a laugh. “Your precious Laida probably died in her mother’s womb.”

Ardenis turned and punched Hector in the face so hard, he flew back and landed on his ass. The action hurt neither of them, except for perhaps Hector’s pride.

Hector stared up at Ardenis with a gaping mouth. “Are you out of your mind?” He scrambled to his feet. “I’m going to the council.”

“No, you will not." He stared down at Hector. "I know a secret about you involving someone in Acantha. A girl.” Amalia would kill

Ardenis if she found out he'd voiced her secret, that Hector was once in love with her, but Hector deserved it. *Manipulative bastard.*

Hector narrowed his eyes, but took a step back. He glanced nervously around them. "You can't prove it. I have nothing to fear from you." Hector stormed away.

Ardenis shook loose of his anger. He walked home, enjoying the lingering feel of Hector's nose flattened against his fist. If only he'd inflicted pain.

Ardenis watched as Faelyn aimlessly wandered the kingdom of Creadel for the next fifty years. Mostly she camped in the woods, or when she reached the desert, she set up a tent each night or slept under the stars. When supplies ran low, she'd venture into a town or village. She always wore a scarf or kept her hair covering her ears. No one recognized her, and it seemed Daltieri had stopped looking for her ever since King Samual died from old age. Dracus, the eldest of Samual's many ill-equipped sons, took his place, but the wanted fliers stopped circulating.

Faelyn celebrated the news of Samual's death by trading her last Alysian coin for new traveling clothes and a bar of chocolate. The coin had become a collector's item in Creadel since Daltieri outlawed anything related to Alysian culture.

Faelyn worked odd jobs during her wandering. For years, she assisted at apothecary shops in towns across Creadel, always on the move. She stopped practicing swordfighting—she'd had to leave her sword behind—and she stopped smiling. The happiness she'd lost when she left the safety of the farm made her lifeless and aimless. She hardly used her magic, and Ardenis saw it become harder for her each time she did.

Life and time seemed to pass her by while she remained in a fog of fear and denial. But she didn't age, for which Ardenis was grateful.

Someone shook Ardenis from his watch. He blinked allowing

Thera to leave his vision. Amalia stood before him with a huge grin that did not reach her eyes.

"I'm going to be born. I feel it. It's my time."

Ardenis gaped, speechless. Amalia frowned. He stood abruptly, causing her to take a step back. "What did you just say?" His voice carried through the tower, sparking interest from those around them.

Amalia jerked her chin toward the exit, and he wordlessly followed her into their favored rose garden. He focused on the perfect weather to keep himself from blurting questions. Only springtime in Thera seemed to mimic Acantha. During Thera's spring, Ardenis could imagine how it might feel to live in the mortal world. He couldn't appreciate the connection now as he followed Amalia to a stone bench. The pain was already building.

"It's true. I'm going to be born." Amalia glanced at him, eyebrows drawn. Her pleading eyes begged for understanding and acceptance. "Are you happy for me, Arden?"

Ardenis held his hands in the air, as if that could encapsulate all the questions roiling inside him. He decided to start simple. "Why? Why now?"

"Why ever?" The defensiveness in her voice was plain. "I don't know. Something just spoke to me. I feel it's my time. I think... I think Faelyn needs me."

He dropped his arms. She'd said the one thing she could have to convince him not to argue with her. He'd do anything for Faelyn, even sacrificing his best friend to Thera. He couldn't speak, only study his hands while he worked up the courage to be the friend Amalia needed. To be the friend she deserved.

"I will miss you terribly." His voice came out nearly a whisper. The words didn't feel close to adequate. He couldn't look her in the eyes. He gripped the edge of the bench, knuckles white under the strain of his unvoiced pain.

Amalia laid her hand on his. "I'll miss you, too, Arden. You're the only reservation I have about leaving, but still I feel I must. There's a tug pulling me, and I've little time."

"When do you leave?" He held his breath.

"Immediately."

His air rushed out in a great whoosh as if he'd been punched. He found the courage to meet her eyes, and they looked pained, creased with concern and radiating sadness. This was hard for her. He wouldn't make it harder.

"Well then." He shoved off the bench. "I'll walk you there."

Amalia gave a small smile, and they walked side by side to the transfer hall. He held his stomach as the pain doubled when she didn't argue for more time.

This was serious. She really was leaving.

Several watchers who'd overheard the news from her in the tower waited to say goodbye. They wore their oblivious smiles and wished her a good journey. Idonea embraced Amalia, then returned to the transfers to oversee their operations. When the last well-wishers cleared away, Ardenis walked Amalia to the short line within the transfer hall. Not many Acanthians wanted to be born during these hard times on Thera.

Amalia glanced at Ardenis almost shyly, unwilling to meet his eyes. He pulled her into a tight embrace and held her for a long time, not caring who saw. She was the best friend he'd ever had. She'd saved him from exile. More than that, she'd saved him from himself. He would have been lost many times without her. She'd kept the loneliness and pain of losing Laida at bay.

Who would fill the pain of losing Amalia? This was the last time they'd ever see each other.

"Ardenis," she said with her chin on his shoulder, "remember it's not your time. Trust your instincts, as I'm trusting mine. We're part of something bigger, you and I."

"I don't know what I'll do without you."

"You'll just have to find someone new to drive insane." Amalia pulled back and smiled.

He gave a disheartened chuckle. She placed her hand against his cheek, then turned and walked toward the gateway. Everything was happening too fast.

"Travel well, my friend." His eyes burned.

Under the guidance of Idonea, Amalia stepped into the gateway. A few seconds went by, then a few minutes.

Nothing happened.

He'd never seen it take this long.

Amalia cast a worried glance at Ardenis, who looked at Idonea. Idonea, in all her emotional unawareness, merely smiled, unfazed by the delay. Ardenis turned, ready to retrieve someone from the council to witness what was happening, but then Amalia gasped behind him.

He spun back in time to see her expression, unlocked by the connection to the mortal world. She looked nearly the same, having long been exposed to the emotional influences of Thera, but there was a new kindness in her eyes, an almost innocence he'd never seen before. She held his gaze. The bond of friendship emanating from her nearly brought him to his knees. It came hand in hand with her sadness at leaving.

"We were right, Arden. It is better." She smiled, and then she was gone.

Ardenis clung to the railing, unable to move away. Laida's parting had been much harder to bear, but he'd had months to prepare for that inevitability. Amalia was there and gone in an instant. Another person he loved, leaving him forever. How much more could he take?

Tears blurred his vision. All the thoughts he dared not speak aloud to Amalia, lest he upset her or sway her from a decision she'd already made, came swelling to his mind. Who would he laugh with now? Who would ever understand his obsession with watching Faelyn or his pity of Hector, or his capacity to love in a world where love was forbidden? No one. Who could he poke fun at, and who would give him feisty attitude in return? No one. He had no one now.

He was utterly alone, doomed to fake his way through this existence, pretending to be someone he wasn't.

He raised a hand to his aching heart. There was one way to end the pain. He could get in line and be born right along with her. All his problems could be solved, and the solution was but mere steps away. He moved forward toward the gateway, then stopped.

Amalia knew he'd feel this way. She knew he'd be tempted to leave, and it'd been her last wish for him to stay. He sagged as the breath rushed out of him. She was right. As much as Amalia felt a pull to Thera, he felt a pull to stay. Even through the loneliness, his place was in Acantha. It wasn't his time.

His hands fell from the railing, and he shuffled out of the transfer hall.

There was only one thing that could comfort him now, so he returned to the watch tower.

Faelyn was working in a bar in a small town called Newberry on the west side of Creadel when something happened he'd never thought he'd see.

CHAPTER EIGHTEEN

Faelyn filled metal mugs with ale from a barrel behind the sticky bar. Of all the things she'd done to cure her boredom and drive the bad memories away, working at the bar was the worst. But, when coin ran low...

The men inside were already loud, competing over who could drink the most before running out of money or the contents of their stomachs. More patrons filed in, eager to escape the cold of winter.

She scoffed to herself. These people didn't know cold. Creadel's winters hardly compared to those of Alysies.

Jarold, the owner, took orders at the bar, attention half on the customers and half admiring her and the other barmaidens. Faelyn ignored him. She'd worked here for a week, thinking maybe she'd learn how to manage a bar. Not that she'd ever settle down long enough to run one, but it was something new to add to her long list of useless skills. Jarold was hard-pressed to answer her questions, but she'd seen enough already to know this wasn't for her.

Faelyn filled the mugs, hurrying to move out of the way for the next barmaiden, who tapped her foot with impatience. She carried the tray across the room to one of the loudest tables in the bar. These men weren't regulars—most of the patrons in the bar she'd seen every day that week. These seemed to be passing through.

"Just look at her," one of the newcomers said, watching her approach. "Someone drop something so she has to pick it up." The men laughed.

Faelyn seethed. She'd listened to them banter for the better part of an hour, and she was almost at her breaking point. She dropped off the ale with a glare and retreated to avoid conversation.

The biggest man sported a mustache and a leather vest. He was balding, and layers of grease weighed down what hair he had left. He sipped at his drink and leered at her from across the room.

She wiped a table clean from a group who'd just left. An utter waste of time. She'd leave now if she didn't need the money so bad. Tips became more plentiful as the night wore on, she'd discovered. She missed her nursing job. She'd done that for five years before moving on. She was still pissed that, when she'd asked, they told her women weren't allowed to become doctors.

The loud table with the greasy man—Brent, they called him—joked about what they'd like to do to her, getting bolder with each affront. She patted her leg, feeling the reassuring bulk of the knife strapped beneath her short skirt. Oh, how she missed the days not so long ago when not even barmaidens wore such scandalous clothes. The current style featured skirts that barely covered her knees and a too-small tunic that laced too tight at the top.

She finished wiping down the table of bread crumbs soaked in spilled ale and turned to find Brent standing right in front of her. She had to look up to meet his leering eyes.

"You're a quiet one." The scent of whiskey on his breath overpowered her. "The boys and I would like you to come over and talk with us." He looked her up and down, his eyes lingering.

Faelyn rolled her eyes and stepped away. Hurting them would be too easy. Besides, Mary wouldn't have approved, and she was the voice in the back of her head, helping her make good choices. "If you want more ale I'm all ears, otherwise, no thanks." She stepped toward the bar. He grabbed her butt from behind, pinching hard.

Before he knew it, Greasy Man Brent's head slammed against the table she'd just cleaned. He howled in pain as she held him there, his wrist bent painfully behind him.

She knew just how to twist it to snap the bone. Mary would understand.

Faelyn leaned over to whisper in his ear. "You don't touch me." She bent his wrist further back for emphasis. She sensed his growing anger at having a simple barmaiden overpower him. He wanted retribution. There could be none of that. He was ruining her tips. Faelyn called forth magic, using her despair and anger to send dark feelings of fear into him. "Ever."

He nodded into the table.

"And tell your boys the same."

"Is everything all right?" A man asked behind her.

Faelyn released Brent, expecting one of his friends, but they stood at their table, slack-jawed, some with knives drawn, some without. Brent rolled off the table and stumbled over to them, rubbing his wrist.

The hostile silence of the room dissipated, returning laughter and conversation.

She faced the newcomer. His face was the first thing she noticed, lean and stubbled. He appeared as young as she did, early twenties, with broad shoulders and smooth skin. His short ebony hair hung over kind, hazel eyes, and she had a ridiculous urge to sweep it back for him. High cheekbones and a strong jawline highlighted his perfect lips as they formed a slight smile.

She was staring and shifted her gaze to his clothes. Black robes hung down to his ankles, and he carried a staff. She felt the magic in it. She knew that magic. That magic was present the day she'd lost everything. The day her life changed forever.

She grabbed her dagger from its sheath and brandished it, backing up.

"Hey!" The mage's staff lit up, and his eyes widened in surprise. "I'm not going to hurt you. I planned to help, but you took care of that ass well enough." Several more robed figures surrounded her, just out of reach, all wielding staffs full of the same glowing magic.

Faelyn breathed, trying to calm her high-strung nerves. This man was not the same one she'd seen with Samual. This mage didn't help overthrow her kingdom in a day. But it was clear he hailed from the same school. Thomats, the school of magic her father had always denied her in Alysies.

The mages, both men and women, five in all, stared warily.

One of the women, short with flowing red hair, lowered her staff and stepped forward. "It's okay." She glanced at her companions. "Look, it's pretty intense in here. We saw what that man did to you. Are you okay?"

Faelyn lowered her knife. "I'm fine. Sorry. You startled me is all." She looked at Brent's table. He sat back with his friends, pointing at her and plotting to hurt her after she left, though he couldn't know she heard him. She narrowed her eyes.

Redhead mage cleared her throat. Faelyn sheathed her weapon, and the glow dimmed from their staffs now that a knife wasn't being pointed at them.

"Are you all here to drink? What can I get you?"

"We *are* here to drink," the handsome mage hedged, "but we've happened upon something more interesting. Is there somewhere we can talk privately?"

Faelyn felt the eyes of her temporary boss, Jarold, on her from the bar, so she flashed him a quick smile of reassurance.

"No. There's nowhere." Certainly not her makeshift home, in the dense thicket of the woods outside of this unforgiving town. Where was she, anyway? *Who cares.*

"Okay." Handsome stepped closer, lowering his voice. He locked her in with his penetrating gaze. "Tell me, how did you do that magic just now?"

Faelyn blinked, heart racing anew. "Look, I can't talk to the customers. Just give me your order, and I'll be on my way." She backed up a step.

"We'll order drinks, but when your shift is over, we'd really like to talk with you. We're bound for Thomats School of Magic in New Daltieri."

Faelyn cringed. She hated that name. Every time anyone used it was an insult to her family. No one alive called her kingdom by its true name anymore. She refused to call it New Daltieri no matter how much time passed.

She shook her head, ready to deny Handsome yet again.

"I feel it's no coincidence we've crossed paths this night." Handsome's mage staff glowed slightly as he spoke.

Faelyn sighed through her nose. "Your order?"

He exchanged glances with Redhead and their fellow mages, then they sat at the empty table and ordered a round of ale.

Before she walked away, Handsome spoke up. "I'm Kian, and this is Niri." He gestured to the redhead who gave a nod. "Mason, Avier, and Miyah." The mages inclined their heads in turn, radiating a mixture of curiosity and distrust.

Faelyn adopted a bored expression. "Great." She walked to the bar and got in line for the tap. She glared at the back of a hussy of a barmaiden who liked to sleep with the patrons for extra tips.

Jarold crossed his arms and cleared his throat. "You will not hurt the customers, Ali." He used the false name she'd given him. She stared at the floor, trying to appear appropriately abashed. "This happened yesterday too. They're gonna grab ya once or twice when they get the drink in them. It's your job to show them a good time. A little grabbin' won't hurt ya none. Once more, and you're outta here."

Faelyn remained silent, glaring at the floor. The urge to grab Jarold and show him how it could hurt filled her mind with a satisfying scene. Her penetrating gaze burned a small black hole in the wooden floor.

Jarold didn't notice the new addition, or the wisp of smoke. He grunted and walked away.

Faelyn looked up and caught Kian's knowing stare from across the room. He didn't blink, only quirked his head to the side to let her know he knew. Damn him and his unusual magic-detecting ability.

"Go, Ali. Hurry up." The barmaiden behind her shoved her by the shoulder, and Faelyn realized she'd been staring again. It was her turn for the tap.

Her face heated as she filled five mugs full of ale, narrowly avoiding the urge to make them all foam.

She carried the tray around the bar and wound her way through men belting drunken folk songs, and barmaidens throwing themselves around for tips. Faelyn felt more awake, more aware than she'd been in the past couple of decades. She had to admit something rang true in Kian's words when he said their paths crossing was no coincidence. Not that she believed in fate or any of that. If she believed in fate, she'd have to admit she was doomed to a life of misery, and she couldn't do that, even in her depressed and indignant state of mind. The group of mages had simply piqued her curiosity, but she wouldn't speak with them.

Faelyn hadn't encountered much magic in her travels. She'd seen tricks performed by traveling showmen. Sometimes she hitched a ride, paying her way with small bits of real magic to pose as a magician. If they wouldn't accept her as a performer, she'd trade manual labor, or an apothecary concoction—sweet grass ground to a powder, infused with her healing magic to make people feel better. She'd tried healing them with only magic, and learned the hard way people felt safer with the ruse.

Despite her devotion to living alone—a lingering punishment to Ell for forcing her into this kind of existence—Kian and his group intrigued her. She wanted to hear what he had to say. That irritated her.

She plunked down the tray, splashing ale across the table. She did not look at any of them as they reacted to the spilled ale. Especially not Kian. She turned to wait on the next table.

"We're staying at the inn next door. I'll wait up for you. No matter when you decide you're ready, you can find me." Kian's feelings of curiosity rose above the rest.

Faelyn swore he sent something else purposefully into his being. An aura of urgency perhaps? Definitely something to tempt her further into coming.

Did he know she could sense his emotions?

Faelyn scowled and missed what the new table ordered. She spent the rest of the long night thinking about the mystery of Kian. Her tips were especially low when she counted them at the end, and then Jarold took his cut. She'd have to work another day in this heaping dunghill before she had enough to move on.

She was tired, dirty, and she smelled. She was in no state for a midnight meeting with a handsome mage.

Good. Time to get it over with.

She threw on her worn cloak, pulling it tight. The winter nights just loved to bite through her clothes, especially with the wind's help. It gusted as she pushed open the door.

The scent of sour whiskey and grease accosted her before a hand clamped over her mouth. She'd forgotten about Brent and his grand plans. The point of a knife stuck her back, but didn't break the skin. Brent—panting and glancing from side to side—and two more of his thugs surrounded her, and they dragged her to an ally between Newberry Inn and Jarold's bar.

Newberry. That was where she was.

The man holding her mouth and arms backed up against the inn's rough wooden wall. Faelyn would have sighed if she could. If the anger rising in her wasn't outweighing her annoyance. She let them drag her out of the public eye, not that there was much public this time of night.

Bad things tended to happen when she lost her temper, so she clamped down on her anger.

Brent approached, smirking. She expected some kind of speech, but instead he thrust his hand under her skirt, grabbing her knife. He held it in front of her.

"Thought I forgot about this, eh? You're just like all the others. Easy prey."

Faelyn's anger exploded from her tight control. The magic clamped onto her rage, and she let it loose. Brent screamed as his hand caught fire, flames licking over his fingers and up his arm. The knife thunked to the ground.

The man holding her shouted, but didn't loosen his grip. Faelyn used his surprise to slam her head back into his nose with a crunch. He cursed and let go. While he stumbled back, she grabbed the knife in her boot and slit his throat.

Brent's friends threw him down, beating him with their coats.

They helped him do this. Her magic set them on fire, too.

Brent writhed on the ground beside them as his friends stilled, dead. Still, the anger in her wasn't sated. With an enormous effort of will, she extinguished the flames. Brent lay weeping over his disfigured arm. Faelyn approached him, knife at the ready.

"Don't kill me, please." He begged her with snot and tears running down his face. "I didn't mean nothin' by it. I didn't know you were a witch."

A witch? "I told you not to touch me. You meant to do terrible things to me. I can't let you do those things to anyone else." Her voice sounded cold. She stared down at him. Guilt and remorse tried to flood through her, but she blocked the emotions with a stab of the knife into Brent's heart. He wouldn't hurt anyone again. He fell over dead, and she let out a weary sigh. The anger abated as quickly as it had come, leaving her drained.

A sharp gasp sounded behind her. She sensed Kian before she turned. He stood next to the opening of the ally, staff aglow, hair and robes billowing in the wind. She met his eyes. His magic spiked, and before she could react, she collapsed to the ground into blackness.

CHAPTER NINETEEN

Faelyn awoke, keeping her eyes closed and immediately continuing the breaths of deep sleep. The wind whistled as it whipped against a nearby window. She was no longer outside. She lay in a soft bed beneath a thick blanket. She was warmer than she'd felt in weeks. No light penetrated her eyelids, so it was still night.

Soft breathing and the rustle of a quill scratching against parchment sounded nearby.

"I know you're awake," Kian said.

Faelyn frowned and sat up in the bed.

"I thought I was doing a decent job. How did you know?" She wrapped the blanket around her shoulders against the slight chill in the room.

He closed the book and smiled. "You snored when you were really asleep."

"I did not!" she said, and he laughed.

She scrunched her eyebrows. Something about Kian disarmed her, but it wasn't magic. His staff wasn't glowing.

She looked at her surroundings. The room was small, with scant furnishings, just the one bed and a writing desk where Kian sat. A small lamp was the only source of light. "You brought me to the inn?" Something about being alone with Kian in his room awakened her senses.

"Yes, I'm sorry. You were out of control, and I had to do something." He studied her.

"I blacked out..." The last thing she saw was Kian and his glowing mage crystal. "Wait, did you put me under some kind of spell?" She'd never heard of such a thing.

"I don't know how you haven't been discovered by a school yet, but your magic is very powerful. You let it go unchecked tonight. Your anger fueled it, and you killed four men. Do you remember that?"

"Of course I do. They meant to harm me! I'd kill them again given the chance." Faelyn stood and threw the blanket back on the bed.

"Where are you going?" He dropped the quill.

"To hide the evidence, of course." She reached for the door.

"Already taken care of."

"Then I'm leaving. Thanks for rendering me unconscious and bringing me to your secluded room alone and watching me while I slept." She looked down at herself. "At least I'm still in my own clothes." She shuddered, unnerved. She had no idea how Kian had been able to use magic against her, and she wasn't about to stick around so he could do it again.

Kian jumped up from the tiny writing desk, his book tumbling to the floor. "Wait, please. I'll leave if you want. I know the aftereffect of what I did leaves a violent headache." He smiled, abashed. "I do apologize for that."

Faelyn felt no headache, to which she attributed her quick healing.

"Normally, people sleep all night after that particular spell."

Faelyn shrugged. "Fine, then leave, I suppose."

"You're not making this easy."

She suppressed a smile. She found she enjoyed making Kian

squirm. It had been a long time since she'd felt so at ease with someone, enough to be herself despite his unnerving magic. Even during all those long years on the farm, she'd shaped herself into someone whose personality would better fit in. Accommodating, nonconfrontational, hardworking, eager to please. Maybe she was all those things, but around Kian she was allowing herself to be much more without any conscious effort to do so.

The fun couldn't last. Nothing did. So why not enjoy it while it did?

"Okay, Kian. You wanted to talk, so let's talk." She sat back on the bed and wrapped the warm blanket back around her shoulders. Newberry Inn was a far better place to sleep than her shelter in the woods, but it still had its drafts.

Not all of the tension left Kian's shoulders as he sat back in his chair. "I think you should come with us. Back to Thomats."

Not a chance. "And why is that?"

"I have a gift for sensing the magic in others. I've never sensed a magic so strong before. I don't even have words to describe it. It's pure and... elemental. It feels clean, somehow." He rubbed his hands on his bouncing knees. "Where do you keep your mage crystal?"

"I don't have a crystal. I don't need one." She felt an odd need to reveal all her secrets to this perfect stranger. Another one of his tricks?

"You don't have to tell me. I'm simply curious." His hazel eyes locked on hers.

She found herself lost in their bottomless depths, forgetting how to speak.

"All right, next question, and I hope you'll forgive me for saying so, but I've never seen ears like yours before."

Faelyn's hands shot to her ears where they remained safely hidden beneath her long hair. She jumped up on the bed, looking down on Kian with eyes narrowed in fury. Her ears were the only thing left to tie her back to who she really was. She pulled her magic forward, readying to defend herself.

Kian snatched up his staff reflexively, and the crystal flared. "Hey!" He held it in front of him. "What did I say? Calm down. Your magic is spiking."

"What do you know about my ears?" Faelyn shot the words like arrows.

"What? Nothing! Your hair shifted when I carried you up here."

"Who else saw them?"

"No one. Once I got you up here, I sent my friends to take care of those men. Believe me, they weren't happy about it." Kian narrowed his eyes. "Burying bodies in the middle of the night is not exactly what mages do in their spare time. We did you a favor."

Anger flowed out of her, chased off by guilt. Kian had done more than just a favor. No doubt they'd all get expelled from the school if they were caught. Probably worse.

Of course, if he hadn't rendered her unconscious, she could have cleaned up her own mess. The truth she didn't want to admit was, she should have found a way not to kill the men.

She lowered her magical defense just a bit, pulling back the amount she'd readied.

Kian relaxed his staff to his side, sensing even this subtle shift in her.

She frowned. "My ears are a sensitive subject."

"I see that." He gestured to where she still stood atop his bed.

She stepped down in front of him, aware of how close he was. "This is hard for me, but I want to trust you, and I don't want to kill you, so I'm going to be honest, and I need you to be honest with me in return."

He still retained a hint of anger in his stern eyes and set jaw. "Well, in exchange for your trust and my life, I vow to tell the truth." The sarcasm was lost with his irritated delivery. But she felt his sincere heart.

Faelyn's gaze drifted to the floor. Kian could be a friend to her, but things were starting all wrong between them.

She took a deep breath and stuck out her hand. *Here goes nothing.*

"My name is Aliyah, but people call me Ali." Not *too* much honesty, anyway.

Kian looked at her hand and then took it slowly. He felt warm and comforting.

She pumped her arm up and down, then let go. "I hail from southern Creadel on the outskirts of the Sengi desert." She'd done her nursing there so she knew enough for it to be plausible, and it wasn't populated enough for most to have ventured there. "My parents passed away some years ago, and I was left with nothing, so I've been wandering ever since."

Kian smiled. "Nice to meet you, Ali. I'm Kian, as you know. Kian Foster. I'm from Creadel as well, but I grew up south of here near Terca. My companions and I were on holiday, but are on our way back to continue our studies. I've been at Thomats for ten years now, since I was twelve, but I have a long way to go."

Faelyn returned his smile. "And what do you plan to do when you're finished?"

"I want to teach there, which is why I've been studying so long. The school pays me to recruit for them on breaks because of my unique ability." He winked at her.

Faelyn frowned, a familiar sadness creeping over her. "Is that why you're interested in talking to me?"

Kian's brow wrinkled. "Well, yeah." He shuffled his feet. "Partly." He set his staff back against the wall. "There's something in your voice that draws me to you."

"So you're trying to recruit me?" She crossed her arms.

"Come back with us. Meet my professor. If you don't like it, you could always leave. But I think you should at least learn some mastery over your magic. You let your emotions rule you, but that's nothing that can't be fixed with some discipline."

Faelyn bristled, her pride stung. She'd done all right on her own. Besides, she couldn't afford to go to some fancy school anyway.

"Don't take offense," Kian hurried to say. "I've just never met anyone like you. My words are getting in my way." He sighed and sat down in the chair. "We leave in the morning, so I really should get some sleep. I'll bunk with Avier, and you can stay here." His eyes opened wide. "Unless you'd prefer to go home, I mean. Jeez, you probably wouldn't want to stay in this rundown place when you could be home. Can I escort you anywhere?"

Faelyn smiled at his plain unease. She opened her senses and felt his honest concern for her wellbeing and comfort. Kian could be trusted.

"I tell you this not to earn your pity, but because I think we could be friends and I want to be honest with you." She plopped back on the bed. "I have no money. I've saved some from my tips at the bar, and I've enough to survive on, but that's it. My home for the past week has been the woods outside of Newberry." She looked away from his eyes that had turned pitying despite her warning. "Before that it was the open road. I don't lead an easy life, but it's my own fault." She studied her hands. "Anyway, I couldn't afford to go to your school even if I wanted to. But thank you for the offer. Perhaps we'll meet again someday."

Sadness radiated from him. She tasted a sense of loss from him and wondered if he felt the same from her. Loss of what might have been. He stared without speaking, but the silence was full of what neither of them would say.

"I was born this way, Kian. My ears, my magic. It sets me apart from others—makes me different. My whole life I've wondered why, but that's a question I fear will never be answered." She reached and took his hand. "As your new friend, I must plead with you to keep what you know about my appearance to yourself. It could be life-threatening to me if it got out."

Kian squeezed her hand and opened his mouth to speak, but she cut him off.

"I can't answer any of your questions, so don't try to force me."

"I was simply going to say, your secret is safe with me. Like I said, I feel it's no coincidence our paths have crossed. I believe in the Fates." He let go of her hand, but Faelyn felt his reluctance. "As for tuition, the school funds the way for those with strong magic, and yours is particularly strong. Can't have mages running loose with no training, right? Otherwise someone could get hurt."

Faelyn felt her guilt anew. Kian gave her a tight smile.

"So, will you come with us?" Hope bloomed in his pretty eyes and layered the air around them.

There seemed no reason to refuse now. Except for the fact she hadn't stepped back into Alysies since she'd fled. And even all these years later—seventy, eighty?—she could still be in danger there.

"Okay. I'll come." She smiled and shook her head. She must have been out of her mind to agree to this. Yet, it felt right. It was the first thing in so many years that Mary would have been pleased with.

"All right!" He jumped out of his seat in excitement and hugged her.

Faelyn's eyes went wide, but then she leaned into his strong embrace, hugging him back. He didn't let go, so she cautiously, briefly, rested her head into the crook of his neck, breathing him in. He smelled of musk, and travel, and friendship, and knowledge, and hope. It had been a lifetime since she'd been so close to someone else. The nearness of him filled her up, and her heart softened.

Too soon, he let go. He cleared his throat and stepped back from the bed. "Well, I'll rouse you in the morning, then. Goodnight." He hurried out the door before she could reply.

Faelyn smiled and climbed under the covers. With only a few hours before dawn, it would be a long day, but Kian's friendship gave her something to look forward to.

The door flew open, startling her. Kian darted to her bedside. Faelyn's heart sped up.

He grabbed his staff from where it sat propped against the wall. "Sorry. I can't believe I forgot this. Goodnight." He rushed back out the room and closed the door behind him.

The blanket shook with Faelyn's silent laughter as some of the bitterness of the past years melted away.

CHAPTER TWENTY

Faelyn was up before dawn after only a few hours of sleep, and she crept down the hall. She knew immediately which room Kian slept in, sensing him as she passed. It was as if she had learned his magical essence and become attuned to it. Whatever it was, she breathed in the gentleness of it. The forewarning was also very convenient.

Drawing her cape tight around her, she stepped outside, shivering in the cold air. A layer of frost blanketed the town. No one walked the streets at this early hour. She crossed the dirt road and slipped behind the bakery. The rich smell of baking bread set her mouth watering. It'd been a while since her last meal.

Faelyn listened for sounds of pursuit, then quickly hopped the bushes dividing Newberry from the woods. She sprinted to a grove of thick trees and rounded them, side-stepping thorn bushes and saplings. Ducking beneath the branches she'd carefully propped up into a makeshift shelter, she picked through her latest bag, already packed for a quick departure. Shivering, she changed out of her barmaiden outfit and discarded it in the dirt. She smiled and kicked the insulting uniform, sending it flying into the trees.

Over a fresh tunic, she hung a delicate silver chain, weighed down by the pendant she'd made from her mother's turquoise stone. Ready, she shouldered her bag. Keeping her father's circlet posed a risk, but it was safest with her.

The snap of a twig made her draw her knife. She sent out her hearing, holding her breath. Her heart raced.

Kian's presence preceded the glow from his staff. Faelyn sheathed her knife and approached him at a crouch, concealing her footsteps with a bit of wind magic. A mischievous smile played on her lips. She'd teach him for following her.

She crept closer, hiding behind a tall bush. When she felt him on the other side, she jumped out.

"Caught ya!" she yelled. But he wasn't there.

Her eyes widened. She felt him right in front of her, but couldn't see him. She glanced from side to side.

Kian appeared, bursting out laughing.

Faelyn yelped and jumped back.

He grabbed his stomach, doubling over. He tried to talk through his laughter, but it was unintelligible.

Faelyn scowled. "Show off. How did you do that?"

"Magic," he said, waving his hands mystically through the air. He laughed all over again.

"Fine." Faelyn stormed off toward the town.

Kian stumbled through the brush behind her. "It's about bending the light with your magic to hide yourself. You'd have to be able to control light, though."

She stuck her chin up. "I can."

"Then it's something you'll learn at Thomats, if you work hard enough."

Faelyn clenched her fists and vowed right then and there she'd learn Kian's trick before they even reached Thomats.

When they arrived back at the inn, the sun had risen enough to send the frost glistening and the townspeople out of their homes.

Niri, the redhead, Mason, Avier, and Miyah stood outside, bleary-eyed, with their packs and staffs, blowing warm air into their cupped hands. At Faelyn's approach, they glared.

She stopped yards away. "Looks like they mind more than you let on, Kian." She resented him all over again.

Kian stepped in front of her. "We have a long way to travel, my friends. Ali wants to learn to master her magic so what took place last night doesn't happen again."

Faelyn huffed in irritation. She didn't need Kian to speak for her. "I'm sorry you all were brought into it. If Kian hadn't knocked me out, you'd never have been involved."

Kian frowned.

Niri's eyes softened. "It's all right, Ali. I would have done the same thing."

"Yeah," Mason said. He stepped forward and offered a smile that almost reached his dark eyes. "They deserved it."

A shout sounded from inside the inn, followed by the innkeeper bursting out the door and running down the street.

"And now it's time to go," Kian said. The others nodded and rushed to follow. Kian led them up the dirt road heading north.

Faelyn shifted the strap of her bag higher on her shoulder and matched their quick pace. She was certainly no stranger to walking long distances, though she missed her faithful friend, Clip Clop.

They walked in silence for the better part of the morning. Kian ignored her except to pass her a fresh chocolate chip scone. He winked, then walked ahead of her.

She felt Mason's eyes on her and realized she'd been staring at Kian. She glanced at Mason, a heavyset mage who looked not yet twenty, and he shook his head and faced forward again.

She shrugged and bit into the scone. Sweetness flooded her mouth, and she moaned.

Niri giggled.

Kian burst out with a chuckle, and after that, the group went to talking.

Faelyn licked the sweetness off her lips. "Where are you all from?"

Niri dropped back next to her. "We're all from the same part of Creadel, north of the Sengi desert. That's why we started traveling together early on."

Avier smiled. "I've only attended Thomats for two years. My parents moved to Creadel from Salaya."

Faelyn's eyebrows rose. Avier's unique accent confirmed he came from the tropical island in the south. She hadn't heard anyone speak like him since she was a child in her father's court.

Faelyn studied her new travel companions. They wore black mage robes, even in travel, carrying their staffs and packs, but unlike Faelyn, their hair was trimmed and pristine. Their skin smooth, without calluses. They carried themselves, heads high, with an air of confidence. They had money, for sure. Except for maybe Avier. She sensed he looked upon her more as an equal than the others. Magic swirled in all of their blood, a prerequisite to qualifying for Thomats, but it ran deepest in Kian.

Kian and Miyah walked closer together than the others. Faelyn's shoulders dropped in dismay. She had the misfortune of observing their behavior from the back of the pack.

"I can't wait to get to the border and stop for the night." Miyah put a hand on Kian's shoulder.

Faelyn's blood and magic boiled. Kian finally looked back at her, eyes wide. Faelyn stuck her chin up and reminded herself to calm down.

Kian stepped away from Miyah, and they didn't walk as close together after that. Friendly conversation ceased, and Miyah scowled for the next ten miles.

When they stopped for meals or to rest at night, Faelyn put her energy into attempting Kian's light-bending magic. She held a leaf, or a stick, or her hand out in front of her and opened her mind to the element of light. She felt the magic running through her, sending adrenaline coursing. Try as she might, she couldn't direct it to do what she needed. There was something about it she was missing. She set the first leaf on fire with the heat of the light energy. She extinguished it before she thought anyone noticed, but felt Kian's curiosity from across their campsite.

With a fire going and food dispersed from the supplies, Faelyn sat alone. Though they were mostly polite, the group had yet to accept her as one of them, because she wasn't. Kian didn't sit next to her as she'd hoped. Despite the number of companions, she felt more alone than she did traveling by herself.

She finished her nut-filled travel bread and a piece of dried beef, then lay back to watch the stars. Her breath puffed out into the chilly night, and she was thankful for the fire. They'd assigned a rotating shift to ensure it remained lit throughout the night. Faelyn had second watch. When her turn came, she intended to do it solely with magic.

With one hand behind her head, she used the other to stroke the hibernating grass, growing the wildflowers whose seeds lay dormant underneath. She sat up, pleased with the purple patch of violets. It was always a surprise what she'd get, but she'd made up a guessing game to see if she could learn the type of flowers before they bloomed. She'd guessed right this time.

Her eyes found Kian's where he sat beside the fire. It cast across his face in a quiet glow and sent the shadows to dance between them.

He stared at her. Into her.

She tasted his awe and intrigue. Then she noticed it had gone silent around their fire. The others stared too.

"That's some talent you have there, Ali," Miyah said. "How did you do that without a staff?" She added a log to the fire and didn't wait for an answer. "This is a real find for you, Kian."

The reminder that she was simply a potential recruit to Kian made Faelyn turn back to the stars. She shouldn't care what she was to him.

"Those are wonderful," Avier said in his thick accent. "They make me anxious for spring."

Mason and Niri affirmed they were impressed as well. Kian stayed silent, but she felt his focus like her own personal campfire, warming her.

Acantha above. When had she become so desperate for attention?

After a solid minute, Kian stood and walked over. He crouched next to her and picked a violet from the bunch, then carefully tucked it in her hair without exposing her pointed ear.

"Beautiful," he said, though he looked into her eyes when he said it.

Warmth seeped between the tiny cracks in the ice over her heart. That one word held more than she ever thought she'd feel again. She didn't trust it.

From across their campsite, Miyah snapped a twig, seething.

Kian shrugged and walked back to her.

Faelyn couldn't begin to guess why he wanted to keep his distance, why he'd want Miyah's affections over hers. The warmth in her chest retreated. It was for the best. Everyone she ever loved, she lost.

They traveled for a week before reaching the town at the edge of the woods between Creadel and Alysies. They planned to stay at the inn —Kian offered to pay for her—and get an early start through the woods the next morning. Faelyn could not take her eyes off the tree line.

Was it too soon to go back? She counted over and over in her head how long it had been. She left Alysies on her eighteenth birthday, spent thirty years on the farm, then nearly fifty years scrounging her way around Creadel. That meant she was ninety-eight years old. The reality made her dizzy. She didn't feel or look a day over twenty-four, if that. No one from when she lived at the castle would still be alive.

Her hand covered her mouth. Lord Calem would be long gone, if he'd even survived the siege. Swordmaster Benton, too. They'd saved her life that day. Her eyes stung with tears.

"Ali?" Kian said.

Faelyn stood outside the door to the inn, her gaze locked on the forest to the north. The trees shifted as if welcoming her home. She turned her back on them.

"Ali?" He placed a hand on her shoulder making her jump. "Is everything all right?"

The others had gone inside already. "Yes. I'm fine, Kian. Just nervous, I suppose." She took one last look at the woods.

"Don't worry. The people of New Daltieri aren't so bad if you travel in a group. Just keep a sharp eye on your belongings. Poverty is widespread there, and you can lose everything if you're not careful." He chuckled. "But I forgot who I'm talking to. I'm sure you can hold your own."

Faelyn nodded numbly. Poverty was not the norm when the kingdom was under her father's rule, though he certainly did his best to make it so. The people were suffering.

She followed Kian into the inn, and he showed her to a room up a flight of stairs. After dinner with the group, Faelyn used the rest of the evening to practice bending light. She focused her magic on the light from the lantern in her small room, pouring all her efforts into it. Finally, a single beam diverted in a different angle. She jumped for joy, grinning. Her efforts were far from accomplishing what Kian could do, but she was closer.

The use of magic left her tired, so she gave up to try again another day and went to bed.

CHAPTER TWENTY-ONE

When Faelyn fell asleep, Ardenis moved his gaze to Kian. He didn't like the boy one bit. Every time he stared at Faelyn, and every time she stared back, blushing and pretending not to care, his blood boiled. Faelyn looked at Kian the way Ardenis had always longed for Laida to look at him.

When Kian touched her or complimented her, Ardenis did everything to read more into the situation, to prove Kian meant foul play, but there was nothing. Kian had been honest about everything; his past, where he came from, how long he'd been at Thomats. Ardenis found his parents' estate; a palace north of the salt plains, as fine as any king's. They were powerful rulers in Creadel, and it was only a testament to Kian's character that he hadn't flaunted that fact.

Ardenis snorted. He still didn't like him. He'd nearly fallen out of his chair when Faelyn had nuzzled Kian's neck back in Newberry.

Kian hunched over a desk in his room at the inn, writing by lantern light in his journal. Ardenis read over his shoulder, skipping the details of their travel.

I don't know what is wrong with me lately. I can't get Ali off my mind.

I feel her doing magic in her room right next to mine. Her power is beyond compare, but she doesn't seem to realize it. No one simply grows flowers in the middle of winter, not without exhausting themselves, and she did it without a thought! And without a mage crystal to pull in and direct the magic around her, so she claims. But where could she be keeping it? Never, in all of history, have I heard of someone performing magic without a crystal.

My heart does strange things when I catch her looking at me with her turquoise eyes. But her ears, and the weight she carries on her shoulders... Something about her says to be careful. And Mother and Father wouldn't approve. Well, what do they know?

She's winning my heart, and by the things I sense in her, I hope she feels the same.

Bastard. Ardenis shook his head.

How could she fall in love with someone like him?

Later at home, he imagined what Amalia would say if she were here to lend a much-needed ear.

He chuckled. Almost as if Amalia hadn't left, Ardenis pictured her lounging lazily in his living room, rolling her eyes. She'd ask if he expected Faelyn to go her whole life without ever meeting someone. Then she'd point out the obvious, that at least Kian was a decent person who was smart and had made good decisions in life.

Ardenis glared at Amalia's favorite chair. "Whose side are you on? Can't you just agree he's a bastard and make me happy?"

He knew exactly what she'd retort. "Fine. He's a bastard. A smart, handsome, rich, powerful, kind bastard."

The memory of his dearest friend eased his heartache, and he found himself smiling. "Thank you. That's all I ask."

Faelyn and her band of mages got an early start the next morning. She shouldered her pack, standing apart from Kian, much to Ardenis's delight. They walked down the road headed north toward the forest. No one spoke, which was their usual custom this early. Kian offered Faelyn a chocolate chip scone, but she shook her head. The concern was plain in his eyes—the same concern Ardenis felt—but Faelyn was fixated on the trees.

Her steps faltered just before entering the woods, and she stumbled, nearly falling. Ardenis could imagine how hard this was for her, to return to a land full of so many dark memories. He wanted to help her in some way, so it irritated him to no end when Kian fell back and offered his hand.

Faelyn took it, smiling gratefully, and they passed into the woods together, hand in hand. They walked that way until they stopped to rest and Ardenis had worked his robes into clumps in his fists. They didn't hold hands after that, but they walked together more often than not, and soon Faelyn was laughing again.

The only thing preventing Ardenis from cursing Kian's name to the Hereafter was Faelyn's blatant happiness and ease in Kian's presence. The person she had been growing up, the spirited, 'won't take anything from anyone' girl was back. It had been a long time since she'd laughed or smiled so openly. Despite the circumstances, it warmed Ardenis's heart. He'd never admit it out loud, but he owed Kian for some of the sunshine coming back into Faelyn's life.

When they crossed out of the woods, Kian offered Faelyn his hand again. This time, she had no trouble entering her kingdom.

The trouble came when they reached the first town and Faelyn discovered what Ardenis had already seen with his own eyes. Half the town's shops were boarded up, including the inn. Not many townspeople walked the streets, and those that did wore dirt-stained threadbare clothes against winter's chill, begging from shop to shop for coin or food. Faelyn covered her mouth at the sight of a young girl running barefoot trying to beg for work from those that hadn't abandoned the town. Faelyn took her last bit of food and shoved it in the girl's eager hands.

As hard as it was to watch Faelyn grieve for her once-prosperous kingdom, it was what she needed to see.

Faelyn and the mages slept in a barn they rented from a desperate widow.

Several more rundown towns later, the first flakes of snow fell as they crested the hill and reached Thomats School of Magic.

Faelyn gaped, looking over the land and the school grounds, eyes gleaming in pleasure.

Ardenis smiled at her reaction. Even under the current economic circumstances of former Alysies, Thomats had maintained its health and notoriety. It had been constructed on a plateau centuries ago based on an ancient architectural design that had fallen out of style in Thera, but not in Acantha. As a result, the school, with its columns and white walls, looked much like a typical Acanthian building.

The campus was comprised of one main building with branching wings, and housing in the rear of the property. It had its own stable and gardens. It was definitely one of the grandest places in Thera, almost more so than Pavora, where Faelyn was born.

"It's so beautiful." Faelyn's eyes swept over the grounds. Sculpted bushes that bloomed in the spring lined the road. She didn't seem to notice Kian watching her, smiling with joy at her astonishment.

Kian didn't seem to notice Miyah's frown of displeasure as she watched him watching Faelyn.

Ardenis smiled, glad to see Faelyn finally living her life. For too long she'd pretended the farm was where she belonged, but seeing her now confirmed that wasn't true. The Fates had given her special gifts, and Isaac should have sent her to Thomats long ago. Perhaps he wouldn't have been murdered if he had.

Like always, Ardenis's first thought was to rush out and tell Amalia of Faelyn's progress. Each time it hit him in the gut that Amalia was gone. He'd spent more time at the baths since she'd left him. He looked for her often on Thera, but his search had proved as impossible as he knew it would be. He found his comfort in Faelyn.

If she gained admittance to Thomats and learned to use her magic consistently, she'd be that much more prepared for her future. Besides his love, his instincts still pulled him to watch her. Her purpose in history was still ongoing. Her inevitable destiny lay at the end of the path she now walked.

CHAPTER TWENTY-TWO

Many years had passed since Faelyn left her home in Pavora, but the sights and sounds of the castle were still fresh in her mind. Perhaps her father, King Isaac, had let the castle go to ruin in her living memory, but she'd never seen anything like the Thomats School of Magic. It wasn't locked in by walls or battlements. It was light, open, and pristine. Each section of the building was surrounded by beautiful white columns bordering covered porticos, where a sea of students in black milled about. Their voices carried over the spray of a tall fountain and the crunch of her boots over dormant winter grass.

Faelyn wordlessly followed the mages, trying to take it all in and avoid picking at her tattered clothes. She shifted her bag to cover a mud stain, then rested her hand to cover a hole in the bag. Their steps quickened, bouncing with anticipation as they neared. When they crossed into the courtyard of the biggest building, Miyah, Niri, Mason, and Avier said their goodbyes.

"It was a pleasure getting to know you, Ali. I hope to see you around the school." Niri grinned, and Faelyn smiled in return.

Miyah, who'd quit talking to Faelyn since Kian held her hand, glared and walked away beside Mason.

Avier gave Faelyn a hug. "I'm sure you'll be a great success. Come find me anytime." He shook hands with Kian and walked toward a different part of the campus.

Now alone, Kian turned and beamed. "It's not modern or anything, but it's the best school on the continent for learning magic. If there were a better one, that's where I'd be."

"It's amazing," Faelyn sighed and shifted her stance. "I followed you all this way. What now?"

"Are you hungry?"

Starved. "Not really."

"Well, I am. Let's get out of the cold and get something to eat, then we'll find Professor Wemnar. He's mentored me since the beginning, and is very kind. He can help you with admissions. We arrived just in time. Classes resume in two days."

Faelyn nodded, at a loss for words. Talking to Kian's professor about her magic was a big step from attending classes. She'd been tutored privately as a child in all the regular subjects, but was she ready to commit to becoming a student here?

She hugged her arms and followed Kian to a set of double doors almost lost among the vastness of the building. The warmth of indoors caressed her cold cheeks. A long hallway with marble tile stretched forever in front of her. More students in black robes bustled around them. As she walked, the chorus of voices became louder, accompanied by the smell of fresh bread and roasting meat. They entered a large room filled with long tables and students of all ages eating alone or in groups.

Kian stood in line in the back of the room and filled a wooden tray with double of everything; stew, bread, hunks of cheese, peach cobbler, and apple cider. Faelyn's mouth watered. He paid for the food and found an empty table. She wasn't quite sure where to sit. Her feet shuffled. Next to him? That would seem forward. She sat across from him.

He gave half the food to her.

"I said—"

"It's been a long journey of dry, stale meals. Please, eat." Kian ate without reserve.

Faelyn watched him with a small smirk, then ate as well. The food tasted amazing after the weeks of travel. When she'd eaten most of it, her muscles unwound, and some of the tension left her body. She felt more relaxed. Bolder.

"Why do you carry a staff?" she asked.

Kian stared at her half-eaten cobbler. She pushed it over to him, and he grinned and dug in.

"The staffs are how we access our magic. Without them, we are useless. The ability may have been born into us, but it's the power inside the crystals that lets us access it. There's tales of the rare exception if the mage was very powerful, but they're only children's stories." He met her eyes.

"Why not wear the crystal as a necklace or something?"

"I asked my parents that when I was little. Years of magery tradition, combined with the fact we can't physically touch our crystals without the possibility of death," he touched his staff next to him with his elbow while shoveling the last bite in, "and this is the result."

Faelyn stared at the staff, a dark knobby wood, most likely walnut, with a rounded top and blue glass peeking out from within. The crystal pulsed when she focused her magic on it. It was a pleasant feeling, like a caress.

Kian blinked and looked at his crystal, then back at her. "What you are able to do is unheard of. It's otherworldly. I've no doubt you'll get the tuition expenses covered. Just don't forget me as you rise to the top, eh?"

Faelyn felt her cheeks burn. "You're just being nice." She smiled and ducked her head. "But I do have something to show you."

She picked up her empty cup of cider and held it out on her palm.

Concentrating, she opened herself to her magic and focused on the elements. The cup disappeared.

Kian jumped. "Holy Hereafter!" His mouth dropped open. "It took me two years to master that trick."

"I would have figured it out sooner, but you left out a clue."

He closed his gaping mouth. "Yes, I did. But I didn't think it mattered. I would have never thought you could control fire, aether, earth, *and* water magic. I never thought you would figure it out."

"You forgot air magic." She winked when his eyes widened in surprise. "It's a combination of bending the light and reflecting it off the water in the air." She smiled, proud of herself. She let the cup reappear and set it on the table.

"Most impressive, young lady."

Faelyn started, knocking the empty cup. An old man stood beside their table. His long gray hair framed his full face, complete with stern eyes fixed right on Kian.

"You're not a teacher yet, Kian. We've had this discussion before. You're not to teach magic until authorized to do so."

Kian grinned. "She taught herself that one, Professor Wemnar. Meet Aliyah."

The professor gave a warning shake of his finger to Kian, then turned a crinkly-eyed smile on Faelyn.

"Are you joining our school, Aliyah?"

Faelyn swallowed her nerves. "I have some questions, but I may consider it."

Wemnar chuckled. "Good. Never commit to something before you know what you're signing up for. Since you're finished eating, may I suggest we visit in my office before Kian starts licking his plate?"

Faelyn laughed, and Kian ducked his head, placing his plate on the table. "It was one time, Professor. Am I never going to live it down?"

"Perhaps. Mages do live long lives." Wemnar raised a robed arm, waving for them to follow.

His affection for Kian warmed her to him. She sensed his eager excitement to talk to her, though his advanced age helped him hide it. Wemnar caught her eye, and Faelyn wondered if he felt her exploring his emotions.

Faelyn and Kian walked side by side behind Wemnar. They ascended two flights of marbled stairs, then down a long hall. Wemnar opened a white door, one among many.

Wemnar's office was neat and tidy, with floor-to-ceiling bookshelves, an oak desk in the middle, and cushioned chairs.

He took his place behind the desk. "Kian, it's not necessary for you to remain here. Aliyah can find you when we're done."

Faelyn's heart skipped a beat. Alone? She glanced at Kian. Why did he have to leave? And how on Thera would she find him later? Kian's thoughts must have been in line with hers.

"She traveled all the way from Creadel with us, Professor. She might feel more comfortable if I remain with her."

"As always, Kian, your recruiting skills are unmatched. But a potential student's business is her own." He narrowed his eyes at Kian, who took the hint.

Kian walked to the door. "I'll be in my room at the Academ dormitory, the furthest north before the teacher housing. Anyone can direct you there, and then just ask for me." He offered her a small smile before shutting the door behind him.

Faelyn stared at the door, worrying her lip, unsure if she shouldn't follow.

Professor Wemnar cleared his throat and gestured for her to sit. "I must say, that's quite a gift you have, Aliyah."

"You can call me Ali if you wish." She sat, folding her hands in her lap, trying to appear calm. If she didn't get into the school or didn't like the situation, she could always leave and be a wanderer again.

"Ali," he said, trying it out. "I may seem an overbearing old mage, but really I just want what's best for my students. I've been at this school a long time, well before you were born."

Doubtful. Faelyn shifted in her chair.

"I've learned the value of patience over the years, and so it may seem I'm not eager to barrage you with questions." He leaned forward, eyes sparkling. "That would be untrue. I'm brimming with many questions about you."

She'd sensed as much, but her heart picked up speed. She half-forced, half-prayed her magic to stay dormant. "And if I don't desire to answer your questions?"

"Do you desire admission into Thomats School of Magic, Aliyah?"

"Yes."

"And do you have the financial means to cover tuition and lodging?"

Faelyn gritted her teeth. "I do not."

Wemnar raised an eyebrow. "Please don't take offense. I'm simply trying to establish common ground." He sat back in his chair. "Based on what I've seen and what I can sense from you alone, I'm considering sponsoring you for a scholarship, but I need to ask some questions first. It is up to you to answer or not."

Faelyn nodded.

"Where do you keep your mage crystal?"

"I don't have one." She expected him to press her, but he simply nodded and went on.

"Where are you from?"

She proceeded to give him the same story she'd given Kian regarding her fake Creadel origins, though unlike Kian, she sensed Wemnar searching her words with his magic. Searching for truth. There wasn't an element she could think of to use to block his efforts. The best she could come up with was to use the undertones of the wind to distort the feel of her words, altering the force and air currents to match his projected reactions. He had to believe the lie. Sweat prickled her skin.

"Stop." Wemnar raised his hand, cutting her off midsentence. He shook his head back and forth for several seconds. "Unbelievable," he muttered.

"Professor?" The old man was crazy, or he was on to her.

He chuckled. "You felt me testing your words. And used the wind to counteract my magic? I'm not sure if I've ever seen that done before." He shook his head again. "Who trained you, and why aren't you allowing me to test the validity of your information?"

Faelyn's shoulders slumped. This was never going to work. She couldn't lie to him, and he already didn't trust her. "I don't know what to say, Professor. No one trained me." He tested her words again, but she didn't attempt to block him this time. "My father refused to let me attend class here despite my gift, though my professor at the time thought it was a good idea. I've had to learn everything on my own."

"Who is your father?"

"No one with any magic, that's for certain. Both my parents died long ago. I've no one." Nothing had ever been truer.

"You don't have to tell me everything, Aliyah, but I've no doubt you'll get your tuition if you give enough. You need to consider what your story is going to be. Because people will ask. No one in the history of this school has ever possessed a gift equal to the one you potentially hold. I say potentially, because it is up to study and to push yourself to the greatness you can achieve here." He sat back in his chair and adopted a faraway gaze. "There is someone from history who could do much magic without a mage crystal."

Nervous energy shot through Faelyn's body. She patted her hair over her ears, then swept her hand down her messy braid to hide the action.

"She hailed from A..." His eyes shot to her. "A place from another time." His head shook. "Alas, she died long ago. Before my days." He met her eyes. "It's amazing you've come this far without training. Why, you're lucky you haven't killed anyone. Respect your gift. Use it wisely and carefully, for the good of others more than yourself."

Faelyn's heart soared with relief that he didn't suspect her, and joy that she may belong. "Thank you, Professor. I will."

"Give me the afternoon to talk to admissions. We'll find you temporary lodging. Until then, you're free to wander as you please."

"When should I return?"

"With a gift like yours, I'll find you when I know something more." He chuckled. "Until you learn how to block me."

So he could sense her like she could sense Kian. Wonderful. She'd have to figure out how to douse that beacon.

Faelyn gave a quiet sigh as she opened the door back out to the hall. Kian made finding him sound easy, but her ability to sense him only worked so far.

She sensed him near and looked up. He sat on a cushioned bench a few doors down, grinning.

"Would you like a tour?" He held up a thick black cape. "I found this for you. The snow's coming down a little harder, and I know you're not used to this kind of winter, being from Creadel."

Faelyn stood still, staring at Kian, vision blurring. Very few people had ever been so nice to her in her life, especially those who'd seen her ears. Her heart swelled and melted in the same instant.

Kian dropped his arms. "Or I could leave you alone." He stood.

Faelyn hesitated, then walked to him and hugged him. Her face met his warm neck, and she breathed his alluring scent. "Thank you," she whispered.

She sensed his surprise, but he hugged her back. She accepted the cape from his hands. "Let's go."

Kian showed her the entire campus. The main building held most of the professors' offices, the largest dining hall, admissions, and many classrooms. The wings housed more classrooms. The boys' dormitory sat separately toward the east, and the girls—where Faelyn would likely stay—on the west, each with their own smaller dining hall. Closer to campus, but directly north, lay Kian's co-ed dorm for advanced students. When the snow became too thick to keep exploring, Kian led her through a side door of the main building, where a sweet aroma overtook them.

They entered a small, cozy room with curtains of red with golden hues and tables and chairs not unlike a fancy tavern. Kian bought her hot chocolate with whipped cream, and she sipped at the rich, velvety flavors.

He nudged a chocolate chip scone toward her. "I remember how much you enjoy them." They both laughed.

Kian sidled next to her, instead of across. As they spoke, he scooted a hair closer. Faelyn's heart pounded each time. She couldn't deny her attraction for him, the way his hair fell in his eyes. The way his tongue casually licked the cream from his lip. The way he focused on everything she said, it was all more than a little alluring. But, was this what she wanted? She just got to Thomats, and the last person she trusted with her heart had ruined more than just her life.

She shifted away from Kian, just a bit. He stopped midsentence, pain flashing in his eyes and countenance. It nearly broke her heart. She didn't want to hurt him.

By the time Professor Wemnar's assistant found them, their shoulders were pressed together, and their hands almost touched on the table.

"Aliyah?" She nodded. "Professor Wemnar says you are needed in admissions." He turned and left.

Kian rolled his eyes. "That's Alex. He's a little nervous around beautiful women."

Faelyn shook her head.

"Come on, I'll show you the way."

Kian led her down a series of hallways, which instantly had her lost. They slowed when the floor became a darker shade of marble, and the walls changed from white to dark wood. The ominous feel made her stomach flutter.

"Here we are." Kian gestured to a set of double doors.

Faelyn walked past, intent on hiding her fear.

Kian stopped her with a hand on her shoulder. “Don’t worry. You wouldn't be here if they didn’t want you.”

She gave a quick nod and entered the room.

A young woman wearing black robes rested behind a desk similar to Professor Wemnar's. She looked up from a book. “Aliyah?”

Faelyn nodded.

“I’ll inform them you’ve arrived.” She stood and entered a door behind her, reappearing a few seconds later. “You can go in.”

“Who’s in there? Is this how I apply for the school?”

The girl sat back on the desk. “The admissions board is in there. This is how they review special recruits for admission. I’m Babette if you need anything. Good luck.” The girl, Babette, smiled and picked up her book.

Faelyn sensed nothing malicious from the girl, but her palms grew slick. What would they ask her? She took a deep breath and walked through the door.

The room was large, but the only thing in it was a long desk with eight men and two women sitting behind it along the back wall. Gold embroidery decorated the hems of their black robes. There was no place for Faelyn to sit, so she walked to the table and stood before them, wishing she’d at least brushed her hair.

She recognized Professor Wemnar, and he winked.

An elderly professor in the middle of the group spoke. “I am Professor Fenedict, Head of Admissions. I understand that you wish to be admitted under full scholarship to Thomats School of Magic. Is this correct, Aliyah?”

Suddenly unsure what to do with her arms, Faelyn crossed them, then let them hang like dead weights at her sides. “It is.” Her heart raced.

“I’m going to ask you a series of questions to evaluate you as a potential student. First off, are you in possession of a mage crystal?”

Why would they start with that? “No, I am not.” She felt ten different mages probing her response. There’d be no lying today.

“What is your purpose in coming here?”

Good question. She struggled to come up with an answer that was both honest and meaningful. "I desire to learn more about myself and my abilities. I want to learn my limitations and gain some control over my magic." There, that sounded eloquent.

Several of the mages nodded, including Wemnar.

"What is your background? Where did you learn to access your magic, and why do you need a scholarship?"

The questions she'd been dreading. She took a deep breath. "My mother died giving birth to me, and my father neglected me as a child. He was murdered before my eyes on my eighteenth birthday." She glanced down, trying to control her emotions under the barrage of magic probing her words. "I was left with nothing but a few coins, and those quickly ran out. While wandering Creadel, Kian found me and convinced me to come here." She met each of their eyes one by one. They stared with open curiosity. "My magic is a part of me, and always has been. I've never known a day without it."

Fenedict exchanged glances with the man on his right. "Very well, then. Lastly, we'll need a demonstration, of course."

Holy Hereafter. "A demonstration?" They were going to have to be more specific.

"Yes." Impatience and condescension dripped from his tone. "Show us what you can do. Prove why we should fund you to attend our school."

Faelyn bristled at the phrasing, as if she was nothing but a poor beggar leaching off their charity at their discretion. Pride stung, her eyes narrowed, and she called her magic forward.

She clenched her fists, then lit herself on fire. A fire that neither burned her nor the floor around her.

The mages jumped up, each of their staffs alight with magic. One doused Faelyn in water, snuffing out her flames and soaking her from head to toe. Jaw set, she used the wind to dry her clothes and gave a tight smile.

The mages stared at her, wide-eyed and speechless. Even

Wemnar had his mouth dropped slightly open. Her pride still not quite satisfied, she decided to go for one more.

"I also learned a fun trick on the journey here." She made herself disappear completely.

Shouts of surprise rang out, but Wemnar smiled his crinkle-eyed smile. His staff glowed brighter as he toyed with the light, ruining Faelyn's trick and revealing her again.

She grinned.

"That's quite enough, Aliyah." Fenedict pulled his chair out forcefully and sat back in it. The other mages followed his lead. "You've made your point. You've obviously studied at a mage school in Creadel. Now, where are you hiding your mage crystal?"

Faelyn crossed her arms again. "I don't have one. I didn't even know of the concept until I met Kian." The magical probing made her wince.

Fenedict frowned. "Is there anything else you already know how to do that you'd like to divulge?"

"That's the extent of it. Oh, except I can also grow things." How she missed growing things and the simple days of the farm.

"So your powers are limited to the elements."

Faelyn wanted to like Fenedict. He was in charge of her fate, after all, but he was making it difficult.

"I've never thought of it, but I suppose so."

"We've seen enough. You may go. We will inform you when we've reached a decision."

Faelyn left the room, nodded to Babette behind the desk, who didn't look up from her book, and left the admissions office.

She didn't know what to think of the process so far. She hadn't really meant to lose her temper and light herself on fire, but maybe it was best to be honest about her capabilities. If forced to hide her true nature, she'd only be holding herself back.

At least the magic had worked the way she wanted this time. And they seemed satisfied enough with her vague responses about her past.

Kian would know if her demonstration was over the top. She headed toward the main hall of the building, hoping to find him. Instead, a squadron of soldiers armed with swords and black armor strode through the hall. They were lined in rows of ten stretched out from wall to wall.

Their armor featured a golden raven with wings spread in front of an obvious rendering of the Northern Mountains. Faelyn scrambled backward, using the light to make herself disappear.

These soldiers were from Daltieri.

Faelyn backed against the wall, her breathing ragged. Images flashed in her mind from that horrible day Daltieri destroyed her life. The soldiers marched past, and she prayed not to be discovered.

"This wing's clear, sir. Moving on to the west wing," a soldier said.

Faelyn's muscles locked tight. When they were gone, she dropped her magic, trying to remember the way out of the building. She laid a hand over her racing heart.

"Are you okay, Ali?" Niri stood beside her, making her jump.

"Niri! We're under attack. We must find Kian." She tugged on Niri's arm, but Niri did not move. "Come on!"

"Ali, we're not under attack." Her tone was placating, as one would speak to a caged animal.

"Did you not see those soldiers?"

"I did, but they aren't here to hurt us. They wouldn't attack their own school." Niri shook her head. "I forgot you're not from here. You're trembling."

Faelyn took a deep breath, trying to calm down. "Why are they here in Alysies? I mean, Thomats. Why?"

"They make a regular appearance here, and everywhere in New Daltieri, really. King Seber sends soldiers to maintain order and ensure we are safe and keeping our high standards. It's nothing to worry about." Her tone was matter-of-fact, as if this was indeed a regular occurrence.

"What happens if someone fails to maintain the high standards?"

Niri's lips formed a worried line, and she glanced down the hall.

So, the invaders ruled by fear.

"Sorry, Niri. The soldiers were a sight I'd never expected to see. It's been a long day. Professor Fenedict and a panel of mages are discussing if I'm to be admitted."

"Do you have a place to sleep?"

"No. I'll figure something out."

"Why don't you stay with me for now? My roommates haven't returned yet, so you can have your pick until admissions makes their decision." She nodded encouragingly.

Grateful, Faelyn smiled. "That would be wonderful."

"Great. Have you eaten?"

Faelyn shook her head, so they ate in the dining hall. As she licked chocolate pudding off her spoon, she smiled, marveling over Niri's kindly chatter and her willingness for friendship. Making friends had been near impossible growing up at court. Of course, here at Thomats she wasn't the shunned princess with the freak ears. Niri didn't know her true past, or who she really was. Niri didn't know anything about her, and yet was still willing to extend so much kindness. Faelyn's heart thawed, and it wasn't from the warm cider.

After dinner, Niri led her to the girls' dormitory on the west of campus. The rectangular building was comprised of white-washed brick with a pair of marble columns flaking the main doors. It rose several stories and, as Faelyn found out, each room held four bunk beds.

Faelyn chose the empty top bunk, simply because she'd never slept in a bunkbed before, and snuggled down under the covers, exhausted.

Niri's magestaff glowed, and a second later, an extra blanket floated up to Faelyn, landing across her knees.

"Nice trick," Faelyn said.

Niri shrugged from where she stood by the other bunk bed. "I can't grow flowers, but I can levitate things. Though, I'm also good at research, genealogy and such." She paused. "Ali?"

"Yes?"

"I'm sorry we didn't speak much on the trek here."

"That's okay. It's probably my fault. I'm not used to having people to talk to." Or making friends.

Niri fidgeted with her mage staff. "I didn't want you to think it was because of what happened at Newberry."

Faelyn tensed.

"I really don't hold it against you. Kian took care of most of it. He told us how they'd attacked you, giving you no choice." Niri set her staff against the wall and met Faelyn's eyes. "I'm glad you're here. You'll learn better ways to punish those who mean to do you harm."

Faelyn nodded tersely. She hadn't thought of her actions affecting anyone but herself. She sat up. "I'm sorry, Niri. Truly. You're right, I'm looking forward to learning more control, and hopefully making friends, if they admit me."

Niri gave a sly smile. "Then can I ask you a personal question?"

"Sure." Faelyn lay back down on the soft pillow.

"Are you in love with Kian?"

Faelyn's half-closed eyes shot open. "Umm." She had no idea how to respond. It wasn't love, she wasn't ready for that. Attracted to him, for sure. Having a lot of fun getting to know him. But, love? She wouldn't be the first one to make that leap, not after all she'd been through.

Niri burst out laughing. "Hey, you don't have to white-knuckle those blankets. It's just a question."

Faelyn relaxed her grip and breathed. "It's too soon to say." She grinned. "He's amazing, but I'm not sure yet."

"That's good. I think it's best not to rush into these things. Just be careful, okay? He and Miyah have been dating off and on for a while. They aren't together now, of course. But Miyah can be... possessive." Niri burrowed under her covers on the bottom of the other bunk. "Also, Kian's been my friend a long time. I'd hate to see him hurt because you both rushed into things."

Faelyn considered Niri's words. She didn't give a damn about Miyah's potential jealousy, but she'd hate to take things further with Kian and have it end in heartbreak for either of them. She almost laughed at herself. Of course it would end in heartbreak. He'd grow old and die someday while she remained young. Could she love him enough to overcome that kind of pain?

Faelyn rolled to her side. "I know enough about Kian to know he doesn't deserve to be hurt. I would never wish him ill. For now, I'd like to get to know him better and see what happens."

"Good answer." Niri fanned her red hair over her pillow and pulled the blanket up to her chin. "Goodnight, Ali."

"Goodnight." Faelyn lay awake thinking of Mary and wondering what she'd say to all this talk of boys and love.

CHAPTER TWENTY-THREE

A pounding on the door jolted Faelyn from sleep. The light of dawn seeped through the window. It took a moment for her to remember where she was. Niri grabbed her staff and rolled out of bed, stumbling in her haste to answer the door. Faelyn sensed who it was just as she opened it.

Niri scrubbed at her face, red hair sticking up in every direction. "Is everything all right, Kian?"

He brushed passed her with disheveled hair and crazed eyes. "I've been trying to find you, Ali."

Faelyn jumped off the top bunk. "You have?"

"All night!" Kian pushed his hair back.

Niri put her hands on her hips. "Really, Kian? All night?"

"Yes! Well, not *all* night. I may have fallen asleep for a little while. But, anyway, why didn't you come find me?"

Guilt heated her cheeks. "I'm sorry, Kian. I'm not used to answering to someone. Niri offered me a place to sleep. I should have found you." Having friends was more complicated than she imagined.

Niri backed up to her bed, then fluffed her blanket smooth.

Kian grabbed Faelyn's hand. "I was worried about you. You don't need to 'answer' to me. I just wanted to make sure you were safe somewhere warm."

As sappy as his words were, she didn't mind, and found them endearing. What did that mean?

Kian's eyes softened. "I feel responsible for you, since you followed me here."

Faelyn pulled her hand away. "I'm here for me, Kian." She sighed. "I'm sorry for making you worry."

He flashed her a handsome smile. "Come on, admissions has made their decision, and they've summoned you."

Faelyn exchanged a glance with Niri and grabbed her meager possessions. "Thanks again, Niri. I hope to see you later."

"Good luck," Niri called as the door closed.

Kian waited while she readied herself in the shared bathroom. Outside, the cold morning air bit at Faelyn's thin travel clothes. She wrapped her new cloak around her. The path had been shoveled overnight and was bordered by piles of snow. The sun hit the frosted crystals and sent them shimmering like diamonds in a sea of alabaster.

"Can I ask you a question, Ali?" Kian walked beside her on their way to the main building.

"Yes." That didn't mean she had to answer.

"How old are you?"

Did he suspect something? "How old do you think I look?" She'd love to know. It would give her a better idea of where she fit in this world.

He shook his head. "That's a question that will get me in trouble. No way."

"I promise I won't be upset. I genuinely want to know your opinion. And it had better be honest and not just what you think I want to hear."

"Twenty-two?" Kian cringed.

Faelyn smiled. "Close. I'm twenty-three."

"I'm twenty-two, so we're almost the same age."

"I thought so."

"When's your birthday?" he asked.

"Not until March."

She could have made up a date, but she didn't want to lie any more than necessary, or give more real details that could link to who she really was.

Faelyn and Kian arrived at the back of the main building, and he held the door open. Faelyn knew where to go, so she led the way.

Kian stopped at the admission's door. "I'll wait here this time."

Faelyn smiled and entered. The same girl from before, Babette, sat reading a book. She didn't look up.

Faelyn walked into the room less nervous than she should be. They'd already made their decision. There was nothing more she could do. The mages watched her approach—some with smiles, some with scowls. The Head of Admissions, Professor Fenedict, neither smiled nor frowned, but his expression set her teeth on edge—arrogant and superior. Wemnar sat at the end, holding back a smile.

"It has been decided to grant you admission into Thomats School of Magic," Fenedict said with resignation.

Faelyn's heart soared. Through a great force of will, she kept her feet planted and her face safely neutral, but inside, she was grinning like a fool. She hadn't realized how much it would mean to be accepted.

"You've been awarded a full scholarship, including room and board. You will be placed under Professor Wemnar's sponsorship."

Faelyn looked at Wemnar, and he couldn't contain his smile anymore.

"Due to the advanced stage of your magic, we have decided to place you in the Academ's dormitory. You will begin your classes at the lower levels, of course. Your professors may pass you along at their discretion. A stipend will be granted to you each month. It will last if you're frugal." He peered down his nose. "All of this is conditional upon your good standing here at Thomats, including academic performance and personal conduct. We may remove this scholarship at any time if we feel you're not a good investment. Do you have any questions?"

Faelyn was dumbfounded, eyes widening with each word. Tuition, food, money, and a place to sleep. They were going to pay her to learn to use her powers better. She'd never felt so blessed. "Thank you, Professors. This means so much to me. I've wanted this my whole life." Not entirely true, but it sounded nice.

At that, Fenedict smiled. "Good luck, Aliyah."

Dazed, Faelyn turned and walked out of the room. She couldn't wait to tell Kian and Niri.

"Hey, wait!" Babette called from the desk. She raised a large pouch and jiggled it. Heavy-sounding coins plunked together from within. "This is for your books and supplies, including clothes and such."

Faelyn took the heavy pouch, bouncing on her toes. It was more than she'd seen in a long, long time.

"Come back the first of every month for more." Babette handed her a sheet of paper. "These are your classes." She waved and went back to reading.

Faelyn read over the list.

Mage Staff Execution

Magical History

History of Daltieri

Magical Defense 1

Magical Offense 1

Faelyn planted her feet on the ground. *What? History of Daltieri?* Never in the Hereafter could they force her to take that class. Besides being the enemy, they'd erased all traces of Alysian culture and history from any text Faelyn had been able to locate. And that included any mention of Faelyn, her mother, or the battle that lost them their kingdom, other than a quick reference about how Daltieri liberated a suffering kingdom.

Faelyn clenched her fists. "Babette, who do I talk to about changing some of these classes?"

The girl didn't look up. "You can't change them. These are required courses for every student."

Before she could respond, Wemnar walked through the door, followed by some of the other mages. "Well, Ali, are you pleased?" He smiled.

"I'm very grateful, Professor. You must have pled my case, and I can't thank you enough." She waited until the others were gone. "I do have a few concerns about my schedule, though. I do not wish to study History of Daltieri."

"Ah, well." He rubbed his neck. "I'm afraid that's a requirement no matter which school you attend in this kingdom. By king's command. It's considered treasonous not to attend."

Faelyn scowled, fury chasing away joy. Curse that wretched kingdom to the depths of the Hereafter. Over and over and over again. She'd never attend that class. Let them come and make her. She took a deep breath. "Is it something I can wait to take?"

Wemnar peered down his nose. "I don't see why not. As long as you take it before you graduate."

"Great, then I'd like to change my schedule. Also, Mage Staff Execution? I don't require a mage crystal to access my magic. Why do I need this class?"

Wemnar took the paper from her and squinted as he read. "Hmm. You're right. It's a required course, but we've never had a student who didn't need a mage crystal." He chuckled. "I'll see what I can do about exempting you. It will take board approval, and I doubt they'll agree in an afternoon. Attend tomorrow's class, and I'll see where we stand. Maybe you'll learn something."

Faelyn accepted her schedule back with a nod of thanks.

After she traded out History of Daltieri for Elemental Magic, a class she felt more than a little excited about, she finally left admissions. As promised, Kian sat waiting in the hall.

He stood when he saw her. “Well?”

Faelyn grinned, waving her schedule and jingling her new money pouch. “I got in! And on a scholarship.”

“I knew you would.” Kian took her up in a big hug, spinning her around and leaving her breathless.

He set her on the ground, but didn’t let go. His eyes locked onto hers, then they fell to her lips.

Before Faelyn could consider it, Kian leaned down and pressed his lips onto hers. He tasted of honey and something distinctly Kian. A fiery warmth shot through her veins. She pressed her lips against his, and he pulled her tighter to him. Dizziness threatened to erase all rationale.

Kian straightened. The corners of his mouth rose into a warm smile. “Looks like you have some shopping to do. Want my help?”

Faelyn found her breath. “That would be great. Can you also show me around the Academ and help me find my room? Maybe introduce me to my roommate?”

Kian pulled back with wide eyes. “They gave you a room in the Academ?” He whistled. “They must have been very impressed. What did you show them?”

“Oh, this and that.” She shrugged. “I showed them your trick.”

Kian laughed. “That will do it. Let’s go to town for supplies.”

Kian led Faelyn off school grounds and down a trail banked by snow. More than once, his hand brushed against hers sending tingles up her arm. She didn’t give in to his subtle hints he wanted to hold her hand, and soon they reached a small town at the bottom of the valley. The stacked-stone houses with slanted roofs covered in a thick layer of snow painted a quaint picture. Smoke rose from the chimneys, and wagon wheels carved frozen ruts in the street.

"It's so peaceful here." Faelyn hopped over a slushy puddle

beside the road. "Nothing like the poverty we encountered along the way."

Kian walked beside her, watching her. "The school goes to great lengths to make sure the students have a safe place to go, and the town helps attract prospective students." He glanced around the mostly empty street, then lowered his voice. "King Seber doesn't tax the school and its town like he does the rest of the kingdom. But at a price. The mages are at his disposal."

Faelyn straightened in alarm. "I would never work for that pig!"

Kian grabbed her arm, pulling her close. "Careful! You'd be hanged if a soldier heard you say that."

Faelyn wrenched free.

Kian shoved his hands in his pockets. "You're a citizen of Creadel, anyway. King Jeffe wouldn't allow King Seber to force you against your will." He quirked a hesitant smile. "I doubt anyone could force you once you graduate."

Faelyn scowled, but allowed Kian to lead on. They passed several shops including a bakery and an armory, before reaching a bookstore. The rest of her anger melted when they entered the warm, cozy atmosphere. It was a charming store, with tightly packed shelves mazed around the small area. Kian helped her pick out the right books, which cost over half her stipend.

He led her to the shop next door, then stopped, rubbing the back of his neck. “Typically mage crystals are handed down from generation to generation, but...”

“Magnus's Magery,” Faelyn read aloud from the carved wooden sign above the door. She halted. “I don’t need one of these. Professor Wemnar is going to exempt me from the class. I only have to attend until the board approves it.”

Kian paused with his hand on the door handle. “It could take a while. You’ll need one until then.” He opened the door.

“No. I don’t want one.” It would be a waste of precious coin to invest in something so unnecessary.

“All right, no staff.” Kian closed the door. “Robes!”

By the time she'd bought two sets of black robes, shoes, a quill, ink, parchment, and extra clothes, Faelyn's money was gone. She'd have to replace her holey bag next month.

She came out of the last store, smiling behind an armful of bags and boxes. She hadn't owned so many things since she'd been a lady of the Alysian court. "I hope my room has blankets."

"It will. The rooms are equipped with most everything you'll need. Except this." Kian grinned and pulled his arm from behind his back. In his hand was a pot of dirt. He held it out with an eager grin.

Faelyn raised an eyebrow. She studied the pot, then freed a hand, placing it against the side. She gasped. The seeds within the dirt begged for her touch. She concentrated, and soon they sprouted, continuing to bloom into beautiful purple lilacs.

"It's perfect, Kian. Thank you."

"A small welcoming gift. Come on, let's get back."

Kian took Faelyn to the Academ dormitory. The person behind the front desk, whom Kian said was in charge of the safety of the students, gave her a key and told her where her room was. She nearly bounced down the long hall, carrying her new and old items. Kian smiled through a grimace, under the weight of all her books and heavier purchases.

She opened the door, and it swung inward. Her new room was small, a single bed with bedding folded at the foot. It had a good-sized writing desk, a wooden chair, and an empty bookshelf. The room was clean of dust and cobwebs. She set her satchel and boxes on the floor and walked to the curtainless window. The view left much to be desired—the girls' dormitory across the way, plain white against the even whiter snow. She missed the forest.

"Academ students get their own rooms. Mine is two floors up." Kian sat the lilacs on the windowsill. The touch of color and the warmth in his eyes were the perfect antidote to lift her spirits.

Faelyn's room, quiet and devoid of the usual chirp of insects or gusts of bitterly cold wind, gave her a good night's sleep. The next morning she donned her new black robe, sized just for her. She felt ridiculous. The robe hung loose on her body and flowed down to her feet.

Professor Wemnar hadn't managed to exempt her from Mage Staff Execution, and it was her first class. Kian told her where to go, so she entered and sat in the back of a sizable room with four rows of tiered seating. She crossed her arms as more students in black filed in. A couple of them shot furtive glances her way, then sat elsewhere. They gave her wary looks, and no one talked to her. None of them were a day over twelve, and she was the only one who didn't bring a staff.

The professor, long black hair tied back in a tail, walked in with his own staff and took his place at the front of the room. He wore the relaxed expression of one who'd taught for a lifetime.

"Good morning, students." He took a step from the chalkboard and thumped the ground with his staff. The room quieted. "I'm Professor Cody. For some of you, this is the first time you've ever held your own staff. I find it's best to assess your ability and comfort level before we continue, so we'll start at the back and work our way forward. Pour your mind into your mage crystal, and use your magic to make it glow."

Of course, he'd start on the back row. The first person to go lit her crystal up with a smirk.

The second person licked his lips under all the attention. He gripped his staff and closed his eyes, scrunching his brow in intense concentration. The professor let him work on it for a good few minutes. Beads of sweat broke out on the boy's face.

"Feel the magic around you through your crystal. You can do it."

The boy nodded, and a moment later, a small glow appeared. He beamed and lost the magic.

After a few more amateurs went, it was her turn. Faelyn sat in her chair with her arms crossed. The children stared.

"Where is your staff?" the professor asked.

"I've no need for one." *Or this class.*

Professor Cody narrowed his eyes. "You will not disrespect my classroom, Aliyah." So he knew her name, at least. "You may be new here, but that excuse will only take you so far before it's considered insubordination." He took a step closer to the front row of students.

She stared, unfazed by his methods of intimidation. This was no way to start her first day. "I mean no disrespect, Professor. I don't need a staff to access my magic."

"Nonsense!" Professor Cody's roar made the children jump. "Without a staff, you can't access magic and will not pass this class."

Faelyn bristled. He didn't need to shout. Had no one told him? Or did he not believe her, as most claimed. He'd likely pegged her as a troublemaker and was trying to make an example of her. She stared at Professor Cody and concentrated on the mage crystals in the room. Their power called to her, though it was nothing stronger than what she could access without them. With a thought, she lit them up simultaneously, turning the room as bright as a sunlit day.

The children screamed and ducked. Professor Cody raised his staff to defend himself against attack. The magic, like invisible moths to a flame, was pulled from the air and gathered around his glowing crystal. Quickly, it bubbled around him, waiting to be directed.

Wincing, she extinguished the lights. That was definitely not the reaction she had expected. She waited patiently for him to recover and realize what had happened.

When the yelling and the panic died down, the children slowly took their seats, heads swiveling every which way. Professor Cody dropped his defensive spell, the magic dissipating into the air—a very interesting process to watch. He stared at her. Simply stared.

Faelyn opened her senses to get a read on him. She sensed awe and astonishment mixed with anger of the purest kind, and a hint of jealousy. Anger would win out. He had an example to make of her.

"Most impressive and unnecessary. You are dismissed from my class. Indefinitely."

Faelyn nodded. She hadn't expected anything less. She gathered her bag still packed and walked out of the classroom. The children watched her with gaping mouths. After the door closed behind her, conversations burst into life, trailing her well down the hall. It took Professor Cody some time to regain control.

She found her next classes much more interesting, if very basic. In magical history, she learned the school had been in existence for over two centuries. In magical defense, she learned how to create a shield against weapon attacks by condensing the element of wind into a tangible wall, like a bubble. That wasn't part of the lesson, but the professor had used it to show off for his new students—to demonstrate what they could learn by the end of the class—and she picked it up.

In magical offense, she didn't learn much, except that she'd eventually use her elements in a more controlled way and not just when angry on a massive destructive scale. When she'd finished her last class for the day, her rumbling stomach sent her to the main dining hall. She made it a few paces toward her anticipated slice of pie with cream before Professor Wemnar's assistant stopped her in the hall.

"Professor Wemnar summons you to his office." The young man, Alex, waited for her to follow.

Faelyn looked past him, smelling the fresh aroma of chicken soup. She sighed. "All right."

She trailed Alex down the hall and up the stairs, though she remembered the way. When she opened the door, she was met by Professor Wemnar's narrow-eyed expression of disapproval.

"Sit down," Wemnar said when the door shut behind her.

His commanding tone made her immediately want to do the opposite, but she complied, folding her arms tight over her chest.

"Professor Cody advised me of what you did in his class today. As your sponsor, your actions directly reflect upon me." He stood from his chair and leaned toward her over his desk. "It is strictly forbidden to access magic through another's mage crystal."

She nearly flinched from the anger in his words. “Professor Wemnar, I didn’t—"

He held up his hand, silencing her. “I convened with the board on your behalf and pleaded your ignorance of the rules. They’ve agreed not to expel you on your very first day of class, and to give you another chance.”

She couldn’t withhold the irritation in her tone. “I did not access magic through those children’s crystals. I don’t know why it’s so hard for the people in this school to understand, but I do not require a staff to access my magic.” If she could have stomped her foot to emphasize the last words without seeming to act her appeared age versus her real age, she would have. “I’m sure to Professor Cody it appeared I had—without touching them, I should add—but that is not the case. I merely used my light magic to make their staffs glow.”

Wemnar sat slowly back in his chair. He stared at her, drumming his fingers against the desk.

Finally, he spoke. “You are a mystery, to be sure. I’ve not pressed you for more than you are willing to share, though I feel that is a great deal. There is a familiarity about you that I’ve not permitted myself to pursue. If you are to continue here, you must learn to operate within the delicate balance that is our school. I’ve no doubt you can benefit greatly.”

“Then put me in classes befitting my ability.”

“Don’t be too eager to rise to the top. Kian told me something of the manner in which he found you. You’ll need the basics if you’re to learn the kind of control necessary to become a great mage.”

Faelyn crossed her arms.

“That being said, you’ve been exempt from all required mage staff courses.”

She smiled openly. Professor Wemnar's frown turned slowly up, then he winked.

“Professor,” Faelyn said thoughtfully, “I’ve always had a passion for swordfighting. Are there any courses offered in that field?”

“This is a school of magic, Ali. If you want to waste time with something as simpleminded as swordfighting, you'll need to find tutelage elsewhere."

Faelyn frowned. Simple swordfighting had saved her more than once. "Then may I have permission to practice on my own?"

"Your personal time away from classes is your own. Do with it what you will. But don't lose sight of your purpose here, Ali. Don't give the board cause to end your scholarship."

Faelyn inclined her head and left his office, meandering her way back to her dorm. What was her purpose here? To prove to herself she could gain admittance? To prove to Kian she was just as good if not better than him? What she'd told Professor Fenedict was more than true. She needed to learn control and respect for her magic. Maybe the skills she learned could help if she ever decided to do something about people like the starving little girl they met on the way here—people who suffered under the Daltieri regime.

Faelyn tried to brush those thoughts aside, but they took root. She was staying. So long as she avoided the Daltieri soldiers, she would feel safe here, with a warm place to sleep and regular meals. And Kian.

She smiled and stepped outside into a courtyard thick with snow. The chill wind made instant goosebumps, stealing body heat from the loose folds of her robe. Her thoughts turned to Pavora, her home from so long ago. Perhaps the knowledge she gained at the school could be used not just to help people, but to reclaim her kingdom.

She nearly laughed at herself. Those were the thoughts of a hopeful child, blissfully ignorant of reality. Faelyn was no child, and the reality was that even with all the magic in the world, she was just one girl in a kingdom that had forgotten her, and long forgotten the good name of Alysies. The tyrannical control Daltieri possessed, the total oppression and fear, was a force too great to counteract.

CHAPTER TWENTY-FOUR

The sun had finally pushed through the harshest of the cold winter, breaking through the gray, gloomy clouds. Faelyn sat on the edge of the fountain, still kept dry for the winter, stretching her legs. Her black robe soaked up the heat, and she could almost pretend it was spring.

Several students ran about the sodden grass, laughing and chasing one another. Kian was in class in the west wing, assisting as a teacher. She couldn't wait to see his smile when he found her waiting for him.

Faelyn's sensitive hearing picked up Miyah's scoff from several yards down the path. Faelyn kept her eyes closed, face upturned to the cheery sun. It'd been almost a month since she arrived at Thomats, and Miyah still resented her for Kian's attention. From the stomping beside Miyah, it sounded as if Mason walked with her. Their steps and muttering drew closer, but Faelyn didn't open her eyes. With any luck, they'd pass and leave her be.

Yeah, right.

"Just look at her, all smug in her charity robe." Miyah couldn't know Faelyn heard every word.

Faelyn tightened her grip on the fountain's ledge.

Mason snickered. "You know what to do if you ever want revenge."

Faelyn gasped and opened her eyes.

"We'd only be implicating ourselves, moron." Miyah lowered her voice. "Watch this."

Miyah stepped close enough for human hearing. "Oh look, Mason, it's Ali." She turned toward the covered portico flanked by columns that led to the double doors of the west wing. "I bet she's waiting on Kian."

Mason smirked.

Faelyn sighed and stood. "Good morning Miyah, Mason. Enjoying the unseasonably warm weather?"

Miyah took a step closer. "Kian would be better off with me, you know. I don't get kicked out of classes. I have a title, and land in Creadel. What do you have?"

Miyah had been building to this moment for weeks now, but she wouldn't give in. The pain and jealousy rolling off Miyah was proof enough the girl didn't deserve Faelyn's retribution.

Faelyn raised her hands in a placating gesture. "I'm sorry you're hurting, Miyah, truly. We might have been friends if you could see past this. Kian and I aren't dating. And besides, it's up to him who he chooses. That might not be you, but in time, you'll learn to respect his wishes and move on."

Miyah gritted her teeth and tilted her staff forward. It glowed as she gathered magic.

"Maybe that didn't come out as I intended." Faelyn offered a wince.

"Respect his wishes?" Miyah snarled. "Big words from a freak." Her magic increased.

Faelyn frowned. There was that word again, as inescapable as her painful past. She couldn't interpret Miyah's magical intent—she hadn't taken that class yet. Just in case, she used something she'd learned in elemental class combined with magical defense, and created a shield of air around her.

"Don't do anything stupid, Miyah. You could get expelled." Mason put a hand on her shoulder.

She shrugged him off. "This was long overdue."

Kian came out the double doors, grinning as he glimpsed Faelyn. His gaze drifted to Miyah, and his bright smile parted into a small gape. He ran forward, dodging students, mage staff glowing. "Miyah, stop!"

Students jumped out of his way, gawking.

Miyah blinked, startled into dissipating some of her built-up magic. Whatever she was planning, it took a lot of energy.

Faelyn held her shield, watching and weighing Miyah carefully. Kian put himself between them.

Miyah growled with irritation. She didn't have a prayer of besting Kian. She released her magic, shoulders drooping from its taxing use. To the gathered students, her hanging head might appear derived from shame or embarrassment. Faelyn sensed fury underneath the act.

Kian's staff dimmed. "Why would you do something like that, Mi?" His voice was soft, pitying.

Tears welled in her eyes. "You've barely spoken to me since we've returned. Are you really picking her over me?" She threw her pointed finger like a dagger.

Kian faced Faelyn, an irresistibly handsome innocence on his face. His eyes danced with hidden joy. "If she'll have me." The words were a statement of his intentions, and Faelyn sensed the burning desire underneath.

Faelyn held his gaze. She brushed her long hair over her shoulder, giving herself time to think. Was she ready for this?

Miyah rolled her eyes behind Kian. "Freak."

Faelyn straightened. Yes, she was ready to move beyond friendship with Kian. She nodded, cheeks warming.

Kian's half-smile grew to a full-on grin that made Faelyn's heart sputter. He turned around, but Miyah had already stormed off. Mason cast them a grimace, then chased after her.

Beaming, Kian jogged toward Faelyn, stopping a few feet away. He stood there, eyeing her meaningfully. "You mind dropping your shield?"

"Oh!" Faelyn let go of her magic, and Kian took her hands.

"I'm so happy you said yes. I was planning on asking you a more proper way later today, but this works. Now we can enjoy my surprise as a couple." He kissed her on the mouth.

"I'm happy too, Kian," she said, and meant it. They weren't just empty words to fill the gap with what she was supposed to say. Not this time.

She felt the urge to hug him and didn't fight it. She wrapped her arms tightly around his torso, and he relaxed against her. The motions didn't feel as natural as she expected. She cared for Kian, so maybe it would become easier in time.

She nuzzled his chest. "You have a surprise for me?"

He pulled back, eyes twinkling. "Yes, we're going on an outing later. No need to bring anything, just wear your sturdier boots. Can you meet me here after fourteenth bell?"

"Yes, I'll come right after class."

"Great." Kian gave her a quick peck.

Maybe he'd dated others before her, but she wasn't so accustomed to the fast pace. The casual intimacy was something she'd have to get used to. Courting had been so much simpler when no one wanted anything to do with her.

He beamed. "I'll see you this afternoon."

"Wait." She pulled him back. "What about Miyah?"

"Miyah? I'm sorry about her, Ali. I made it clear to her we were not a couple anymore after you and I first met. I've never seen her act that way. I'm sure it won't happen again."

"No, I mean, what kind of spell was she planning on using?"

Kian sighed. "She was going to transport your robe away." He brought his hand up to cover a smirk.

“Leaving me in nothing but my undergarments?” Faelyn gaped. That vicious little...

Kian nodded behind his hand.

"I didn't know someone could do that."

"Transportation is Miyah's special gift. It's not as common as elemental magic."

She pursed her lips. "Where would my robe have gone?"

"Wherever she wanted it to, depending on how much effort she put into the spell. The distance is limited by the energy it takes." He lifted her chin. "I'm not sure your shield could have prevented it, but I've never seen it tried." He shrugged. "See you this afternoon?"

Faelyn nodded, and he bounded away. She'd have to study how to counteract that kind of magic, and any other kind she didn't already have in her arsenal.

Faelyn bounced in her seat, unable to even pretend to take notes. She stared out the window at the students passing by. The fourteenth bell had already rung, but Professor Teomar was still lecturing. Under normal circumstances, Faelyn wouldn't mind. She loved her elemental class, and the professor was discussing how the absence of heat produces cold—something to experiment with later.

The professor’s black robe hung loose on her thin frame as she gestured to the board. “Once you remove enough heat, you can freeze anything. One only needs to be master of fire, which several of you are.” She nodded to the class, her gaze landing on Faelyn. “This principle is applicable in a multitude of situations.” The half-bell chimed from the clocktower. “Okay, mages dismissed.”

Faelyn scooped up her bag and rushed out the door ahead of the class. She jogged-walked all the way down the hall, out the main doors, and cut across the grounds to the west wing courtyard. She didn't bother putting on her cloak; the sun had warmed the day enough to be tolerable.

She spotted Kian pacing by the fountain. He looked up and smiled.

"So sorry! Professor Teomar kept up the whole class."

Kian wrapped his hands around her hips.

Faelyn flinched but covered it with a smile. She'd have to get used to being close to people again.

"If I had remembered you were in Teomar's class, I would have known to expect you late." He laughed. "She's an excellent professor, but long-winded. And she prefers the fire element, which I do not have." He squeezed her waist. "Ready to go?"

"Where are we going?"

He placed his finger to his lips and winked.

Faelyn rolled her eyes, pretending to be unimpressed. Truthfully, she was buzzing inside. No one had ever planned a surprise for her, except Mary on her birthdays.

They dropped off Faelyn's school bag, and after taking a moment to freshen up, they headed away from the school. His fingertips grazed her hand before he took it, twining his fingers with hers.

A pleasant tingling wound up her arm until encircling her whole body. He squeezed her hand, and she squeezed back.

They walked downhill, passing between bare trees and leafless bushes, distant villages and farmland on the horizon. After a couple miles, she couldn't resist.

"Now will you tell me where we're going?"

Kian swung their arms. "There's a town north of here—"

"Rosen." Faelyn had never been, of course, but she'd been taught some about every note-worthy city in Alysies. Rosen was known for its beauty, nestled at the bottom of Thomats' plateau, in a small valley before the earth rose back up again.

"Yes, you know your geography."

She nodded. At least Daltieri hadn't changed the names of the towns.

"Now that we've reached the bottom, it's only another two miles until we skirt around the base and reach the town."

She'd always wanted to see Rosen. The pictures in her books boasted waterfalls, lush vegetation, and gorgeous architecture built into the side of the hill. The opulence made it a popular place for a holiday escape, even in winter when the townspeople decorated with flowing banners and little touches to await the bursting colors of spring.

A skip entered Faelyn's step. The exercise felt wonderful after sitting through so many classes, cooped up in the routine of the school. And she was with her *boyfriend,* no less. If only they had the time and money to stay the night—in separate rooms, of course.

As they neared, the sun lowered in the sky, and fog crept in. Soon they reached the outskirts of the town, marked by the end of the gravel road and the beginning of a street paved with stone broken up in several places.

Faelyn hopped over a patch of rubble. "They haven't kept the roads up very well." Ahead, she saw the outline of buildings blanketed by mist.

Kian stared intently in front of them. "No. I hear the town was beautiful once."

Faelyn turned to him. "Once, but not anymore? Why not?"

"I don't know. It's been like this since I started at Thomats." Kian shrugged. "But there's one good thing that hasn't changed. Come on, I can't wait." He tugged her ahead, and Faelyn increased her speed, heart racing.

The rustle of bushes drew her gaze. A woman stood in front of a makeshift house, holding the hands of two young children. She wore nothing but a burlap sack, with a dirty face and wild hair. The three of them stared, wide-eyed.

The people in the pictures had always dressed so fine, with bright colors and lordly opulence.

"Watch your coin. They won't bother you if you don't talk to them. But we can't stop here." Kian pulled her ahead.

Faelyn reached into her pouch and pulled out a handful of coins. She set them by the road, keeping her distance from the family. She backed away, offering a warm smile while they stood watching warily. Kian and Faelyn continued on, not waiting to see what became of the coins. He didn't say anything, but she felt his pride.

The sight as the town came into full view chilled Faelyn's blood. Her eyes strained through the fog as they crept closer. Some of the buildings, once tall wooden structures with glass windows, had collapsed. The piles, worn by age and weather, had been picked through, but not cleaned away. Homes and abandoned shops displayed missing paint, boarded windows, and patched roofs.

"What happened here?" she whispered. "The people, the place. I don't hear any waterfalls."

Kian eyed her with concern as she numbly followed him down the path. Hills still rose on either side of the main street, but nature was overtaking the neglected town.

"It's much prettier in the spring. The river is dry because of the dam, but there's the lake beyond. That's not where we're going, though. We're almost there."

The winter trees were as dead as the town, and yet there were still so many people. They stepped out of the foggy shadows or peered through broken windows, watching them. No one begged for coin, and Faelyn wondered why until the faint glow of Kian's staff caught her attention—a warning only.

Her hand slipped back into Kian's. Around a curve in the road, which followed the path of an indeed dried-up river, sat the least rundown patch of buildings she'd seen. A town square. The white and blue paint still remained over most of them, and the vines hadn't choked the rest away. Here, people wore drab roughhewn tunics or dresses, but clean faces and combed hair.

"The Running Dove," she read from a red sign hanging above the door. "I've heard of this place." The restaurant was old and about the only thing still recognizable. Time had not been kind to the once beautiful town.

"That's where we're going. They have the best food for many miles, and it's inexpensive, too." He acted as if the oppressive countenance radiating from the people didn't choke him, as it threatened to choke her.

Townspeople moved out of their way, as if touching them would bring a plague. No one would meet their eyes.

She spoke into Kian's ear. "Why do they act that way?"

"The townspeople associate us closely with the king. Mages are often used to put down rebellions. I'm sure this place has seen a few in its day."

Faelyn's eyes widened with each word. She shook her head. "That's horrible."

Kian patted her arm. "It's okay. Let's enjoy our meal."

How could he think of food in the face of all this ruin? Her fingers curled into fists. The king had done this, King Samual, and now his vile descendent, King Seber. What she'd seen on the journey to Thomats had been but a sample. This was the new Alysies after Daltieri.

Was it her fault? Had her cowardice and inaction for all those years brought ruin to her once beloved kingdom?

She followed Kian through an open doorway, barely noticing the cozy interior, a hearty fire and lanterns casting an orange glow. She didn't smile as the overly-friendly host immediately showed them to a table in a prime spot by the warm hearth. Her mind whirled.

She slumped into the chair beside Kian, staring at her folded hands. Kian cast her worried looks while ordering drinks.

By right, these people were hers to rule, and she'd abandoned them. The fearful stare of the villagers weighed down on her, and she deserved it. She was their enemy. Not because she worked for King Seber, but for reasons much more heinous. They'd needed a leader, and she'd run away.

"Ali, dear, is the smoke bothering you? We could move to another table." Kian took her hand, rubbing his thumb over her skin.

Faelyn blinked and looked up. "Smoke?"

"Yes, you're crying." He lifted his arm, catching tears on either side of her face.

"It's not the fireplace. I'm just... I can't believe how destitute these people are."

A server wearing a stained apron interrupted her thoughts. "Welcome to The Running Dove, young mages. What can I get you?"

Faelyn glanced at the menu on the table and ordered the first thing she saw. "Roasted hen, please." She wiped her face, taking sips of cold well water.

"Ham for me, good sir. And how do things fair in Rosen?"

Faelyn looked up.

The man, grey on top with an abundance of wrinkles, scratched the back of his neck. "Well enough, I suppose. It's been a harsh winter, but we're glad for this milder day." He met Faelyn's gaze and smiled.

Underneath his friendly veneer was a desperate man ready to crack.

She would be his queen if she hadn't run away, if she'd fought for it. Could be his queen still, if she learned the proper skills and raised an army.

Faelyn reached out her hand, and the man took it without hesitation, his smile growing. Keeping her eyes locked on him, she drew magic to her and sent it into him in the form of peace and contentment. His eyes widened, arm going slack, then his body visibly relaxed, years of tension easing away.

"I'm sorry times in Rosen are so hard. Let us both pray to the Fates for better days ahead." She released his hand.

The man nodded, eyes glistening, and pulled his hand to his heart. He cast a quick glance at Kian before departing.

"What was that all about?" Kian's tone chafed. "You shouldn't use magic so casually, so carelessly."

Faelyn shook off the haunting feelings of Rosen and turned her attention to him. "I've observed a few things since coming to Thomats. One of the most intriguing is how a proper mage, one with a mage crystal, uses magic. They pull it from their surroundings, channeling it through the crystal. The magic builds until they have the necessary amount, then released. Unlike the build, the release—or execution of the magic—requires much more of the mage's energy."

She sipped more water. "It doesn't work the same for me. It's as if my crystal is internal, and the magic comes from within me. It is a part of me. There's no building it up, it just is. That's a long way of saying I don't use it casually or carelessly, but intentionally. And, like a child learning to walk, Thomats is helping me expand skills which have always been there."

Kian's lips turned up. "I love to hear you speak. You're so eloquent, like you come from the past."

Faelyn winked.

"I'm sorry, Ali. Using magic is something we're cautioned not to do until we're properly trained, especially outside the school. It's not forbidden, merely frowned upon. It's a notion that's hard for me to let go."

The man returned with their food, setting it on the table with a slight bow. "No charge tonight for the young mages."

Faelyn shook her head.

"I'm Farero, the owner, and I insist." He bowed again and left with a smile.

The smell of the delicious hen, stuffed with spices and vegetables teased her senses.

"Kian?"

"Don't worry, we'll leave double."

Faelyn beamed, proud of his decision. He leaned over for a slow, tortuous kiss, and then they ate. It was the best food she'd had in years.

As promised, Kian left double their tab. The view of town going out was as depressing as it was coming in. They walked quickly to avoid being caught in the dark. Kian's glowing mage crystal helped.

Faelyn stole one more glance back before the town was out of sight. The sad state of the once glorious village, and the sad eyes that tracked their progress, hardened her resolve.

Five years. She'd give Thomats five years to teach her how to be the best mage she could be, and then she'd do what was necessary to win her kingdom back. She owed that to these people. Her people. And she owed it to herself.

CHAPTER TWENTY-FIVE

Ardenis swelled with pride and relief that Faelyn had settled into Thomats. She should have been sent there long ago, then she could have avoided some mistakes, like killing those men back in Newberry. Thanks to her fool of a father, she'd been denied many things, but was finally on the right path.

Even Kian with his lavishing attention didn't bother him. Much. Though Ardenis had nearly ripped the door off its hinges when he'd stormed out of the watchtower the first time Kian kissed her. He shuddered.

Kian saw to her needs and made her smile, and it became gleefully obvious she didn't care for Kian as much as Kian cared for her, even as time went on. Though, her advanced age probably had something to do with that. Kian was infatuated.

She would eventually be alright, if she could let go of her injuries. The pain in her eyes as she walked away from her first class, walked away from rejection, wasn't of her doing. It was a pain born of harder times. And now it had changed. No longer did her eyes reflect sadness, but a new determination.

Day after day, Ardenis stared into the watch window, looking out for Faelyn. She came through her first winter at the school with the highest marks. The classes were too easy for her, and she tried to get her professors to pass her early, but under the direction of her sponsor, Professor Wemnar, they would not. Ardenis commended Wemnar's persistence against the stubborn force that was Faelyn. The basics would do her good, no matter how eager she was.

Time had not taught her patience.

As Faelyn advanced into the next classes, and then the next, her own magical strengths and limitations led her to specialize in elemental magic. She couldn't read minds or control people, she never mastered transporting objects or creating things out of thin air. But in elemental magic, Wemnar had no choice but to pass her ahead; she was as advanced as some of the masters at the school.

She learned many skills, spells, and techniques, but most of all, she learned control. Ardenis beamed every time her magic came when she called. She didn't allow it to take over in the face of her anger—she could work up a temper when she entered the sparring courses.

At the end of Faelyn's fifth year, Kian achieved his goal to become a teacher at the school. Faelyn attended the ceremony, smiling with bright eyes as Kian accepted the professor's insignia and was given the assignment to teach the element of light to the intermediate students.

He acquired a humble house on the outskirts of the school amongst the rows of teacher housing. Keeping track of his actions, it became apparent Kian was about to do something unforgivable.

Faelyn rushed to the stage to meet Kian as soon as the graduation ceremony ended. He bounded from his chair straight to her. He took her up in a tight hug, lifting her off the ground.

"I'm so proud of you, Kian. You earned this."

He grinned, eyes alight. "Well, you helped. I wouldn't have

completed my dissertation if you hadn't taught me that new way of harnessing light to create energy."

Faelyn shrugged. She'd surpassed Kian in many things, but not everything. He still had more control, even if he didn't command as many elements. Though, anger no longer controlled her magic. During their time of growing closer and getting comfortable with him, she'd never quite figured out how he'd put her to sleep the first time they'd met.

Kian took her hand. "Come on. I have a surprise for you."

Faelyn smiled. "For me? I'm not the one who just graduated."

He said no more as he led her through the throngs of people congregating around him and across campus to his new house among the teachers' dwellings. The wooden cottage had quaint shutters and a single bedroom. Kian led her up the small porch and used his key to enter. The small kitchen and dining area were clean but bare of any homey touches.

He walked her to the middle of the empty sitting area and faced her, taking both her hands. His nervousness filled the air like the uncomfortable heat from sitting too close to a fire. It made her own nerves respond in kind.

Faelyn raised her eyebrows. "Umm..."

"Let me do this my way."

He got down on one knee, a tradition as old as time itself.

Faelyn gasped. This couldn't be happening.

"I feel I have everything I've ever wanted in life, save for one thing." His lips formed a shy smile. "I promise to always take care of you and not be upset when you finally surpass me." He flashed a grin at the joke.

Faelyn's heart hammered in her chest. As much as she loved Kian, was she ready for this?

Kian reached into his robe and pulled out a small black box. "I promise to put up with your stubborn pride and let you win all the arguments. Most of the arguments. Please do me the honor and say you'll be my wife, Ali."

Ali.

It was like a cold bucket of water dumped onto her stolen happiness. He'd asked Ali to marry him. But she could never be Ali, not truly. He didn't know who she really was. Faelyn of Alysies, heir to the throne—even if she hadn't called herself by that title in decades.

He handed her the box without opening it. She held it in her hands, looking into his hopeful eyes, and wondered if it would be worse to refuse him now or later.

This sweet time with Kian, it had all been a fantasy. This wasn't her life.

Marrying him wasn't an option. He'd grow old and wither away, and she'd stay young and there was no hiding that. The life he craved couldn't be his if she agreed to this. She could never be who he needed her to be, the wife he deserved by his side.

She tensed, but he spoke first.

"One's mage crystal is a sacred and precious thing. It belongs to the mage and should not be accessed by anyone else, as you know. But what you probably don't know, having been exempt from the classes, is that there is a single exception to that rule." He nodded at her to open the box.

She studied the simple package and all it promised and implied. An image of them dancing, laughing, together flashed in her mind.

Ever so slowly, she lifted the lid. Inside was a ring with a single gem framed in white gold. Her breaths turned shallow.

"This is a piece of my mage crystal," he said softly. "You've captured my heart, Ali. Accept my crystal as a symbol of my love, which shines on you from all directions."

Tears slid down her face. Such a big sacrifice he'd made. She felt him in this ring, his essence, his pure love for her. There had to be a way to make it work.

He watched her expectantly.

She took a shaky breath, her pounding heart threatening to betray her fear. Could he accept her if he knew her truth? Her ears—a secret he'd kept all this time—were not even a small part of it.

Through her love of learning magery and her happiness being with Kian, she'd almost forgotten a promise she'd made herself. Five years. Her five years at Thomats were up, and she was supposed to leave and reclaim her fate.

"Before I can accept this ring and the honor of becoming your wife, I have much to tell you." She owed him this, and he could be trusted.

She sat cross-legged on the floor of his new home, pulling Kian down with her. His brow creased with worry. She tasted his trepidation in the air.

He waited patiently while she took deep breaths, emotion and adrenaline competing to ruin her composure.

"You must promise, no matter what you decide, not to reveal what I am about to tell you. Even if you choose not to marry me, I will have your oath of secrecy."

"Of course, Ali, of course. I promise to keep what you are about to tell me a secret. On my life and honor." He squeezed her hand, and the power of his promise thrilled through her, resonating deep in her bones.

The weight of what she was about to tell him was almost enough to stop her. For so long, it'd been her secret, and her secret alone. It had kept her safe and the pain of her cowardice buried deep. Now that she was on the great precipice, about to tell everything to the man who loved her, it wanted to burst out of her. A secret, too big to be kept hidden all this time. Would he blame her for running and hiding, as she blamed herself?

She swallowed against the dryness in her throat, chin lifting with a readying breath. "My name isn't Ali. It's Faelyn. Faelyn Eva Rylandor."

Kian sat up a little straighter. "You lied about your name? And all these years we've known each other? Why?"

"To protect my identity." Her eyes bore into his, holding hope she could make him understand.

"From who?"

"The kingdom of Daltieri."

"I don't understand. Are you in trouble with the king? Are you an outlaw?" His arm twitched as if he wished to withdraw his hand, but he held it in place.

"Have you heard of Alysies?"

Kian jumped where he sat and looked around the room, as if fearing she'd been overheard. She'd used her hearing long ago to ensure no one approached.

"That name is forbidden here." The pressure from his fingers as he squeezed her hands mirrored the anxiety in his tone.

"Forbidden?" Faelyn laughed a dry, mirthless laugh. "I'd assumed it forgotten, but never imagined it forbidden." No one spoke of Alysies, but anyone alive would have been born under the rule of Daltieri. "And what do you know of Alysies?"

Kian dropped her hands. "Don't speak that name. We'd be imprisoned. You could ruin everything we've worked for." His words, usually so kind and calm, snapped like a whip.

Faelyn's blood boiled. "I've never heard someone utter anything more ridiculous." She set the box with the ring in the empty space between them on the floor before her control fled entirely and she threw it at him.

Her people had been punished for even speaking the name? And now it was forgotten, lost like sands in time. Daltieri had gone to great lengths eradicating her roots.

Kian placed his hand tenderly against her face. "Please, Ali. Tell me what you are trying to say. You're worrying me. Your magic is flaring." He peered into her, his eyes and mouth threatening to crumple. He was a man on the brink of a great pain, one that he felt coming but tried to stave off.

She pulled away from his touch. "Even here in privacy, you ask me not to speak of Alysies?" The words snapped out in frustration.

"Though I'm from Creadel, I still have a healthy fear of it, and it gives me grief to hear you use it now. Soldiers are never far, and I will not see you harmed."

Her fists clenched until her nails dug into her skin. The training she'd received was the only thing keeping her from setting the house on fire. Never had she felt the years separating the two of them so keenly. The world had truly forgotten her kingdom.

She loosened her hands. If she didn't calm down, she'd deliver her information all wrong, and the sacrifice of so many years of secrecy would be for naught. It wasn't his fault—she wasn't angry with him.

Closing her eyes, she took deep breaths. "And what do you know of Alysies?" She refused to be cowed.

Kian flinched. "I know it used to be the ground we stand on. That Daltieri conquered it long ago. It was ruled by a horrible king who let it turn to ruin, and he died without an heir. King Isaac was his name." He went on. "They don't teach of any history before The Purge here. All I know is what I've heard by word of mouth and what little I learned from school in Creadel."

She winced against his words, but Kian only knew what he'd been told. The Purge. Faelyn hated the title given to mark the beginning of New Daltieri. Two little words to sum up the inexplicable pain that altered the course of history and her life.

"King Isaac of Alysies was my father. He was murdered before my very eyes by King Samual of Daltieri over eighty-five years ago—during The Purge." She wrapped her arms around herself. "My father was hours away from pronouncing me heir. Daltieri conquered my kingdom for its riches and trade routes, and has exploited and impoverished my people ever since. Clearly there is no end to their tyranny."

Her people. Had she ever called them that before? But that was who they were, and a fierce need to protect them from further harm overtook her.

Kian's eyes grew bigger as she spoke, but she impressed upon him the truth of her words, so as outlandish as they seemed, he wouldn't be able to deny them.

She held her breath, waiting for his response.

Kian grinned. “You’re joking. I can feel you trying to make me think this is all true.”

She narrowed her eyes and shook her head.

“Then you must be mad.” He stood, moving closer to the door and grabbing his magestaff. “Absolutely mad.”

She stood and stared at his robe, unwilling to meet his face. “I’m telling the truth, Kian.”

“Oh, I believe you think you’re telling the truth. Mad people are incapable of distinguishing reality from the worlds they’ve created in their minds.”

His words stung like a slap. More than that, they cut her deeply, and she found herself with a hand to her chest, holding the pieces together.

His eyes widened. “I’m sorry. I’m hurt. I didn’t mean it.”

“Do you think I’m making it all up just so I don’t have to marry you? I followed you here, trusted you, stayed true to you. Now I bare my soul, my pain and agony and living nightmare, and you throw it back in my face laced with burning venom?” Sadness shrouded her like a fog, and her hand drifted to the floor.

Kian’s brow bunched into remorse. “I know, I’m sorry. It’s just difficult to imagine.”

She was a fool to believe she deserved the happy ending. Even if he could push past the pain of rejection and see she spoke the truth, they could never marry. It was for the best. Everyone she ever loved died.

Faelyn picked up the box. He accepted it as she slowly passed it back to him. When she spoke, her quiet tone carried the weight of her profound emptiness. “My past is my burden, as is my long life. It’s better this way, Kian. Find someone worthy of such an honor as your hand. Someone you can grow old with. Someone not cloaked in death and sadness. My fate lies elsewhere.”

“Ali...”

Faelyn wiped a tear with the heel of her palm. “Yes, that is my name. Please forget what I've told you. And please don't ever speak to me again. I don't think I could bear it."

He reached for her, but she backed away. The right words from him and she'd say yes, dooming them both to a life of misery. Before he could speak, she turned and rushed out the front door, letting it slam closed. Tears blinded her as she ran away from a life she could never have.

Again. She was running away again.

The one place safe outside of Kian's arms called to her, and she fled to the embrace of the woods behind the school. Dodging students and the feel of Kian's pain, she leaped over underbrush and branches, her robes snagging on briars until she stopped, breathless and sobbing. She had outrun the weight of who she was for so long, but it had caught up to her. It crushed her. Tilting her head back, she glared at Acantha. Was she doomed to a life of solitude and loneliness? Even after a century, she couldn't accept the idea.

Who was she meant to be?

Faelyn tensed as her keen hearing picked up the crunch of boots on leaves. Kian knew her well. Her foot inched forward. The temptation to go to him was almost too great. Instead, she used air to create a veil, hiding with magic too strong for him to detect. He called her name, Ali, over and over, hardening her resolve with each utterance. Each time was another stone cast, rippling the pond, ruining the false image she'd thought she could trick herself into believing was real.

When at last he'd gone, she trudged to her room and considered packing. She'd acquired many things, gifts from Kian or items bought with her stipend. Her most precious and secret items she hid under the floorboard, a key to nowhere from Calem, a pouch with her parents' rings and turquoise necklace, and her father's circlet. She pried up the board and grabbed the circlet. Head hanging, she dropped to her bed, examining it, turning the single sapphire this way and that in the fading light of day as it streamed through her window.

Could she face Kian if she stayed at Thomats? She didn't feel ready to leave yet; there was still so much left to learn.

Faelyn didn't hide the circlet or look up when Kian entered the room, closing the door behind him. He propped his staff beside the door, then sat heavily on the bed beside her, rubbing his eyes. They were red and shining.

Rather than letting her resolve crumble by gazing up at his handsome, anguished face, Faelyn stared at her father's circlet.

"I've seen this. In my history books from when I was a child in Creadel," he said, voice rough. "The circlet was coveted for its role in history, but it went missing."

"You shouldn't be here." Her voice was a whisper under the weight of despair. "I don't know what to do now, Kian. I won't stand in the way of your chance at happiness. Maybe I should pack my things and leave." When he didn't say anything, she looked up.

Silent tears welled in his eyes and threatened to spill over. "I'm so sorry, Ali... Faelyn. I don't know what to think. But you can't leave. You haven't given me a chance to understand before making a decision that affects us both."

Her heart melted, lips parting. She couldn't stand to see him in pain. His sadness stabbed like a knife to her heart. "We can't be together, Kian. Besides the simple fact we can't grow old together, my destiny lies elsewhere." The truth of those words burned in her chest. This wasn't her life. She couldn't be a teacher here alongside him or a teacher's wife. Her lack of aging was bound to be noticed eventually. The time at the school was but a stepping stone, though a step toward what, she didn't know.

She went on. "Danger will always follow me. It may not seem this way to you, but it was so recent that these events happened. I could still very well be identified." She sighed heavily. "You know I love you, and I would marry you if not for the burden I carry."

"I have heard of you. I have. It was said Isaac had a daughter, sickly and deformed, unfit to rule. I just... it's such a fantastical story." He took the circlet from her hands and clenched it so tight,

Faelyn feared he might snap it in two. His shoulders slumped, and he set it gently on the bed behind her. He pushed her carefully styled hair back behind her pointed ears.

She couldn't help but lean into his familiar touch. Her lips parted, aching for one last kiss. He'd never judged her, called her a freak, or shown the slightest revulsion to her appearance. Even now, he didn't question why she'd never claimed her throne. He simply loved her for who he thought she was.

But she wasn't that person.

He grabbed her and pulled her tight against him.

She allowed herself to sink into his familiar embrace, placing her head against his chest.

He lay his face against her golden hair. "I don't understand, Al—Faelyn. You... How could you be here, attending school like any other student, when such atrocities have been done against you? Acantha above, the very soldiers who took your kingdom from you march on these grounds. You've never let on. I never suspected. Never."

She squeezed him, giving him the time he needed to process this new knowledge.

"You're a powerful mage," he said. "Why don't you fight back?"

She lifted her face. There was no blame in his countenance, only worry and confusion. "Fight back? You're the mad one. What could I do against an entire kingdom? I'm just one person. Daltieri has its own mages, employed out of this very school, and could easily command more based on the tight control I've seen of the kingdom's leadership." She shook her head. "No. There will be no fighting back." Not yet. She dropped her arms from around him and picked up the circlet, wrapping it in cloth. "I have to pack."

Kian's eyes went wide, and he grabbed her arm. "No, Faelyn. Please stay."

"I can't. I don't think I could be around you and not be with you." They couldn't go back to the way things were, and she'd only stand in the way of the life he should have.

"Then I'll leave," he said in desperation. "You belong here."

Faelyn scoffed. “I can’t let you give up on teaching, on everything you’ve ever wanted and worked for.”

He squeezed the fabric on her arm. There was a desperation on his face that betrayed just how scared he was of losing her. “We’ll both stay. Then I’ll come with you when you need to move on from the school. Teaching isn’t as important to me as you are.”

“Don’t make this harder than it has to be, Kian. This is your world, and I don’t belong in it.” Her racing heartbeat betrayed her sensible words. Kian was on the edge of convincing her to stay. The only choice was to get away before it was too late. She wasn't supposed to marry Kian, for more reasons than she could name.

Kian threw his newly awarded professor insignia to the ground and pulled the box from his pocket. He plucked the shining mage ring and grabbed Faelyn’s hand. Too shocked to resist, she stared as he slipped the ring on her finger.

His essence filled her, spreading from head to toe, like diving into icy water. She gasped, her hands shooting to her face. She felt him as she never had. His raw emotions of love and fear swarmed her, blinding her with tears. He stood before her, breathing heavily, watching with wide and desperate eyes. He held his hands out, not touching, but ready to catch her if she fell, or grab her if she ran. Like a second skin, his essence wrapped around her, given life with their bond.

“What have you done to me?” The connection trapped her, suffocating her under the weight of his whole being. It was like being imprisoned in a room where her body burned for air and each lungful wasn’t enough.

“The shared crystal binds us together. I can feel you, too.” He panted and stepped closer. "So much power. So much pain." He caressed her face. “I’ll give my whole life to you.”

And she felt it was true. The weight of him became more bearable, but there was a wrongness in the connection that wasn’t simply the new sensations of Kian.

Her head shook frantically from side to side, and she tried to pull off the ring.

Kian's hands covered hers. *Don't. The bond takes time to get used to. It won't feel so new in a little bit.* "It'll be okay. You know me now. You hear my voice in your mind, and feel the truth of my heart."

Mindspeak? Her limbs shook.

He smiled, but frantic distress ran underneath. She felt it with more than just her fae senses. It hit doubly hard because of the ring. He wanted her to stay, needed her to love him as much as he loved her.

But she didn't. A sob escaped her.

She didn't.

"I feel your doubt, Faelyn, but we belong together." He didn't stumble over her real name. "I'll help you win back your kingdom, then we can rule together. Is that what you want?"

What did she want? She wanted what anyone would want. What she couldn't have. Because her people needed her, and she owed them her complete attention.

She had to get away. "I can't, Kian. I'm so, so sorry." She used his light trick to disappear from sight, then layered it with a thin shield so he couldn't bend the elements to reveal her again. Yanking the ring off her finger, she clenched it in her fist. At once, she felt whole again, no longer tied to Kian's emotions or influence. She only felt him as she always had.

"No!" He pierced the room with mage light, then when that didn't reveal her, he grabbed wildly around the room.

Tears streamed down her face as she dodged him, stepping to the door.

Kian lunged violently, heartbreak evident in his wild eyes. "Please, wait! Don't do this. I'm begging you."

When she reached the door, she found he'd blocked it with a strong water-screen. Her air and light magic cut right through it. She was outside running before his yells of anguish began.

Her form whipped wind against those she passed on her blind

retreat. There was no plan except escape. Tears of anguish assaulted her, as did Kian's agony. It raked over her heart, threatening to pull her back into his arms, until she was finally, blissfully, out of range.

She found herself at Niri's door. Niri had graduated as an assistant professor just last year and lived only a short distance from Kian's new house.

Niri took one look at Faelyn and pulled her into a tight hug. She made strong tea and was a sympathetic ear while Faelyn told her the only details she could—that Kian had proposed, and Faelyn had realized she didn't love him in that way, and so she'd left him.

Niri listened with understanding and empathy, letting Faelyn sob herself into exhaustion. When there were no more tears, Niri made up a cot with warm blankets and soft pillows by the fireplace, lit to keep the chill of early spring at bay.

After Niri went to bed, Faelyn studied the fire as it crackled and consumed the wood. Something jabbed her side, and she reached into her pocket. Kian's ring. She closed her hand over it, not daring to put it on. In her haste, she'd forgotten to give it back. It indented her skin where she squeezed it tight in her fist. She placed it back in her pocket and snuggled deep under the covers.

Tears all gone and her body warmed by the fire, an odd sense of peace filled her. The loss of Kian was keenly felt, but the decision was right. He could move on from her, and her secret and her life would remain safe. Perhaps she was never meant to love.

Most importantly, she hadn't run. Not this time. Tomorrow she'd return Kian's ring, return to her room, and plan. It would be hard to face him every day, but she had to. Her future wasn't to keep pretending to be part of this fake life. She'd started something at Thomats, training for a future where she might be of use to her people. She wasn't going to stop now.

Faelyn's gaze strayed to the window. She stared up at Acantha and drew strength from the stars, which seemed to radiate their love.

CHAPTER TWENTY-SIX

Faelyn awoke when the late-morning sun dropped below the window ledge, its rays burning behind her eyelids. She sat up with a start, remembering where she was. Agony washed anew when the memories of the previous day came crashing over her.

Niri wasn't home, so Faelyn tidied up the blankets and pillows. She'd slept longer than intended. Eagerness hurried her actions. She had to return Kian's ring, as hard as it would be. She'd throw herself into learning and training. Magic, swordfighting, history, warcraft. Those things would be her priority now. It was the only way she'd be able to cope with seeing him around school.

Faelyn sensed Niri's anxiety even before she entered the house. Faelyn finished tidying up and met her friend at the door.

"Feeling better?" Niri's red hair was plaited over her shoulder, and she wore black robes with thin silver thread along the hem. She handed Faelyn a box of something sweet-smelling. "I brought pastries." Her kind voice couldn't disguise the strain in her eyes.

Faelyn set the box on a table. "What's wrong?"

Niri's eyes lined with tears. "Kian's gone."

Faelyn stilled with shock.

"He packed his things and left before sunup." Niri sniffled. "He didn't even say goodbye. I was on my way to talk to him when Professor Wemnar stopped me in the courtyard. Kian asked him to send his apologies, that he had to leave before anyone talked him out of it." Niri paused to wipe her eyes. "He resigned as teacher and is returning home to Creadel."

Faelyn covered her mouth. "No. He can't give this up. He's worked too hard." She brushed past Niri and practically sprinted toward the school grounds.

"Wait!" Niri called after her, but Faelyn kept going.

Kian couldn't have got far, at least not far enough that a hard day's ride couldn't make up for. Faelyn didn't own a horse—it'd been years since she'd ridden—but she'd steal one if she had to. She'd done it before.

Halfway to the stables, she spotted Professor Wemnar stepping quickly to intercept her. It would be easy to outrun him, as old as he was. His long, gray hair shook loose around him in his haste, and she slowed, pivoting to meet him. She'd hear what he had to say. It would only be a minor delay in finding Kian and sending him back to Thomats where he belonged.

Students in black robes meandered around them, in pairs or groups, walking well-worn trails in the grass or on cobbled pathways, heading to class in their familiar routines. None were aware of the crisis that was Kian giving up on his dreams. And it was all because she couldn't love him enough to choose him over her people. Even though he'd never asked her to do that, that was the choice she'd made.

Professor Wemnar caught up to her in the center of the empty grass field between buildings. The stables stood mockingly in the distance. His disapproving eyes said enough, and she stayed silent while he caught his breath.

"You're forbidden from following him," he finally said, voice stern.

She almost narrowed her eyes. Her temper wanted to accept his challenge and leave. Professor Wemnar deserved more respect than that. "I've hurt him, but that doesn't mean he shouldn't be here where he belongs. It should be me that leaves if one of us has to." If she had felt any sense of Kian's intentions to leave, she would have been gone in a heartbeat. What was he thinking?

"He told me everything."

Faelyn gasped. "Everything?" Kian said he would always protect her secret.

"Yes, I know about your fight and how you don't love each other like you once did." His eyes softened, and Faelyn nearly fainted with relief. Not that she didn't trust Professor Wemnar, but it was safer if he didn't know. "Love comes and goes, but Kian's decisions are his own, and we must accept them for good or ill." He crossed his arms.

Faelyn crossed hers in kind. "You can't believe that. His decisions are his own, yes, but those who love him can't allow him to make bad choices just for the sake of letting them be his."

Professor Wemnar stared at her.

"I know you love him, too."

He finally sighed, arms slackening to his sides. "Yes, I do. And it pains me to see you two at ends." He placed a gentle hand on her shoulder. "But that is life. We are a product of our choices. I wouldn't erase the bad decisions I've made because they've shaped who I am and led me here." One side of his mouth quirked up. "My point is, even if Kian is making a bad choice, it's his mountain to climb. Who knows what he'll be when he crests the other side, or how the future will change because of what he does now?"

Faelyn's gaze drifted to the ground where it blurred. All her own bad decisions paraded through her memory. She hadn't yet crested the mountain of her choices. But choosing to stay at Thomats felt like the right choice. She needed to be as strong as she could if she was to ever take back her kingdom.

"You're right, Professor. I'll let him go."

He stepped back, clasping his careworn hands. "Kian will be okay. There's quite the need for teachers in Creadel, you know."

Faelyn nodded. "I know." The guilt still stung, but Professor Wemnar had tempered it. And renewed her decision to stay. "Can I ask a favor?"

He blinked at the sudden shift in conversation. "Of course."

"I want to find a swordmaster to train under."

His eyebrows rose. "Mages have no need of swordcraft outside of those conjured by magic. Besides, it's outlawed without express permission by the court of New Daltieri."

The name chafed her skin. "It's a useful skill, one that can be used with conjured swords as well. Surely you must know someone?"

He studied her intently, almost reading her with magic, except he didn't have his staff. "There is someone. He hasn't trained anyone in a long time, not since Monhaber closed. His family hailed from there, but now live nearby."

Monhaber? Where did she know that name? Faelyn's breath caught. Monhaber was in Daltieri, the greatest army preparatory facility they had. It's where her old swordmaster, Benton, had trained. Calem had trained there as well, because it was the best.

"Don't get your hopes up." Professor Wemnar's lips thinned. "His name is Donoven. He's a horse breeder now. And it will be near impossible for you to be approved for training, even as a student of magic." He glanced around them. "Why the sudden interest?"

Faelyn studied him. It would be so nice to trust someone else with her secret and maybe get some help, but she couldn't. The school reported to the king, and she'd only be endangering him.

She shrugged. "Just a passing fancy."

"Hmm. Well, good luck. And leave Kian be. He'll be fine." He gently patted her hand. "You'll be okay, too, you know."

She swallowed and nodded. Grief made it difficult to breathe through as they parted ways. Kian had been a huge part of her life these past years. Giving him up wouldn't be easy. But she wouldn't waste time being idle.

She had to prepare.

CHAPTER
TWENTY-SEVEN

Ardenis didn't know what to feel. He wanted to cheer and cry at the same moment. Kian had asked Faelyn to marry him, and she'd rejected him. Ardenis had never seen such uncertainty in her, such agony, and he'd seen her suffer much in her long life. He, above anyone else in Acantha, understood that pain. To give up love—in any form—for the greater purpose was no small thing. Watching Faelyn make the same choice made him cringe from the pain of his old wounds.

Ardenis pitied Kian because he also knew the feeling of the one you love choosing something else over you. Laida had made the decision to leave Acantha. She made the decision with an emotional veil over her eyes, unaware of Ardenis's love for her, but that didn't make the pain any less real.

He also couldn't deny that he wouldn't miss seeing Kian's stolen kisses, adoring gaze, or the way he lay claim to Faelyn.

When Faelyn finally settled at Niri's for the night and gazed up toward Acantha, Ardenis only felt one thing. Love. Though it was well into the night watch, he sat at the window, gazing into her eyes.

With tears still staining her face, her lips twitched up in a small smile he liked to think was meant for him.

He fantasized about being born on Thera and searching the lands until he found her. Or maybe she'd find him. They'd fall in love and it would be perfect for a while. Would she make the same decision if he had been in Kian's place? Would she leave him for his own good?

If things were different, and he'd had that chance to be born during her time, he would never stop looking. Until his dying breath, she would be his sole purpose.

Ardenis had watched her until she fell asleep in the light of the dying embers.

CHAPTER TWENTY-EIGHT

The pretty spring day made the trip outside of school pleasant, even as apprehension weighed Faelyn down. She walked a dirt road, avoiding rainwater trapped in crevasses rutted by wagon wheels. Birds chirped from trees that were bright green with new leaves. Wildflowers grew along the edge, tiny blooms of yellow and white. She finished the last of a chocolate chip scone under a blue sky filled with white, fluffy clouds. If she'd known it would take this long to reach Donoven's home, she would have borrowed a horse. The ex-swordmaster liked his seclusion, apparently.

It was hard to enjoy this rare moment of peace when Donoven's answer determined whether she could stay at Thomats. Proper training was necessary if she were to fight an army, more than just the magical kind. She'd go anywhere she needed to get it.

Thomats had allowed her to study each area of her magic—earth, wind, water, fire, and aether. She'd learned as much as possible in the short years. While not deemed ready to pass the tests for master mage in any area, she'd gained knowledge and control.

Her capabilities were limited only by her imagination, Professor Wemnar once told her.

Midstride, Faelyn stopped short and tilted an ear ahead. People. A lot of them. Stepping in uniform.

She cursed and jumped off the road, landing in a cold puddle that soaked her trousers to the knees. There was only one reason for so many—an army—and she wouldn't be caught by them. Magic warmed her as she used Kian's trick to hide from sight. Two empty holes existed where the water was displaced around her legs.

The company drew closer, and she prayed to the Fates not to be spotted. The first of the group rounded the bend, confirming her suspicions. Daltieri soldiers. Row after row rode in a never-ending stream of black and gold-leathered armor just a stone's throw in front of her. The water rippled as the ground shook with their passing.

Where were they going? This road led to the school, but it also forked to many other paths. None of it could be good.

Faelyn's senses prickled. There was a mage among them. Their mage crystal called to her, though they had not yet passed into view.

She stretched her hearing as far as it would reach. Overwhelming noises assaulted her—the plod of hoofs over dirt, the splash of puddles, the clink of armor and swords, idle chitchat among the ranks.

The mage rounded into view. She didn't recognize him. Lean and bald, he wore black robes with gold insignia embroidered along the hem—a master mage. His robes hung down over a chestnut mare, reins held loosely in his hand, and magestaff secured in its holder. Two men wearing gold spaulders over their black armor—generals—flanked him on horseback. They steadily approached Faelyn's watery ditch.

The hairs on the back of her neck stood up. A master mage would detect her. She pushed more magic into hiding herself, hoping he wouldn't sense it.

Faelyn held her breath as they approached.

The mage lifted his chin, suddenly alert in his saddle. His eyes darted around, seeking her. Faelyn's heart hammered against her ribs. She hadn't done anything wrong, but they wouldn't see it that way. If they found her, she couldn't allow them to catch her.

As the mage passed Faelyn, his head whipped from side to side. He turned in his saddle, but couldn't find what he was seeking.

A general eyed the mage warily, then scanned their surroundings. "Something amiss, Panook?" He placed a hand on the hilt of his sword. His horse puffed a breath beneath him. The mage watched the trees and didn't say anything. "Panook?"

"No. Nothing." Panook shifted in his saddle.

The general grumbled. "You're just tired. We all are. Crushing these upheavals one right after another gets wearisome."

"You'd think they'd wise up. Surely by now, word has got around of what happened with the other towns that rebelled," the other general said, shaking his head.

The first general smirked. "Once we make an example of Cristanfani, the others will fall in line. We won't have to worry about collecting taxes much longer."

Fury replaced fear, washing deep over her. Cristanfani. Faelyn knew that town, a peaceful place, popular for its fur trade. It was once a prosperous Alysian town. Was it still, or had Daltieri broken their spirits as it broke their backs?

Her limbs shook with rage. This was no company to put down a simple unrest. This was an army big enough to wipe Cristanfani off the map.

Faelyn steadied her heart and called her magic, pulling it from deep within her, letting it build and build. The Daltieri plague could not be allowed to carry out their orders. One more person couldn't be hurt because of her lack of action. One more coin couldn't be allowed to pass into the hands of her enemy.

She could do this. She could stop this army. She had to.

As soon as the last soldiers passed beyond her, she released the magic, focusing it, shaping it with calm intent just as she'd been trained. The magnitude of the magic nearly dropped her to her knees. She panted, directing it true.

The ground beneath the soldiers' feet began to tremble, and relief eased the tightness of her chest. Birds fled the trees in waves, dotting the sky. Heads swiveled, but they didn't stop marching.

"Watch your formation, soldiers," one of the captains yelled.

Barely holding on to the magic keeping her invisible, Faelyn stepped out of the puddle and onto the road, leaving wet bootprints. She crouched with her hands on the dirt, eyes closed in intense concentration. Her part of the road stood still, just the faint rumblings from the ground ahead.

The generals halted in the distance. With a grunt of effort, she pushed even more magic, ignoring the wave of exhaustion that slammed into her and made her vision blacken at the edges.

The road grew from trembling to violent shaking. The vibrations ran all the way back to her, buzzing through her boots to the soles of her feet. Soldiers ran, scattering and falling to the ground in fear.

"Hold!" The taller general tried to maintain order while gaping as the ground cracked around him. "What is this, Panook?" Faelyn picked up his panicked voice even this far away.

Wide-eyed, magestaff in hand, Panook looked back in her direction. Did he sense her? Surely he must. It didn't matter. The army couldn't be allowed to continue.

Cracks became gaping holes in the ground. Soldiers screamed as they fell in.

"Panook!" one of the generals yelled, a command to do something.

The master mage spun around, facing her, and spurred his horse into a gallop. Soldiers darted or fell out of his way.

Faelyn tensed. He was coming for her. He knew she was here. The master mage's crystal glowed brightly as he readied a spell to destroy her.

His powerful horse leaped over bodies and fissures, finally

breaking free of the quake. Her hooves found sure ground, and Panook urged her into a gallop, his staff held high.

Faelyn checked her invisibility. It remained intact. He couldn't know what he sought, only that she was there, somewhere.

Just a little bit longer. If she could hold the magic a little bit longer, the army would be weakened enough not to follow her or harm any more Alysian towns.

Sweat beaded on her forehead, and her fingers dug into the soil. Her invisibility flickered and went out, leaving her completely exposed.

Halfway to her, Panook sneered. A wave of flame burst from his staff. It spanned the width of the road, rushing toward her with the force of a hurricane.

She didn't think. With a cry, her magic centered on the mage. A great wall of earth rose in front of him, dwarfing even his horse. The flames rolled over it like a flood. Panook yelled in wide-eyed terror, but then she lost sight of him behind the dirt and fire.

Seconds to spare, Faelyn threw herself flat on the ground, tightening her shield. Time stood still while the flames surrounded her, passing over and around her in a tidal wave of heat that blocked out the sky and seared her skin even through the shield. How long could the mage keep them up? Forever? Sweat coated her body. The air grew thin.

Her magic regathered slowly. Just before she released a blast of air to divert the flames, they stopped. Cool, fresh air prickled her hot skin. She looked up to see Panook's horse darting away through the trees, riderless.

Panook had retreated back to his army, now regrouping. The quake had ceased while she was distracted. One general remained at the head of a fraction of their army. And they all saw her.

Her breaths came in pants. She couldn't run—she'd never make it.

"Charge!" the general yelled, sword raised.

The soldiers—maybe a hundred—drew their swords and ran.

Adrenaline and fear fueled her magic now. Faelyn dug her fingers back into the earth and screamed. The ground beneath the enemy broke apart. Earth cracked and rose to the sky in shards, only to fall into the depths of great chasms.

Soldiers and horses ran for their lives. Falling rocks crushed them, or they tumbled into the rubble. Those that continued toward Faelyn were swallowed by the ground. She pushed herself to the breaking point. When the shouting stopped, Faelyn cut off the magic. She collapsed.

Its absence was like losing a limb. Black spots swarmed her vision. She managed to stand, shaking on trembling legs. Dust and smoke clouded high into the sky, and what once was a road was now cracks and piles. Nothing remained but rubble and dead bodies. The trees and flowers burned.

The world fell silent but for her broken pants.

Her heart raced anew. She couldn't stay. Someone would have heard. There could be soldiers left, Panook even. They would find her.

Faelyn ran. She ran as fast as her shaking legs could go, stumbling every few steps. The only measure of comfort was that this army could do no more harm.

The road back was impassable, and there were no sounds of pursuit. No sounds of anything. Despite the real danger, she was proud of herself. She never could have done something like that before Thomats, and even Thomats had underestimated her capabilities. Never again.

The meadows and trees tilted and spun around her, but she pushed on, still following Professor Wemnar's directions. There was no going back the way she'd come, and she didn't know these roads well enough to divert without getting lost.

She continued on to Swordmaster Donoven.

The time had come to stop running from who she was.

She was the heir of Alysies.

The time had come to fight her way back.

CHAPTER TWENTY-NINE

Faelyn gained ground, putting distance between her and the massacre, still heading toward Donoven's home. There was nowhere else to go.

When she could go no further, she dared to stop and rest, using a small pond to wash off some of the dirt. What she needed was a week's worth of food and water, and some sleep. But she couldn't allow Daltieri to delay her goals. She eventually crested a hill and walked a narrow road that ended at a rundown two-story house with a large front porch and chipping paint. Horses dotted a rolling pasture that stretched for miles beyond. The proof of her havoc hung in the far distance as smoke and dust whorled in the sky. A barking dog ran to greet her. Faelyn patted its head, then walked to the front door.

She placed her hand casually by the hilt of her knife and knocked. Within seconds, a man threw open the door and shoved a blade against her throat, stopping just shy of breaking her skin. Faelyn resisted flinching. With no magic, she was powerless against him, but she stared coldly, testing his emotions. Anger. Annoyance.

"Who are you, and why do you trespass on my land?" Though

the man looked young, his gruff voice and countenance seemed beyond his years. He held his sword with all the confidence of someone who knew how to use it, and his muscled arms and ready stance told her this was Donoven. He wore a stained tunic and trousers, not bothering to shove dark, disheveled hair from his eyes.

"I'm Ali. I'm seeking Swordmaster Donoven." She stared straight into his eyes. His face gave no reaction.

He studied her for half a second longer. "No." He slammed the door in her face.

She sighed and pounded on the door with the hilt of her knife, then stepped off the porch. Weapon raised, she bent her knees, readying for an attack. The world spun at the edges, but she ignored it.

It'd been a long time since she'd handled a weapon—since before Thomats—but her muscles remembered.

Donoven flung the door open. "Be gone with you, girl, or I will run you through." He stepped off the porch and swung his sword in a sweeping arc.

"You could try." Faelyn smirked, crouching lower. The thrill of the fight and her boldness chased some of the exhaustion away.

An eagerness lit Donoven's eyes and countenance, but then he frowned. "Go away." He turned around.

"Afraid?" Faelyn asked, baiting him.

Back to her, he paused. Once more, he entered his house and closed the door. Faelyn rose from her crouch, body heavy. She hadn't expected that.

A retort died on her lips when the door opened and he tossed a second sword at her feet. "Let's see what we've got."

Faelyn sheathed her knife and lifted the sword from the dry, patchy ground. The weight of it pulled at her exhaustion, but her heart kicked into gear. This was her chance. "Let's do this."

A fierce smile came over Donoven, and he leaped off the porch with surprising grace. He brought his sword down hard. It would have split her in two, but she raised her sword and blocked. The blow knocked her nearly to her knees. She pushed against the weight of fatigue and regained her balance. Faelyn blocked his second attempt to cleave her in half at the waist. They fought, circling each other and trading blows around the yard.

Her magic, what little had built back up, lay waiting, but she didn't call it. Skills learned long ago rekindled and burst through her arms and legs. The thrill that she hadn't lost everything gave flight to her movements. It was a dance long forgotten.

But she slowed. He noticed the opening and swiped. She barely blocked in time, but then countered with a swing of her own that had him retreating a step. She smirked, and there was almost approval in his eyes.

Her arms drooped, heavy with the weight of the sword. She wouldn't be able to continue much longer, but that didn't scare her. Disappointment was her first thought. She hadn't had this much fun since besting her water professor in a water fight last fall.

Her slowness left open a killing blow, the perfect chance for Donoven to end the bout. He didn't take it. Gone was his irritation, and he became more a partner than an enemy. Faelyn dared to hope she'd won him over.

Her weariness caught up to her. She slipped on a patch of loose gravel. It threw her timing completely off. Donoven clashed swords with her, circling his sword around hers until he popped it from her tired grip. It clanged to the ground, too far to reach. He held the tip of his sword to her neck.

Breathing hard, sweat dripping down her face, she smiled. "Swordmaster." She bowed with her eyes, sparing her throat an impaling.

Donoven frowned, but lowered his sword. "Your technique is sloppy. And ancient." He circled Faelyn while she stood in place. "You're out of shape and clumsy." He stopped in front of her. "You aren't completely without skill, but I don't train anyone. I work with horses now." He turned his back on her and walked to his house, barely winded from the fight. "You seek Dalisted's near the Daltieri capital. That is where people with the will learn to fight." He spat on the grass.

"I'd sooner be dead than go there." Conviction and anger rang in her voice. "They murdered my family. Teach me the skills I need to avenge them. Teach me to be a leader."

One of Donoven's eyebrows rose. "How do I know you're not a spy, sent to ensure I'm not breaking my mandate?"

"Mandate?"

"That's right. King Seber closed my family's school which we ran for generations, then outlawed me from training anyone again."

Faelyn's teeth ground together. She pointed to the horizon without looking. "That's not a forest fire. I stopped a contingent of soldiers on my way here. They were on their way to destroy people for trying to feed their families."

His eyes widened, staring at the dusty mess and back to her. "You? By yourself?" Disbelief colored his tone.

She nodded.

He shaded the late-afternoon sun from his face, squinting into the distance. "You've risked your life telling me this."

"And I'm asking you to risk yours to help me. Weaponry and warfare."

He met her eyes and nodded. "There's something greater at work here. I will teach you all I know."

CHAPTER THIRTY

Ardenis's heart dared to settle as Donoven accepted Faelyn as a student. It had been too much to handle, watching her almost die at the hands of the fire mage, then still go on to challenge Donoven.

Faelyn had taken him by surprise yet again. He hadn't realized she'd made the decision to fight back, and pride radiated through him. She was incredible.

And she was nearly ready to step into the role she was born for.

She had learned of magic from Thomats, and now she would learn the art of war. Her moment in history, which would define her more than the sum of her past mistakes and hardships, was upon her.

Donoven and his family offered Faelyn food and rest, then gave her directions back to Thomats by a different road. She promised to return the next day, then set out just as the sun began to dip toward the horizon.

Ardenis pulled his gaze back to examine the damage. The trees still smoldered, and the road more closely resembled a war zone. Villagers had swarmed from every direction to investigate, including some mages from Thomats. Bodies were already being carted away. Further out, a small group of New Daltieri soldiers raced at breakneck speed to the site.

Ardenis tensed. If Faelyn didn't hurry, they'd intercept her.

He tracked her slow progress down the darkening road. Despite the rest, her weariness was plain.

Hurry!

The soldiers rode hard. Faelyn meandered sluggishly. She wasn't going to reach the turnoff in time. They would be upon her soon.

Ardenis gripped the marble ledge. Then the watch window went black.

He was thrust from Thera in a shocking rush that took his breath away. His vision filled with the white-domed room of the watch tower. An echo of gasps rang around the room.

What was going on? He stared into the marble watch window, trying to focus on Thera and back to Faelyn. Where landscape and mountains should have filled his view, he saw only blackness. He looked up seeking Amalia's eyes, remembering with a pang she wasn't there. Whispered conversations broke out among the watchers.

This couldn't be happening. Was Faelyn okay? Did she get away?

As the conversations died out, one by one the watchers looked to him. He shifted in his seat. They were waiting for him to have all the answers. Maybe they believed the gossip, that he had Head High Councilwoman Rhea's favor, even if the opposite was true. The need to step up and assure them all was well swirled through him. He could be a leader, just like Laida. The thought bolstered him, and he stopped fidgeting.

But there were no answers to give. He cleared his throat and gazed with all his might back into the watch window. He cried out in relief when he once again saw Faelyn. She ran down the road, away from the soldiers who hadn't spotted her. Safe. He looked up.

"It's okay. It's working now." His stomach turned with

suppressed fear. "I will endeavor to find the cause of this disturbance."

The watchers smiled, relieved, and resumed their watches. He didn't know what had caused the momentary blackness, but it scared him. Nothing like it had ever happened in all his long years as a watcher.

Faelyn slowed her run to a brisk walk. She didn't stop until she reached Thomats, slipping inside under the cover of darkness. She had just collapsed onto her bed when the watch window went black again, forcing him out of Thera.

Ardenis's eyes went wide, and he stared across the pool. Something was gravely amiss. He stood, and the night watchers tracked him, some with curiosity, some with clear worry.

"I will report this to the council. Continue focusing on your watching should the window become functional again." He gave a curt nod.

Outside the tower, he stepped quickly toward the council hall. A bright moon and twinkling stars hung in a clear sky, lighting the way. His path intersected Idonea's.

"Idonea, how are you?" Ardenis smiled through his worry. Idonea Transfer Leader returned his smile, looking as carefree as anyone who didn't carry the same emotional burden. They walked together, and he welcomed the distraction. She was his friend, even if not as close as Amalia had been.

"Well met, Ardenis. We're having some trouble at the transfers. I'm on my way to the council with my report." She tucked stray strands of black hair behind her ears as she matched his pace.

He pulled at his sleeves, dread rising within him. "What kind of trouble?"

She glanced over, her relaxed disposition unphased. "It's hard to say exactly. I could be imagining it."

Ardenis gritted his teeth. "Imagining what?"

"Well, on a couple of occasions, there was a delay in the transfers, or so it seemed to me. People stepped into the gateway to go to Thera, but it took longer than usual."

"Has that ever happened before?"

"Never."

They walked on in silence. Idonea may not be worried, but worry akin to panic increased with Ardenis's every step. He'd seen it happen before. With Amalia.

When they arrived at the council courtyard, the sight of others arriving sent his palms sweating. Ardenis recognized people from almost every area of Acantha; genealogy, recreation, even someone from the kitchens arrived and lined up to speak to the council.

Mina Enforcer sat behind the foyer desk. She smiled as they piled into the room, and nodded toward Ardenis. He was the fourth person in line to talk to her. They were all polite and pleasant, despite the frightening circumstances that brought them together. It reminded him to remain calm and maintain tight control of his emotions.

Despite the number of people, and the fact he wasn't first in line, Mina said, "Ardenis Watcher Fater, the council will see you."

Ardenis nodded his thanks and entered the council room. The dark wood paneling seemed even darker somehow. He took his place behind the podium while the council members settled into their seats. They muttered amongst each other.

He shifted his weight.

Averick Head Councilman stood before his chair, front and center of the rest of the council.

"Ardenis Watcher Fater, what news do you bring?" Averick clasped his hands before him, his face blank of emotion.

Ardenis paused. Averick normally greeted him with a smile, and never asked after news, but more specifically asked after the happenings of Thera. The council already knew something was wrong.

"I wish to inform the council of two unusual occurrences in the tower today." Ardenis waited until Averick nodded to continue. "While in the middle of a watch, the window went black. All watchers were denied a view of Thera." Whispered conversations broke out amongst the council. "It happened a second time before I came here."

Averick looked back once at his council. "Anything else you'd like to add?"

"Can these occurrences be explained?" Ardenis asked.

Averick's mouth thinned as if weighing what he would say next. "We are looking into what happened, but thus far there seems to be nothing of concern. The council will convene."

Ardenis inclined his head and departed the building, giving a brief smile to Idonea. He returned to the watch window, which was thankfully working again. No further incidents occurred that night, but it didn't help settle his nerves. Averick was wrong. There was every reason to be concerned. But what could be causing it?

Was it related to magic? For decades, there had been a decline in the number of magic wielders born on Thera. Usually, it preceded a magical occurrence, like an explosion in the mage population, or when Faelyn was born. Almost like the world was saving up magic to give to something else.

But maybe it was more than that this time. Was the dissipating magic of Thera also affecting Acantha?

And if so, what could they do about it?

But what if it was *his* fault? He continued to break the rules every day, loving Faelyn as he did. Could it be his fault things were out of balance?

He trudged home from the tower and through his door, eyes dragging the floor, and began to undress. He didn't notice there was someone else in his home until she spoke.

CHAPTER THIRTY-ONE

"Ardenis Watcher Fater," she said from the dark corner of Ardenis's home. "We have much to discuss."

Ardenis jumped, nearly falling over as his eyes adjusted. "Head High Councilwoman Rhea." She sat at his table, in the exact chair she'd sat in when she'd warned they'd be watching him, many years ago. She turned up the flame in the lantern while he hastily threw his robe back over his body, blushing, though nudity wasn't supposed to bother him.

His heart picked up. He couldn't fathom why she'd be in his house. He'd done so well. He hadn't shown any strong emotions or outbursts. It had been years since any confrontations with Hector. Perhaps Rhea had heard about his stress over the watch window failing, though he thought he'd done well to hide it.

"How can I help you?" He stood awkwardly in the doorway to his bedroom.

She sat straight-backed, hands folded in her lap. The silver emblem of a Theran globe with a gavel above it gleamed in the lantern light against the ocean of her blue robe. Her hair was in a tight bun at the back of her head.

"You look surprised to see me, Ardenis." Rhea leveled her cool gaze on him, yielding no hint as to the reason for her visit.

Ardenis looked down, unsure how to respond. Of course, he was surprised. Entering unannounced wasn't the custom, even for a high councilmember.

Rhea laughed. "It's quite all right. I meant to surprise you. I want our meeting to remain secret, and I want you to be honest with me. Please. It's my request and my command."

Ardenis's eyes widened. A secret meeting? Rhea's words hinted at lies and deceit, foreign concepts in Acantha.

She looked hard at his face, then stood and walked toward him, stopping at a respectful distance.

"Ardenis. Something is amiss in Acantha. I need to know if you're behind it." Two high council enforcers stepped from Ardenis's bedroom, making him jump again.

His heart took off, and his muscles tensed to flee. He backed away from Rhea and her enforcers, noting they were the same two who'd dragged him to the transfer hall to be born after he'd been framed for starting a fire to burn down the transfer hall. These enforcers had been all too happy to comply until Amalia proved his innocence.

"I haven't done anything, Rhea. I'm a loyal citizen of Acantha. I've witnessed separate incidents which gave me cause for alarm, and I reported them to the council." He balled his hands into fists. "If someone is behind what's happening, it's not me." At least, he hoped not.

A thought occurred to him. "Have you sought Hector?" Ardenis had seen nothing but good behavior from Hector, who seemed to have taken to being a watcher with ease. But that didn't mean he could be trusted. It didn't change what he'd done to Laida when he tried to prevent her from being born as the first elf.

Rhea stepped closer and stared into Ardenis's eyes. He didn't flinch, didn't blink, and bore her scrutiny, feeling her testing the truthfulness of his words. After a long moment, she sighed and her shoulders drooped.

She turned to her enforcers. "Wait for me outside. Stay out of sight." They nodded and left Ardenis's house through his back terrace.

Stay out of sight? Had Rhea been emotionally influenced? He told the truth, but her scrutiny proved she believed him capable of lying. She knew what it meant to lie.

Rhea stared at his floor saying nothing.

Not sure what else to do, Ardenis walked to the cabinet and prepared two cups of tea.

Rhea accepted hers with a silent nod of thanks, taking several sips. "I'm sure I seem much changed since we last met, Ardenis. It has taken a toll on me, reading through Gharum former Head Councilman's journals. Such vile corruption. I feel it's altered me, in a way."

Could that be why she showed this new capacity to lie? Had Gharum influenced her, even in exile? Those journals should be burned.

With a tightening of his lips, Ardenis tried to convey his sympathy without admitting to understanding her feelings out loud. Her suspicion of his emotional awareness was far better than openly admitting it, even if she seemed to need someone to relate to. Just moments ago, she was prepared to have her enforcers seize him if he'd admitted involvement with whatever was wrong in Acantha.

No, he couldn't open up to her. Even if Amalia had left a void needing filled. This was the woman with supreme authority over all that took place in Acantha. If she answered to anyone, it was a power higher than Ardenis knew.

He spoke to fill the awkward silence. "The watch window went black. Never in all my years have I seen that happen. It happened at least once more since then."

"It's happening everywhere," Rhea said. "Not only in your region of Acantha." They exchanged a long glance. "I've searched my memories back to the beginning of the human race and can recall nothing like this ever occurring."

Ardenis could only stare. Why was she here? Why was she sharing this information with him? This should be a conversation between her and her council, not a watcher. "I witnessed a delay at the transfer hall today. It took longer than usual for the borns to make the transfer."

Rhea nodded, setting down her teacup with the soft clink of porcelain. "Yes, it's not just the watch windows. Even the smallest functions. The fires that blaze at the council hall flickered in and out. The food we so enjoy stopped replenishing itself, then started again. Genealogy records blurred into nonexistence, then reappeared." She reached forward and gripped his hand hard across the counter. She dug her nails into his skin.

He gasped. He felt something foreign—unpleasant and alarming. Pain. It radiated in his palm. He jerked his hand from her grip, rubbing the pink line, and backed away. His voice dropped to a whisper. "It's not possible."

She watched him rub his hand. "It comes and goes. Like I said, Ardenis. Something is amiss in Acantha. If you know something, you have to tell me. I'm begging you. Our entire existence could come undone if things continue to progress this way. If Acantha fails, so too does Thera."

Ardenis shook his head, heart pounding in his ears. Acantha couldn't come undone. It was a premortal realm in existence to supply souls to Thera. Bad things could happen, certainly, but nothing to end existence as they knew it.

But he couldn't tell Rhea it might be his fault—that loving Faelyn in a world where it was forbidden might be throwing Acantha out of balance. Without a doubt, she'd force him to be born. She'd blame him. Besides, he'd loved Laida before she became Faelyn, and that had never caused these kinds of problems.

"What if it has to do with magic?" he said.

She tapped her sandaled foot on the hardwood floor.

He barreled on. "You've seen the reports of fewer mages in the world. Magic seems to be dying out. What if that's tied to Acantha somehow?"

"This cycle isn't unusual, Watcher Fater. It has never affected Acantha before." She paused. "Though this does seem to be a lower than usual cycle. Not since the elf was born."

"I thought so, too." A lie. He'd been too busy watching Faelyn to notice if the number of mages born was fewer than the usual low.

She glanced at the front door. "It's worth looking into. Any other theories?"

Only one, but he wasn't about to tell her it might be him. The occurrences weren't progressing. Rhea had time to riddle out the cause, and maybe it wouldn't worsen. It was her job, after all, to take care of Acantha. He was just a watcher.

"No, that's all. I'll keep a lookout for anything amiss and report it to the council immediately."

Rhea slammed her palm against the table, rage flashing in her eyes. "Don't lie to me, Ardenis. I know you've been emotionally altered. You'd protect yourself over the survival of two worlds?"

Ardenis gaped, blinking in admonishment. So much emotion.

Her hand dropped to her side, and when she next spoke, the anger was gone. "You're famous, Ardenis. A hero after stopping the destruction of the transfer hall from that fire. The people look up to you, some even more so than they do the council." She took a deep breath, then released it in a sigh. "Please report anything amiss to *me*."

He inclined his head, reeling from the shock of her anger and the lingering feel of pain in his palm. She flipped up the hood of her robe and left out his back terrace, following where her enforcers had gone.

Ardenis collapsed into the nearest chair. He couldn't deny the evidence that Acantha was in trouble. Rhea must suspect him of the cause. Had his decisions caught up to him? It'd been so long since Laida had gone, but that was not where his love for her had ended. He also loved Faelyn.

He rubbed his eyes. A tiredness he'd never felt before came over him. The strain of the watch window and then processing the news from Rhea was too much. A tinge of fear shuddered through him as he rubbed his hand where her nails dug in. Surely, he wasn't to blame for the wrong in the world.

CHAPTER THIRTY-TWO

The weeks progressed, and the watch window did not go dark again. Ardenis thought he must have imagined his conversation with Rhea, or hoped so. He watched Faelyn, who'd been training and studying with Donoven, growing stronger. He kept a lookout for anything unusual, even questioning people he saw at the public baths, inquiring if they'd noticed any strange activity. He was often met with blank stares.

Feeling more at ease, he walked into the tower for his day watch. The watchers all stood, gathered around the watch window. He pressed between them, peering in, and his mouth dropped open.

The pool had a thin crack running along the length of the bottom. The blackness of it stood out in sharp contrast to the white marble.

The watchers stared curiously at it, whispering among themselves. Hector and Cadence sat in their chairs, speaking quietly to each other.

"How did this happen?" Ardenis didn't waste time whispering.

The group broke apart to take their seats.

Cammon, a trustworthy watcher, spoke up. "The night watch

said it occurred last night, during a time when the watch window failed to operate again."

"Does anyone have an idea why this is happening?" He was met with slow blinks. Ardenis glanced sharply at Hector.

Hector lifted his chin.

"Hector? Any thoughts?"

Hector sneered. "I wasn't here. How should I know what caused the crack?"

Ardenis turned to the others. "Has the council been informed?"

"Oh, leave us all alone, Ardenis Watcher *Fater*." Hector's voice was venom, a mockery of Ardenis's title. "You're no more in charge here than I am."

The watchers eyed each other, unclear how to respond to someone challenging Ardenis's authority. Showing such emotion.

"I think—" Ardenis stopped himself. He was about to threaten Hector with reporting his emotional state to the council. Anger and threats were not the Acanthian way. Amalia would have been proud. "I think something this serious should be reported to the high council. Continue your watches."

One by one, they focused on the watch window, heeding his leadership. Whether Hector believed it or not, every one of the watchers followed Ardenis's lead. Hector stood away from his chair in spite.

Ardenis ignored him. "I'll be back soon." He turned and left the tower.

It was a long walk to the head high council. Dread numbed his vision to all but the stones beneath his feet. Acantha was breaking apart before him, and he was no closer to figuring out why. He feared beyond anything that it was his fault. The emotional instability within Acantha had not started with him, but he still felt central to it somehow. Rhea was right. Seeing the proof in the cracked watch window had convinced him of that. If what he knew could be the cause of the destruction of two worlds, he had to be forthcoming.

Nora Enforcer's smiling face greeted him in the high council foyer when he finally arrived. "I need to speak to Head High Councilwoman Rhea. Privately."

Her smile faltered. "She's in a session at the moment. The high council has been very busy solving this riddle. It will be some time before they are finished."

"Then I'll wait. It's urgent."

Nora nodded, and Ardenis sat on a dark wood bench along the wall. For an hour, he alternated between sitting and pacing to the sound of Nora's scribbling quill. After another hour, he announced he was going for a walk and left the council hall behind.

People he didn't recognize milled around the courtyard. They smiled in polite greeting, but no one talked to him. They didn't know him as a fater like his own region did.

He examined the columned council hall, so much like Thomats School of Magic, and mirroring his own council hall. Just behind the building ran a wall comprised of a thick grove of trees extending beyond either side of the council hall. The trees served as a fence separating the council from the rest of Acantha, and for the first time, Ardenis wondered why.

He ignored an impulse to approach the tree line and made his way to the bulletin board. Scanning the local Theran news was a much-needed distraction from the stress of his visit.

The people in northwestern Thera, though not quite as populated as Ardenis's hemisphere, were doing well. They'd formed permanent settlements in places near water, and large trade routes. The current interest was in a family who led one of the largest permanent settlements, similar to how a king would in Ardenis's northeast hemisphere. Or how Faelyn would if she ever became queen.

After two hours of meandering, Ardenis thought he'd go to the Theran Museum. He hadn't been back since he'd been with Laida. Too many difficult memories. He'd warned her to watch out for Daltieri, but of course, she didn't take any of those memories with her when she left.

He glanced up to find Rhea walking toward him. "You seek my private audience?"

He met her halfway. "I've dire news to report."

Rhea's eyes looked more careworn in the sunlight. "Dire news you can't share with the rest of the council?"

Ardenis paused. "You came to me in secret and asked I not mention our meeting. It seemed to me I would act with the same caution."

"Very well. We will go to my home." She turned and walked away, leaving Ardenis gaping.

The council lived a separate existence from the rest of Acantha, especially the high council. No one saw where they lived. They even dined separately. Rhea paced away, and Ardenis hurried to catch up. He followed her back through the council building and down a hall that wrapped around the perimeter and led to a back door. Beyond that door would be the council residence.

"Are you sure there isn't a better place? I thought it was forbidden for people like me to go beyond the wall." Even after he became emotionally altered, he never thought to ask why they lived separately. It had always been that way.

"For people like you, it is not forbidden. For most others, it is."

Ardenis was completely confused. "What do you mean, 'people like me?'"

Rhea gave a tight smile. "Come, you will see." She opened the door, and Ardenis stepped into a different world.

The houses, row upon row, were as different from each other as night and day. Gone were the unending whitewashed houses of Ardenis's world. Instead, the houses varied in color, from brown to blue to pink, as well as style, from brick or wood, to columned. Even the yards varied, some had grass like Ardenis's, but some had flower gardens or rocks. Every style or architecture the watchers had ever shown Acantha was represented here, all at once.

"I don't understand, Rhea. What is this?" He fought the urge to grab her arm for support. The colors seemed to spin in his dizzying vision.

"I will tell you a secret, Ardenis. But first you have to tell me yours. Come to my home." Rhea waved him on, and he followed slowly, taking in this diverse new world. He couldn't even compare it to Thera. Thera didn't have this much variety, or such vibrant colors. This place defied all the rules of uniformity Ardenis had known his entire existence. It shook him so badly that he tried to focus on the things that were the same. The cobbled path beneath his feet was the same. The houses were aligned in rows just as they were on the other side of the trees.

He tried to imagine he was in a Theran city, and it eased the tightness in his chest.

Rhea's house was right across the path from where they entered. It had two levels, and was colored a sensible tan, though even that was jarring from the familiar white of the homes in Acantha. The front room was carpeted, featuring lace curtains and plush seating. Rhea gestured to a couch, and Ardenis numbly took a seat. She brought him a glass of lemon water, and he gulped it down.

Rhea chuckled. "You should see the look on your face, Ardenis. You look terrified."

He took the glass from his lips. "I don't quite know what to think. Why are the houses all different?" The walls of the dim room were covered with pale yellow flowers.

"No, no. Me first." She sipped her own water and then set down her glass. "What did you wish to tell me in private, Ardenis?" She sat forward, eyes unblinking, as if daring him to change his mind.

For a moment, he couldn't recall his purpose. His world seemed to have turned upside down, and he couldn't remember what was important anymore.

"Have you come to tell the truth?" she prodded.

The truth? Was that wise? He took a shaky breath.

She continued. "I can't promise what you say won't have consequences, but what are consequences if it can save us and Thera? And Laida," she added quietly.

His back stiffened. So she already knew the truth, but perhaps needed to hear it from him. Did she really believe their situation to be that dire? Or was she manipulating him, using a threat to Laida's safety to make him talk? No matter, she'd hit on the one way he was guaranteed to divulge.

He'd come here to tell her the truth. If he was in any way the cause of this, it was his duty to stop it.

"I will help in any way I can." He met her gaze. "A crack has formed in the watch window. A black gouge along the bottom where there wasn't one before. It occurred last night when the watch window failed again."

Rhea's body stilled. She swallowed. "It has already begun. Tell me what you know." Her calm voice held an edge of panic.

He nodded and took a deep breath. "Before Laida was born, I learned of love by watching Thera and became emotionally altered." He paused, waiting for Rhea's outrage or judgment, but she waved for him to go on. "I worry that bringing emotions into Acantha may be the cause of what's happening." He looked up. "I fell in love with her." His heart ached anew with his confession.

"You fell in love?" Her eyes went wide.

His heart kicked up in pace. "Please, if I must be forced to be born, let it be in my own hemisphere."

"Acanthians can't fall in love. It's not possible in this world."

Dread washed cold over him. "But I did." Hard. And he wasn't the only watcher that had experienced love. Amalia had loved as well.

"Maybe you only think it's love because you've seen more of Thera than anyone. I'll explain what I mean." Rhea sat forward in her chair. "You've told me your darkest secret, now I'll tell you mine." She straightened. "All council members are emotionally altered."

Ardenis's eyebrows shot up.

"All of us. We've been exposed too long to not be. We live a life of exception, separated from the rest of Acantha because of it, but, we can't fall in love. We know of it thanks to Watchers, but aren't capable of really understanding or experiencing it. The emotional veil doesn't lift until we leave. Which is why I don't think you're truly in love."

He sat back in shock. It made sense about the council, but he couldn't see it before. "How do you know?" She didn't blame him, but she thought he didn't truly love Faelyn.

No one in the vast expanse of time had ever been more wrong.

Rhea took another casual sip of water, as if she wasn't proclaiming a perspective-shattering secret. But was her hand shaking? "I know you're not the cause of our disruptions simply by being emotionally altered. Otherwise, something like this would have happened eons ago. Is there anyone else you know of who is emotionally altered?"

He forced his thoughts passed Rhea's revelation. "Amalia, but she was born already."

"Hmm. Anyone else?"

Ardenis shook his head.

Rhea's shoulders drooped slightly.

He raised his hand. "Wait, yes. Hector. But you already know about him." His hands formed fists. "Though everyone seems to have forgotten he tried to burn down the transfer hall so Laida couldn't be born." He gritted his teeth.

"I thank you for your honesty, Ardenis. The council will uncover what's happening in Acantha." She stood, so he did too. "Should you have need to seek me out again, feel free to come into the council residence. However, I must demand you not tell another about the council's secret. It would not bode well for Acantha to have its citizens become emotionally altered. That is why we maintain a separate existence. And why the watchers who fall victim to the emotional charms of Thera are forced to be born."

Ardenis gulped.

"Do not fear, Ardenis. You have proven you're able to handle it.

Others, however..." She trailed off in thought, then met Ardenis's gaze. "You may go. Please report further incidents to me."

He inclined his head and let himself out. He was once again shocked by the diversity of the houses running up and down the stone pathway. The sun shone high, making the colors all the more vibrant. The councilmen and women he glimpsed on the street still wore the same blue robes, yet were somehow different. He watched a woman walk toward him for a long time until he figured it out. Her head was down, and her hands were shoved in her pockets. She looked... sad.

A man on the other side of the street walked with a skip in his step and a grin on his face. These were emotions he didn't see in Acantha, only Thera. In the council residence, they didn't need to hide their emotional awareness. There was much he could learn if he stayed. The smell of roasting meat wafting from the dining hall tempted him.

But, he had a job to do. He'd promised Amalia he'd always do his duty. He'd promised Rhea to help solve the mystery. And he'd promised Faelyn he'd always watch over her, something he hadn't been able to do today.

So he shoved his hands in his pocket and let his head droop until he passed through the door back into the council hall. Then he took his hands from his pockets and lifted his chin, ready to face the world.

CHAPTER THIRTY-THREE

Spring turned into summer, and Ardenis cataloged and reported every instance of the watch window failing to Rhea. His heart stopped each time. The incidents were regular but not increasing in frequency, and the crack in the watch window didn't grow. When he dug his nails into his skin he no longer felt any pain. Acantha hadn't ceased to exist, but the cause of the strange occurrences remained unknown.

He even had a couple Fatings of the future, but nothing significant, as they never concerned Faelyn. They both centered around the northeastern kingdom of Kestrea, for some reason—a prison escape, the birth of a new prince.

Under Donoven's tutelage, Faelyn became a master swordswoman. He pushed her hard, inventing new challenges. She drilled, trained, and studied war day and night, learning to fight with both hands. Donoven even let her incorporate magic. Ardenis paid close attention, learning right along with her. If anything came with him to Thera, maybe swordfighting would help one day.

Faelyn was strong and determined, but for what end? Ardenis could only hope. He hated what Daltieri had done. Seeing the decline of the once-prosperous kingdom which should have been hers only intensified that hate. He was glad Faelyn finally felt the same.

He sat watching Faelyn wield fire as a blade when something happened that hadn't happened in a long time. His instincts nudged him in a different direction. He focused in on them and sensed a thread pulling him away from Faelyn. He hunkered down, refusing to move his gaze from her. It became an almost physical strain. By the end of his watch, his weary muscles barely carried him home.

He sat down to his watch the next day, and the pull was worse. It had him in its grip, and he could ignore his instincts no more.

He sighed in defeat and closed his eyes, willing his instincts to take him where they wished. When he opened them, his vision zoomed away from the trees and fields of Donoven's family land, across the border into Alysies, and west to the shores of the Tribunair Sea.

A grand stone castle stood at the top of a towering cliff. Waves crashed against its base, and seagulls cawed above. A valley of rich greenery extended from the castle and down a gentle slope. Tattered banners of blue and yellow whipped about in the sea breeze.

Ardenis knew this place. Seaside Keep. This was once Lord Calem's castle, after his father died in the aftermath of the battle against Daltieri. He'd risked his life to help Faelyn to safety, and lived to return to his castle by the sea. The Purge, Daltieri had dubbed it. The day they rid Alysies of its lackadaisical king and imbedded a new ruler.

The irony was that Daltieri had the chance to do some good in Alysies because, truly, Isaac was hurting the kingdom more than helping. But Daltieri squandered that opportunity and exploited Alysies for its riches. The rich and powerful always desire more riches and power.

Seaside Keep still flew the family colors, but the grounds were unkempt—crumbled statues, cracks in the stone walls, a stable with a sunken roof. Weeds choked gardens bordered by untrimmed hedges. No one milled about the castle grounds. It appeared deserted.

The invisible thread tugged Ardenis further still, coming from inside the castle. He shifted his vision to within, where the scene painted a different story.

A man wearing thick leather practice armor with a sword strapped to his side bustled down a stone hallway. The warm glow of lantern light bathed a hall lined with thin red carpet. His footsteps accompanied the sound of a distant rumble. He stopped at the top of a set of stairs and was met by two more people, a man and a woman, dressed similarly. They nodded to each other and descended the stairs. Corridors led away, but the group kept going down. The rumble grew, changing into the sound of swords clanging and people shouting. They were well below ground level. This part of the castle hadn't existed one hundred years ago.

When the stairs finally ended, the group dispersed into an enormous cavern bustling with activity. Ardenis's eyes opened wide. Groups of people in practice armor were led in drills, while several pairs dueled one on one. Hundreds filled the space. Maybe thousands. Torches lined the walls and large barrel fires were placed throughout for light. Thick cloth draped over much of the exposed rock, but the noise of an army training for war still echoed loudly.

Above all the shouting, one phrase resounded.

"Free Alysies!"

Ardenis trembled with excitement, grinning from ear to ear. There was no denying what this was. Lord Calem had kept his word. He'd promised to raise a force to help Faelyn regain her kingdom, and he had.

Though Lord Calem was long dead, and these people would assume Faelyn to be as well, they were clearly training for war. He'd seen it repeated in history over and over. Daltieri had grown too demanding. They'd pushed and punished the people of Alysies to the breaking point.

Ardenis wanted to stay and study the preparations and inner

workings of this operation, but the thread still tugged him. This room wasn't what his instincts had brought him to see. Whatever it was, it was above him now, somewhere in the main part of the castle. He drifted upward through the layers and levels, viewing barracks and a mess hall, an armory and then a regular basement full of discarded furniture covered in a thick layer of dust.

Back in the lower levels of the castle, his instincts guided him through a hall and into a library.

A young woman wearing a tan dress with a bodice laced in the front sat in an oversized chair. She looked to be about fifteen. Her legs were crossed underneath her, and a leather-bound book sat in her lap. She shoved her chestnut locks over her shoulder and skimmed the page with her finger. When she reached the end, she flipped it and continued on to the next.

She appeared to be no one of consequence, but so had Faelyn's mom, Eva, when Ardenis's instincts first led him to her.

The watch window flickered to black, and Ardenis lost his vision of Thera. He groaned with irritation and sat back in his chair. The other watchers in the room sat patiently, knowing the window would resume functioning in moments. At least Hector was absent, and Ardenis wouldn't have to endure his seething glares.

Ardenis rubbed his eyes and then stared into the clear water, ignoring the black fracture at the bottom. Minutes passed, and then the familiar glow returned. His focus went straight back to the library of the castle on the sea. The girl was talking to an older man with a graying beard and a round belly, the open book clutched to her chest.

"I don't care if you'd rather not. You have to." The older man paced the floor in front of her. His stern voice belayed no argument.

The girl clenched her teeth and tore her gaze from the man. "I already know what I'll see. New Daltieri's overseers with their whips at our peoples' backs while they slave from sunup to sundown. You said it yourself, Father. The blood tax is out of control." She slammed the book closed, then slid it across the table.

"Enough with the theatrics, Amerae. You know what's at risk if we don't perform our rounds. Surveying the work does more than appease King Seber." He stroked his beard. "Don't think of it as a way of supporting New Daltieri by our obedience. Think of it as another layer of deception to conceal what we are doing here. Whether you believe it or not, it will do our people good to see you by my side."

Amerae groaned. "I just found this new book. I really need to continue reading." She held it up, but her father didn't look at it.

Ardenis read the cover. It was a banned book. *The History of Alysies.*

"Can't Trey or Marus go instead?"

Her father threw up his hands. "They are training, girl."

Amerae turned away. "Wish I was down there," she muttered.

"You're always down there. It's good to take a break from training every now and then. Get some fresh air." He narrowed his eyes. "Now let's go."

Ardenis leaned forward, enthralled. His instincts had never led him astray. There was a reason he was here, if he could resist the temptation to watch Faelyn long enough to discover it.

Amerae huffed and stood, following her father through the castle and out the front doors. An open carriage pulled by two gray horses awaited them. They climbed in, and a driver accepted the reins from the stablehand. They drove down a narrow dirt road flanked by the green of the sloping valley.

Amerae said nothing. She leaned against the side of the carriage, sulking, staring at the passing trees and rocks. At the bottom of the valley, the farmland began. Several people worked row after row of freshly tilled dirt. They wore stained clothing, pulling seeds from dirty aprons and planting them in even intervals. Men and women held their aching backs and wiped sweat off their brows. The workers only glanced as the carriage passed, but the overseers stared long and hard—one for every ten rows of crops.

Amerae's father tallied something on parchment. It took Ardenis three fields to realize he tallied not the projected yield of the crop, but the number of overseers.

Amerae watched on, the bitterness in her eyes growing as they traveled. Ardenis thought her anger stemmed from being forced on the outing. When she sucked a breath through clenched teeth at the sight of every child amongst the bunch, he knew he'd misjudged her character.

"It's not right, Father. The children should be educated, not forced to labor to pay a tax they don't understand and did nothing to deserve."

Her father frowned. "I know. Take these memories and let them harden your resolve, daughter. Alysies will be free."

"And when we come out of hiding and win our great war, who will lead? You, Lord Father?"

Her tone was taunting, but Ardenis sensed the real curiosity burning behind the words. He held his breath, waiting for her father's response.

"Perhaps." He stared straight ahead, not giving into what sounded like an argument they'd had many times.

A whip cracked, bringing them up short. Amerae grabbed her father's arm. An overseer stood behind a man on hands and knees, his face contorted in agony.

"I can't stand this, Father." Tears welled in her eyes. "Do something."

He schooled his features and patted her hand. "You know I cannot. To interfere with the king's business would be to bring his wrath upon my land, and I cannot have us discovered."

"It's madness!" She pulled away from him. "This is our land. We should say what goes."

"Keep your voice down." He peered down his nose at her. "This land hasn't been in our family's control for decades, but if you don't expose our secret with your ravings first, it will be ours again."

Amerae turned away without responding, the same bitterness entering her eyes.

When they returned home, she gave a perfunctory hug to her father and slipped away, back to the library. The book sat on the table where she'd left it. She pulled it into her lap, opened it to the middle, and resumed skimming the pages.

Toward the end of the book, when she'd reached the section on Alysian rulers, she gasped and broke into a wide grin. Her careworn face turned youthful and radiant. She flipped the pages past portraits and lists of accomplishments until she reached the end. There was a portrait of King Isaac. He sat atop his throne wearing his golden circlet—now in Faelyn's possession—and a stern face. The artist had been kind, portraying him as a serious king instead of the detached fool he'd become.

The opposite page featured a portrait of his beautiful wife, Queen Eva. The artist who'd rendered it had talent, but no master painter in all of history could have captured the life and vivacity of Faelyn's mother. Even still, Ardenis stared at the painting in the book. He could almost picture Eva running wild and free, hand in hand with Damian among the fireflies and old oaks that existed only for them in that moment.

Amerae scooted to the edge of her chair as she read aloud. "Children. King Isaac Rylandor had but one child, Faelyn Eva Rylandor. King Isaac died during The Purge with no named heir." Amerae looked up and frowned. "That's it?"

She flipped the page, then her hand shot to her mouth. There before her was a perfect rendering of Faelyn, pointed ears and all. Faelyn sat in a chair wearing a pink rose-colored gown. She looked just as Ardenis remembered from when Mary had forced her to sit for the portrait, days before her eighteenth birthday. She didn't look much older now than in the picture.

"Faelyn Eva Rylandor. Mother, Queen Eva, died at birth. She was born with a deformity thought to render her incapable of ruling. The condition—elongated ears, and magic without use of a mage crystal—was termed 'fae,' named after Faelyn, the first and only person to exhibit such a deformity."

Amerae traced her fingers delicately over Faelyn's face, caressing her smooth golden hair and around her blue-green emerald eyes.

Ardenis read the rest of the small section of information below the picture. It talked about her fear of courtly duties, and that she used her magic to attack people at random during her childhood. It stated she fled the castle during The Purge and drowned in a river. Ardenis sighed. History was often written by the winning party of a disagreement.

Amerae sighed as well and set the book on the table. She stared at Faelyn's picture for a long time. Ardenis watched as her face went from downturned hopelessness to flinty resolve. She shoved off the chair.

"I don't care," she said to the empty room, then stomped out of the library carrying the book. She left the stone corridor and entered the castle foyer, which extended three stories tall. An armed man stood at attention near the front doors.

"Bade, where is my father?" she demanded.

The guard didn't blink or turn her way. "Lord Calem is resting, My Lady."

Lord Calem! So, they were direct descendants of Faelyn's long-ago friend. A slow smile spread across Ardenis's face. Maybe they would help Faelyn. Maybe that was why his instincts had led him here.

Amerae turned on her heel and headed to the back of the room, then climbed a set of stairs to a balcony. From there, she walked to the end of a long hall, hesitating at a thick wooden door—Lord Calem's office—where voices filtered through.

"The entire Daltieri regiment, just decimated?" Calem, Amerae's father, sounded stunned. "Who led the incursion?"

"We don't know. Our spies are looking into it, but it's a mystery. We know the soldiers were on their way to quell an uprising in Cristanfani, but they never made it. They were attacked by powerful mages. There were few survivors."

"Find out who's in charge. They sound like formidable allies."

Amerae finally knocked, and the conversation cut off. The second man answered the door. He was dressed in crisp clothes, almost uniform-like, with short graying hair and a blank expression.

"General Huntington," Amerae said. "Is my father busy?"

"Come in, daughter," Calem said from inside the room.

"I'll report when we have more information." General Huntington nodded to Amerae and left, closing the door behind him.

Lord Calem sat at a desk, pouring over ledgers by the light of a window set into thick blocks of stone. He smiled behind his beard when he saw his daughter, then frowned at her expression.

"What now, Amerae?" He pushed the paper aside though it couldn't move far with all the maps, books, and clutter covering the surface.

"I found a book in the library called *The History of Alysies.*" Her voice rose with excitement, and she clutched the treasure close. "It says King Isaac had a daughter who escaped The Purge."

Calem pointed. "You should not be carrying that around. It's one of the few not destroyed by Daltieri."

She hugged it tighter. "I'll put it back. But, what about King Isaac's daughter?"

Calem raised his eyebrows. "Yes, your great great grandfather, who I'm named after, helped her escape. He's the one who started all of this, as you know." He swept his hand to the ground below him. "Though, in his time, it never took hold."

"Why not?"

Calem stared down at his work. "King Isaac was not a good ruler, and many things went unchecked in his kingdom. I suspect some even celebrated a new ruler at first, not knowing what was to come. The fact that he died without naming an heir was his biggest blunder. I've often wondered if we would be in this mess if he had." His gaze became far away, then he picked up his ledgers and began reading again.

"Father, I want to go on a quest."

"Alright, dear, just be back before dark."

"No." She stomped her foot. "Look at me."

Calem dropped his palms onto the desk and looked down his nose at her.

Amerae didn't blink. "I've had a thought. You'd make a good ruler, but what if we found a descendent of the Rylandor family. Someone with a rightful claim to the throne. There has to be someone, somewhere with a connection. The other lords may contest your rule, and we may end up in a civil war once we reclaim this kingdom."

Ardenis's eyebrows rose. *Clever girl.*

Calem was quiet for some time.

Amerae fidgeted slightly under his scrutiny.

"You surprise me, daughter. Your mind is more political than I realized." He smiled. "And here I thought you were only interested in besting your brothers at the sword. What you suggest is not a terrible idea. We've searched before, but it wouldn't hurt to try again." He turned back to his desk. "I will discuss it with General Huntington. If he agrees, we'll pick a man, perhaps a team, to seek out a potential heir. King Isaac had an uncle. And Queen Eva had a half-sister. Perhaps we can trace the line from there." He stroked his beard in contemplative thought. "Though, no doubt Daltieri did their best to destroy any possible heirs."

Amerae gritted her teeth and took a deep breath. "I want to go, Father. It was my idea."

Lord Calem didn't look up. "That isn't going to happen, Amerae. For several reasons."

"But—"

Calem slammed his fist on his desk and stood, scraping back his chair. "This kind of quest would take years. It's dangerous and could put you in the enemy's sight. Your place is here, to grow into adulthood and marry a lord's son, making an alliance for our cause."

Ardenis suspected as much.

Amerae clutched the book tighter to her chest. "Father." Her sharp tone promised argument.

His cheeks turned red. "If the bloodsucking Daltieri bastards captured you, they could torture you for information that would ruin a century of progress. I'll repeat myself once more, and never again. You will *never* be allowed on this quest. Now go. I have work to do."

Amerae's eyes filled with tears, but she turned and left the room without another word.

Ardenis tracked her up a flight of stairs and down a hall to her bedroom. He didn't disagree with Lord Calem. Though she claimed to know swordfighting and showed intelligence, she was inexperienced, and a young girl in a man's world, not even of age. Her father wasn't wrong to forbid her from going. But Ardenis's instincts had brought him to her for a reason. She'd discovered Faelyn in the book. It had to mean something. Fate was at work.

Amerae changed from her dress into a tunic and sturdy cotton trousers. After rolling her dress up, she placed it in a travel bag along with a few more articles of clothing, a coin pouch, and a dagger. She plaited her hair in a single braid and donned leather armor. Her movements were quick and purposeful. Some of the anger and hurt left her eyes as she gathered her things. She hid the pack at the back of her wardrobe, then left her room.

She descended the stairs all the way down to the cavern filled with soldiers and made her way to a rack of swords. After testing a few, hefting and swinging them, she chose one to her liking and sauntered over to an empty practice ring. She stood waiting, not saying a word, but the hard expression on her face said it all. She wanted to do battle.

"What are you doing down here, Am? It's your rest day. Now go rest." General Huntington stepped away from supervising a duel in the ring next to hers. He carried himself with his shoulders back, chest up, and an air of authority.

"I went to the fields with father today. I need this."

He nodded as if that was all the explanation required, then returned to his circle. A leering young man stepped up to Amerae, sword raised. His shoulders were broad, his arms thick, and he was at least a foot taller than her.

She stared at him with narrowed eyes and gave a small sigh—a combination of loathing and resignation.

"I thought you'd learned your lesson last time, little girl." He circled the ring.

Amerae tensed.

He gave a mocking bow. "Oh sorry, I mean, Your Ladyship."

"This little girl nearly kicked your ass last time, Michael. If you're back to let me finish the job, you're even dumber than I thought."

He growled and attacked with a broad swing.

Amerae was fast. She twisted and swung, slapping his practice armor.

He clenched his jaw and turned to meet her attack. They traded thrusts and parries, Amerae throwing her rage into her movements and Michael reciprocating with his own anger.

They grunted when their swords clanged together, then broke apart, moving faster and faster. Amerae huffed, grimacing, but she slowly drove Michael back to the edge of the ring.

He cursed and hastily pivoted, leaving his flank exposed.

Amerae smirked and struck his side. His arms shot up to catch his balance, but he stumbled out of the ring.

Michael rose to his full height, anger plain on his face. He tightened the grip on his sword, raising it, then his scowl became a grin. He started laughing.

Amerae straightened from her defensive crouch and returned his smile.

"Ah, Am. When did you get so good?" He laughed again and wrapped his arm around her shoulder.

"Well, I learned from the best." She winked. "My older brothers." He gaped, pretending his pride had been hurt, and she chuckled. Their eyes held each other for a few moments. "Our place, tonight?"

"Of course." He stared at her mouth, then lifted his arm from her and shook his head. "I think I figured out how you beat me."

"There's more where that came from." She blushed and walked away, putting her sword back on the rack and ascending the stairs.

Ardenis found himself grinning.

Amerae dressed in a gown of dark green embroidered cotton, redid her braid tight to her skull, and made her way to a dining hall decorated with simple landscape paintings and a carpet over the stone floor. Brass chandeliers lit the rectangular space, and a long table extended over half the room. Silver platters topped with lids sat at four of the chairs. Already seated, Lord Calem held his wife's hand. Across the table, Amerae took an empty chair next to a young man.

"Where's Marus?" Amerae raised an eyebrow.

"Your brother has been sent on an important task." Lord Calem lifted the lid off his silver platter, revealing an entire roast guinea hen with steaming vegetables.

Amerae ignored her plate. "What task?" She glanced at the young man, Trey, who dug into his food with a sullen expression.

"Word has reached us we might not be the only force rising against Daltieri. I sent him to gather more information."

"A force under whose leadership?"

"A mage by the name of Kian Foster of Creadel. That's all I know."

"A mage?" Amerae grinned and speared a glazed carrot.

Ardenis closed his gaping mouth. What had Kian been up to?

"I heard you sparred that Michael boy again, Amerae." Her mother daintily cut into her chicken, only briefly looking up. Still youthful, she wore a modest dress that buttoned to her neck. Amerae could have been her twin, with their matching hazel eyes and high cheekbones.

"And I won." Amerae smiled, adding salt to her peas.

"I don't like how much time you're spending down there."

"Mother, we're about to be at war. I have to keep up my training." She perked up. "I also spent time in the library today. I've convinced father we should consider finding a descendent of the Rylandor family, someone the people can rally around with legitimacy to the throne." She shrugged. "It would solve the problem of exactly who would be the leader should we win."

"*When* we win, I think Father should rule as king." Trey waved his knife in Calem's direction. "It will be *his* glory, anyway."

Ardenis frowned.

"He does have a point." Amerae's mother nodded.

Amerae nudged her plate away. "Several others will try to lay claim to glory, especially those who would join once the tide turns in our favor. There are plenty of lords ruthless enough to challenge our gathered force, especially after we've bore the brunt of the battle. It's the perfect recipe for a civil war."

Her family stared at her, each frozen in their place. Lord Calem smiled and shook his head.

Amerae's clever, know-it-all attitude and assertive behavior reminded Ardenis of Amalia.

The scraping of forks and knives across plates resumed.

Her mother took a sip from her goblet. "When you put it that way, a descendent does sound appealing. Someone young so we can help guide their rule?"

"Yes. I was thinking of tracking down Faelyn's descendants. They'd be the closest to the throne," Amerae said.

Calem frowned. "Faelyn died before she had any children. And you're not going."

"I'll go," Trey said.

Amerae glared at him. "It's my idea, I'm going. Not you."

Calem slammed his hand on the table, rattling the dishes. "No you are not. Now get out of my sight."

Her mother's brow creased with concern, but she didn't contradict her husband.

Amerae, likely used to his outbursts, didn't balk. Instead, she tore a leg off her bird, grabbed a slice of bread from the basket, and left the room. She came back within seconds and collected the whole plate, then left again. Her eyes softened from anger to ease as she wound her way down to the dusty basement. She circled around a high stack of furniture to where a blanket was spread. After setting down the food, she lit a couple of half-melted candles, bathing the space in an orange glow.

When Michael came, she jumped up with excitement and ran into his arms. He crushed his lips against hers. When they broke apart, they sat on the blanket, and she presented the food to him. He grinned and ate, savoring every bite.

As the food dwindled, Amerae's shoulders drooped, her face downcast.

"I'm going away for a while, Michael, and you can't come with me."

He set down a chicken bone. "Where, and why not?"

"I'm not sure where yet, and you can't come because it's something I must do on my own." She looked up at him. "I don't know how long I'll be gone. It could be years." She reached for his hand and twined her fingers with his. "But I hope not."

"Did his lordship finally find some noble to marry you off to?" Jealousy stained his tone.

"My father doesn't know I'm going. In fact, he's forbidden me to go. I'm leaving tomorrow in secret."

"What?" Michael got on his knees. "You're running away? You'd go against his wishes and leave me as well? Why? For what?"

"To find an heir to the throne of Alysies."

Michael frowned. "But there is no heir. If there was, Daltieri would have killed them long ago."

Amerae huffed.

Michael leaned forward. "And let's say you actually track someone down with ties to the throne. They might not even want to join our little cause. Alysies is dead to all but a small few. Oppression is all our people know, but even that is less scary than change."

She scooted back. "It saddens me to hear you say our cause is little. It's my life, Michael. My family's. Yours and your family's. What we're doing here... it will change the world. You don't witness the suffering I do firsthand. Yes, change is hard, but this kingdom has been beaten down by our enemies for so long, surely change can't be scarier than what we've endured."

Michael hung his head. He reached out and cupped her cheek without meeting her eyes. "You're just one girl, Amerae. If the task must be done, let someone else do it. You're too young."

Amerae hissed and stood, backing up. "So, the big and mighty seventeen-year-old thinks he knows better than me?"

"You're fifteen, Am. You're just a baby."

Ardenis's lips pinched together. He was fond of Amerae. Michael shouldn't speak to her so. The ideas swirling in her head about an Alysian heir and her stubborn conviction were proof enough of why his instincts led him to her. But, fifteen? She was awfully young.

"Why do you say such hurtful things?" Her eyes welled with tears, and she shook with fury.

"I'll say whatever it takes to keep you safe. When are you leaving?"

Amerae hesitated. "Two weeks from today, when the weather warms up a bit more."

Michel shook his head. "You don't trust me, and all because I don't feel it's safe for you. You said you were leaving tomorrow."

Her chin jutted. "Why, are you going to stop me?"

"Perhaps. Or perhaps your father will."

"What is wrong with you, Michael?" Her lip curled in disgust. "You'd tell my father and sacrifice our relationship, perhaps even your standing in the army if my parents found out about us? I'm going to bed before you can spout any more nonsense. Goodnight."

Amerae walked past, and Michael stopped her with a hand on her wrist. "I'm begging you. Don't go."

She ripped her arm from his grip. "I said goodnight."

Ardenis watched Michael after Amerae left. He paced, mumbling to himself. His steps, shuffles at first, became more distinct until his head snapped up, and he stomped up the stairs.

By the time Michael found Lord Calem and told him he'd overheard Amerae making plans to leave, she was slipping out of the castle with her bag and sword, and *The History of Alysies* tucked safely away. She saddled a horse from the barn and was riding by the light of the moon before Calem stormed into her empty room.

She headed south, away from where Faelyn was at Thomats, and Ardenis nearly pulled out his hair. The odds were always stacked against Faelyn. He couldn't guess what guided Amerae. Her wits and the Fates, perhaps.

Ardenis left the tower and headed to the high council hall to make his report. He desperately wanted to share this new development with Rhea. If this girl, Amerae, were to discover some distant relation to the Rylandor family, Faelyn could lose the throne before she even had the chance to claim it for herself. Amerae, who was the same age Amalia would be at this time...

Ardenis paused midstep, struck still with the thought. Could Amerae be Amalia? A slow grin spread across his face. Maybe he hadn't lost his friend after all.

Ardenis went straight to Rhea's house. He was no longer discomfited by the strange neighborhood or the frilly décor of Rhea's sitting room. She stopped offering him lemon water, for she preferred his visits to be brief. He'd tried to inform her once of the happenings of Thera, but she stopped him, saying he could report to his own council with that news. He'd been disappointed, but not entirely surprised. He wanted a friend to replace Amalia, but Rhea couldn't be that friend.

"Ardenis, thank you for coming. I'm sorry for the necessity of the verbal reports, but as you know, my faith in Acanthians has been shaken since my dealings with Gharum." Rhea perched on the edge of her chair, hands resting in her lap, her face a mask of calm.

Ardenis knew her better by this point. The way she glanced at the door in irregular intervals meant that she was particularly harried today, and probably in a hurry to return to the council. He did not envy her the job of head high councilor.

"The crack in the watch window grew longer this week." He launched into a quick recap. "The number of blackouts has increased as well, but only by three per month according to the watchers' consolidated reports."

Rhea frowned. "Your findings are in line with what I've been told from the regional councils. Anything else? Anything at all that strikes you as important?" She asked this question each time he came, and each time the answer was the same.

"No, nothing."

"Please let me know if anything occurs before our next scheduled visit. As always, thank you for your help."

Ardenis nodded and went back to his part of the world, the troubling occurrences on his mind.

CHAPTER THIRTY-FOUR

Ardenis watched Amerae as she spent many days on the road, camping as she went, even through rain and bad weather. She wisely avoided any inns where her age and gender might attract trouble. Ardenis couldn't help but smile when it became clear where she was heading.

Straight for Kian's estate.

It took Amerae close to three weeks to travel south across Alysies, through the woods and into Creadel. Between watching her travel and studying Faelyn's training with Donoven, Ardenis checked in on his old nemesis.

Kian, or rather Lord Kian, had inherited his family's estate when his parents passed away, though he'd refused to return. Now he fit right in as if he'd never left, overseeing a property worthy of the title of palace.

Due to the proximity of Kian's land to the Sengi Desert, his palace was built out of large bricks fashioned from sand. It gave the structure a far more inviting appearance than the rough timber and cold, cut stone of the typical Alysian estate. There were no walls topped with battlements, just a sprawling estate with a flat lawn of tough grass suited to the hotter climate.

Guards and servants bustled around every corner, and there was a curious cache of weapons and supplies overflowing most of the storerooms. The more Ardenis discovered, the clearer it became that Kian would never return to Thomats. He'd made new plans and thrown his dreams away for the woman he loved. Ardenis would have done the same.

When Amerae rode her horse up the long gravel road which led to the palace, a squad of guards clad in sleeveless leather jerkins and wielding spears intercepted her. She wore a clean dress of loose ivory to fight the heat, and it fluttered in the wind.

Ardenis's heart quickened. This meeting seemed Fated, if indeed Amerae would be allowed to see Kian. And if she did, oh, how much closer might she be to finding Faelyn?

"Name yourself." The lead guard pointed his spear while two others secured her reins.

Her horse stomped and flipped its ears back. Amerae regarded the guards with wary irritation.

"I'm Lady Amerae Kinsman of Alysies. I seek audience with Lord Kian Foster." She lifted her chin.

The guards exchanged looks of surprise. Ardenis mirrored their wide eyes. Did Amerae realize which kingdom she'd claimed? It was reckless, as she didn't yet know where Kian's allegiance lay.

Despite the confident words, her exhaustion was made plain by her slow blinks and the fact she hadn't immediately reached for her sword. It had been a long journey, and it was well into summer. Sweat beaded at her neck, rolling down her back beneath her dress. Heat shimmered off the rocks in billowing waves.

The lead guard jerked his head toward the palace, and another guard broke away, running back to the estate. Amerae tipped back her water skein, sipping the last few drops. Ardenis didn't know what that kind of heat felt like, but it didn't look pleasant.

After several sweltering minutes, the guard returned. "Lord Kian is intrigued by where you're from. We will escort you to the palace."

They didn't give her reins back, but led her horse to a stable further up the road. She dismounted and reached for her pack. The guards intercepted her and searched the bag, pulling out her dagger before handing the bag to her. She snatched it from their hands.

"The sword stays with us."

Amerae scowled, but handed over her sword and followed them into the palace. Compared to the bright sun outside, the entry hall seemed dark. The windows were small, high up and through the thick stone to keep out the heat. Interspaced torches lit the interior, casting orange light over the large, tall space. Palms in colorful pots sat atop smooth granite tiles surrounding a spraying fountain.

At the doorway, a servant offered Amerae a bowl of water with flowers floating on the surface. Amerae stared blankly until the servant also offered her a towel, then she correctly dipped her hands into the bowl to wash the grime of travel.

The servant led Amerae to a room down a step just off the entry hall. Round alabaster columns flanked the open entrance. The room boasted tall ceilings and woven fans rotating by pulleys and ropes leading to where a servant turned a small crank. Guards in the same sleeveless armor stood at every corner and entrance.

Kian sat alone on a red sedan, sipping from a glass. His fine silk clothes rested perfectly against his fit body. His beard was short and neatly trimmed over a bitter face, chiseled from the hard lessons life had taught him.

A tray with inviting glasses of water and a bowl of fresh fruit sat on a long, low table. Kian stood when he saw Amerae. His eyes took her in but revealed none of what thoughts may have been going through his mind.

Ardenis didn't know what to expect of the outcome of this meeting as past and potential future collided.

Amerae's hair was braided eloquently and draped over the shoulder of her dress. Her face was clean of travel grime, if not sweat.

Surrounded by the luxury of the palace, she looked striking in her warm-weather attire. It didn't help much to disguise her age.

"Welcome. I am Kian. Please sit." Kian gestured to an empty armchair across from the table. "No doubt you're thirsty. The summers here are brutal compared to Alysies." He showed no hesitation on the word but studied her as she took her seat without reacting to his casual reference.

"Yes, I'm not accustomed to so much heat." She took a glass, condensation beading from the cold water within, and sipped.

"No need to be formal. Drink up."

Amerae gave a tight smile and drank, draining the glass. Kian refilled it from a pitcher, but she left it untouched on the table.

"Alysies. That's a dangerous name where you come from. Who are you?"

"As I told your guard, I am Amerae. More specifically, Lady Amerae Kinsman of Seaside Keep, daughter of Lord Calem Kinsman."

"A lady of the New Daltieri court. And why are you seeking an audience with me, Lady Amerae?"

Amerae cringed. "I prefer to think of myself as a lady of the Alysian court, one that I hope to see restored in my lifetime." She paused, expectant, but Kian did not betray any emotion to her admittance of open rebellion against Daltieri rule. Ardenis, however, beamed at her bravery. "I've heard a few rumors I hope to confirm are true. If they are, I could really use your help."

"What rumors?"

Amerae stared at Kian for a long time. He bore the scrutiny with increasing impatience. Ardenis waved his arms, pointlessly urging Amerae to speak up. Kian's love for Faelyn could be trusted, if nothing else. Though, it was right for Amerae to be cautious.

Amerae spoke quietly. "What are your feelings regarding the word Alysies? I see you have no trouble using it, anyway."

Kian folded his hands over his middle. "Much the same as yours, I suspect."

Her eyes alighted with hope. "I've heard you're raising an army.

At the same time, I heard of an attack against a band of Daltieri soldiers. Was it you?"

His brow furrowed. "Your sources are well informed, Lady Amerae, but you aren't being as cautious as you should. You've already revealed too many secrets to a stranger you shouldn't trust."

Amerae blushed fiercely, eyes on her glass. "I trust in the cause. I trust that I know things can't continue as they are. I trust my instincts."

Kian smiled faintly. "What is it I can help you with?"

She seemed to gather her courage. "I'm seeking to quell a potential civil war in Alysies..." She glanced at the guards and lowered her voice to a whisper. "If New Daltieri's rule is ever toppled, I fear what may happen. I intend to find an heir to the throne. The Alysian throne. Someone with a rightful claim through traceable lineage to provide an undisputable rallying point." She pulled her pack in front of her and rummaged around. "All I have to go by is this." Amerae pulled the precious book from her bag and flipped it around, revealing the title. *History of Alysies*.

Kian gasped.

She opened it to the back, right to Faelyn's picture.

Faelyn's hair flowed in loose waves, half unbound, half up, falling over the shoulders of her rose-pink coming-out ballgown, now out of fashion and antiquated. Her turquoise eyes shone with a light the artist had captured just right—a young woman about to finally receive a piece of what she'd desired. A meeting with her father that would never happen. A friendship in Calem that would be cut short. A first kiss in Samual that would turn her life to ruin.

Kian's stern composure cracked. His face went white as a snow bank in the mountains of Daltieri. Snatching the book out of Amerae's surprised hand, he brought it close to his face. He slunk back against a cushion as if he could no longer support his own weight.

Amerae stared at him with wide eyes. Kian smiled and traced his fingers over the page.

"I need help, Lord Kian." Amerae's voice broke through the ominous silence in the room. "I don't know what's going on or where to go from here." She bit her lip. "Please, I've come so far. Help me."

Kian finally looked at her. "Do you truly believe Daltieri's rule over Alysies will fall?"

"I do," Amerae said carefully. "It must."

"And what makes you so certain?" He sat up, forcing his features into a less eager expression.

"We have word of upheaval within the towns. The people are not happy. They suffer. Daltieri has finally bled the kingdom to action."

"It wasn't me who defeated the soldiers."

"But I thought it must be you. Are you not raising an army to help Alysies?" She gripped her knees. "If not you, then who?"

Kian stared at Amerae and let out a long gust of air. He picked up his staff where it sat propped against the armrest, and its mage crystal glowed. "If you will allow me to use a bit of magic, Amerae, I will read your intentions. If I find you've been truthful, I promise, you will be well rewarded with the information you seek."

Ardenis found the entire conversation extremely irritating. Kian had all the knowledge Amerae needed, and more. But for obvious reasons, neither one could trust the other. Ardenis let out an audible sigh as Amerae balked at the glowing mage crystal. She stood and retreated a few steps, and Ardenis saw all hope for Faelyn to receive the help she needed disappear into oblivion.

Next would come the part where Amerae decided she doesn't trust Kian at all and flee the palace of sand.

But, Amerae surprised him. She clenched her jaw and marched determinedly back to Kian.

"Okay, do it. I've come this far. Everything I've said is true. Go ahead." She sat back in her chair.

Kian nodded his approval and stood over her. His imperfect crystal glowed bright enough to bathe the room in light. He concentrated hard, looking deep into Amerae's eyes. She winced a few times, but then it was over. The light dimmed back to the orange glow of the torches.

Kian dropped his tough veneer and smiled. “You are very brave, Amerae.”

She took two deep breaths, calming herself. “For one so young, right?”

“No. Not many willingly agree to this, but most have something to hide. I can sense you’ve spoken the truth. In exchange, I will share something with you.”

Amerae leaned forward, eyes eager.

“I do know who defeated the soldiers. She created an earthquake that hit only the road where the soldiers stood. There is only one person I know of that is strong enough to unleash a force of that magnitude, with that kind of control. Only one person with the motivation to do so. She’s who you need to find next.”

“She sounds powerful indeed. What's her name?”

Kian grinned. “Queen Faelyn Rylandor of Alysies.” He picked up the discarded book and tapped Faelyn’s picture.

Amerae dropped her hands in her lap. A sound of exasperation escaped her. “You’re mocking me. You think this is all a joke, don’t you?” She stood, her voice rising. “I’ve forsaken everything to come this far—my family, my safety. I've put my entire life down for the cause. I do not appreciate your ill-advised humor. If Faelyn didn’t die at The Purge, she’d have died of old age decades ago.”

She grabbed the book from him and stuffed it in her bag.

“Lady Amerae, Faelyn’s not dead.” The tenderness and longing in his voice were unmistakable. Even after all that had happened, he still deeply cared for her. “Of course, I have no way to prove it, but it’s true.”

Amerae didn't slow her determined stride out of the extravagant room.

Kian stood but didn't pace after her. “Tell your father he has friends in the south when the need arises.”

Amerae stopped in place and spun around. “What do you know of such things?” Her words hissed like poison, with fear and surprise.

“These guards aren’t just for show. There are secrets here, not unlike the secrets at Seaside Keep. I pray my sources don’t know the full extent of your progress, because if I know, Daltieri knows.”

“Our sources found out about you easy enough.”

“Your time to act is growing short, but you are not alone.” He approached and placed a hand on her shoulder. “You have friends in the south when the need arises. Our queen resides at Thomats School of Magic. She has a ring with a piece of my mage crystal in it. I could communicate with her through it, except she’ll never put it on.” His eyes creased in sadness. “But you, you’ve come this far. Perhaps you can go a little further.”

Amerae swallowed. “It’s not possible.”

The corners of Kian’s mouth tugged up. “She’s one of a kind, Lady Amerae. You read about her magic and beautiful ears in that book. She’s also blessed, or cursed, with long life. We were both students at Thomats. Faelyn told me everything. She wants to fight for her kingdom, but she’s been alone for so long with no one on her side, she doesn’t know where to start. With my army and your army combined, we stand a real chance of helping her. You must go to her and convince her she’s not alone. We’ll stand behind her for a free Alysies.”

Amerae’s eyes wavered with tears. Even Ardenis felt the weight of Kian’s words. “I will do as you say. I will find her.” Her face dropped and tears slid down her cheeks. “I can hardly hope that what you say is true, that our rightful queen still lives.” She looked up. “But I feel it is. I feel maybe I’ve always known, that maybe I was born for this purpose.”

“We all have our purpose here in Thera. This is just a part. Now, rest and replenish, then you must continue your journey.”

Ardenis could barely disguise his smile. Amerae was a million steps closer to finding Faelyn. All Faelyn needed was a push.

Someone to tell her she had the support she feared missing. She'd have the army she always wanted.

He managed to make it back to the privacy of his home before he pumped his fists in the air, cheering for the turn of the Fates. The pieces made long ago, but broken, were finally coming together.

CHAPTER THIRTY-FIVE

"That's it, Ali. Good!" Professor Wemnar mopped sweat from his brow with a handkerchief. Faelyn stood near him in the stone courtyard outside the cafeteria at Thomats. It was ridiculous how they had to wear these heavy black robes, even in summer. Even the fountain seemed to protest the unusually warm day, the stone fish dribbling water from their mouths with a slow gurgle.

Faelyn channeled more magic into the metal barrel that rested a safe distance from anyone, producing enough heat to melt rock. Though most students had returned home for the summer, she'd still drawn a crowd. The students cheered as flames shot up from the barrel, and Wemnar beamed with pride. He'd taken on a lot of her advanced magic training. When she wasn't studying with Swordmaster Donoven, her excess energy went to this, with barely time for sleep.

She'd never felt so alive.

Another flame shot up from the barrel of rocks to the resounding cheer of the students.

"Direct it," Wemnar warned. "The heat needs to stay condensed."

Faelyn nodded, panting under the hot midday sun. This was a lesson in control. She'd been doing tasks like this for hours now, expanding the limits of her magic. Exhaustion crept up, but she was almost there. She could sense the properties of the rocks begin to break apart under the barrage of heat. Hopefully the barrel would hold up.

Boots stomped across the stone, heading in their direction, and Faelyn flinched. Her concentration slipped, heat escaping into flames that shot high above the crowd. New Daltieri soldiers. They'd been an increasing presence at the school lately, recruiting mages for their regime and threatening those that refused. They also interrogated everyone about the mysterious nearby earthquake.

Professor Wemnar frowned when he finally noticed them.

"What's all this commotion?" one of the soldiers asked when they reached the group, a captain. "Stop this at once."

With fear in their eyes, the students scattered. Faelyn controlled the flame and increased the magic.

"It's a training exercise," Wemnar explained. His weariness coated the simmering air.

The captain eyed Faelyn with suspicious distrust. He wore black Daltieri leathers, but no helm, and a stubbled beard "I said stop."

Faelyn ignored him, pushing the final wave of heat into the rocks. They melted in each other, becoming a glowing red liquid at the bottom of the barrel, which must have been made of metal strong enough not to be affected. She smirked.

Wemnar's answering smile was wary, warning in his lined eyes.

The captain put his hand on the hilt of his sword in warning. The four soldiers with him tensed.

"I'm done." Faelyn cut off the magic. Dizziness assaulted her, but she stood tall. Taller. She couldn't be cowed by them.

"Very good, Ali," Wemnar said, trying to take back control of the situation. He flapped his robes to create a breeze. "Let's do our next exercise inside, shall we?" He motioned her to the nearest building, but the captain held up his hand.

He eyed her up and down, and she considered briefly how much trouble it would cause to direct that rock-melting magic to his uniform. "Where were you when the earthquake occurred?"

Faelyn raised her chin.

"I've already told you, Captain Dunnard, Ali was with me." Wemnar bustled toward Faelyn. "All of our students have been accounted for, several times."

She kept her free of surprise. He had vouched for her. Why, and what did he know?

"Watch your tone," one of the soldiers said.

Captain Dunnard leaned over and spat into the barrel. It sizzled and popped on the hardening lava. "Our king could use your abilities, mage Ali. We'll be watching your progress closely."

Faelyn clenched her fists and bit her tongue. Nothing good could come of her opening her mouth. But the soldiers walked away.

Wemnar let out his pent-up tension in a long sigh. "That was a near thing. Next time, try not to look like you're contemplating murder."

Had it been that obvious? "Why did you vouch for me?"

Wemnar mopped his brow again. "I have a wild theory, but now is not the time or place." He nodded toward the retreating soldiers.

He was no fool, and clearly, she could trust him. So what if he'd learned her great secret? Still, her heartrate ratcheted as she glared daggers at the soldiers' backs, tracking their progress toward the building. They finally went through the doors and disappeared, revealing a young girl in travelworn clothes. The soldiers had blocked her from view, but now she was impossible to ignore.

Tall and lean, sword at her hip and chestnut hair braided tight behind her, she stared at Faelyn with tears running down her cheeks. She clutched a book to her chest like it was the most precious thing in the world to her.

Wemnar said something, but Faelyn didn't hear. She tasted the air around the newcomer, and it was full of profound happiness and even more deeply, a reverence she had not encountered since the days of her father's court.

"Ali, are you listening to me?" Wemnar trailed off, noticing where Faelyn's attention was.

"Thank you for the lesson, Professor." Faelyn didn't wait for a response before crossing the courtyard to the girl.

The girl found her feet and met Faelyn the rest of the way, awe in her hazel eyes. "It's you. I found you." She glanced around, then slowly turned the book to the front cover. *History of Alysies.*

A pit opened up inside Faelyn, and she was falling into it. This girl knew who she was.

The instant urge to deny her true identity almost burst out unbidden. But something stopped her. The girl wasn't standing there accusing Faelyn, judging her or pursuing her for capture. There wasn't a hint of the disdainful anger that had always accompanied who Faelyn was. The opposite, this girl *loved* her.

"Hide that book," Faelyn said quietly. "Let's go."

The girl somehow fit the book into her travel bag, then followed Faelyn across campus and into the dorms. Faelyn thanked Acantha that so many traveled for the summer, and that the soldiers all hid from the heat. Inside the building, the coolness licked the back of Faelyn's neck and eased her burning skin. Once in her room, Faelyn locked the door and threw up an air shield to veil their words.

This was going to be an important conversation.

"You're very brave to travel with that book." Faelyn sat on her bed, crossing her legs beneath her, and waved the girl toward the writing desk that had the only chair in the room. "What's your name?"

The girl blushed and slowly set down her pack, then perched on the edge of the chair. The feelings of reverence were evolving into resolve. "I've traveled far to find you. I'm Lady Amerae Kinsman of Seaside Keep."

Faelyn blinked, studying the girl anew. Kinsman of Seaside Keep?

That was Calem's family name. Calem, the only boy at the castle who'd ever shown her kindness. The young man who'd saved her life at the expense of his own. That would make this Lady Amerae a lady of Faelyn's court, if she had a court.

"And you're Faelyn Rylandor, our rightful queen." Amerae said the words so fervently, yet so sincerely, as if she'd accepted them as fact long ago.

Faelyn's quick intake of breath was the only show of surprise she let slip, but warmth bloomed from the open pit inside her. No one had ever called her that. "How did you find me?" Her voice scratched with suppressed emotion. Amerae knew her. Knew her and loved her for who she was. Nothing about any of this said it was a trick.

Amerae pulled her bag over and took out the book, flipping the pages to the back. She turned it around, and there was Faelyn's portrait wearing the beautiful gown Mary had painstakingly hemmed. The painting only existed because Mary had forced the court to commission it. They would have been happy to forget she existed.

"Lord Kian Foster told me where to find you," Amerae said, closing the book. "I just can't believe you're real."

"Kian?" Faelyn covered her mouth.

"He told me to tell you to put on his mage crystal, that he has news."

Faelyn's hand dropped, and her lips thinned. Having Kian's unrequited feelings invade her mind wasn't something she wanted to do twice. He knew where she was when he wanted to share news.

Amerae went on, talking more excitedly as she grew more comfortable. "I have news, too. We've raised an army to battle the New Daltieri rule and reclaim Alysies, but we need you, Queen Faelyn. The people are ready to fight back, but we need a leader."

Shivers chased up Faelyn's spine. So much information at one time. "This is too much. An army... at Seaside Keep?" Her gaze drifted across the room. Amerae only spoke truth. Faelyn needed an army, and one had been laid at her feet. But, "Do they know about me?" If

Amerae figured it out, then Daltieri could too. They had spies everywhere.

And would this army accept her leadership?

"Not yet," Amerae said. "But they will." A fierce look of conviction took over her face. Such was her confidence that Faelyn almost believed it could be true. Almost.

She wasn't ready. There was so much more to learn from Swordmaster Donoven. And she hadn't even completed the tests to become a master mage. What kind of leader could she be without proper training? Another year wouldn't change anything, and she'd be much better prepared.

Faelyn opened her mouth to tell Amerae she wasn't ready, but Amerae spoke first.

"Where have you been all this time?" Her eyes reflected all the pain the Alysian people had endured in Faelyn's long absence. It was as if Amerae was just realizing that her queen had been here her whole life and had done nothing to help them.

It gutted Faelyn.

It couldn't hurt more if Amerae had taken her sword and sundered her in two.

The weight of her failure shocked her silent. She hadn't realized how outside the suffering of her people she'd placed herself, even when it had stared her in the face. Now here was someone, a lady of her court, who already loved her without hesitation, asking the question Faelyn had spent decades running from. Yet there was no blame in Amerae's countenance, just pity, as if she already suspected how hard Faelyn's life must have been.

The Fates had placed Amerae in Faelyn's path, of that she was sure.

Tears welled in Faelyn's eyes. She couldn't play the part of a dignified queen in the face of so much raw emotion.

"I'm a coward." She wiped her eyes dry. This was no time for self-pity. "I told myself it was for the kingdom, because I was the sole surviving heir to the throne. When I realized I wasn't aging, I wandered, waiting to outlive any Daltieri who would remember me."

Amerae listened in stoic silence, eyes creasing in sympathy that mirrored her essence, sympathy Faelyn wished she didn't feel. Faelyn didn't deserve it. And here she was, unburdening herself to a stranger. Except Amerae didn't feel like a stranger. She felt like an old friend.

Amerae scooted her chair closer to the bed. "For what it's worth, I don't believe you're a coward. You needed to survive to save us another day."

Faelyn nearly shrank. Amerae's words of affirmation only hurt her more. "I wasn't idle. I learned new skills that I told myself would one day help our kingdom. But the truth is, the kingdom hated me. The court refused me my title. The people—even my own father—treated me like an outcast because I was born different." She pulled back her hair, revealing her ears. Angry tears leaked down unbidden. "I was scared. Even if I could have found a way back, there was nothing left and no one to support me."

"See?" Amerae said, barely glancing at Faelyn's ears.

"Those things don't matter, Amerae. They are just excuses. What is my life worth if I don't use it to better the lives of others? There are so many things I could have done more than doing nothing. My title was a way to excuse my poor choices. My aloofness was a way to ignore what was happening in my own kingdom, to my own people." She roughly scrubbed her face dry. "I'll regret it all my days."

Amerae took her hand. Her fingers were callused and warm. "Alysies wasn't ready for you yet. And maybe you weren't ready for us. We didn't know how much we needed you. But we do now. Come with me to Seaside."

Faelyn squeezed her hand back, sending the same feelings of love she still felt from Amerae, even after admitting her failure. "Of course, I'll come. You bring me the best news. If I wasn't crying so much, I'd be shouting from the rooftop." Their laughter broke the heavy mood. She couldn't change the past, but she could change the future, and maybe begin to heal a wound she hadn't known she still carried. "This is what I've been waiting for." She shook her head in amazement. "This could be our chance."

"It *will* be, Queen Faelyn." Amerae grinned.

"It will be." Faelyn hugged her, whispering, "Thank you for believing in me."

Afterward, Faelyn settled Amerae in to stay and rest for the night, and they discussed plans for travel. Amerae wanted a few days' headstart to break the news of Faelyn's discovery to her father, which worked well for Faelyn because it would take time to finalize things with Swordmaster Donoven and Professor Wemnar. The journey to Seaside wasn't overly long from Thomats, and she sent a letter with Amerae that would hopefully help.

Faelyn saw Amerae off the next morning, a brief goodbye to someone she felt would be a lifelong friend.

CHAPTER THIRTY-SIX

The weight of Faelyn and Amerae's meeting made Ardenis's chest burn in a way it hadn't in a long time. He just knew, be it by instincts or intuition, that he'd witnessed a historic moment. A turning point for both of them, as well as for Alysies. More than that, he'd seen his two most favorite souls in all of existence converse and embrace for the first time since leaving premortal Acantha.

And it was as if they knew each other.

Most strangers didn't behave as if they were continuing a conversation they'd had only yesterday. Yet Faelyn and Amerae did. The power in their words struck Ardenis deeply.

Was it always that way when you met someone you knew before you were born?

It was inevitable that Amerae's good luck would run out. That was how the Fates worked, especially for the good ones. Ardenis began his watch one day to find Amerae riding into danger she couldn't see coming.

Amerae approached a blockade—placed there due to recently heightened measures to control who passed the major roads of New

Daltieri. Faelyn's earthquake had rippled across the kingdom, it seemed. A crude fence spanned the length of the road, with a moveable section in the middle to allow travelers through.

By the time Amerae realized she should turn her horse around, it was too late. At least a dozen Daltieri soldiers guarded the road. She pulled her horse to an abrupt stop. With a gulp, she joined the short line of civilians waiting to pass.

At the front of the line, a man and his teenage son cast nervous glances from the bench of their wagon. Two soldiers lifted a burlap cloth covering their goods and poked around. One of them pocketed a couple apples from a crate.

"We're on our way home. Just come from Thomats selling our crops at market," the father stated in an even voice. The son sat very still.

The soldiers waved the wagon through, and the son let loose a gust of air.

A man by himself, travel-weary and on foot, was next in line. He stated he was on his way to his lord's house to pay dues. They took his name and some coin, then let him go, as they did for the next three parties, and then it was Amerae's turn.

"Dismount. State your name and business." The soldier—a faceless young man in black Daltieri leather—spoke with the bored tone of one who'd repeated a phrase until it lost all meaning.

Amerae hesitated for only a beat, then dismounted, smoothing her riding clothes. "My name is Amanda, and I'm on my way home."

A different soldier grabbed her bag from the saddle and dumped the contents on the ground. Amerae's clothes, food, knife, and meager coins hit the dusty road. With a loud whomp, *History of Alysies* hit the ground. Amerae's head swiveled, and her hand jerked to her sword, halting at the last second.

Ardenis tensed.

The soldier picked up the book and flipped it over to read the cover. His eyes went as wide as the grin on his face. He rushed over to a captain overseeing the blockade, pointing and whispering. Amerae's breathing grew shallow.

A prayer formed on Ardenis's lips.

"Detain her!" came the command.

Amerae grabbed onto her saddle and threw one foot into the stirrup. Strong hands of half a dozen soldiers pulled her sprawling to the ground. They held her down, scrambling to remove her sword.

The captain, marked by his single golden shoulder spaulder and commanding presence, loomed over where she lay pinned to the road by rough hands. "Where did you get this book, young one?" He dangled it above her in his meaty fist.

Amerae's head swiveled side to side like a caged animal desperate for escape.

Lie, Amalia. Lie.

"I... um." Her voice came out a nervous squeak.

"Speak up. Quickly." He drew his sword and pointed it at her chest.

She flinched back, then stopped. Ardenis saw the exact moment when Amerae's determination overruled her fear. Her mouth snapped shut, and her eyes narrowed.

The captain saw it too.

He turned to his men. "Bind and gag her. Take her and this book to the Rosen outpost and lock her up. No food until she talks."

The captain watched as they hauled Amerae to her feet.

She glared daggers at him.

"Trust me, young one. We can get you to talk." He smirked.

She spat, and it landed on his dirty trousers. Rage filled his face. He stomped toward her, winding his hand back to strike.

Ardenis stood from his chair, anger flaring.

"Captain Van, you'll want to see this." Another soldier approached carrying a letter. Faelyn's letter. "We found it in her bag."

Captain Van lowered his hand. Ardenis shook as he sunk back down.

Van snatched the letter and tore open the wax seal. Ardenis read as he did.

CK,

I apologize for sending a letter in my stead. I will join you shortly. Your daughter is very brave and can be trusted. Everything she tells you now is the truth. The time has come to fulfill our destinies.

The letter was unsigned. Clearly, Faelyn took precautions should Amerae be caught with it.

Van's eyes narrowed. "CK? Show this to the commander when you reach the outpost."

"Yes, sir." The soldier nodded.

The book and letter went in the saddlebag of one of the riders. They bound Amerae's hands behind her back. She didn't struggle until they stuffed a dirty rag in her mouth, tying a cloth over her mouth to keep it in place. They threw her into the back of a barred wagon and slammed the door shut. Kneeling in moldy hay over splintering wood, she glared through the bars. The soldier clicked the lock in place without a second glance.

Amerae struggled, working her mouth and tilting her head side to side. Little by little, the cloth slipped off and dropped around her neck. She spat out the rag and slumped against the bars. Silent tears slipped down her cheeks. The wagon rolled forward, increasing speed and sending dust in the air as trees whipped by.

Ardenis's hand went to his chest. He couldn't predict what might happen to Amerae. Her age and innocent appearance might have helped her before, but now they would use them against her. Would anyone in Daltieri's army connect it back to Calem Kinsman?

Either way, Amerae might be put to death for her trouble, and Faelyn would never know.

Amerae shifted, fitting her bound hands between the bars behind her for comfort. She closed her eyes and bowed her head. She took a hitching breath, opened her mouth to speak, and then the watch window went black.

Ardenis blinked past the burning in his eyes and continued to watch. The view of Thera did not return.

The room remained quiet as the watchers patiently waited for the window to work again. Time ticked by. Something was wrong. It had never quit working for this long before. He looked up to where Amalia used to sit, meeting the eyes of Wes. The disappointment that flooded Ardenis was quickly replaced by the realization that all the watchers were looking at him. For guidance.

He had no idea what to do.

CHAPTER THIRTY-SEVEN

Midswing, Faelyn gasped, her sword of flame dissipating.

"Lady Fae! Are you well?" Donoven rushed to her side, sheathing his sword. He grabbed her arm, then turned toward his house. "Steisha, come quick! Bring water."

"No, I'm fine, Swordmaster." Faelyn's voice came out harsher than she intended. She couldn't say what had made her react that way—tiredness maybe. Donoven had pushed her hard today, cramming her head full of warfare and weaponry, even letting her use magic. Strengthening and honing her abilities and mind. They only had a couple days left before she would leave for Seaside Keep.

Donoven crossed his arms. "All right. If you're fine, then what just happened? Why is your face so pale?" He hadn't shown this much concern when he'd nearly crippled her last month.

"Is it?" She wiped away sweat before it trickled into her eyes. "I need rest is all." The sun waned on the horizon, sending beams of orange across the sprawling fields. Crickets chirped loudly around them.

With a wary look, Donoven bowed at the waist. Faelyn bowed in tandem, then marched her way from the dusty yard in front of his home. Steisha, his wife, met her on the porch with concerned eyes, a cup of water, and a bundle of bandages.

"Did you cut him again, dear?" She glanced out to her husband, her tone more curious than worried.

"All is well, Steisha. No need to trouble yourself." Faelyn smiled at the kind-hearted woman to reassure her, but didn't pause as she stowed her weapon and swigged the water. Donoven's two young children giggled from the window.

She would miss this family. They'd treated her as their own, but she might never see them again after this. Donoven hadn't asked what the urgency was when she said she had to leave for good in two days, merely planned a rigorous schedule to cram as much as he could in their time left.

"Dinner's on the table, anyway," Steisha said. "Then off to bed with you. You look pale." The trek back to school was far enough that Steisha had long-ago declared the spare bedroom as Faelyn's. She'd stayed over frequently when she didn't have classes to rush off to.

Despite Donoven's assurances, Steisha hurried to check on her husband. Faelyn smiled warmly. Theirs was a love to envy.

All through the next two days, the nagging feeling she should be elsewhere ate at her. It only increased the more she ignored it, distracting her. During their studies of the art of war, Donoven smacked the side of his dagger on the table, making her jump. She realized she'd read the same paragraph countless times and hadn't heard his question. During training, her gaze would drift to the horizon, earning her a sharp whack to the ribs with the broad side of Donoven's sword.

"Another year would be better," Donoven said at the end of their time. They'd just finished clearing the dishes from the evening meal. "You've still much to learn."

"I can't put my task off any longer. It's always been one excuse or another for me, but I'm done with that. I'm ready." Faelyn hefted her small pack and bowed to the swordmaster. "Thank you for everything."

Donoven bowed back, then paused. "I know who you are." Faelyn raised an eyebrow, and he shrugged. "My family ran Monhaber for generations until King Seber shut it down." His face grew angry for a moment. "They may have wiped the name Alysies from history, but it still burns bright in many places. You should have taken more care to conceal your ears, my queen." His eyes twinkled.

Faelyn stood still, too shocked to react. Emotion constricted her throat. How long had he known? "If it is within my power, your family's legacy will be restored." A bold decree for someone without a kingdom, but it felt right.

Steisha, tears spilling over, pulled Faelyn into a tight hug. "I believe in you, my girl. You'll make this a better place yet."

It was late when Faelyn finally left, hurrying home in a daze. The road she'd destroyed had been repaired, but she didn't dare go that way now. Donoven had shown her a faster way back after their first spar.

The sun was well gone by the time Faelyn crested the hill to the school. The heat of day had been chased away by the night breeze, chilling her bare arms. The grounds were empty but for the occasional student out to raid the kitchens for an evening pastry. Nothing seemed amiss—no great disaster awaiting her discovery. Still, the sense that she was needed didn't let up. It only increased the closer she got to her dorm.

Faelyn slipped through the door into the small room that had been her refuge these past years. Everything looked as she had left it. Her eyes fell to the floorboards which hid Kian's ring. She'd refused to put it on, but maybe that was foolish. In reality, she didn't want to face the heartache—how he'd thrown away his dreams because of her.

But that didn't make it any less true.

Reaching under her simple bed, she pried two boards loose and rummaged among her hidden items until she touched a velvet pouch. She pulled it out, then sat on her bed and dumped the contents in her hand. Her heart lurched at the sight of her treasures: her parents' diamond and sapphire rings, Calem's key with the ruby in the handle, and the turquoise stone imbedded in silver and hanging from a thin silvery chain. She kissed the necklace and hung it around her neck. She tucked almost everything else back in the pouch, then turned her attention to the remaining object.

Kian's ring. A single gem encased in white gold. A piece of his mage crystal. Turning the ring over and over in her hand it felt warm to the touch. It'd be so easy to slip it on her finger. Should she? Why did she feel so compelled?

She didn't love him anymore, at least not more than friends. Life had been so simple during their time together, but time had proven she'd been fooling herself into thinking her love for him was lasting. It wasn't. This was reality now—an existence in which she prepared for a future that might never come to pass. But not loveless. She felt love from Donoven's family and now Amerae, and from those she'd met along the way. And they too would grow old and die while she remained young.

Faelyn held the ring out, poised to slip it on her finger. Kian was her good friend, and he might be in trouble.

She pushed the ring into place, dropping the barrier against him. Gasping as the familiar rush of Kian's being filled her, she felt his utter surprise and joy.

Faelyn, oh, finally. How I've longed for this.

Her muscles tensed against the rush of emotion from him. Love, desperation, and a great urgency.

Are you safe? He was desperate for the answer.

Faelyn cleared her throat, then felt foolish. She focused on the crystal and sent her thoughts to him.

I'm safe, Kian. I'm still at Thomats, but not for much longer. Her thoughts ended there, not knowing what else to say. The awkwardness of the whole thing washed over her. This was a bad idea.

No! Don't go, please. There are so many things I need to tell you. He paused, but Faelyn felt it was so he could decide where to start. *I went home to Creadel, but I didn't become a teacher. I've spent this time raising you an army, Faelyn.*

Her mouth dropped open. The overpowering silence was filled with Faelyn's complete shock. It took several moments to think through her many reactions and settle on the right one.

An army? He risked his life with the very thought of rebellion, let alone actually amassing any kind of resistance. And on Creadel soil. Where did he get the troops? He'd brought a whole other entire kingdom into this fight, whether intentional or not. It was mere months ago he couldn't even hear her utter the word Alysies, and now he'd raised an army to fight for it?

Why, Kian? You are supposed to be a teacher. It was the only question she had energy to form, but she sent her feelings into it so he would know what she meant. Why do any of this for her?

You know why. The sadness in his voice cut through his thoughts. *I can tell you don't feel the same. My feelings have not changed. They'll never change. I love you. You needed an army to fulfill your dreams and your destiny, and that was never going to happen on your own. Now you have two.*

He knew she didn't feel the same, and he didn't care. So this is why Amerae told her to speak to Kian. *Amerae told me about Seaside. It's hard to believe.*

I'm so glad Amerae found you, and even more glad you put the ring on. Amerae's in trouble. I received word she's been captured. She's being held at Rosen.

Faelyn gasped. *No!* Amerae couldn't be in trouble. She was the key to all this. The letter. The book.

I'm too far away to help, but you're so close... she knows everything, Faelyn, and she's so young. If they torture her... They both winced internally. *The book she carries has your picture. It identifies you as Isaac's daughter.*

I understand. Faelyn jumped into action. She dumped out her pack and crammed it with provisions. Plans and thoughts swarmed her. Two armies. She had two armies prepared to fight in her name. Donoven's strategy training kicked in. *How many are you, and how long would it take you to get to Seaside Keep?*

We have five thousand infantry, two thousand cavalry, and around fifty mages already sworn and trained to fight. More would join. The people are angry. When you declare open rebellion, more mages from Thomats, and even civilians will join. He paused, thinking. *We could be there in a month.*

So many! But it wasn't nearly enough.

Her mind ran off in a million directions. All of her training and preparation, her wishing and hoping for this opportunity, and it could really be true. A Daltieri lord—Lord Jamison—sat on her father's throne overseeing things in Alysies. She could march the armies on her birthplace and take back what was rightfully hers. With just the thought, her spirit lifted.

Faelyn.

If she were queen, she could undo so much of the damage done to Alysies.

Faelyn.

Her starving people, not much more than slaves, would know once again what it meant to thrive.

Faelyn. This time the interruption was laced with annoyance and a sense of urgency.

What, Kian?

If Lord Calem hears of this, and I'm sure he has, he will preemptively march to get his only daughter back. The Seaside army will be exposed. It will ruin everything.

Her resolve hardened, fingers curling around her pack. *Then it's up to me.*

CHAPTER THIRTY-EIGHT

Faelyn rode as fast as her borrowed horse could carry her without wearing down. She'd kept her traveling clothes so as not to tie anything back to Thomats, and secured her sword—a gift from Donoven, made from the finest materials at the hands of expert craftsmen. The dawning sun rose higher into the sky, and trees blurred by with each kick of her horse's hooves on the dusty trail.

Rosen was so close to Thomats. Amerae must have been captured shortly after leaving, and that was days ago. Had they tortured her? Did she still live? Faelyn prayed Amerae had been strong enough to withhold her secrets. Was she still in Rosen? What if Kian's information was outdated or wasn't accurate? But no, instincts told her she was on the right path.

At the next breakaway, Faelyn veered her horse right and raced on, looking for the first signs of the town. She hadn't returned since her date with Kian—it hurt too much to see what her absence had done to her kingdom and people. More proof of her cowardice.

Smoke on the horizon caught her eye. Thick black curls of it cut through the otherwise empty, brightening sky. This wasn't chimney or campfire smoke.

Faelyn sent strength, courage, and a little bit of healing magic into her horse, and they barreled down the trail. When screams of panic reached her sensitive ears, she contemplated dismounting and traveling through the cover of trees to avoid detection. A male's cry of torturous heartbreak cut through any plans of caution. She raced the rest of the way down the path, careening around bends and dodging branches.

The tree line thinned, then broke, revealing the shabby town. As before, crude wooden buildings stood in a line along a dirt road with gaps in between where homes had long collapsed. Abandoned shops and boarded windows led the way to the center of town.

Closer to the town square, Faelyn found the source of the smoke. Fire blazed in a giant barn, flames and smoke pouring out the hayloft. Townspeople shouted, running back and forth carrying pales of water, while others pointed, gawking at a different commotion in the center of the square.

Still outside the chaos, Faelyn craned her neck, but couldn't see beyond the jostling horde. She dismounted and dropped the reins. Her horse trotted to the nearest watering trough in front of a dingy tavern. Ears concealed beneath her hair, Faelyn stepped to the back of the crowd unnoticed. Edging to the front of the circle, she stood shoulder to shoulder, boxed in by villagers. The coarse reek of smoke hovered in the air.

In front of the only stone building—a prison, by the bars for windows, that hadn't been there the last time she'd visited—kneeled a young man, hands tied behind his back. Blood ran down his face and smeared into his brown hair. Tears ringed his defiant eyes, and his broad shoulders quivered, straining against his bonds. Two captors in black pointed swords at his chest.

Daltieri soldiers.

There was no sign of Amerae.

Faelyn's jaw clenched. She scanned beyond the square to the

burning barn and the rest of the town. More Daltieri soldiers walked the crowds, intermingled amongst them and doing nothing to put out the fire. She seethed. Had Daltieri found yet another way to corrode this once-prosperous town by turning it into an outpost? A central location, close to the mage school, upon which they could quell any more so-called upheaval.

The prison blocked her view, but it was easy to imagine the Running Dove with its kind owner overrun with Daltieri filth, demanding drink and sullying everything with their poison.

A soldier stopped not five yards from her. Her nails dug into her palms. Anger replaced the fear that had once plagued her at the sight of them. The townspeople's voices cut in around her.

"Did you hear? He started that fire."

"Some of the horses are still trapped inside."

"No Daltieri citizen would do something so cruel."

"But, why'd he do it?"

Who was he?

"Bring her." This voice rose to Faelyn's ears above all the rest. Those two words dripped with dark menace, of expectation and anticipation. The Daltieri soldier who uttered them stood across the square by the door to the stone prison. He stared at the young man with cold calculation in his dark eyes.

Along with the shoulder spaulder to show his rank as captain, the soldier wore the standard Daltieri black tunic under a black leather vest. In the center was a gold crest of a raven, wings spread wide, with the North Mountain range behind. It was a newer look, probably to instill fear into their enemies with a show of wealth and ruthlessness.

Faelyn was not afraid.

Two soldiers hauled out a girl too weak to stand on her own. Amerae! Faelyn gasped and took an involuntary step forward. The townspeople watched her warily.

The soldiers each held one bloodied arm, not even bothering to tie her hands. Her travel clothes, barely recognizable under blood and filth, were half torn from her shoulder. Her face was swollen, and her bottom lip split. She wore no shoes, and her hair was a matted mess.

Faelyn shook with anger. It took everything in her not to charge the square. If Amerae hadn't been broken, they could still lead the army in a surprise attack. There had to be a way to rescue Amerae without attracting attention—maybe once the crowd cleared.

The captain held up his hand, and the soldiers threw Amerae to the ground. She landed facedown, sending up a cloud of dust, and didn't move. Faelyn hissed, earning sideways glances.

"Amerae!" The young man shot to his feet and managed one step before his guards caught him and shoved him down. He yelled obscenities and struggled to stand until the point of a sword pressed into his neck.

The captain watched on while the soldiers raised the young man back to his knees.

"What did you do to her, you filthy pieces of shit? I'll kill you all!" He spat, earning a knee to the face. "Amerae!"

Amerae stirred, raising her head and squinting in the smoke-covered sun. "Michael? Oh no, Michael. What have you done?" The grief and regret in her ragged tone were crushing. Her arms trembled as she tried to push herself up.

Amerae knew this boy. He loved her. He'd tried to rescue her using the fire as a distraction.

The captain bent down and grabbed Amerae by the back of her mangled hair, forcing her to face Michael. She cried out in pain. Faelyn inhaled through clenched teeth. She couldn't just stand here.

"Now, *Amerae*, you will tell me everything I want to know, or you can watch me torture your lover to death." The captain's tone promised violence. "Where did you get that book, what are you hiding, and most importantly," he put her mouth right up to her ear, and she flinched, "where can we find Faelyn?"

She whimpered, and he smiled. He was enjoying this moment of triumph.

He didn't factor in Faelyn. Secrecy be damned.

Faelyn balled her hands into fists and stepped forward out of the watching throng. People gasped when she kept going, muttering as her boots crunched over the gravelly square. The captain’s head snapped up. A fiery breeze blew Faelyn’s unbound hair back, exposing her ears.

Let them see. Let them finally know her. They should have killed her when they had the chance.

The captain's eyes went wide, and then wider still as he likely put the pieces of the puzzle together.

Tears flowed down Amerae's cheeks, forming new tracks in the blood and grime, rolling over her quivering smile.

Faelyn stopped halfway between her and the ring of villagers and drew her sword. “Let them go.”

"Seize her!" The captain dragged Amerae back by her hair, reaching for his sword.

Amerae screamed defiance and clawed at the captain’s hand. He let go, and she dropped to the ground in a heap.

Beside a gaping Michael, the guards tensed. Soldiers came running. They pushed paths through the confused villagers, but one was closer than the rest. He charged from behind.

Faelyn’s breathing evened out. Anger sharpened her focus. Her muscles tensed. All the knowledge and training her swordmasters and professors had drilled into her coiled within, waiting for the moment to strike. The world slowed.

Pounding footsteps quickly approached. Without turning to look, she made a quick backward jab. Her sword met flesh. He fell to the ground at her feet, scattering the pebbly dust.

Villagers screamed, bolting away from the square. The captain jerked his hand, motioning for the other soldiers to hurry, but they were further away and hindered by the crowd. A sense of urgency guided her choices. The longer she took retrieving Amerae and Michael, the more their chances of escape plummeted.

She held her sword out, which glowed from the heat she channeled into it, and marched straight for the captain. Two soldiers launched themselves at her. She bashed the first one's weapon away, then swirled to bash the second's, muscle memory taking complete control. They stumbled slightly from the force. She lunged, slicing through their armor like butter.

The captain balked and hauled Amerae up, holding his sword to her throat. Real fear showed on her face, but along with it came a glint of defiant hope. This girl was tough.

The captain sneered. "Stay back, or she's dead."

"Don't hurt her," Michael screamed, voice hoarse. His guards shuffled in place. The town was in chaos with villagers abandoning the barn to flee for their lives, the heat and smoke of the raging fire curling over the square.

Faelyn paused, narrowing her eyes at the beads of perspiration running down the captain's face.

"You're her, aren't you?" His tone dripped with contention. He squeezed Amerae closer, and she let out a cry of pain. "You're the Faelyn from the histories." He laughed in disdain. "Or you're the spitting image of your great-great-great grandmother. Either way, you're mine now."

Amongst the screaming and pounding of running feet, the swish of leather armor from three soldiers charging sounded from behind. Faelyn pivoted, raising her sword. The first soldier aimed a blow to her head. She swiped her red-hot sword through the air, cutting his weapon in two. As the tip of his blade fell, she kicked it on the blunt end, sending it flying like a dagger. The piece embedded into the second man's eye socket just as he lunged to strike.

The first soldier's head rolled to the feet of the scrambling, shrieking villagers. Only one soldier remained. His wide eyes matched the terror rolling off him in waves. He glanced at his captain, then swung his sword in attack. She ended him with a quick thrust through the heart.

Her eyes closed as his body slumped to the ground. So much

killing, and this was only the beginning. War was terrible, she'd learned. But now she had the power to make things right.

She tightened her grip on the sword and forced herself to look upon the fallen. Then she broke into a run, straight for Michael's guards. He wrenched his bound arms out of the soldiers' grasp, throwing himself to the ground.

They backed away, hands in the air.

"I said seize her!" Spit flew as the captain snarled. He held Amerae up against him like a human shield, back against the stone prison.

The guards advanced. It was over quickly, and Faelyn was forced to take two more lives. She couldn't think on it now. Rope sizzled as her sword burned through Michael's binding. He rubbed his wrists, staring up at her. With her boot, she nudged a fallen sword toward him. He picked it up in a daze and stumbled to his feet.

The frantic clang of a bell cut through the chaos of the square. The rest of the troops were being called. Time was up.

"You have nowhere to go, freak, and I will not easily part with my prize." The captain shook Amerae, demonstrating his hold. He pulled her tighter against him, then traced the tip of his nose from Amerae's jaw to her hairline.

Amerae cried a horrible, anguished sound that spoke of a pain deeper than surface wounds. But he hadn't broken her. Not yet. He raised his sword from her neck, intention clear. He meant to end her. Amerae snarled in defiance, reaching up so fast the captain didn't have time to dodge the punch to his face.

That was all the opening Faelyn needed.

With a simple thought, she cut off his air. He jerked and lost his grip on the sword and Amerae. Both fell to the ground. Michael rushed to her side. The captain clawed at his throat in a futile effort to breathe. The sight wasn't nearly satisfying enough for what he'd done, but Faelyn needed him to live.

She tucked the hair behind her ears and turned so all may see. "Hear me now, Daltieri." Her voice carried past the square, quieting those who scrambled and screamed and commanding the charging soldiers' strictest attention. "I am Faelyn Eva Rylandor, daughter of King Isaac, granddaughter of King Tristan, and the rightful queen of the kingdom of Alysies, a kingdom forgotten in history, but not in spirit." She peered around. Even the soldiers trickling into the square halted their pursuit. The captain fell to his knees, turning blue. "Tell your Daltieri king that a free Alysies is at hand. I will have my revenge."

The square remained silent. Faelyn returned the captain's air to him. He pitched forward, gasping and coughing, clawing at the ground and taking huge gulps of air. Faelyn quickly gathered her horse and crossed to Michael, handing him the reins.

"Can you run?"

He opened his mouth to speak, but no words came. Instead, he nodded.

"Good." Faelyn knelt by Amerae, wrapping an arm around her.

Amerae attempted to stand, glaring murderously at the captain. "Please, my queen, I can do it. Don't trouble yourself."

Faelyn's heart skipped a beat, and she paused. The title, though she'd just claimed it and Amerae had used it before, still took her by surprise. Amerae's spirit, however, did not. Faelyn smirked and kept hold of the girl, leading her to the horse. She directed simple magic to Amerae's swollen face and split lip. The rest of the injuries would have to wait until they were safely away.

The captain sat up, still gasping. "Kill—." His words were choked off by violent coughing as he still struggled to regain his breath. "Kill them, what are you doing?"

Around the square and interspaced between the citizens, the Daltieri soldiers blinked as if coming out of a trance.

"Now, we run." Faelyn lifted Amerae onto the horse, Michael steadying her.

Amerae gripped the reins in feeble hands. The young people exchanged weak smiles behind their injuries.

Faelyn slapped her horse on its rump. It took off, cutting a path between the last of the people, heading back the way Faelyn had come. She grabbed Michael's hand and pulled him into a run, letting go when he matched her pace.

"Get them," the captain shouted. "Get them!"

Michael ran impressively fast for his injuries, but still, he lagged behind. Amerae rode out of sight, and Faelyn was forced to drop back to keep pace with Michael. It wasn't long before five soldiers and the captain chased after them on horseback, gaining fast.

Michael gritted his teeth, panting and pumping his arms and legs. He wiped blood from where it dripped in his eyes mixed with sweat. He wasn't going to make it.

The soldiers rounded the bend behind them. Faelyn stopped and turned. With a huff of exertion, she sent a gale of wind at them. They flew backward off their horses, sprawling to the ground amidst toppled trees. The horses bolted away, right into the path of an entire company of soldiers racing up the trail.

"Acantha above, can I get no help from the Fates?" she muttered. She took a deep breath, extending both arms out to the side. With a great cry, she clapped her hands together in front of her. Wind blew down the trail, knocking every tree from her to the soldiers into the path. She lost sight of the enemy behind debris, flying tree limbs and dust rising to the sky.

Faelyn smirked, pivoted, and ran up the trail. She caught up to Michael, and much further west, they caught up to Amerae. She'd stopped at the crossroad, her horse pawing to keep going back to Thomats. She swayed in the saddle, eyes closed.

Faelyn offered her and Michael a quick drink and some dried meat from her saddlebag. They stuffed it in their mouths, hardly chewing.

"We have to keep moving," Faelyn said. "They won't give up so easily. We've given them much reason to chase us."

Heading west, toward Seaside Keep, they traveled until night fell, forcing them to stop.

Faelyn found a resting spot behind a boulder as tall as her.

Michael collapsed on the rough forest floor of leaves and twigs and fell instantly asleep. Faelyn eased Amerae down. Even sitting up, the poor girl's eyelids drooped, but Amerae forced them open.

Faelyn was not surprised after what she'd learned about the girl's character.

Faelyn sat and watched her expectantly, offering her a biscuit and more water. The moon overhead gave little light, but Faelyn had no trouble seeing the hero worship in her eyes.

Amerae raised her head. "How did you find me?" Her voice sounded hoarse, as if from overuse. Like she'd been screaming for days. She leaned forward to pass back the waterskin, and a hiss escaped her. She winced and grabbed at her chest.

A cracked rib? She was tougher than Faelyn thought.

Faelyn sent her hearing to the east, focusing, listening, and was rewarded by the comforting sounds of night predators hunting prey, the trickle of a nearby stream, and the rustle of leaves in the breeze. She strained for signs of pursuit that so far hadn't come.

"Lie down, Amerae." Faelyn kept her voice gentle, trying to comfort this girl who she already considered a friend. "I will answer your questions, but first, lie down."

Amerae complied, letting out the faintest sigh of relief. The captain had her chained up. This must have been the first she'd been able to do this small thing.

Faelyn scooted through dirt and leaves to Amerae's side. She placed one hand on Amerae's forehead and the other on her stomach.

Amerae trembled at the touch, but Faelyn was gentle and felt her relax under her care.

As they taught her at Thomats, Faelyn concentrated, channeling her anger and anguish at the treatment of Amerae into her magic. A white glow emitted from her palms. Amerae gave a quick intake of breath as the healing washed over her.

The magic worked its way through Amerae's body, finding the damage and slowly repairing it, bit by bit, piece by piece. Cuts, bruised organs, a cracked rib. There were more than just physical wounds to heal, but that healing would come with time. When Amerae's body was whole, but weak, Faelyn removed her hand from Amerae's stomach and placed it over the girl's heart.

"I found you this time, Amerae Kinsman, daughter of Calem, Lady of Seaside Keep." Faelyn spoke in soft, soothing tones, sending feelings of peace and safety to accompany her words. Beneath her hands, Amerae moved with silent sobs. "But it's you who saved me. Your quest is complete, and you're safe. Sleep now, sister. Sleep."

And Amerae did, a smile on her lips.

Faelyn slumped back, winded from her use of magic, and studied the girl. Amerae had inherited many traits of her long-ago friend, Calem. From her chestnut hair and small nose, to her high cheekbones and smattering of freckles. The girl was clearly stubborn like her forefather. And brave, so brave.

Faelyn smiled as the memories came back to her. The way Calem never spoke harshly like the other boys. The way he'd insisted she leave the kingdom, to come back and save them another day.

This girl, Amerae, was going to change everything. She'd endured much to bring Faelyn such incredible news. Two armies! Two people from different times who loved her and believed in her and what she could offer, how she could make a difference. After all those years of hiding from who she was, then preparing for a future she never truly thought possible. Now, thanks to Amerae, it was. It was every bit possible.

Faelyn pulled out Kian's ring from her pocket and slipped it on. *Kian.* She waited a few moments.

Faelyn? Kian's thoughts seemed muddled with sleep.

It's time to march. Meet me at Seaside Keep.

CHAPTER THIRTY-NINE

They traveled for three weeks over plains and rolling hills to reach Seaside Keep. It could have been swifter, but Amerae was still healing, and Faelyn made them visit the major towns inhabited by Daltieri soldiers. There, they set fires to Daltieri compounds and wreaked havoc, avoiding the innocent citizens—the first step in fighting back. They backtracked in untraceable patterns to throw off the enemy.

The townspeople, who knew nothing but oppression and heavy taxation, needed to see that someone was on their side. If they had hope that things could change, more might join the rebellion. This way of life didn't have to be the only way. Daltieri need not take their land and resources any longer.

"That's an awful lot to place on a few fires and general mayhem," Amerae replied as they rode the final stretch to Seaside Keep on horses stolen from the Daltieri.

Bringing up the rear, Michael snickered.

Faelyn frowned. Apparently, with the return of Amerae's strength also came snarkiness. "Don't forget about the armories we broke into, and all those confiscated weapons we returned to the townspeople." She was just happy to finally be moving forward. Even if the only thing it ended in was her death, she'd taken a stand and was finally doing something worthy with her life.

The salty scent of sea air and the distant cry of gulls greeted them. Faelyn breathed it in deep, feeling more at ease. It'd been too long since she'd seen the sea.

Lined up in a row, they kept the horses at a slow walk down the steep trail that ran alongside craggy boulders and scraggly bushes that scratched at their legs. A cliff towered above them on one side, blocking their view of the ocean.

Michael, who rarely spoke due to some kind of deep reverence, said, "I'll be glad to be home. We've trained for this all our lives, Am, never thinking—but always hoping—it'd be us who live to see such times. I, for one, will be happy to be out of that hole and finally doing something." He caught Faelyn watching him from her saddle and averted his eyes—as if he expected to be rebuked for speaking out of turn.

Faelyn smiled to reassure him, but he didn't see. It was easy to sense his nervousness around her.

She'd been no one her whole life, even when she was a child and people knew who she was. Being in charge, being a leader, was going to be hard to get used to. She imagined a lot of pretending at first, playing the part of the great queen she wanted to be. This was her destiny. That didn't mean it came naturally. The people at Seaside Keep didn't know her, but they were about to. All of Thera was about to.

"I wish I'd gone back for the book." Amerae fidgeted in her saddle, and Faelyn raised an eyebrow. "The book, the History of Alysies, had your picture in it, describing you as King Isaac's daughter. Without it, I'm not sure how we'll convince anyone you're the true heir." She groaned. "All that history, gone! The book's probably in some ritualistic Daltieri bonfire now."

Faelyn had forgotten about the book in their hurry to leave. Such a tragedy.

She looked ahead as they approached a break in the brush and boulders. "I have a few things that might help."

"Like what?" Amerae asked.

Faelyn barely heard her. She stared down into the valley, lips parting. An army of thousands spanned along the base of a towering keep with the ocean beyond. A patchwork of tents with waving banners of blue and yellow lined in never-ending rows. Soldiers in leathers sat around cooking fires or trained in sword-to-sword combat. The distant clamor of swords and commands carried on the sea breeze to Faelyn's ears. A score of cavalry, more than Kian said was possible, stood mounted, as if readying for battle at that very moment.

"Oh no," Amerae groaned. "Father's called in the troops."

"Halt!" Five soldiers dressed in over-polished armor jumped out from behind boulders on the rocky path and surrounded them.

Impressive. Faelyn had been too intent on the sight before her to notice them lying in wait. Her small group raised their hands, showing they were unarmed. The soldiers took her reins, swords ready to attack if necessary.

Flickers of recognition passed among the soldiers.

"Am? Michael?" the tallest soldier asked. He dropped Faelyn's reins, then his face broke into a grin. "Where the hell have you two been? The whole army is preparing to rescue you, Am. They had to execute the overseers so they couldn't report us. Lord Calem is pissed!"

Amerae gasped. "The overseers are dead? There's no hiding this now. That stubborn... I can't believe he'd risk the army to save me." Amerae clenched her reins. Her horse sidestepped beneath her.

Faelyn nodded. "If he discovered you were captured, Amerae, he didn't have a choice. He'd have to assume Daltieri knew about Seaside."

The soldiers narrowed their eyes.

Amerae clenched her jaw, gaze flinty. "They tried their best, but I never talked."

"And who is this?" the shorter soldier asked, studying Faelyn. A helm hid his features, but she sensed his wariness.

"I am Faelyn Eva Rylandor, Queen of Alysies. Allow us passage so I may speak to Lord Calem." The words felt foreign on her tongue. The awkwardness of saying them tried to rise up and ruin her bravado, but she stared at the soldier with a steely glint, warning him not to challenge her claim or authority.

She was born to this, even if she'd spent her youth being denied it, and forever running from it. The title was rightfully hers, but to claim it now almost felt false. The people needed her—Amerae was right about that. The pitiful state of her kingdom could only lead to unsung heroes felling each other for power in the wake of any rebellion.

The tall soldier's sword drooped. He tilted his head toward Amerae.

"Let us pass, Rayber." Amerae sounded annoyed, but Faelyn sensed her fear of his resistance.

Rayber nodded slowly, then backed off the path. "Let them through."

The other soldiers stepped away until they disappeared behind the rocks—sentinels, ready for whoever should come this way. Faelyn had learned of their role and importance during her time with Donoven.

Rayber sheathed his sword. "I don't know what you've been up to, or what you think you found, but good luck to ya, Am. Michael. I wouldn't want to be in your shoes right now."

Amerae gave a tight smile, then they rode the rest of the way down the trail into the valley of the army. Hundreds of heads turned their way, but no one else tried to stop them. They gave their horses to a stablemaster at a dilapidated barn nowhere near big enough to house the cavalry seen from afar.

The castle itself was impressive, one of the biggest she'd seen in recent days. Though, that didn't mean much. Dark gray stone interrupted the empty sea sky. It was almost as she remembered from pictures, except there were rough patches over part of the slanted roof, lichen covering large swaths of the walls, and the landscaping had not been tended. Weeds took over the grass, and sculpted trees and bushes had long gone wild.

The three of them walked passed a pair of surprised guards flanking a large entry door and entered Seaside Keep.

"Trey! Marus!" Amerae embraced two young men who ran to meet her.

They were no doubt her elder brothers. They hugged her, checking her over for injuries, then stepped aside with a warning glance behind them.

A burly man with graying hair and a countenance of fury strode toward them. Large fists rigid at his sides, he breathed sharply through his clenched teeth set in a face so red with anger, it was nearly purple. His blue tunic and vest strained against his girth. Lord Calem. Calem's progeny, even if not in physical features or personality. The knowledge filled Faelyn with a twinge of sadness for her long-lost friend.

Michael hung back, trying his best to blend in with the wall. Amerae raised her chin and stared her father down, the epitome of someone ready to take whatever her father's anger wrought. The hint of fear beneath her brave veneer was palpable.

"Are you pleased with yourself, daughter?" Calem stopped a pace away. "Do you see what you nearly made me do?" He roared, sending echoes around the bare foyer. "An entire army assembled, ready to intervene and ruin everything, all for your ghost chase. How could a daughter of mine be so foolish? *How?*"

"Father." Trey stepped forward, hands raised. One dagger-sharp look from Calem stopped him.

Warning bells went off in Faelyn's mind. This was Calem's army, not hers. She needed him to fight in her name, not have the army divided or its leadership challenged. "Don't do anything you might regret, Lord Calem." Faelyn stepped to Amerae's side, hoping her age in years overshadowed her youthful look. She'd appear only a few years older than Amerae.

His eyes widened, then narrowed. "And who is this? The long-lost heir to the throne you nearly destroyed trying to find?"

Amerae started to speak, but Faelyn stopped her with a hand on her shoulder. "I do apologize for the trouble caused, but Amerae does not come back empty-handed. I am Queen Faelyn Eva Rylandor, long-ago friend of your forefather."

Calem's lips pushed out and down into a frown.

Faelyn used his angry silence to her advantage. "By my gift or curse, I've been given a long life. I was there the day my father, King Isaac, was murdered by a Daltieri prince. Now the time is right for me to come back, to fight for a free Alysies."

Calem glanced back and forth from Amerae, who held her breath. A slow smile spread on his face. "Ha! Haha!" He doubled over laughing in one of the worst displays of ignorant mockery Faelyn had ever seen.

Before he was done, Faelyn fished an object from her bag and held it in the air. When Calem dashed away fake tears and opened his eyes, the key given to her so long ago dangled in front of his face. Its thick brass finish unmarred by time, the ruby glinting in the handle.

Calem sobered immediately, going still with shock. "Where did you get that?" His tone lost all trace of anger and mirth. The words came out low and gravelly.

Amerae and her brothers locked eyes on the key, transfixed.

"Your forefather, Calem, gave it to me, the day he helped me escape from Pavora lest I be captured and killed by Daltieri soldiers in my own castle." She stared at him hard, holding the key between them and thanking the Fates it meant something to him. This man controlled an army raised in her kingdom's name. If he couldn't learn to trust her, the war was already lost.

He swallowed. "Give it to me."

Faelyn hesitated. She could easily get the key back if he tried to keep it, and it belonged to him anyway, so she passed it to him. He snatched it and turned it around and around in his hands. He held it up to a window, squinting, then tapped it on the wall. She wanted to ask what the key went to, but she feared Calem would see her lack of knowledge as evidence she stole it somehow.

Amerae's eyes were wide, glued to the key. Faelyn glanced at Michael, who shrugged.

“It’s the right shape.” Calem’s voice sounded hollow, dazed. "Follow me."

Faelyn followed, anxious to finally have some answers after all this time. Michael and Amerae trailed behind with her brothers. Faelyn got her first real look at the inside of the keep. The foyer ceiling went at least two stories high, with a simple candle chandelier and arched windows letting in meager light. The space was free of any grand tapestries or ornamentation, but for one threadbare rug on the floor. It was clear every coin went to funding the massive army and none of it wasted on frivolity.

They ascended a double staircase leading to a balcony overlooking the foyer, then down a long hall with wood flooring and stacked stone walls. Clean, but ancient lamps provided minimal lighting. At the end of the hall, Calem entered a set of doors leading into what must be his personal office. It was overflowing with papers, books, and maps. A cluttered wooden desk sat near an empty hearth.

Calem walked to a table by the curtained window. It was covered with a dusty cloth and mounds of clutter—a lamp, quill, loose papers and books, and a small statue of a couple embracing, probably a remnant of décor before whoever had spent the effort just gave up.

To Faelyn's surprise, Calem swept his arm across the table, knocking all the items to the floor. Books tumbled and glass shattered. Faelyn imagined the porcelain couple now in pieces and pursed her lips. Then Calem ripped the cloth off the table. Dust flew into the air in a thick cloud, then cleared to reveal a padlocked chest.

Calem looked at the key. He stuck it in the lock and turned. The padlock clicked open. Calem faced them slowly with a gaping mouth. He'd gone from red to shocked white. He stumbled, and Faelyn reached out to steady him.

Amerae's brow furrowed in evident confusion. "Father?"

"I can't believe it's possible, but the key is genuine." Calem fiddled with the lock. "This doesn't prove anything."

So he wasn’t convinced she was telling the truth. It was almost satisfying he didn't believe her to be who she said she was just yet—the mark of a good leader. The only evidence he'd seen was a key, a key that could have come from anywhere.

"Let's see what's in that chest." Faelyn did not smile, and her heart pounded, eager and excited to have the mystery solved. Calem was a proud man and might view her smile as a mark of youth, rather than joy.

Calem held the key up to the light. "The chest has been sitting here a long time. I remember asking about it as a child, testing different keys, but nothing ever fit. It’s never been opened. My father told me I couldn’t without the key.”

"You always told us the same,” Amerae said. “Open it, Father,"

Calem slipped the lock from the clasp. He leaned his weight into the lid, and it protested with a loud creak. Faelyn edged closer to see inside. The top was a layer of papers, crinkled and yellowed with age. Calem pushed them aside to reveal heaping stacks of gold bars.

"Acantha above," Calem whispered. "This could fund the entire battle."

Faelyn didn't look at the gold for long. A drawing, half hidden under other papers, featured a girl with long hair and pointed ears. She gently pulled the paper out, revealing a picture of her, decades ago and looking exactly the same. She hadn’t realized Calem could draw. Tears prickled her eyes as the drawing touched something deep within her heart.

Calem pointed with shaking fingers. "That's you. This is signed by my ancestor, Calem the First." He stepped backward, hand outstretched behind him until he found a chair and slumped into it.

The rest of the group crowded in.

"Queen Faelyn, look." Amerae pointed to another yellowed paper.

It was a letter. Faelyn reached for it. The ink had faded considerably, and it was hard to make out as she read aloud.

"To my son, Richard,

You of all people know the hardships we've secretly endured, trying to win back our freedom. I am dying, Richard. I know you don't believe she lives, but I've never lost hope that our queen survived and will come back to us. It is my dying wish you seal up the gold we hid from King Samual, along with this letter, to give to Faelyn or her children when they come calling. She'll need it more than we do. I'm sorry I let my life be consumed by the need to fight our oppressors. You were named after a great man who served two great kings in his lifetime. He died defending our kingdom and never compromised what he believed in, and so will I. I hope one day you'll understand. I hope one day you'll forgive me.

Love, Calem"

Faelyn let the paper fall from her fingers. The room was stunned into silence.

Oh, Calem. You never gave up. You've saved me twice now.

He'd devoted his whole life to Alysies, and she'd barely ever spoken to him. She couldn't allow his efforts to be wasted.

Lord Calem stood, shoving his chair back. "If you're our rightful queen, the same Faelyn born to Queen Eva and King Isaac of old, just where have you been all this time? All these years and not even a word from you?" His voice rose, becoming more heated with each breath.

She didn't interrupt, nor did she give into the temptation to flinch under his anger. Because it was true. No one judged her more harshly than she judged herself. She bore every word looking straight into his eyes.

His arms swiped through the air with his words. "Daltieri has dealt out death and destruction, destroying the memory of our proud kingdom. Many alive don't even know the name Alysies, and those that do are afraid of it! Our people are little more than slaves to their whims. And where has our queen been hiding? Living a pampered life holed up with a mighty noble somewhere?"

"Father," Amerae said through clenched teeth.

Calem closed his mouth, then waved for Faelyn to speak.

She took a slow breath, disguising the shakiness. "You have every right to be upset with me. All of you do. I let you down."

Her gaze drifted to the chest of gold, but she forced it back up. "I'll tell you my story not as an excuse for my absence, but as confirmation of my resolve. I left at Calem's urging, pursued by Daltieri soldiers. I sought refuge in Creadel where the enemy nearly discovered me. I was young and naive, and I let my fear and the pain of all I'd lost overshadow who I am. When I finally returned to Alysies and saw the devastation firsthand, I trained for a future I only hoped might one day exist. Then I found Amerae, or in truth, she found me."

Faelyn exchanged a small smile with her. "Alysies needs a leader to bring the kingdom together. That role is mine by birth. Even as I claim it, I vow to spend the rest of my life earning it. Making up for my past mistakes. Making up for my father's past mistakes. I am the rightful queen of Alysies, and I will not falter, nor fail my people again."

Calem shook his head. "You'd use the glory of my army? That my people have given everything for, to raise your good name as queen?"

From the corner of Faelyn's eye, Amerae balked, raising an arm in protest. Her brothers and Michael hung back, bodies tensed for a fight.

Faelyn clenched her fists, taking a step forward. "It is not your place to deny me the throne, Lord Calem." Her magic begged for release, but this wasn't the time. She had to win his allegiance without force or fear. She needed his army, but she'd find a way to win without it if possible. So long as he didn't stand in her way.

He narrowed his eyes. "I may believe you are the lost princess, but you're not queen, not fit to rule. And how would you even begin to earn it? You can't." His words whipped through the small space between them, cutting right into her worst insecurities.

She straightened her shoulders. "An army from Creadel, amassed in my name, will arrive here in a week. Five thousand soldiers, two thousand cavalry, and most important, fifty mages."

Calem's mouth tightened. Gasps from the others filled the room. Trey and Marus exchanged excited grins. Amerae crossed her arms in smug triumph.

Faelyn lifted her chin in silent victory over this small feat. "When the two armies join together, we stand a chance—a real chance—of taking back our kingdom." Her emotions swept away with her words, and she allowed a small glow to surround her.

A little bit of a show wouldn't hurt. It was nothing compared to what she would show them later.

Calem inhaled, stepping away.

She willed her voice softer. "As your daughter said, we cannot come together unless united under one ruler. I will not allow my past mistakes to divide us and ruin our only chance for redemption. I am your rightful queen."

The small light reflected off his awed face in the dark space. He quickly wiped the expression away. "We'll see." It was a start.

Faelyn looked to Amerae, whose tears had spilled over her cheeks. "Daltieri knows my face and my claim, and there's no way they haven't seen my army coming. The enemy has been forewarned. We must plan our attack and be ready to march by the time the soldiers arrive, or risk having them call for more troops from the north." She paused to watch the calculating wheels turn behind Calem's eyes. "They know what it will mean that I've returned."

Calem cleared his throat. "We have maps detailing scout reports on enemy movement. Let's get started."

Already trying to take charge. This was going to be harder than she thought, but Donoven had warned her it would be. The next part would be the true test of the limits to Calem's tolerance.

"In the morning," Faelyn began, "I'll expect you to present me, and swear fealty in front of the army which, forgive me for being blunt, will become my army, under your command."

She watched him, unblinking. Could he acquiesce his rule to a young woman he just met based on a key and a tattered drawing?

The room held its breath.

Calem's chin lifted, and his fists clenched. He stood rooted in place, his face turning red, then purple. His chest puffed up, holding in the outburst he so clearly longed to unleash.

If ever there was a hurdle to taking back her throne, it was this man. Faelyn knew what she was asking—no, demanding. This was his army, an army his ancestors had fought and scraped for. They worked all their lives, generation after generation under the constant fear of discovery with punishment of death. And she just told him to hand it over. If he didn't, a civil war would be next.

"Father, I spoke to Lord Kian Foster myself," Amerae said. "You know his army is real."

"It makes sense," Marus, the oldest son, said. "You once sought someone of noble Alysian blood to have a rallying point. Well, now we do."

No doubt she wasn't the rallying point Calem had in mind. She wasn't someone he could control.

They all watched intently as Calem's red face slowly cleared and his posture loosened.

He appeared to be considering it, but Faelyn sensed his adamant resistance.

He grunted and spoke through gritted teeth. "We haven't come so far because I'm an ignorant man."

"Let go of your stubborn pride, Father," Trey said, then winced. "You can't deny who she is, just like our people won't."

Calem growled at his younger son. "If we win this war, I want a place in the new court, a place of position and power."

Smart man. "Of course, Lord Calem. You will retain your lordship status over Seaside Keep and all its holdings, in addition to anything seized by Daltieri since their invasion. If you desire a higher position, then you must earn it. Through my good graces."

Calem stared, fingers rubbing together, studying her as if he couldn't believe those words came out of her youthful mouth. His jaw clenched.

Faelyn stepped toward him. "I appreciate the delicacy of the situation, but we must be able to trust each other. We are working together toward a mutual goal, a free Alysies. I will not be caught up in a game of political pandering while we have bigger issues to contend with."

Calem turned away from her.

Her temper flared, but she tamped it down. "I will give you and your family privacy. Come, Michael." Though Michael hid it well, Faelyn felt his profound relief at leaving.

The air outside the office was cool, free of the heat of repressed anger. Faelyn sighed, suddenly exhausted.

Amerae's mother and a servant waited down the hall. Michael excused himself, and Faelyn was shown to a room, sparse, but clean. They mercifully left her to rest. The bed was twice as big as her bed at Thomats, with soft sheets and fluffy pillows. She fell into the bed, replaying her conversation with Calem.

She'd done the best she could. He was as stubborn as his daughter, but she was glad he hadn't let her off easy for abandoning her kingdom. She'd never be done paying that debt.

It didn't escape her attention that Calem hadn't agreed to swear fealty to her.

She'd earn his allegiance somehow.

CHAPTER FORTY

The next morning, Faelyn arose with the sun, its rays just peaking over the distant valley through her window and chasing away the morning fog.

Tossing open the small wardrobe, she chewed her lip. What to wear? A borrowed gown to look the part of a queen? A soldier's uniform?

Through her father's lack of effort during his reign, he'd taught her one thing—image was everything. She had to set herself apart from everyone. This would be a pivotal day, as she expected every day in the foreseeable future to be.

A gown then.

She borrowed one from Amerae's mother. The servant referred to it as "old fashioned." Its burgundy velvet lacked adornment, but fit well enough for the purpose with only minor pinning. The neckline scooped only just below her collarbone, as she preferred.

For the first time in a long time, Faelyn fixed her hair as she wanted to, without having to pin it *just so* to hide her long ears. She worked the comb through the strands, smoothing it and gently working out the tangles with her fingers. The motions sent her chest aching with memory. Once, it was Mary's hands helping her with such loving care. "Wear your differences with pride," she said. Faelyn smiled. Mary would be proud of her today.

Surrounded by the memory of Mary's love, Faelyn finished sweeping her hair up and back, exposing her neck and ears.

Once dressed, Faelyn took four things from her bag for her presentation to the army: her mother's ring, her turquoise necklace, the royal crest ring, and her father's circlet, which sat securely on her head thanks to her hair plaited in place. It was only right both her parents be with her.

She held her skirt, pretending to be the fine lady she was not, and walked regally down the steps into the foyer. Calem, in his general's attire of polished steel with double blue braids, waited for her. He stood beside his wife and sons, and a cleaned-up Amerae who looked striking in a green silk dress with billowing skirts. Faelyn smoothed down the plainness of her dress.

Their eyes snapped to the circlet on her head, and the blue Rylandor sapphire. A slow smile spread on Amerae's face, quickly becoming a grin as she glanced at her parents.

Then, everyone bowed at the waist, servants, guards, and soldiers alike—everyone except Calem. Faelyn's hurt lurched. Maybe she could actually do this.

Faelyn nodded as if she was above it all—*hardly.* She used a bit of water magic, cheating really, to form shimmering ice crystals in whorling patterns on her skirt and bodice.

There, not so plain anymore.

She followed them outside to a landing positioned up the stairs from the valley. It was a clear day, the sun already warming the air though it was yet morning. Seagulls cawed in the distance, and a breeze brought the salty scent of the ocean. The army was assembled in row upon row of soldiers at attention. The sight was astonishing. Faelyn gulped, hoping her eyes weren't as round with panic as they felt and that her hands remained steady.

The emotions swirling from the men and women before her

ranged from many things, but the underlying feeling was hope. Whispers continued amongst the clink of armor.

"They say she's our queen. Look at her crown."

"Alive all this time?"

"The commander's daughter found her."

"I don't believe it. It's a hoax."

"Look at her ears! It's really her!"

Calem stepped to the railing. Faelyn held back, waiting for him to announce her. All those faces, all turned toward her, curious and hopeful. She willed her knees to steady and her heart to slow, rehearsing in her mind what she'd say.

"Today," Calem began in as loud a voice as possible without screaming, "our cause has taken a drastic step forward. We are not alone in our efforts. We've received word, and plans are now underway to take back what is ours."

The soldiers cheered, their voices echoing over the castle walls.

Calem waited patiently for them to finish. "A legion of allies will soon arrive. We are to treat them as such. They will help us with our cause. The time for redemption is near." He scanned the ranks. "Dismissed."

There was an awkward silence before the captains repeated the order, and the soldiers reluctantly broke formation.

Calem left the balcony without acknowledging her, and without giving her the chance to speak.

Defeat and crushing embarrassment washed over her, leaving her feeling ridiculous in her fancy golden crown.

The line had been drawn, and she was on the wrong side.

The following days passed by in quick succession. Faelyn barely had time for sleep. When she wasn't with Calem, poring over maps and reports on enemy movement—Amerae's rescue had certainly sent them moving—she met with the generals in groups and individually, winning them over with her fae charm and gaining their insight. In between, she monitored the soldiers' training, offering tips to the captains and encouraging specific soldiers by name when she could.

Heads turned to follow her wherever she went, so she held her chin up, bearing the confidence her rank and skill afforded her. She didn't reprimand Calem for what he'd done. It wouldn't help, and it was only a matter of time before she'd convince him there was no alternative. She couldn't deny the excitement that grew within her every passing day. This would be *her* army, and their moment to shape history forever.

Calem was at least beginning to trust that she knew what she was talking about when it came to strategy, though she often deferred to his good judgment. Her training was no match for his real-world experience. Relinquishing some of the control to him seemed to help his attitude toward her.

One afternoon, she spoke with General Huntington, a ruthless, but loyal man who'd escaped a difficult childhood in the fields and bore the scars to prove it. Leaving his tent, she passed his training soldiers and was shocked to see Amerae and Michael going blade-to-blade. They had a thin ring of spectators, grinning and cheering them on. Sweat rolled down their faces, but the undeniable glint in their eyes spoke volumes. They enjoyed the thrill of the fight. And they were *good*. She stepped closer to watch.

Faelyn had never asked Amerae about her life, assuming as the daughter of a lord, she'd spent her time on the political side of the war, meeting dignitaries and gaining allies. She should have known better. Calem's life's work was this army, and Amerae was his daughter. Faelyn knew all too well the feeling of wanting to earn a disapproving father's approval.

Amerae and Michael circled each other wearing identical smirks of confidence. Quick as lightning, Amerae struck out. Michael rushed to counter her hit. The clang of steel kept time to their fast pace and heavy breathing. Amerae jerked back, narrowly avoiding a slice across her armored abdomen. She lunged, striking Michael in the side with her blunt blade, winning her the match.

The gathered soldiers cheered. Amerae grinned and bowed, exchanging a look with Michael. Faelyn couldn't help the pleased smile on her face. She'd identified half a dozen errors in Amerae's form, but that was dozens less than the average soldier.

Faelyn drew her sword, happy to be wearing trousers and leather armor. "Amerae."

The soldiers jumped and parted—bowing slightly, Faelyn noted with no small satisfaction. She stepped forward into the ring.

Michael grinned in anticipation and backed up to join the growing group of onlookers. Amerae bowed with delight.

"You're very good, Amerae. I had no idea. Daltieri would be quaking in fear if they knew how skilled this army is." Appreciative cheers and backslapping broke out among the men and women watching. Faelyn raised her sword in the air, an invitation. "I can make you better."

Amerae smirked good-naturedly. "We'll see." She tapped Faelyn's sword, and the duel began.

Faelyn waited, sword raised, watching the impressively subtle shifts in Amerae's movements as she tensed to attack. Amerae flinched to feint left, then struck right. Faelyn countered, then parried. The dance took off in a whirlwind of blows and shuffling feet. Her heart sang with the thrill of a challenge.

Amerae's movements were slower, weighed down by her inexperience, but not by much. The blows hit impressively strong. Faelyn found herself truly working not to be injured. She'd been tempted, but so far avoided using any magic in self-defense.

The crowd cheered when Amerae's blade nearly chopped off Faelyn's arm. She twisted away and blocked. Then they cheered even louder when Faelyn slashed at Amerae's ankles. She jumped right over the blade. Faelyn barely withheld using wind to knock her to the ground. Her training with sword and magic was second nature now, and she actively focused on not using it.

The bout went on, and Amerae tired. Soon she wouldn't be able to defend against the barrage of blows Faelyn laid out for her. Faelyn struck repeatedly, purposefully. Amerae blocked the hits with fierce determination, no longer able to go on offense. She backed up until she almost reached the edge of the ring.

Amerae gritted her teeth, eyes darting for an opening. In a final, desperate move, she flinched, feinted left, then struck right, only to receive Faelyn's sword biting into her forearm.

To the credit of Amerae's strength, training, and stubborn determination, only a quiet hiss of air escaped her teeth. She recovered and continued the fight.

Faelyn grunted against the attack. "Good, Amerae. Very well done."

The soldiers cheered, but the fire did not leave Amerae's eyes. Blood dripped from her wound to soak into the soil.

They locked swords. When Amerae was off-balance, Faelyn threw her backward. The girl stumbled several steps, sword and arms flailing.

"Enough." Faelyn raised her sword in the air. "I concede." The wound needed tending.

Amerae's temper was at its peak. Faelyn was pleased to see her hone her anger as a weapon but now was not the time. Amerae charged, sword held in both hands, hilt tucked to her side, point forward like a battering ram. A second before she connected, Faelyn jumped, flipping high over Amerae's head, then twisting in the air. She landed facing Amerae's back where she was stumbling, having expected to run Faelyn through.

Faelyn smacked the flat side of her blade on Amerae's shoulder. Amerae cursed and threw down her sword. The soldiers went insane, money exchanged hands, but Faelyn ignored them. She hadn't meant to upset Amerae. She'd forgotten how temperamental youth could be.

"Amerae, look at me." Faelyn sheathed her sword and stepped closer.

The girl turned, head bowed. When she looked up, her eyes shone strikingly gold in the paleness of her face. Her anger slowly left as Faelyn stared into her, saying nothing. Her sleeve was now good and bloody. Amerae's face went white. She took a single step and collapsed.

Faelyn lunged and caught her, slowly lowering her to the ground.

"Fetch a healer!" someone shouted.

Amerae gripped Faelyn's arms. "I'm sorry, my queen. I shouldn't have lost my temper. I'm ashamed."

Faelyn smiled. "I have that same temper at times." She placed her hand casually against the gash in Amerae's arm. "You're tough, Amerae, and very skilled. Your father should have made you captain long ago, a problem I will remedy shortly. But first." As before, a white glow emitted from Faelyn's palm, healing the wound beneath the sleeve.

The gathering crowd cried out in surprise, stumbling against each other. As the white light flared out, color returned to Amerae's face, and silence descended over the crowd.

Faelyn stood, taking Amerae's hand and hauling her up. Amerae pushed her sleeve up high to reveal the dried blood and healed wound, nothing but a pink line. Cheers broke out among the soldiers. They pointed and shouted, pumping fists in the air. Their captains, some of whom had attended, barked them back to whatever task they'd been shirking. They scattered in a thunderous retreat.

Beside General Huntington's tent in the distance, Lord Calem and his sons—both generals in the army—watched the scene unfold. Michael came to her side, and they walked with Amerae back to the keep.

Faelyn let the soldiers' enthusiasm fade behind her. "Be mindful of your temper, Amerae, lest it distracts you. As I well know. And on the battlefield, as well as off, remember not to flinch before you feint. Bluff with full confidence. It will serve you well."

She sounded like Swordmaster Donoven, so serious and formal. But that was the role she had to play now. She hoped he'd be proud.

"Thank you, my queen. I've never fought anyone with your skill before. You move so fast." There was more jealousy than awe in Amerae's tone. Amerae had kept things more formal between them since they'd returned, but maybe that was best. At least for now.

"I've had many years to perfect my technique. And all for Alysies. Let's hope it proves to be enough."

CHAPTER FORTY-ONE

The next day, Faelyn was distracted. Kian drew closer. Though it was hard to know how close, she felt it. She could have put on his ring and asked, but the thought made her gut clench. She paced her room, eyeing her wardrobe. Her choices were limited to a travel outfit, a simple dress, and her new fighting leathers, but it took a quarter-hour to choose what to wear.

Faelyn sighed and snatched the dress. She could ask for more, had been offered more, but what was the point? The dress would remain here when their armies marched into battle. There'd be no use for dresses.

She might as well make a good first impression with Kian's army. With Kian as their leader, they likely already knew who she was. *He must pay them well.* Creadel had no part in this fight, had never done anything against Daltieri other than shore up their own border, and the soldiers couldn't have come from Alysies.

A servant helped Faelyn with her hair and the buttons on the dress, tsking at the plainness once more. Faelyn fitted her father's circlet—her circlet—to her head. Hair pinned up, her ears were more prominent than ever in the mirror. Her face was still youthful and unchanged, but not her eyes. The weight of all she'd endured and the knowledge she'd acquired rested in her eyes. Not by shadows or wrinkles, but a subtle encumbrance in the turquoisey-green, and the way her face held a stern expression that mirrored the way she felt —resolute.

She blinked and marched out of the room. No one waited to follow and obey her commands, as she remembered them doing for her father. They didn't treat her like their queen. They looked at her with awe and respect, they followed her leadership and guidance, but she had yet to completely win them over.

Faelyn approached a guard in the foyer. He didn't move from his post, but bowed his head. "Inform Lord Calem the rest of my army approaches. Send a runner to alert the generals."

The guard only hesitated for a moment. "Yes, Your Majesty." He bowed again and took off.

Faelyn stood in place, blinking in surprise. No one had addressed her by that title, the same title her father carried all those years ago. But she wouldn't make his same mistakes. She wasn't above her people. She was one of them.

Faelyn stood on the front landing while the sun rose higher in the clear sky, forgetting to eat, strategize, or politicize under the weight of the knowledge that Kian drew closer. Calem must have believed her because he had his army amassed in front of the castle, dressed in full armor, ready to make an impressive greeting for Kian.

Finally, a horn sounded, signaling the army had been spotted. An hour later, Faelyn watched from the window as their banners of blue and silver rose above the distant crest, furrowing in the wind.

Blue and silver. Alysian colors.

A smile played on her lips, even as her heart raced. The army gleamed with polished steel, marching in step in perfect lines. More and more soldiers came over the hill making for a show everyone stopped to see. Faelyn didn't notice Amerae, Calem, and Michael had joined her until Amerae brushed against her.

Then, there he was. Mage staff in hand, he rode hard, cutting a line through the ranks to reach the front of the line and his generals. Even from this distance across the field, he looked unusual out of his mage robe. He wore armor to match the rest of his army, as did the mages he brought with him, riding at the rear with their staffs.

As Kian approached the keep, he removed his helmet, revealing loose ebony hair nearly down to his shoulders. He stared at Faelyn with a joyful gleam in his hazel eyes. She wanted to return it, but was frozen where she stood. She'd wronged him, even if it was for the right reasons. Yet he'd remained a loyal friend. He'd accomplished so much in the short time they'd been apart. And it was all for her.

Lord Calem stopped in the doorway. It was unmistakable when his breath caught in his throat. He scanned the horizon at the leagues of soldiers in their shimmering armor. Faelyn studied him until he finally drew his awed gaze from the horizon. She sensed hope and begrudging respect from him before he descended the stairs to greet Kian.

The Alysian soldiers parted for the two lords. Calem and Kian bowed, then shook hands. After introducing each other, they exchanged pleasantries, but Faelyn didn't listen for the pounding in her ears. Why was she so nervous? When Kian's vast army finished gathering, he finally focused back on her. He smiled and ascended the stairs, shaking his head. She sensed his happiness, and none of the sadness or anger she'd expected.

When he reached the landing, he dropped to one knee. Then so did his entire army. The clink and scrape of armor as thousands kneeled at once stole her breath away and thawed her limbs. Their movements were so precise as to be rehearsed.

"Queen Faelyn Eva Rylandor of Alysies." Kian spoke loud enough for all to hear. His mage crystal glowed. "I bring you your army and swear featly to you as my queen. I testify that I, with my own eyes, have witnessed your unchanging grace and beauty. The Fates have prepared us for these times, and you are the chosen one to lead us to victory."

Her chest swelled, tears stinging her eyes. This was all a dream.

From the side of her eye, Calem twitched, then approached the railing. “The rumors are true. Our queen has returned to us. I stand before you to testify the truthfulness of who she is. Daughter of King Isaac Rylandor, she is Queen Faelyn of Alysies!"

Excited whispers rushed through his army. Faelyn was afraid to breathe for fear of shattering this new reality.

Calem grunted down to one knee and bowed his head. "I, Lord Calem Kinsman of Seaside Keep, swear fealty to you, Queen Faelyn of Alysies. My army is yours to command, to win back our kingdom."

Like a wave in the sea, one by one the Alysian soldiers followed, lowering to their knees. Faelyn spotted Michael on the front row, smiling, and sensed indescribable joy from Amerae behind her.

Faelyn closed her eyes, forcing the tears loose. Alysies needed this moment. She needed this moment. It wasn’t a dream. It was a beginning.

Bending down to place a hand on Calem’s shoulder, Faelyn smiled. She stepped past Kian to the banister overlooking the amassed soldiers. Thousands of men and women kneeled before her, watching her in silence with bated breath. She scanned their faces. Some were very young, no more than fifteen or so. Interspaced among them were their generals and captains, identifiable by the blue braids on their shoulders.

And all were ready to die for a better world at her command.

Her hands gripped the stone banister. The only sound was the fluttering of the banners in the breeze and the distant waves crashing against the jagged cliff below.

And Faelyn's heart as it beat for her people.

She filled her lungs with sea air. "Rise."

Thousands stood at her command. Above any skill with a blade, or any magic she wielded, the power at her disposal dizzied her. She'd never dreamed she would see this day. Kian's pride radiating from behind affected her more than the score of eyes trained on her. With great effort, she didn't look at him.

She knew what he saw; Ali, the simple mage in a black robe with a unique power, the girl he'd asked to marry, now a queen on the brink of battle. Faelyn could hardly believe she'd come so far, and all thanks to those who loved and believed in her.

Donoven had given her tips on how to give speeches, what to say, how to keep her head high and gaze locked onto her people. When she spoke, she sent her words on the wind to carry to the furthest soldier, so it would seem she stood beside them.

"Nearly one hundred years ago, Daltieri invaded our kingdom, murdered my family, and stole what was rightfully mine. And what was rightfully yours. With the help of Lord Calem's ancestor, I was able to flee. I harbored the hope, but not the means, to one day battle for a free Alysies."

Commotion advanced through the ranks.

Faelyn nodded. "You know that name. It calls to you, even as it has been forbidden to you. Because Daltieri has worked hard to strike our once free and prosperous kingdom from our hearts and memories, but they did not succeed. I look across your faces, you who've worked your whole lives for this opportunity, proof of Daltieri's failure."

Her voice rose with raw emotion finally fighting its way free. "Now we have come together on this day to wage war against a formidable enemy. Indeed, Daltieri is a force to be reckoned with. For decades, they've stripped Alysies of its riches and spirit, and made themselves strong." A grumble rippled across the valley. "But no longer." She took a deep breath. The magic came easily to bolster her words. "Together we will take back what is ours, and rid Alysies of its oppressors!"

The roar was deafening, shaking the ground where she stood. Faelyn grinned with wild enthusiasm, taking in the assembled soldiers. She gave a quick nod in Kian's direction, then walked into the keep without a backward glance, the cheers still crashing over the castle walls. Calem and Kian followed, in addition to their most trusted advisors and a host of guards and servants.

Well into the foyer, Faelyn turned. "Lord Calem."

Calem blinked, hesitating for the barest second. "Yes, Your Majesty?" He came to her side, and she suppressed the thrill that went through her. He wouldn't deny her as queen now.

"Have someone see to it that the Creadel army is well received by our soldiers. They'll need those fresh supplies and to be directed to their designated area to camp for the night. I will inform Lord Kian of our plans until you return."

"Yes, Your Majesty." He inclined his head, not even gritting his teeth this time, and headed back out the door.

"Lord Kian, if you'll follow me." She didn't meet his eyes—couldn't. Not yet. Not when they had an audience.

Still, the heat of his intense focus remained as he followed her up the stairs and through the long hall into Calem's office, which was now a war room. She requested refreshments from the attending servant, who nodded and left. Faelyn closed the door and remained facing it, taking deep breaths. They were alone.

Her heart pounded, and she fought to get it under control. Speaking in front of thousands of people didn't bother her, but this? He didn't seem hurt or angry still, yet he should be. It felt as if they'd never parted, as if that horrible memory of her ending their relationship had never happened. She turned around to Kian's smiling eyes. It was the most natural thing to go to him, and he embraced her with open arms.

"Ah, Faelyn. You look just as beautiful as when I left. It feels like so much time has passed, yet it's been nothing at all." Kian's baritone voice vibrated through her, and he sighed in contentment.

His hug warmed her to her bones. She rested her head against his armored shoulder. His presence chased her nerves away, but the stirrings she once felt for him did not take their place. She saw him for his soul, for the core of who he was—a friend.

She lifted her head and met his gaze. He loved her still, that much was clear by the warmth in his face and countenance. When his eyes dropped to her mouth, she stepped away. "How are you?"

"How did you expect me to be?" Some of the ice she expected crept into his tone.

Faelyn cringed.

"I knew I'd see you again and get the chance to prove that who you are changes nothing." He studied her. "I've turned myself into what you needed most, but didn't know to ask for. I see it in your eyes, your parting lips, that you want to interrupt and tell me you don't feel the same. That's all right." He clenched his fists, his gaze momentarily flinty. "I'll fight by your side to see those who hurt you pay for what they've done."

His words were hard to bear. She held her hands out in a helpless gesture. "You were supposed to move on, Kian, and forget about me. I didn't want you to hurt or give up your dreams." Her lips trembled with the effort to lock in her emotions.

"I know." Kian's mouth turned up in a gentle smile. He pushed a loose lock of Faelyn's hair behind her ear. "I know you meant no harm, darling. I don't blame you. One thing life has taught me is that dreams can change as we grow. My dream became bigger than just myself. Bigger than you, even. When you are on the throne, Alysies will flourish again. Trade with Creadel will resume, and the threat of a Daltieri invasion will cease. This is how I convinced my king to allow my army to grow unchecked within Creadel. He's turned a blind eye in exchange for this chance."

His words took Faelyn off guard. Was he being sincere? Or was he simply saying what she needed to hear to feel less guilty? Either way, it didn't matter. People changed as they learned more from life. She herself began as a young, naive child, desperately seeking her father's love, to a fugitive on the run, afraid of her past and destiny, and hiding away. Now she embraced that destiny with open arms. What would become of her next?

"You seem so sure we will win." She didn't dare sound hopeful.

Kian walked to the desk, peering at the maps marked with Daltieri's known compounds in Alysies. He took a quill and dabbed it in fresh ink, then drew X's over the compounds in the south. "My army was attacked by random Daltieri patrols and squadrons many times on our trek here, always we tracked them back to their base. We were fortunate to have crossed Border Wood completely before the first attack. Did you notice how we are armored?"

Faelyn's cheeks warmed. "Alysian blue and silver. Nothing to tie you back to Creadel."

"We are an Alysian army now, my queen." Kian set down the quill. "As I was unable to contact you since you never put on the ring after ordering us to march, I took the liberty of eradicating Daltieri's southern compounds as we traveled northwest to Seaside. Squads of my soldiers attacked and drove out or defeated all those I've marked. Some squads have not returned, but I expect them by the time we break camp tomorrow." He came around and sat on the edge of the desk. "I noticed you didn't announce where we are marching. Spies?"

Faelyn crossed her arms. The slight weight of the circlet pressed on her head. "I am always concerned about that. Our perimeter guard has already captured a pair of scouts in Daltieri armor. Their scouts died in the skirmish." She looked away, thinking of Calem. "I don't have the complete support of the army. Though I doubt any would betray the cause."

"I have a guess where we are going, but why don't you go ahead and tell me."

Boots in the hall signaled Calem's approach. Faelyn squared her shoulders just before he knocked. Kian stood from the edge of the desk as Calem and a servant pushing a cart of tea and sweetmeats entered the room.

Faelyn nodded to Calem. "We march for Pavora." She pointed to the drawing of a castle in the middle of Alysies. "That is where Lord Jamison resides and where his loyal Daltieri subjects send the collected taxes before they are transported back to King Seber. After studying the information Lord Calem and his predecessors have carefully collected, we have devised a plan. We drive Daltieri out of Pavora, then afterward, we use the army to cut off their trade routes to Alysies and deal with the local militia skirmishes that will ensue.

Daltieri was once dependent on our seaports and rich timber reserves. They've taken both of those, and I intend to see them restored."

"But first, Pavora." Calem interceded.

Kian took a slow sip of tea, watching Calem over the rim of his cup. Faelyn knew that look and his intent. He was weighing Calem's worth and loyalty. "What are the details, Your Majesty?"

They'd been busy this past week planning and preparing. The fact that Calem had already been ready for battle—loading supplies and sending out scouts for information—because of Amerae's capture had worked to their advantage.

"Lord Calem's knowledge has been invaluable. The scouts have reported increased activity in Pavora. The city is evacuating, for which I am glad, but more Daltieri soldiers from the nearby compounds are piling in. By the time we arrive in a few weeks, they will outnumber us. Even so, we believe we will have the best advantage if we divide. It's not standard tactical procedure, and Daltieri won't expect it, especially now that it's been undoubtedly reported you have joined us here."

"Yes, that could work." Kian nodded his approval.

Faelyn beamed. "The main entrance to the stronghold is to the west. There are two outer walls before you reach the castle." Faelyn pointed at the map.

Calem cleared his throat.

She looked up. "Lord Calem?"

"There is only one wall now, Your Majesty. Daltieri dismantled one of the walls to make room for their garrison about seven decades ago."

Faelyn raised an eyebrow.

Calem watched Kian, weighing him as much as he was being weighed. "When the fall of Alysies happened so fast, it was determined the cause was due to limited onsite troops to respond to an immediate threat. The garrison was erected to keep the army nearby. There is only one wall to breach before reaching the castle."

Kian sniffed and wandered toward the window. In the valley beyond, his army made camp.

Faelyn looked back to the map. "Well, good. I have some ideas of how we will get through the wall. Also, there is a tunnel on the very southern edge of the city that will lead to the castle gardens, if it hasn't collapsed. It's good enough to sneak a small contingent in, but that's all. I will remain with the army. Once we're in, I know my way around."

Calem glanced up sharply. "Faelyn, er, Your Majesty. We discussed this. As queen, as the person who will hold us together should we win, it's best if you remain at base camp outside of Pavora and out of danger."

Kian swiveled to meet Faelyn's gaze and smirked.

Oh, it was so nice to have someone who understood. Kian knew she would never stand back as others died for the cause, just as he recognized Calem wasn't entirely ready to relinquish control. Or glory.

As Calem was looking straight at her, Faelyn hid her smile. "I highly value your opinions in all things, Lord Calem, and will take them into consideration when making hard decisions regarding my army and my kingdom. But as I've told you before," she stepped closer, "I will be on the front lines. My presence will be essential to our victory."

The tension eased from her shoulders when Calem immediately bowed his head. "Yes, Your Majesty."

Kian nodded his approval.

Despite Calem's resistance, Faelyn found she liked him. Respected him. He could have fought her right to rule until the bitter end, but though it wasn't without difficulty, he saw reason and chose what was best for Alysies. That, more than anything, proved his loyalties were in the right place.

The rest of the day was a whirlwind. The generals and commanders of both armies met with Faelyn in the grand dining hall to discuss plans. They called it *grand* because it was one of the only finely decorated rooms in the keep, with a long polished oak table and hanging tapestries disguising the grey stone walls.

Afterward, Faelyn walked the camp, greeting and examining the new army. Kian's soldiers wore expensive armor—one piece that snapped together with hinges, leaving little room for the enemy to find purchase. Upon leaving the keep, two guards bowed and took a position behind her, bringing an amused smile to her lips. They were beginning to take her seriously.

Her studies had taught her that without enough food, their army wouldn't last. Lack of provisions could bring a campaign to its knees faster than any enemy. They would not resort to hunting, so they would bring all they'd need. She passed by crates of food stores, barrels of water, wine, and oil, wagons filled with swords, armor, construction materials, medical supplies, wheelwright and blacksmith's supplies.

Supplying an army was a massive undertaking. She thanked Acantha again for all the hard work done in her long absence. She owed them much and vowed not to let them down.

Faelyn nodded in acknowledgment each time a soldier bowed to her. The feel of the evening air was almost joyous with the relief of finally taking action after preparing so long. The glow of the gathered mage staffs drew her gaze to the outside of camp. Kian’s mages would be crucial. Some would come with her, but most would join Kian’s half of the fight.

Dusk came too quickly, and they were out of time. Waiting another day to regroup was out of the question. Already the Daltieri army prepared for attack. Another day would only make them stronger and give them more time to counterattack.

Lord Calem held a feast that night to honor the new army and their quest. The soldiers received spiced cider and small honey cakes to go along with their evening meal of mutton stew. Faelyn sat at the head of the dining table, trying not to return Kian's relentless regard. General Huntington sat on her left, and they talked of idle things. For a moment, it was as if they wouldn't be marching to battle on the morrow.

After the meal, Faelyn relaxed in a long luxurious bath with lavender oil—probably the last bath she'd have for a while. Back in her room, her heartbeat quickened when she discovered her new armor already carefully laid out. She traced her fingers over its silver planes, the coolness making her shiver.

Tomorrow would be the start of a new era.

CHAPTER FORTY-TWO

The trek to Pavora was far from pleasant. Kian's army marched ahead. Faelyn, Kian, Calem, and several others, including Amerae and Michael, rode in the middle. The rest of the army marched behind them. From this position, the dust raised by boots and hooves and the reek of horse manure were unavoidable parts of life.

Scouts brought regular reports providing assurance Daltieri wasn't marching to meet them and finding suitable places to rest or camp. The sky only poured on them a few times, soaking Faelyn and her horse. She didn't mind. The rain eased the stench of sweat and horses and cleaned her skin of caked dirt. Mostly it was hot. The metal armor absorbed every ounce of the sun's heat, trapping it like an oven.

The endless pattern of flat plains, followed by hills and forests, combined with the incessant commentary from Calem about what he thought she was doing wrong this time was enough to drive her mad. *"You shouldn't ride between the armies." "You should have found a more suitable place to camp for the night." "You shouldn't waste time among the soldiers each night when we could be planning."*

Faelyn sighed. It was almost a relief when, two weeks into the trek, and one week shy of when they were to arrive in Pavora, a Daltieri patrol attacked their scouts.

One of the Alysian scouts came charging back to them, his horse frothing at the mouth. Wild-eyed, he panted. "General Huntington, Daltieri patrol over the next ridge. Twenty marksmen."

The general started to issue an order, but Faelyn spoke first. "Captain Amerae. Take half your squad and handle the threat." Amerae had been made captain just a few days ago, with not much time to train. She needed an introduction to her new role, and this was just the war story her squad would love. They'd never disobey Amerae once they saw what she was capable of.

Calem opened his mouth to protest, but Faelyn flashed him a warning look.

Kian rode away with them, and the rest of the army marched on. Calem scanned the horizon, grumbling to himself about how Faelyn should have sent more soldiers in case it was a trap. Faelyn gritted her teeth against a raging outburst. His doubt at her competence was wearing her long-lifed patience thin.

Michael stared into the trees alongside Calem, fidgeting in his saddle. "She'll be okay, right?"

Faelyn studied him. He'd opened up more since returning to Seaside, though they'd barely had time to speak. "There's a risk in everything we do now, but Amerae is strong."

He nodded. "She is indeed." He coaxed his horse closer, though his eyes stayed on the trees as if searching for Amerae's safe return. "I never thanked you for saving her. For saving us, I mean. She doesn't believe me, but she means more to me than even our cause." He looked over at Faelyn shyly. "So, thank you for bringing her back, and for all you're doing now for her."

Michael's love and sincere gratitude touched Faelyn's heart—a bright spot in a world of darkness. "It's no more than she's done for me."

Before the army left the woods and reached the next ridge, Amerae's squad returned, sweaty, swords bloody, but unscathed. Michael breathed a sigh of relief. Faelyn counted them. Twenty-five. No casualties. Amerae beamed as her soldiers filed back into formation amongst cheers and smiles from up and down the line.

Kian took his place beside Faelyn, fresh blood on his sword, staff in hand. "I looked for tracks. I don't think any escaped. They know we're coming, but I'd like to not tip them off to how close we are."

Faelyn nodded, oddly forlorn. Any loss of life was hard to bear, even the enemy's. She planned to give Daltieri the chance to surrender, though it'd do no good. After all this time, of course they viewed this land as theirs. They wouldn't give it up without a fight.

During their march the next morning, Kian's army branched off where the road forked south. They would travel to the east side of Pavora, skirting around the lake to the castle. She followed Kian for a short while behind his troops. His army rounded a small bend of overgrown brush ahead of them. They were suddenly alone, with only the fading sounds of trudging boots and hooves.

"May the Fates guide your way, Kian. I can't thank you enough for everything you've done." *For me,* she couldn't say aloud. Though it was likely true, Kian claimed otherwise, and she'd let him keep his pride intact. More than that and her eternal friendship, she had nothing else to give.

He offered a warm smile and sidled his horse closer until his knees touched hers. He reached his hand out, slow enough for Faelyn to pull away, but she didn't. Cupping her face with a calloused hand, he said, "I know the Fates guide you, Faelyn." He stared at her lips. "I've never doubted it."

Faelyn saw and felt his intent just before he acted. She should have stopped him, but part of her didn't want to.

He kissed her hard, running his hand from her cheek to the back of her bare neck, pulling her closer. Faelyn kept her hands gripped over the reins, but did not show the same restraint with her mouth. Their lips parted, tongues colliding, sending butterflies soaring through her.

When they broke apart, she was breathless. Kian grinned in triumph. Guilt ate away at her enjoyment, but Kian interjected.

"I know how you feel about me, Faelyn. I may not be as powerful as you, but I am a mage capable of reading people. I won't lie and say I don't love you. Love notwithstanding, we'd make a fine political match between our two kingdoms." He held up a finger, stopping her from protesting. "Don't say no, just give it some thought. *When* you're queen, you'll have plenty to think of." A gleam entered his eyes, so full of confidence. "I'll see you at Pavora. We'll drive those Daltieri bastards back where they belong." He kissed her hand, then spurred his horse after his army, racing out of sight.

The burning in her cheeks slowly subsided as she trotted back to her troops. Kian raised a good point. Creadel would make a strong ally, and he was a powerful lord there. She did love him, in her own way, and they got along well enough to last through the end of his days.

She sighed. There it was. Even if she didn't choose to marry for love, and did so for political alliance, Kian wouldn't live forever, and he wasn't the best political candidate, really. King Jeffe of Creadel had a young son who'd grow into marriageable age in a little over a decade. He'd be a better match for a political alliance. Or perhaps a prince of Kestrea, the peaceful kingdom to the northeast. They at least shared a border with Daltieri and could provide a better measure of control over any future incursions.

Faelyn shook her head. When did her life become plotting and planning, with no room for romance or love? But her life had always been that way. If they succeeded, things would only become more complicated.

She had been too young to understand at the time, but her father endured great stress trying to manage the daily operations of the kingdom. She'd listened from the secret passages as the endless drove brought problem after problem. Part of it was his own doing, problems he created by his inattentive rule.

The reins groaned beneath her clenched fists. She never admitted this before now, but everything she faced was because of her father and his selfishness.

Faelyn trotted her horse up the side of the road, earning bows and smiles from her soldiers. She'd spoken to them all by this point, even if just a passing greeting. By the time she reached the front and took her place by Calem and Amerae, all thoughts of Kian's kiss and romance were gone. If they won Alysies back, then perhaps there'd be time later.

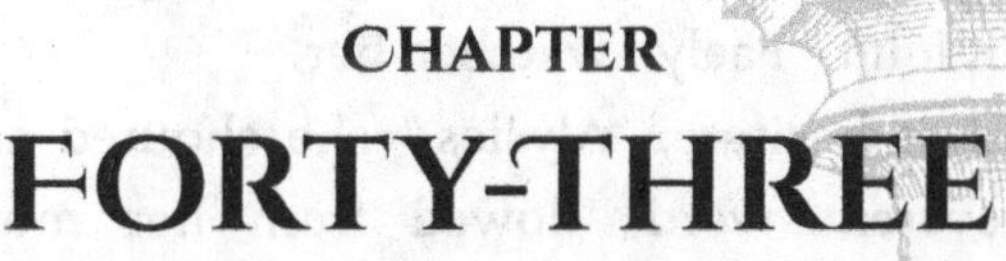

CHAPTER FORTY-THREE

One week later, the afternoon sun dipped toward the trees as they arrived at the wheat fields on the outskirts of Pavora Woods, just east of Oakrin—her mother's birthplace. Only the woods and the town separated them from the castle that was once her home.

Faelyn dismounted, the army making camp around her, and walked closer to the woods. She stared at the trees billowing in the warm breeze, towering dark behind the cleared fields. Old wounds and memories throbbed. Mary had taken her to the woods many times as a child to play and grow wildflowers. Her eyes stung. Her childhood home was but a day away.

Amerae approached on light footsteps, catching Faelyn staring.

"This is where it starts, isn't it, my queen?" Amerae's kind voice cut through the sounds of the soldiers erecting tents and cooking over fires. "From here we will march for Alysies." She said the last very quietly, almost shyly.

"Daltieri has been very efficient cowering the hearts of our people, Amerae. They cowered mine when they murdered my family and tried to murder me. We can't be afraid of them anymore. No longer can they hold control over our hearts."

"I'm not afraid of them, Your Majesty." Amerae's eyes turned hard.

"Then don't let them keep you from uttering the truth, Amerae. Go ahead. Say it loud." Faelyn watched her.

Amerae didn't hesitate. "Alysies," she shouted as loud as she dared. The reverent words flowed from her mouth into the approaching night. "Tomorrow we will win back Alysies."

Faelyn sent it on the wind, reverberating its prayer and promise to the furthest reaches of their army.

Quiet descended upon the soldiers as they soaked up every bit of the emotion that name held. Their fervent whispers as they uttered the word themselves floated around the campsite.

"Good." Faelyn placed a hand on Amerae's arm. "Join me later for the meeting with the generals. I'll send someone for you." Amerae bowed and walked away, leaving Faelyn to study the woods once more.

The first room of the multiroom tent held a low table and small wooden chairs. Faelyn sat at its head, with her generals and Lord Calem seated before her. Amerae was the only captain in attendance, and the youngest person by a decade, besides her brothers, Trey and Marus. Faelyn watched her chest puff with pride. Amerae had earned this right. If it wasn't for her, Faelyn wouldn't be here.

Faelyn sat forward, looking each person in the eye. "I thank you all for bringing us this far. Some of you have been preparing for tomorrow for generations." All eyes were on her. Regardless of their level of acceptance of her leadership, they knew the weight of this moment. The anticipation swelled in the room, and Faelyn used that to bolster her leaders. This would be the last meeting before they marched into battle.

"Our scouts report a massive army at the castle. Our patrols have already killed so many enemy spies. Indeed, Daltieri is a powerful force. Lord Jamison hides behind the impenetrable walls of my castle. They know we are coming, but do they march out to meet us?" Head shaking and grumbling ran around the room. "They've made themselves strong off our people. But no longer. Tomorrow we attack the castle at its western gates. Lord Kian will attack from the east." Faelyn stood, all others following.

Her hands balled into fists. Her eyes blazed with an eon of suppressed anger and vengeance. "No more will we be ruled by soulless, tyrannical oppressors. No more will our people starve while Daltieri leeches our toils. If we die, let it not be from their whips at our backs, but in the pursuit of freedom. We will no longer yield to the control of a foreign ruler. Today we stand together on Daltieri soil. Tomorrow, we fight for a free Alysies!"

The resounding cacophony was deafening, their voices nearly drowned out by the beating of their fists on the table. Faelyn's magic begged for release. Not much longer. She bared her teeth, hungry for the coming battle.

CHAPTER FORTY-FOUR

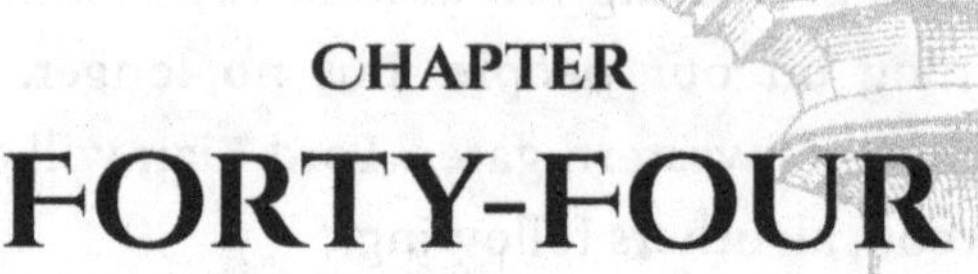

Weeks went by, but the watch window had only returned in short bursts. Not knowing what else to do, Ardenis advised the watchers to continue their normal shifts in the hope the window would go back to normal. The council did not know what to make of it. Similar problems occurred all over Acantha.

Ardenis had arrived early, but there had been no activity. Still, he stared into the cracked pool, praying for a glimpse of Faelyn. Anything could have happened to her at this point. And Amerae. The last time he'd seen her, she was in the back of a barred wagon, on her way to captivity. The stress of not knowing hung over him like a shroud, weighing down his mind and body.

He was about to give up when the watch window flickered to life. Gasps rang around the room, but Ardenis ignored them, throwing himself into Thera. There was no telling how long the vision would last.

Relief flooded him as Faelyn's form came into view. She stood beside a massive tent wearing shiny armor that glinted in the early morning sun. His breath caught. A circlet graced her golden hair.

Her eyes held fierce determination as she overlooked a city's worth of bustling activity. Soldiers ran to and fro, shouting orders, carting supplies, and chopping trees—the makings of a great battle. Even from his seat in the tower, the frenzy quickened his pulse. His knees bounced with his own eagerness. This was her moment. He'd seen her train. She could do it.

Amerae, alive and healthy, approached Faelyn wearing identical armor. "Will we be ready, Your Majesty?"

Your Majesty? What had happened in his absence? Ardenis couldn't contain his awe, or his pride.

Faelyn studied the work before her, wisps of her hair caught in the breeze. "We are ready."

Her voice pierced Ardenis through. How he'd missed that voice. Then she smiled and looked up, right into him.

I see you, Faelyn. May the Fates guide your cause.

The moment was too good to be true. Faelyn's brow creased with concern as she scanned the distant clouds. Then the watch window went out.

Ardenis took a steadying breath. The watchers looked up at him with disappointment. He opened his mouth to assure them all was well, but then the room darkened. His head tilted in confusion. The lanterns remained lit.

"Ardenis." Sam, one of the day watchers, urgently pointed outside the window.

Clouds. In Acantha.

Ardenis rushed to the window. The rest of the watchers crowded behind him. Dark clouds billowed and roiled, covering every bit of sun and blue sky. A Theran storm was coming. Wind whipped through the roses in the garden and rattled the window.

"What do we do, Ardenis?"

"What's happening?"

The questions came in rapid succession with real fear and an edge of panic, more than they should have been capable of in their emotionally neutral state.

Ardenis stared, hoping his terror didn't reflect on his face. Lightning flickered as the sky thickened and swirled. This was dangerous weather, in a place that had seen nothing but perfect sunny days since the beginning of time.

A large cracking sound, the loudest noise he'd ever heard in Acantha, resounded behind him. It was an ear-crushing splintering of stone. The watchers jumped and turned. Ardenis shoved his way passed them in time to see half the watch window break off and crash to the floor. Water rushed out in a tidal wave soaking past their knees.

Ardenis could not believe what he was seeing. His vision blurred. The floor rushed up to meet him, but he steadied himself. Others collapsed. The watch window was ruined. Acantha was coming undone. His heart sprinted in his chest. What had happened? The painful loss of his connection to Thera and Faelyn shuddered through him. Final and permanent. He had to find Rhea.

"Convene in the dining hall until the council sorts this out." Ardenis met the terror-stricken gaze of those closest to him. "Try not to get hurt." He paused, nearly sick. "I suspect the consequences would be dire. Help those along the way needing assistance. We are the most prepared for whatever may be occurring." If the watch window had crumbled of its own accord, Ardenis feared what could be next.

He pushed that fear aside and sloshed through the water. The rest stood immobilized with shock.

Outside, the wind gusted, nearly throwing him over. It chilled his wet robe, giving him sensations he never thought he'd feel in this existence. Goosebumps rippled along his skin, shocking him to a standstill. He ran his hand over his arm feeling the raised hairs, even while rooting his feet against the force of the wind. It howled in his ears, but it was the dark sky he couldn't take his eyes off.

Amalia had been right. Experiencing things through the watch window was nothing like in person. The weight of the building storm pressed on him, the feeling of pressure in his ears alarming.

His chest tightened, and he struggled to draw breath—so many new and frightening sensations at once.

Lightning flashed blindingly bright, striking the tower. The booming roar of thunder immediately followed. The ground rumbled beneath him, sending his heart to his throat. The rest of the watchers came pouring outside, running and pushing. One of them clipped Ardenis, knocking him off the stone path. His wet robes twisted as he stumbled, and he fell. He cried out in pain as his elbow gashed upon a rock.

Eyes wide, he panted for several staggering breaths as the sensations wracked his arm. Pulling his up sleeve, he surveyed dripping blood. Acanthians didn't bleed. With shaking hands, he touched his elbow. The wound stung anew all the way up his arm. He brought his trembling hand to his mouth. The blood tasted metallic.

He pushed off the ground, stumbling upright on the path. A second boom of thunder sounded behind him. The ground shook hard, and he struggled to regain his footing. A great crevice opened beside him, exposing the dirt beneath the grass. The crack extended all the way to the tower, splitting the stone up the side. Shards of rock fell to the ground below. Ardenis's eyesight went blurry as dizziness overtook him.

His body shook in terror as he backed away. Then he ran for all he was worth toward the high council. He dodged Acanthians as they stood staring at the dark sky, huddling against the crisp wind that should have been warm.

When he passed the transfer hall, someone backed into his path, her head tilted up to look at the sky. He ran straight into her, knocking them both sprawling to the ground.

Ardenis rubbed his back. "I'm sorry." He got to his feet. "Idonea! Oh, I'm so sorry. Here." He offered her his hand.

"Ardenis... it hurts." Idonea's brow furrowed. She cradled her hands, red with shallow scrapes where she caught her fall.

"It will be alright. The pain will cease soon." He helped her up and folded his hands over hers. "I must get to the high council. The transfer workers will need your guidance."

Idonea's gaze flicked to the clouds above. "The gateways aren't working, Ardenis. As soon as the sky darkened, no one else was able to transfer to Thera." She leaned closer. "Some haven't noticed, but a crack has formed in the building, precisely where the fire ended before."

Ardenis dropped her hands and shook his head. "Keep trying. I'll be back. Gather at the dining hall if you must."

He didn't wait for a response. He ran.

Along the path to the high council, several other leaders from his region walked to give their accounts. The gravity of the situation must have convinced them to bypass the regional council. Many called out to him, but Ardenis rushed by them all in a full-on sprint. The time for discretion had passed.

When he entered the northwest region, breathless, the clouds didn't appear quite as dark. The people there appeared calm, watching the shadowy horizon with only mild curiosity. The occasional flicker of lightning could be seen only from a distance. Ardenis stared up. The darker clouds hovered over his region, but were slowly building out. They'd be here soon.

He ran the rest of the way to the council hall and burst through the doors. Nora Enforcer looked up from where dozens of Acanthians already lined the foyer. He slowed and tried to hide his panting, edging his way toward the desk. Nora gave him an easy smile, free of the stress he'd left outside.

"Nora, I need to speak to Rhea. Now." Ardenis didn't blink. He wasn't first in line, but Nora *had* to let him in.

Nora glanced at the line snaked around the room. "Of course, Ardenis Watcher Fater." She spoke louder than necessary, emphasizing his position for the benefit of those who may not know him. Even if they didn't know his face, they'd know his title. He was the only fater in Acantha. "The council is in session now, but Rhea will see you next."

Ardenis bit back a groan of frustration. Whatever the person inside had to say couldn't be anywhere near important as Ardenis's information. All this formality and civility when Acantha was coming undone, it was ludicrous. He rocked side to side, eyes locked on the closed door.

The second Ardenis decided to barge in and demand to be seen, the door opened and a man walked out, nodding at Nora. Ardenis rushed by him and entered the council room. He didn't bother standing behind the podium. He stood in the middle of the floor and spoke above the murmur of the council members still discussing the weather. Only Rhea ceased speaking the moment he entered. She watched him with troubled eyes.

"The watch window in the northeast region is no more. It split in two before my eyes as I stood there helpless to stop it." His announcement was met by shocked silence and Rhea's wide eyes. "The transfers aren't working." Rhea opened her mouth to speak. "There's more." He jerked up his sleeve revealing the dried blood on his elbow. "People are getting injured."

Rhea sunk down to the edge of her chair, her eyes not leaving his arm. The silence lasted a breath and a half, then gave way to shouting.

"You know something." Rhea's voice carried to him over the noise, as if he was tuned to her somehow. "What do you know?"

He swallowed. "The darkness and destruction seem to be coming from my region. It's just a theory, but if you were to come back with me, you'd feel the cold wind penetrate more deeply, your body would ache more readily, the darkness felt more thoroughly."

Rhea stood, brushing her robes. The panic in her eyes and fear in her countenance fell off like errant dust. The council fell silent before her.

"The Fates have left us to our own devices. Ardenis and I will investigate the matter personally. I need two council representatives to oversee matters at each regional level." Several hands shot up and

Rhea picked eight council members. "Listen and record, ease any panic, and reassure the people with your presence."

Rhea snapped her fingers, and Ardenis's two favorite enforcers came forward out of nowhere. She nodded to them, and they jogged away. She gestured Ardenis ahead of her. He led the way back to the council courtyard. Right away, the sky looked darker, though it was not yet nightfall. He began the long walk back to his region, but Rhea stopped him.

"This is dire, Ardenis. I know you realize what is happening. Our worst fears are coming to fruition. If we can't reverse whatever is the cause, then this is the end." Her face crumpled, almost as if she might cry.

True fear hit him like a punch to the gut. Never in his mind did he think this could mean the end. He'd counted on Rhea to have all the answers. She was the head *high* councilwoman. There was no one else who could help them. Acantha, Thera, Faelyn, and all he held dear, just gone?

Taking him by surprise, the enforcers appeared, gripping poles that extended from a two-wheeled carriage.

"We will travel swifter this way as I am not the fastest runner." Rhea climbed in, motioning for Ardenis to do the same.

He'd seen these types of carts before, but not for many centuries, not since horses were made popular. Laughter bubbled in his stomach at the thought of the enforcers—these enforcers, who'd once tried to force him to be born—pulling them like horses all the way back to his region. It was borderline hysteria. He managed to shove it down, but barely. The enforcers weren't phased, as if pulling the cart was a common occurrence. It certainly wasn't common in Acantha.

Ardenis climbed in, sitting shoulder to shoulder with Rhea, and then they were off. The enforcers' sandaled feet slapped against the stone pathway, and the buildings sped by. They moved faster than Ardenis would have assumed. People moved out of their path, pointing and gawking, temporally distracted from the disaster looming above, and blissfully ignorant of the disaster to come.

Rhea turned to him, her face inches away. He twisted to look at her. "I pray to the Fates this is not the end of all things, Ardenis. But if it is so, I find myself compelled to tell you I've grown fond of you. Despite the coolness which I've displayed by necessity, I consider you my friend, and your visits have been a pleasure these past years."

Ardenis was touched, in more ways than one. He'd always had the greatest respect for Rhea, but her position prevented him from ever seeing her as anything more than a superior. Now her admission gave him a new outlook—and filled him with dread. It sounded like goodbye. Here was the moment to say all the things they ever wanted to say and never could, before it was too late.

As if to emphasize these thoughts, a crash of thunder made them both jump, and the enforcers ran faster.

"Laida was born as Faelyn on Thera." The words flew out of his mouth before he could stop them. His precious secret. "I know this to be the truth, without a doubt in my mind. And I love her. More than the sky and the sun, more than my duty as a watcher and my very existence, I love her. In a world where I'm not supposed to know what that means, I still love her. And that love is all the more precious and sacred to me because I spent a millennium without knowing what it really means to have this gift, this capacity for it, until my eyes were opened. But I can't believe that is the cause of all this." He gestured to the sky. "I can't."

His eyes stung under the weight of his admission. He stared at the passing trees, awaiting Rhea's shock and judgment.

She placed her hand over his where he'd bunched up his robes in a tight fist, and patted. The friendly gesture eased his grip. "I know, Ardenis. I know you love Faelyn. I've known all this time."

He stared in disbelief. "Then why am I still here? Why have I not been forced to leave?"

"You have a fated born. Your time is in the future." She stared hard into his eyes. "I've told you. It's always been my belief the Fates have a higher purpose in keeping you here, just as you've said yourself." She squeezed his hand in a near-painful grip. "This is that day, Ardenis. Can you feel it?" She raised her hand to the black sky. "You're here to stop this from happening."

Ardenis's eyes went wide. What could he do? Who was he to prevent something so monumental? He shook his head.

"Do not try to deny it, Ardenis. The Fates have prepared you for this since the day they opened your eyes. Not even the council has all the awareness you have. Think! What have the Fates been trying to tell you all along?"

Ardenis felt the truth in her words. His instincts sung to him, nearly vibrating with eagerness for him to fit the clues in the puzzle together. The dark clouds and swirling wind, the lightning and thunder, and the shouting he heard from a distance threatened to overrule his sound judgment.

They neared his region's council hall. The courtyard swarmed with people in blue, all seeking answers and assurance.

"There's no time, Ardenis. Think!" Her voice was a plea disguised by the urgency of her panic.

Ardenis grabbed his head, digging his fingers into his temples, and gasping at the pain.

Then the enforcers screamed. Rhea inhaled. Ardenis looked up to see them pitch over the side of a great crevice in the pathway. He threw out his arm, pinning Rhea against the back of the cart as they fell. Air whooshed by. The poles struck rock, and the cart pitched sideways. Despite Ardenis's hold, Rhea was tossed out. The cart slammed to a rest on its side. He smacked his head against the wall of the cart. The pain was crushing, exploding through his skull and blurring his vision.

He lifted his head to see three prone bodies and a horde of Acanthians standing at the edge of the newly formed pit before he blacked out.

CHAPTER FORTY-FIVE

"Scouts report all clear, Your Majesty."

"Sound it."

At Faelyn's command, three quick blares of a horn rang out across the field. Morning light filtered through the ominous clouds, and the army burst into activity. Men and women poured out of tents and stumbled out of blankets. Fear and excitement singed the air, setting a fervor to everyone's hurried movements.

Time to march.

The captains barked orders. Soldiers frantically buckled armor and packed their gear. Lord Calem stood at her side, chest puffed out as he scanned the progress. They'd drilled this departure many times and in various conditions. The soldiers arranged themselves into companies of one hundred, each with a captain. Each general commanded ten companies.

Faelyn kept one eye on the ever-darkening sky. The distant rumble of thunder promised a heavy rain. She only hoped it would hold out on their journey.

From across the clearing, Faelyn spotted Amerae with her sword high in the air, standing in front of her new company. She fixated on Amerae's voice.

"Soon we will join General Huntington, but not before I tell you how honored I am to be your captain. Your queen fights for you. Will you follow her?" Amerae's strong tone carried pride. Her question was met with resounding roars. She mounted her horse. "For a free Alysies!"

Pride swelling, Faelyn mounted as well. The army broke camp and traveled through Pavora Woods, the atmosphere growing darker as the trees blocked the meager sun. After enduring Calem's protests, Faelyn rode in front. He rode in the middle with their fifteen mages, between the foot soldiers and the cavalry.

Faelyn demanded absolute quiet. Every horse's snort, squeak of a wagon wheel, or clink of armor chaffed. She kept her ears tuned to her surroundings. As much as they were her woods, they were also the enemy's.

She opened her senses, and the air was filled with foreboding. It surrounded them like a cloud, almost as dark as the one above. The woods knew what was coming just beyond their border.

After 'all clear' reports from the scouts, the army passed through the woods sooner than she expected. There stood Pavora. Her hand drifted to her mouth at the sight. Darkness shrouded the capital city like a muted twilight. Lightning flashed in the distance beyond the buildings. *Even Thera feels the coming battle.*

The town had expanded significantly. The woods had been cut back by miles to make room. In place of the clean, simple city of her youth stood a slum. Shoddy homes with rotting wood shingles and patchwork roofs, trash and refuse-filled streets, and hanging cages on every block. She wrinkled her nose against the accosting stench—some combination of human waste and rotting meat.

As reported, the city was mostly abandoned. Only the occasional face peeked out a dingy window as they traveled further into town.

Did these people hail them as heroes, or cower from them as enemies?

Cottage doors hung ajar. Market stalls sat abandoned, fly-covered fish and wares still on display. Faelyn looked back to see one of her soldiers testing the unlocked door of an empty shop. Her reins groaned beneath her sudden grip. A captain under Marus grabbed the wayward soldier's arm and punched him in the jaw. The force knocked him to the ground and sent those nearby laughing.

Good. She loosened her grip. Her leaders should control their soldiers without interference. They were under strict conduct orders. The people of Pavora were their people.

As they traveled, the overwhelming presence of the castle increased. The essence of the enemy soldiers readying for battle, and the anticipation of seeing her home once again, formed a black tidal wave she willingly drew closer to. Daltieri knew they stood the best chance of defense behind their wall, but Faelyn still kept her ears open and regular scouting parties searching for an enemy lying in wait.

Fear and anxiety haunted her soldiers' steps. And something else.

Faelyn's head tilted to the side. It wasn't just the turmoil of emotion and the anger of a brewing storm choking her senses. The air prickled with something that made her palms sweat—a spell being weaved into the air. She was too far away to tell what kind. All they could do was keep going.

Hours passed, then the town abruptly ended at the edge of a small clearing outside the castle wall.

Faelyn's heart pounded in her ears. The last time she'd been here, she tried to set the world on fire—anything to save Mary. This was a different time and place. High on the stone wall, soldiers in black rushed around the battlements like ants on prey. More black figures stood with crossbows. Torches blazed along the wall, bright against the sky's dark background and casting eerie shadows over the stone walls. The heavily reinforced west gates practically glowed with the magic set within. Ramming through would be impossible. Death crows braved the coming weather, circling overhead, already anticipating the slaughter.

Lord Calem rode up beside her, having just arrived. "We're too close. You're going to get us killed." His wide eyes scanned the castle while their army spread out behind them.

Faelyn ignored him and continued studying the scene.

The chants of Daltieri's army echoed across the clearing, along with a rumbling felt from the ground. Faelyn's soldiers did as they were trained, lining up along the edge. She led her horse a few steps ahead to examine her army. It was a most impressive sight. Armor glinted even in the absence of the sun, and banners of navy and silver flapped in the heavy wind. Thousands of soldiers stood at attention, ready to battle for the future. Their determination calmed Faelyn's heart and steadied her nerves, but with the calm came the spell.

From this range, the magic was palpable, like a blanket of static zinging through the air. Her mages eyed her warily. They felt it too.

The enemy lined the battlements, arrows knocked and ready.

Faelyn stared straight ahead. “Steady now.” All snapped to attention as her words carried down the line. “There are powerful mages inside. They've sealed the gates with magery.” She flared her magic, shaping the air around her to create a protective shield.

The world held its breath.

Faelyn watched the castle, concentrating. Waiting. She'd expected them to attack by now.

The wind ceased, and banners went slack.

A loud crash of armor hitting the ground beside her broke the ominous silence. Calem had fallen from his horse. He grasped at his throat. There was no blood. She hadn't seen any arrows loosed.

Faelyn whirled. Her entire army flailed with wild eyes, clutching their necks. Horses bucked, throwing riders to the ground. Calem's mouth gaped like a fish out of water.

They can't breathe!

In a mad panic, Faelyn threw all she could into bringing back the wind. A burst of light tore through her. Strands of hair slipped free as she cast her countermagic. She squeezed her eyes tight with the effort. It felt like moving a boulder, shoving the efforts of countless enemy mages back as strong and as hard as she could. It was her against them—so many of them—but she gained ground, inch by inch. She broke into a cold sweat.

After the longest minute of her life, the wind returned, fiercer than before. It ripped at her braid, threatening to topple her from her horse. She panted, and her skin chilled as the breeze cooled the perspiration from her face.

Lord Calem and the soldiers took deep gulps of breath, coughing and sucking air down as fast as they could. Most of her mages had succumbed as well, and were picking themselves up off the ground. General Huntington struggled to command the soldiers back in rank. Terror showed in the whites of her soldiers' eyes. The enemy had the upper hand, and they knew it. Their cheers shook the air, drowning out the gasping breaths of her frightened soldiers.

They had to breach the wall. There would be no going through the gate. It would take more time than she had to weave a spell strong enough to untwine the mess that protected it, and it would put her too close. In all her studies of historical battles, getting through the wall was the most critical part. It could make or break an army depending on how long they had to lay siege. Faelyn didn't intend to let that stop her.

She didn't come into this blind. Her former home was a near-impenetrable fortress, even without magecraft.

"Siege engines."

The orders ran down the line. The catapults rolled forward, ten in all. They spread across the clearing, stopping short of crossbow range. Soldiers loaded the first stones in place, with more soldiers on standby to reload or repair as necessary. On General Huntington's command, they pulled the levers. Huge boulders launched at the castle walls. Faelyn tried not to flinch as they sailed through the air, hurtling toward *her* castle.

The boulders hit with a weak thud, bouncing harmlessly off. Some even landed short of the wall. Faelyn ground her teeth, squeezing the reins tight when her horse shied from her anger. How many mages did Daltieri have? Powerful ones, too. They'd shielded the entire wall.

Kian's army would never make it through.

Her sensitive ears picked up laughter from the Daltieri soldiers. *Laughter!* They had no fear for their superior position. Of course, they had good reason to celebrate. They believed themselves to be untouchable.

Using fury to fuel her magic, Faelyn lifted her arms to the sky. With a power that rippled the air, she threw her arms toward the ground. A great crack opened in front of her, extending all the way to the castle wall and racing up the side. Daltieri soldiers shouted. The force jostled those on top, effectively removing their superior smirks.

Lightning erupted from the clouds and struck the field, leaving a charred hole. The clap of thunder was near deafening as it careened over the armies.

Faelyn charged, leaving Calem and the army behind. Calem's protest was followed by Amerae's cry as she spurred to follow. Faelyn whispered a plea, and her horse outpaced Amerae's. The girl couldn't protect herself like Faelyn could.

Arrows twanged through the air as Faelyn came into range of the castle. They hit and bounced off her invisible shield of air. The soldiers on the battlements cried out in surprise, shouting for the assistance of a mage.

Faelyn breathed in deep, then unleashed the magic she'd been holding back for days. She concentrated on the discarded boulders, gathering them one by one and raising them through the air. She imbued them with heat until they glowed molten. Her horse reared beneath her, and she willed it calm.

The stones broke apart and reformed into destructive bombs.

Focusing on the thin crack she'd made in the outer wall, she shot forward blasts of rock and fire. They hit and exploded, widening her initial gap.

She smiled through gritted teeth as she regained control of her skittish horse. It was working, even against the mage's shield.

The roaring cry of her army echoed across the valley. Their pounding boots and galloping horses approached, bolstering her resolve. If she didn't breach this wall, they'd be slaughtered.

Daltieri soldiers shot spears. With a thud, they hit, but her shield deflected them. She used the tar they dumped to form new ammunition, sending it sailing at the crack. Her boulders blew apart in ragged chunks, which she added pieces of the wall to and reformed, using it again and again. The crack widened into a sizeable gap.

A rhythmic pounding came from the other side of the wall, like swords clanging against shields or breastplates. To Faelyn's right, the sound of grinding metal made her jump. Wood groaned, protesting. The castle gates opened.

The black and gold army poured out the gate in an endless stream. This was their plan to divert her. Daltieri did not want her to breach the wall. Her army wouldn't be able to fight their way through with any kind of speed before the gate shut again. They still needed another way in.

She redoubled her efforts, hurling the rocks. The gap was two people wide now—not wide enough. Through the jagged edges, she spotted lines of Daltieri soldiers with swords and bows ready for the moment her army stormed through. A few arrows shot from the gap to accompany the ones from above, bouncing off her shield and her rocks. They'd pick her soldiers off if she didn't widen the breach.

She risked a glance backward. Her army had stopped short of arrow range, forming ranks to receive the enemy. Amerae toed the line of safety, watching Faelyn, desperation creasing her brow. The Daltieri army formed similar squads in front of the castle. When the gates closed behind them, they outnumbered Alysies three to one.

Faelyn trembled as fear pumped through her veins. She'd known the odds, but seeing it in person, witnessing the final breaths before the bloodshed... they were not prepared.

Prepared or not, she'd led them to this. There was no turning back. Faelyn took a deep breath and held tight to the reins against the roar of the enemy. Her soldiers lined the valley, facing down Daltieri with fierce determination.

Her army cried out. They raised their weapons and charged. The two armies met, and black converged into silver in an explosion of swords and screaming.

A squad of Daltieri soldiers broke away and charged toward Faelyn—twenty men and women, and one mage, crystal aglow in his staff. The wind swirled around him. *An air mage.* He was trying to disrupt her shield.

She tensed, all effort going into widening the gap in the wall. Her mind raced to form a plan. Help wouldn't arrive before the enemy. Faelyn hefted her sword, years of training resonating through her body. While her shield could deflect arrows, it wasn't impenetrable to the strength of a blade aided by magic. And she wouldn't last draining her magic against an air mage intent on ripping through her shield.

She shot as many blasts of molten rock at the breach as she could before they were upon her.

The first rider in black attacked. She pivoted her horse in anticipation of his swing. Her sword thrust straight through his armor at the neck. The metal helm gave way. She cut through flesh to bone. He slumped off the saddle to the ground.

She ignored his death as the other soldiers surrounded her. The acrid tang of the enemy mage trying to breach her shield filled her mouth. Stopping him was crucial.

She whirled, fending off attacks. A commotion caught her attention. A company of Alysian soldiers rode into the fray, led by Amerae. They'd come to protect their queen, but now they were too close to the wall. Panic raced up Faelyn's spine, threatening to distract her from fending off the enemy. Already, she was stretched too thin.

In the valley behind her, soldiers from both sides cried out as swords sliced into skin and arrows penetrated through the weak parts of armor. The enemy was everywhere. People dying. People screaming. Horses fleeing. The noise drowned out her senses.

Arrows rained out of the dark sky, and some of Amerae's soldiers went down. Faelyn's muscles tensed. Amerae was a whirl of sword and blood from her felled enemies. A Daltieri stabbed her horse which reared, knocking Amerae to the ground. She didn't even flinch. She blocked a downward swing, then got back up and continued fighting, drawing closer to Faelyn.

The main battle finally reached them, swallowing their skirmish into its broken ranks, which meant her soldiers had advanced. Faelyn couldn't turn away to help her people. She had to get through the wall. With the soldiers distracted, and the air mage fending off attacks, the explosions continued. There might be hope for them to breach the gap. It was almost ready.

But then the wall began to mend. The stones formed up and the passage narrowed in the widest places. She cursed, feeling magic pulsing in the air. The Daltieri scoundrels were counteracting her efforts.

She snarled her fury. Like a barrage of arrows, she sent the last of her flaming rocks hurtling toward the Daltieri archers on the battlements. The molten fuel slammed into helms and breastplates, killing or felling the entire section of enemy.

Faelyn hurtled out of the saddle. Her horse ran away, no longer shielded and scared of the fighting that had erupted in all directions. She fought her way to the wall, cutting down enemy soldiers. She stopped mere feet from the gap and threw her arms out wide. Grunting with exertion, she focused her magic on the wall.

She pushed her anger and fear, channeling all she had into her efforts. The enemy's magic zinged, like invisible ropes trying to bind the wall. She could almost see the strands of magic being woven against her. The ropes led a path straight to their wielders. Around five mages, hidden and safe, combining their magical strength to reform the wall.

She pushed against them, only to feel them recoil and double their efforts. The wall closed bit by bit. Faelyn was vaguely aware Amerae and others had surrounded her, fighting off the enemy. White light bathed her, making her an easy target.

Sweat broke out on her forehead. Her limbs trembled. Still, the gap closed. Kian needed them to open the other gate. They were lost if they couldn't get inside. The weight of her failure smothered her. Black spots bloomed in her vision as the enemy's magic threatened to overcome. Was this the Fates' design? Was she meant to suffer her entire long life, always bringing those she loved down with her?

She dragged her eyes to Amerae. The brave young woman fought side by side with Michael, for their lives, for Faelyn's life. This would not be their end. She wouldn't allow it.

"Enough!" Faelyn's scream pierced across the valley, halting the nearby fighting for the briefest of moments. The sound of her panting cut through the respite.

The sky lit up with lightning and finally opened up. Rain poured down upon them, plinking against their armor.

Faelyn ignored the torrent. With a guttural cry, she shoved the mages' efforts back. She clenched her hands to her chest, gritting her teeth. She yelled as she threw her body forward, punching out with her magic as hard as she could.

The wall blew apart.

With a deafening boom, stone and rock tore through the air. Soldiers, friend and foe, dove for cover. The debris rained down in a never-ending torrent. Faelyn barely held her shield against it. When everything settled, the gap was wide enough for her army to march through. She nearly fell to her knees with exhaustion and relief.

Amerae's cry of pain overrode all else. Faelyn turned to see her sprawled on her back, a dagger protruding from her shoulder. The enemy air mage stood over her. His dark eyes shone with hate. He stared at Faelyn through the soaking rain and battling soldiers. His sodden black robe quivered with his efforts as he simultaneously pinned Amerae to the ground with magic, crushing her, and attacked Faelyn's shield. His mage crystal glowed, casting shadows on the blood and rain-soaked ground.

No one could help them. Michael was locked in battle, too far away. The rest were too busy trying to survive against impossible odds. Amerae's hands twitched upward, and her teeth gritted with the effort of trying to rise, but it was futile. The smell of blood and the clang of swords drowned out all else.

Straightening, Faelyn faced the mage full-on. At the risk of weakening her shield, she put all her efforts into her one goal: his mage crystal. She could control it. She'd done it before.

The sneer fell off his face when he noticed her intrusion. His mouth dropped open.

Faelyn used his magic for her own gain. His mage crystal glowed even brighter. The weight visibly lifted off Amerae who used her good arm to reach for her sword just two feet away. The mage fell to his knees under the crushing force of his own crystal working against him. Amerae snatched her sword. With a cry of pain, she sliced him across the throat. Blood gushed as he fell over, choking to a horrible end.

Amerae fell to her side, unconscious. Faelyn hacked through an enemy soldier and rushed the short distance to kneel at Amerae's side, arrows bouncing off her shield.

"Amerae." Faelyn tried to reach her.

Amerae's eyes fluttered open, squinting against the rain pelting her face and the glow surrounding Faelyn. She smiled up at her.

Faelyn reached as if to stroke Amerae's cheek, then diverted, yanking hard and pulling the dagger from her friend's shoulder. Amerae screamed, but it was short-lived. Faelyn's white glow swelled in intensity as she placed her hands and healed the wound as much as she dared with her dwindling magic.

"Am!" Michael skidded to a stop in the mud.

Amerae's company arrived to lend aid, defending her from attackers while Michael hoisted her up.

Even with all her training, Faelyn hadn't exercised her magic to such an extent. Adrenaline couldn't keep up. The battle had barely begun, but already her eyelids felt heavy, and she was thirstier than she ever remembered. It took significant energy just to push on, but then she heard words that nearly brought tears to her eyes.

"Through the breach!" General Huntington yelled, waving them forward with his sword.

The hole was wide enough. Her army regrouped and forged ahead. Faelyn was among the first through the wall, sword held at the ready. The rhythmic pounding of the enemy soldiers awaiting them sounded on the other side. The rain continued to pour, mixing with blood and forming sickening rivulets in the muddy ground.

The courtyard was nearly as she remembered. Though, instead of dirt and manicured gardens, it had been covered with flat flagstones. The only hint of green was in giant stone pots holding plants and flowers, muted in the downpour.

Lines of Daltieri soldiers in black and gold stretched the length of the courtyard. Fresh, frenzied, and bristling for a fight. They extended back to the keep. Behind the barricade of soldiers, stairs led to a second level of the courtyard with the castle turrets rising into the sky beyond.

Deadlier than the soldiers was the line of no less than twenty mages along a stone banister on the upper level of the courtyard. They sneered down at Faelyn's dwindling army, gripping their staffs, mage crystals aglow as they worked their magic. With a shock, Faelyn realized she recognized one of them—Miyah, her rival from Thomats. Kian's old girlfriend. She'd left Thomats years ago, but Faelyn hadn't cared enough to know where she'd gone.

Her heart lurched. Were there others here she knew from Thomats? Would she be forced to battle against a friend who, willingly or not, was here at Daltieri's command?

The smug look on Miyah's face—the cruel set to her mouth and knowing eyes alight with twenty glowing mage crystals at her side—filled Faelyn with terror. Miyah scanned the troops behind Faelyn, and her smile widened into a sickly, mad thing. Magic clouded the air like invisible poisonous fumes, nearly choking Faelyn, but it wasn't directed at her.

Her stomach dropped to her knees, and she spun around. Her army, half arrived through the breach, was locked in place. They were statues—blinking eyes, arms and legs frozen in their running pose, swords locked helplessly in front of them. All of them, spread out across the courtyard, suffered the same struggle. Including Amerae and Michael.

A horn blared, and the enemy advanced. Faelyn attacked the first ranks in a whirling circle of sword and conjured fire, but most skirted around her, going for the easy prey—her immobilized soldiers.

With a roar, Daltieri troops crossed the formidable stone courtyard, swords raised. They swung and stabbed at the Alysian frontline, killing helpless men and women where they stood unable to defend themselves.

Faelyn shook with fury. She widened her shield to rebound her attackers, then focused on the enemy mages. Their combined magic was formidable. Impossible to overcome. The threads of their magic too numerous.

She shot another glance backward, lips parted in the depth of her desperation. The black army moved swiftly. Faelyn's stomach roiled. They were almost to Amerae where she stood beside Michael and her company. Faelyn couldn't get to her, too surrounded by her own attackers. Amerae's wide eyes locked onto an approaching soldier who was intent on cutting her down. Faelyn was watching Amerae's death—strong, proud, brave Amerae.

Knees trembling, resisting the urge to scream, Faelyn fought her way toward Amerae, but her focus was on the closest mage. Rain pouring down on her, her army screaming as they died, she found the trail of his magic. Then it was as if the world appeared through two lenses. In one, Amerae's attacker pulled back his sword to swing for the killing blow, and Faelyn knew she'd never get there in time.

In the other, Faelyn found the mage's crystal. He felt her intrusion, and malicious hate seeped through the trail of his magic. The crystal was too far away to control, but that wasn't her purpose. With a burst of effort, she squeezed and shattered it.

His horror and pain washed over the courtyard. He scrambled for the powerless shards as they tumbled toward the ground, wounding his hands on now-useless glass. It was as if she'd cut off his legs. It was enough. The other mages faltered. The magic holding her soldiers captive released.

Amerae gasped and dropped to the ground. The enemy's strike passed harmlessly over her head. She stabbed her sword up under the black armor, straining until her attacker slumped over dead. The remaining Alysians stumbled to life. They let loose a battle cry that reverberated off the stone, heard even over the constant thunder.

Faelyn cried with relief and focused on the next mage, fighting against fatigue and repelling enemy attacks. Already, the enemy mages regrouped, building up the magic to lock her army in place again. They could be annihilated before she destroyed enough mage crystals to make a difference, but she had to try. Exhaustion slowed her movements. Her white light dimmed.

A sharp pain exploded in her temples. It radiated outward and she fell, smashing her knees on the wet stone. Something slammed into her side, sending pain through her ribs. She raised her head. Miyah stood beside her, mage staff in both hands, poised to strike again. Faelyn's shield was gone. She gritted her teeth and raised her sword to block Miyah's next hit. The staff smashed into her, and her sharp blade cut into the wood and stuck. Miyah yanked it free. She bared her teeth in a snarl.

The enemy soldiers diverted to the Alysian army, wanting nothing to do with a fight between two powerful mages. Faelyn cried out in frustration. She couldn't defend herself and attack the mages at the same time.

Miyah used her special talent to teleport a ball of fire from a nearby torch. She hurled it forward. Faelyn struggled to her feet and extinguished it with a heavy wave of her hand, the flames sizzling in the rain. She tried to conjure her shield, but it wouldn't form.

She swung, whipping her sword through the air. Miyah raised her staff and grinned in malice.

"You're too weak to continue this futile attempt, Ali. I've always known you meant trouble for our good kingdom. And now look at what you've done. You've led them here to die." She shook her head, eyes scanning the massacre behind Faelyn. "Kian should have seen you for what you really are."

Above the rapid beating of Faelyn's heart, the screams of men and women dying, a roar resounded.

Faelyn let loose a shaky breath. *At last.* The other gate had been opened.

Miyah's gaze shot above the courtyard in time to see Kian run a mage through with his sword, staff aglow in his other hand. He was unmistakable in his silver Alysian armor. His helmet did not hide the hard planes of his face.

Miyah's mouth dropped open. Faelyn didn't hesitate. She reared back and stabbed Miyah through her black robes and into her chest. Miyah collapsed to the ground, blood flowing to mix with all the rest.

"I'm sorry you chose the wrong side. It'll be a quick death in honor of our history together." Faelyn sliced off her head before Miyah could heal herself.

Kian's soldiers advanced over the railing and down the stairs, attacking the enemy from behind. Faelyn's soldiers fought with renewed fury.

Amerae was a whirl of death, a beautiful thing to behold. Bolstered by the arrival of the rest of their army, suddenly the odds didn't seem so impossible.

Faelyn caught Kian's eye. He nodded to her. She slipped out of the fray under a portico, going through a familiar door and down a flight of stairs. The coolness of the air caressed her wet face. She rested against the wall, taking deep breaths to steady her heart.

Now it was her turn to change history.

CHAPTER FORTY-SIX

From within the castle, the sounds of battle tortured her—swords clanging viciously, the agonizing cries of soldiers dying, boots pounding against stone as enemy reinforcements arrived. Captains yelled orders on both sides among the continuous twang of bows and the sharp whack of arrows as they missed their targets and bounced off the castle walls.

And the screaming. If only she could drown out the screaming. It was a sound that would haunt the rest of her days, if she lived through this. Even the rain and thunder couldn't cover it. The reality of battle was nothing like reading it in a book. It was nothing like the day Daltieri had invaded her home. That was quick with few casualties. The horrifying sounds almost sent her back into the fray, but she trusted Kian to keep watch over their people while she did what she must inside the castle.

Faelyn's heavy breathing echoed down the dark and empty corridor. She used every precious second to allow her magic to replenish. The narrow tunnel was one of many traversing beneath the castle. It still looked the same, except for a mustiness and a thick layer of grime indicating the tunnels had fallen into disuse. From here she could either descend to the dungeons—a place she'd never dared visit as a child—or continue.

She trusted her instincts.

On light feet, she ran quickly, stopping at every intersection to listen for approaching enemies. This level housed the king's bunker, at least it did a hundred years ago. She'd played in it sometimes, earning a scolding from a random guard. If Daltieri worried about the safety of Lord Jamison, the bunker is where they'd take him. *If* they knew about it. *If* it still existed.

The further east Faelyn went, the more voices she heard, and the lighter the halls became, lit by distant torches. A good sign. Along with more human activity, Faelyn sensed the increasing presence of magic in the air. It confirmed her suspicions, but also meant Lord Jamison was well protected against any kind of attack. By the threads of magic quivering through the air, she estimated at least a dozen mages. All those minions trained at Thomats had been put to use.

She ducked into the shadows, pressing her back flat against the wall. It was impossible. There was no way she'd get through that many. Her hands shook from exhaustion as it was. She couldn't summon Kian. Their army needed him to lead in her absence.

Faelyn clenched her fists. She'd rather die than face defeat, or run away and leave Daltieri to bleed Alysies dry another day. Pushing off the wall, she made her way toward the bunker, turning corners in the familiar maze. The first of the lit torches were spaced out just enough to create dark patches in between. She hurried from one shadow to the next, still conserving her magical strength while it rejuvenated bit by bit.

Around the next corner, she heard the first guard. His sword clanked against metal armor as he paced up and down his section of the tunnel. When he paced away from her, she drew her sword and silently ran up behind him. When he turned, he only had time enough to widen his eyes before she stabbed him through the weak seam in his armored side.

She stifled a cry and eased the soldier to the ground as the life bled out of him, using a bit of wind to send his dying words in the opposite direction. Bile rose from her belly. The young man was barely old enough to be in this fight. All the wasteful killing. Her hand shot to her mouth to cover a sob as the life finally left the young soldier. This guilt was infinitely worse than all those years ago she'd killed those men outside the tavern. Her emotions ruled then. Now the need to free her people ruled.

She could have screamed for the injustice of it all. How many others like him had she already killed today? There had to be many more soldiers in her path to the bunker, waiting to kill her or die trying. She sent out her hearing. The guards increased in number at every turn.

Faelyn rose, gazing at the soldier with fierce regret, memorizing his young face, then walked away. No more. She couldn't take another life like that, even if it meant wasting precious magic.

Before rounding the next corner, she used Kian's trick and bent the light with the moisture in the dank hall, shielding herself from sight. The spell was easy after all these years performing it, but it sipped at her strength.

In the next hall, three guards paced the length, their eyes intent. They were clearly alert, aware of what was at stake if their army failed to stop the Alysian attack. Faelyn crept forward, then waited until the way was clear. She turned sideways, darting between them, and continued down the hall.

Her footsteps shuffled on the uneven stone floor, but the soldiers continued their pacing, unaware of her presence.

Faelyn was torn. With this method, she wasn't forced to quietly murder the young soldiers. But, they were the enemy. When her presence undoubtedly became known, they'd be three more people to fight against, or three more people to run for help, bringing the rest of the Daltieri army upon her.

Foolish as it was, she couldn't kill them in a fight that was less than fair. So her will and love for her kingdom carried her forward, skirting past a dozen more soldiers spaced out in three more hallways, before she stopped, readying herself for the final turn.

Faelyn peeked around the corner, instantly feeling silly—no one could see her. She bit back a groan of frustration. There were ten soldiers stacked up two across. Their shoulders grazed the walls, leaving no room for her to go around. Beyond them, the intensity of the mages protecting the bunker felt like the air before a lightning strike.

The one positive thing in the face of these impossible odds was that Lord Jamison was most definitely in the bunker. They wouldn't waste such precious resources leaving a false trail, not when the other mages were outside, hopefully dying.

Most likely, Lord Jamison didn't know who came for him, or if he did, he didn't believe the stories of Princess Faelyn living all this time. The last thing recorded history knew was that she could barely control her magic.

But how to get past the guards? She'd explored these passageways thoroughly in her youth, and there was only one entrance. There were also no secret passageways this far below the main castle. At least none she ever found.

Faelyn drew her sword. There was no other way. She had to conserve her magic, and she had to get in that room. The thick wooden door beyond the soldiers called to her. Somehow, she knew this was where she was meant to be.

Bracing herself, she took a deep breath and tensed to attack. Pounding feet behind her stopped her short. She swiveled to see a Daltieri runner zooming past the guards heading straight for her. She flattened herself against the wall, narrowly avoiding being barreled over. The runner skidded around the turn, then continued down the hall.

The first pair of guards parted for him.

Faelyn didn't hesitate. With a burst of speed, she caught up to him as he reached the next pair of guards. The rest of the guards rotated, parting to let the runner through like five sets of doors. Faelyn ran right on his heels, passing through without detection.

Almost to the bunker, she nearly stepped on the runner's heels. She pulled back, bumping into one of the guards. He stumbled. His eyes narrowed in a fear-inducing suspicion that sent Faelyn's heart pounding. She didn't want to kill these soldiers.

Hoping the guard wouldn't think twice about it, Faelyn stayed with the runner. He stopped at the door to the bunker which was flanked by two more huge, helmeted guards. The door wasn't quite as she remembered it. It was still wood, but had been painted black with a golden emblem of Daltieri's raven on it. The runner bent over, panting. He managed to stand upright to salute—a flat hand, palm down, hitting the emblem on his chest with the side of his hand.

"Spit it out, man," a door guard said.

"They're in the tunnels." The runner's voice was frantic, and he pointed, bouncing with nerves. "Sammie. He's dead! I found him surrounded by a pool of his own blood." His face crumpled. "Those rebel bastards. Who's going to tell his new wife?" He dropped his arm and leaned closer to the guard. "I think they followed me."

The distant shouts of surprise and clang of swords made Faelyn shuffle back a step. The sound grew louder, and the soldiers shifted, eyeing one another and reaching for their swords.

"You damned fool," the guard said, shoving the wide-eyed runner to the side and drawing his sword. "You led them right to His Lordship."

Faelyn was utterly confused. Who could have come this far unaided? She sent a bit of magic out with her hearing to get a feel for this new attacker.

Amerae. Michael. Kian.

They'd followed her into this madness. And she'd left all those soldiers in their path to fight off alone.

"Remember, Daltierians." The door guard's strong voice carried to his soldiers down the hall. "Protect his lordship at all costs. If we fail, the mages inside will finish them. We will not lose what our ancestors built for us. This land is rightfully ours."

Rightfully theirs? Faelyn clenched the hilt of her sword and widened her stance.

"Attack!" The guard waved his sword, but remained at his post by the door adjacent to the other soldier.

The fighting rounded the corner just as the ten soldiers rushed forward. The first thing Faelyn saw was Amerae's young face, fighting for her life against an enemy soldier. She backed up against his advance.

Her friends were surrounded. Faelyn fixed the door guard with a deadly glare, then dropped her veil. He cursed and lunged for her. They slammed together, blade to blade. His towering strength rattled her teeth. On his second swing, he knocked Faelyn backward with the power in his stroke. She stumbled, but regained her footing.

"Before I kill you," Faelyn said, meeting another thrust, "I want you to know this is my castle, stolen from me when I was barely of age. Daltieri has taken everything from Alysies for too long." She feinted left, but he didn't fall for it and blocked her.

The guard struck in a dizzying series of blows. In her exhausted state, Faelyn only just managed to keep up.

"That word is forbidden, fae. The use is punishable by death, which I will administer swiftly."

At the end of his vicious strikes, he swung a downward stroke like a hammer. The power behind the blow made her stumble, leaving him a perfect opening to end her.

Before she could call the magic to save herself, the tip of a sword appeared through his chest. Faelyn's brow shot up in confusion. The guard glanced down at his wound, then fell to his knees. Behind him stood the other door guard. He pushed his victim off his sword with a heavy boot.

The new guard rose to his full height, staring down at Faelyn. Then he bowed. "My queen, it is my honor to serve you."

Faelyn gaped.

"I'm a spy and a direct descendent of Mary. There is much to tell, and we have no time."

The name of the person who'd been a mother to her crashed over her. "You're a descendent of Mary?" She stared hard at the man in Daltieri black. They had the same hazelnut eyes, but that was all. Should she trust him? Her senses and instincts confirmed he spoke true, but...

Faelyn shook her head. He was wasting time while her friends battled for the chance to get into the bunker. She reached for the door and its brass handle.

"Wait!"

Her hand touched the metal. Light flashed bright as day. She flew backward, blinding pain shooting through her arm and back. The door guard rushed to her side, hands shaking. Faelyn sat up slowly and glared at the door. The pain fizzled out from her body.

"You should be dead! That door is spelled against entrance." He offered a hand.

Remarkably unscathed, Faelyn accepted his help up.

A scream sounded from behind. Faelyn spun around. Kian, Michael, and Amerae stood back to back in a triangle, fighting soldiers from all sides in the narrow hall.

Faelyn tensed to charge.

"My queen, this way." He reached to tug on her arm, then thought better of it. He pointed to a blank wall adjacent to the wood door.

"Yes, but first." Faelyn gripped her sword and charged, running as fast as her legs could carry her.

She reached the first soldier and slashed. Their expensive armor, similar to Kian's army, provided better coverage, and her blow glanced off. He cried out and turned. Faelyn aimed for a weak spot and finished him, moving to the next soldier.

More Daltieri noticed her presence, and two broke from the main foray and attacked. She met Kian's gaze, and he gave her a grim smile.

Sweat dripped off Amerae. Her mouth was set in a determined line as she pivoted and thrust. With an expert move, she knocked her opponent's sword out of the way and into another attacking enemy.

Faelyn stabbed her soldier, then moved aside as another one struck. He missed her and hit the stone wall with a deafening clang. She risked a quick glance at Michael. He moved with efficient speed, equally as talented as Amerae in form. But he was outnumbered. Three enemy soldiers attacked him at once. Michael struck and parried, keeping pace just enough not to die, but he tired. Amerae was too intent on her own two opponents.

Faelyn pushed toward him, deflecting the soldier in front of her.

Kian's eyes widened. He knew. He hedged toward Michael, but more soldiers pushed forward, diverting him.

Faelyn didn't have enough magic yet to help. Panic descended. Her body broke into a cold sweat. With a strong kick, she slammed her soldier back. His head cracked against the wall knocking him out cold. She ran toward Michael. Kian and his attackers blocked her way. She couldn't cut through them fast enough. She reached for the reserves of her magic. There wasn't enough to stop what she saw coming.

"Michael!" Amerae screamed. She snarled at her opponents, fighting her way through.

But she wasn't fast enough.

Michael stumbled, then cried out in pain as he was stabbed in the leg.

"No!" Amerae's mouth dropped open in horror.

Michael's opponents descended upon him. Faelyn lost sight of him in the blood-frenzy.

CHAPTER FORTY-SEVEN

Faelyn lunged past a pair of soldiers—trying to reach Michael—and earned the sharp sting of a slice in her forearm. Grabbing onto Kian's staff, she concentrated. The power rushed to her. She sucked the air from the lungs of every Daltieri soldier still moving. They choked, clutching at their throats. Each one of them fell to the ground, dead.

Faelyn glanced wildly around. She spotted Michael's face hidden beneath two collapsed Daltieri soldiers. His eyes were closed, and blood ran from his mouth.

Faelyn leaped forward and shoved the first soldier off the pile. Amerae screamed. She grappled for the second body, and together they hauled it away. Kian's mage crystal glowed as he attempted to heal Michael, but it was too late. There was no essence to him. His soul had departed.

Amerae crumpled to the floor beside Michael, fingers raking over his bloodied armor. Her breathing came in shallow sobs. Faelyn reached to comfort her, but Amerae shot to her feet and brandished her sword. She put pressure on a wound in her side, wildly scanning the hall, ready to destroy the world with tears brimming her eyes.

Devastation was written on Kian's face.

"Amerae, I'm sorry." Faelyn's words were more than inadequate. Nausea roiled within.

This was her fault.

Her fault. Her fault. Her fault.

She'd shown mercy to her enemy. Michael was dead because of her. Loyal Michael, who loved Amerae even more than the Alysian cause. Her eyes burned. Her body burned with self-hate.

Pain burst from Amerae's essence. She roared, then charged past Faelyn—right toward Mary's descendant at the end of the hall. His wide eyes darted to Faelyn. He raised the sword to defend himself.

Faelyn ran after her. "Amerae, stop! He's on our side."

Amerae skidded to a halt, teeth clenched. She met Faelyn's eyes for a long moment, tears streaming down both their faces. Her sword clanged to the ground, and she trudged back to Michael and dropped to her knees.

"You're bleeding." Kian pointed to Faelyn's arm where her wound wasn't healing.

"I'm okay." *I deserve to bleed.*

He nodded and, stepping over bodies, quietly went to Amerae's side and began healing her wound.

"Kian, I must continue." Faelyn placed a tender hand on the back of Amerae's head as she knelt, sobbing over Michael's lifeless body.

Her fault. All her fault.

"I know." Kian sent comfort and encouragement in his words.

Faelyn turned and followed the false door guard, leaving her friends behind.

"What's your name?" Faelyn asked, voice hollow. They entered the small alcove before the door. The magic was thick, and she couldn't hear anything from inside the bunker.

"Nolan Maddux, Your Majesty." His eyes were grim inside his helmet. "I'm not the only ally. There are some of us who carry Mary's love for you and have remained loyal to an Alysian kingdom. When we heard you were alive, after all this time, we banded together and secretly infiltrated the palace. We aren't many, but two are mages inside that room."

Faelyn's chest ached. Here was proof of how love could bend the will of time, echoing across generations with something as simple as selflessly caring for another person.

"Now come," Nolan said. "I know the way. This door is enchanted and sealed from the inside." He pulled a loose stone from the wall adjacent to the bunker door and stuck his hand in the hole. The clack of a crank turning came from within. A small doorway swung inward revealing a dark, musty tunnel. He hurried down the narrow space, and Faelyn followed. It smelled stale and dry from disuse.

Footsteps resounded behind her. She felt Kian's presence, and behind him, Amerae. Faelyn's steps became surer at the swell of love within her. None of these people owed her anything, and yet here they were, ready to lay down their lives, unquestioningly devoted. It was a love she'd never felt before. A love she'd never known to hope for.

She would earn this love she'd been given. Acantha above knew what she'd done to deserve it, but she vowed to earn it. She'd do better.

"I don't remember this being here before." Faelyn kept her voice down in hopes they still held the element of surprise.

"It was constructed nearly seventy years ago when King Samual fortified the castle. He thought it short-sighted that the bunker only had one way in or out." Nolan turned a corner and kept going, moving quickly in the dark.

Behind her, Kian lit his mage crystal.

Faelyn gritted her teeth. *Samual.* She hated him too much to grudgingly admit it was a good move. One of her many regrets was that old age had taken him before she could.

"What will we find when we get there?" Amerae sounded strong and brave, but her grief echoed in the tunnel.

"The bunker is not a single room, but a complex," Nolan said, rushing through the dusty tunnel. "Think of it as a king's apartment, with servants' quarters and separate rooms. It's meant to sustain the dwellers for an indefinite amount of time."

"Lord Jamison is a coward. I've always known it. This confirms it." Amerae's words snapped like fangs. "Why is he not outside leading his army?"

"Because he's a weakling," Kian said. "Descended from a long line of weaklings. It's why their kingdom won't trade with Creadel. They're worried their people will see how things should be in a kingdom ruled fairly, where the assets from the land are given back to the people, instead of shipped off to feed Daltieri greediness. It's why they beat and murder you when you can't pay their tax increases. It's why we must win today."

"We're here. Quiet now." Nolan stopped in the middle of the hall, facing an unassuming stone wall.

Air whistled through the cracks of the door.

Amerae put a stern hand against Nolan's chest. "How many are in there?" Her words were a fierce whisper.

Kian clenched his staff. He already knew what to expect. He felt the power of the mages just as Faelyn did. Every ounce of her concentration went to restoring her magic and calming her racing mind. Every challenge that had brought them to this point—all the death and punishing trials—was nothing compared to what lay in wait beyond this door.

"The odds aren't good, Lady Amerae," Nolan said. "I'd rather there were more of you."

"This is all that can be spared." Kian gestured toward the door. "Open it."

Nolan nodded and pulled a loose stone from the wall as he had the last door. The four of them drew their weapons, tensing as the crank sounded. Faelyn's heart pounded. Amerae wiped sweat off her brow. Nolan looked to Faelyn, and with her quick nod, he pushed on the door.

Faelyn grabbed his arm as an idea took shape. "Wait!"

He paused, and they all looked at her.

"Kian, can you put a veil up over yourself, like you taught me so long ago?"

"I can," he said with a tilt of his head.

"I have enough to do the same for me and Amerae—stay close to me," she said to her. "Nolan, you're the guard. Go in there and report the slaughter of the men. Try to draw some of the waiting soldiers out. We'll sneak in and see if we can dispatch Lord Jamison before we're detected."

Amerae sidled next to her, eagerness for vengeance plain in her eyes. Kian's mage crystal glowed, then he and his staff disappeared from sight. Faelyn concentrated. It took more effort to shield them both, and even more because she still hadn't recovered her strength, but she managed.

"Go, Nolan. Make it convincing," Faelyn said.

Nolan pushed open the door—and came face to face with the point of ten swords and the glow of five mage staffs. He stumbled a bit, holding his left side with his free hand, and tore off his helmet revealing dark hair down to his chin. He looked younger than she first thought, not even twenty.

"They found their way to the bunker," he cried out. "They... they're slaughtering everyone!" He swiveled his head back and forth, and Faelyn saw a good show of true fear in the whites of his eyes.

The soldiers pulled back their swords. A higher-ranking soldier stepped forward. Golden spaulders on each shoulder, and a gold plume in his helmet. "Did they follow you?"

"No. I don't think so. I got away while the troops were being attacked. Gilmore's dead, General Roque." Nolan pressed forward, still holding his side, and the soldiers parted.

Faelyn, Kian, and Amerae bunched close together, staying right behind him. They barely breathed. Amerae nearly bumped into a burly soldier with a distrustful scowl. Faelyn jerked her back by the arm, keeping a wary eye on the mages. They watched Nolan closely. Two of them looked right at her, sending her heart into a gallop, but then their gazes slipped past.

"How many?" General Roque peered out the door. His shoulders were as wide as two of Faelyn.

"Only ten, but they had a powerful mage with them. She killed six soldiers at once." Nolan moved further into the room, then slumped against the wall. Faelyn and her companions flanked him.

The room was just as Faelyn remembered—a large rectangular box of stone with wooden doorways. Those doors connected to bedrooms and servants' quarters, a small barrack for the guards, an even smaller armory, and a kitchen. All things necessary for protection and an extended stay for the king. Or Lord Jamison of Daltieri.

Chairs lined the wall at random, along with oil lamps. Daltieri tapestries covered the walls and depicted the gold discovery that had turned the tide in their favor. Animal hide rugs decorated the floor. The main entrance to the bunker was triple barred, and the magic felt even stronger from the inside. She would have never gotten through.

General Roque waved over one of the mages. He looked very familiar...

Fenedict! The mage from Thomats who'd been so harsh during her application. His grey hair and thinner frame didn't disguise his familiar permanent scowl. Faelyn tensed. He was very powerful.

Fenedict pressed toward the door. "It's her. I feel the magic she's using. If she makes it past the guards, she might be able to counteract our spell."

General Roque sniffed and glanced at the soldiers. "All right. You twenty take the passage and surprise them. You too, Fenedict."

Fenedict frowned. "I will not put myself in harm's way, General."

Unintimidated, General Roque stepped up, looking down his nose. Fenedict's mage crystal glowed in reaction.

"King Seber commands you, Fenedict. And you have sworn to

devote yourself to protecting your kingdom. I am in charge here, unless you'd like me to retrieve his lordship."

Fenedict's gaze darted to a door in the center of the long wall, directly to Faelyn's right. Her body vibrated. That was where Lord Jamison sheltered. Nolan had picked his resting spot purposely and strategically.

"Fine, General. For king and country." Fenedict followed twenty troops out the secret door, scowling the entire time.

General Roque shoved the door closed and latched it with a thick metal bar. That left only five troops and four mages in the main room.

Faelyn's nerves overshadowed her relief. Like a fool, she hadn't asked Nolan what else had changed. So far, the bunker looked the same, besides the decorations, but rooms or other tunnels could have been added. Lord Jamison could be escaping and she wouldn't know it. They didn't have much time. The soldiers would soon discover their comrades were already dead.

She sensed Kian move away from the wall, and she strained to follow his movements with hearing alone. This plan was seeming more and more foolish. How could she know what he was doing if she couldn't see him?

Whatever he planned to do, she couldn't wait around to be discovered. She tugged on Amerae's arm, and together they edged toward Lord Jamison's room. The door was not spelled, but she sensed several people and a lot of power emanating from within. More mages? She had to end this quick. A blade to his throat, force him to surrender. The four of them wouldn't win the next round if it came to blows.

Faelyn positioned herself to kick in the door. A scream of agony made her jerk back. One of the mages clutched at a hole in his chest from a wound that appeared out of nowhere. He fell to his knees. The enemy blanched and drew their weapons. The room filled with the glow of mage light.

With an exasperated sigh, Faelyn switched the sword to her left hand and linked arms with Amerae.

Another mage dropped with a similar wound in his chest. General Roque began shouting orders. Faelyn led Amerae behind the wide-eyed soldiers who shuffled in place, having no idea what was happening. Faelyn lunged and together, they stabbed killing blows into the nearest two.

The remaining soldiers slashed wildly through the air in all directions, making them impossible to approach. A strong wind gusted in the room, blowing tapestries askew and flickering the lamplight. One of the mages used her magic in a blind panic. She went down next from Kian's invisible sword.

Panic gripped Faelyn's throat. What if these mages were the allies Nolan mentioned? He stood against the wall with a hard grip on his sword, but didn't intervene. Surely, he'd defend them if so. Maybe their allies were in the next room?

General Roque rushed to stand in front of Lord Jamison's door, swinging his sword. "Do something!" he screamed at the remaining mage.

Faelyn jumped back, nearly beheaded by his swinging sword. Amerae pulled away.

"Wait, stay close!" Faelyn hissed, reaching.

Faelyn pushed her magic, but the spell faltered. Amerae appeared standing right in front of General Roque. His eyes widened, and he swung. Amerae jumped back, barely escaping the blade aimed to gut her.

Nolan struck with a quick dash. General Roque swiped at him, and he retreated a few steps.

"I should have known, boy. You were only too eager to volunteer for the last stand." Roque's eyes narrowed as he watched Amerae and Nolan.

The final mage's crystal flared. Out of nowhere, a roaring downpour cascaded over the room. The water destroyed the delicate balance of light and moisture, disrupting Faelyn and Kian's spells.

They were revealed, right before Kian plunged his sword into the mage's back.

Amerae and General Roque erupted into a violent duel. Faelyn had no choice but to take on the final three guards.

She ducked a swing, then stabbed up and under one guard's armor. She couldn't get her sword free fast enough to duck the middle guard. She pivoted, and he stabbed her arm where he'd aimed for her heart. The pain forced an involuntary cry from her lips.

Kian emitted a guttural yell of fury and charged across the room. He cut the soldier down in one swipe. He dispatched the third guard while Faelyn struggled to heal herself. Her palm glowed over the wound, but the light sputtered.

Kian's brow creased in concern. "You're spent. You've done too much." He finished healing her wound for her.

She pushed his hand away. "I'm fine, Kian. Help Amerae."

General Roque and Amerae circled each other. He towered over her in height, arms as thick as her neck. When he swung, she caught the blow with her sword, but the force knocked her back. The anger at being outmatched rolled off her in waves.

Nolan and Kian approached, swords at the ready.

"Don't you dare. He's mine," Amerae yelled, blocking an overhead hit.

General Roque looked up, and that was all the opening Amerae needed. She hit his sword aside, then threw all the strength she had into redirecting her blade in a downward blow. She sliced off his hand. He screamed as his sword bounced off the wet stone floor.

Breathing hard, Amerae pointed her sword to his throat. "Open the door."

His back hit the wall. "Never," he managed between wails of agony. His eyes set into a hard look of resolve.

Amerae pressed her blade into his neck, drawing blood. His cries died out, lips pressed tight.

Kian took his staff and knocked the general over the head. The hard wood thumped skull, and Roque drooped. Amerae shoved him, and he stumbled toward the door.

Faelyn pushed off the wall and joined them. "She said open it."

The general spat.

Nolan ripped a key off General Roque's belt. The lock clicked, and Amerae shoved Roque through the door.

Ten—*ten!*—mages stood in a circle, black robes absorbing the light of their staffs. They wore a mixture of menace, nervousness, and practiced neutrality. In the middle of them, Lord Jamison sat at a small, eloquently carved dining table, eating fancy, delicate pastries as if his life wasn't in jeopardy. His grey beard moved with his slow, calm chewing. His lined eyes and the creases of his mouth were indicative of a man who'd spent a lifetime glaring at others. But his face was relaxed, unconcerned they had made it so far.

"Surrender or I kill him," Amerae said.

Faelyn internally applauded the effort, but it was the hope of youth that it would be that easy. Already Faelyn felt the swell of power from the mages, even if it couldn't yet be seen. They'd come so far just to fail now. Too much was riding on this moment. Too much they stood to lose.

Everything. She'd lose everything if they failed.

Two of the mages were loyal, but Faelyn didn't know which. Could she fight to the death and risk killing a loyal subject? She scanned each of their faces in turn, hoping for a nod or some kind of sign.

Then she saw him. Mason, one of the mages she'd known at Thomats. He caught her eye and tilted his head ever so slightly to his left. Avier! She'd traveled with him from Creadel. She'd always adored his accent, and he'd always been so kind. She couldn't believe her luck.

Kian looked to his friends with an eager smile.

"Kill them," Lord Jamison said, tossing a half-eaten sugared pastry on a porcelain plate. He wiped his hands on the robe of the nearest mage.

Amerae tensed.

General Roque struggled. "The fae's magic is gone. She—."

Amerae slit his throat, cutting off his final words.

The room exploded into chaos.

Amerae and Nolan charged, only to be thrown back by a blast of wind. They hit the wall and collapsed into heaps. Faelyn focused, using precious energy to shatter the closest mage's crystal. He cried out and charged with a sword. Kian quickly disemboweled him. Amerae and Nolan clamored to their feet.

The space became a hurricane of wind and water as the mages wielded their skills. The force whipped Faelyn's hair from its plait. Untouched, Lord Jamison watched impassively from the eye of the storm. There were seven enemy mages left. If she could get to Lord Jamison, she could end it—with the sword, if not by magic.

She surged forward, feet sloshing through collecting water. A mage stepped in her path, air blasting from his staff. She shoved against the blasting winds and sliced her sword into him, so easy compared to the resistance of armor. He fell, and she braced for the next attack.

Her friends each took on an opponent. The enemy mages yelled in surprise when Avier and Mason turned and attacked. Avier tripped his opponent to the ground and pinned her by some invisible force. Kian used water magic against a mage with earth abilities. The mage shook the ground beneath Kian, sending tremors through the room. Kian careened, but kept his footing. He counteracted with blasts of water, dodging back and forth as his opponent struggled to follow.

Amerae and Nolan wielded their swords with blurring speeds. Faelyn's fear spiked at the amount of blood already on them, but their skills with a blade steadily matched the mages' ability.

Faelyn charged ahead, intent on Lord Jamison. Avier called out a warning just as she sensed the shield protecting him. She slammed into it face-first. Agony bounced around her skull. Tears and rain blinded her, and blood gushed from her nose. She fought to recover her wits.

Rain extinguished the lanterns. Only mage light and flashes of spells lit the room. Over the gusting wind and sounds of skirmishes, came the roar of fire. She pivoted just in time. A massive wave of blue flame shot toward her. Breath caught in her throat. She threw her sword up against the onslaught, creating a shield of air. The might of the blaze came from above like a waterfall of flame, forcing her into a crouch. Her shield deflected the searing heat, which boiled the water around her.

When the flames ended, Faelyn released her shield, panting. Her sword drooped, suddenly heavy. The heat seared her skin.

"So, General Roque was correct."

Faelyn glanced up.

Lord Jamison stood above her at the edge of the shield, hands clasped behind his back. "You used too much magic forcing your weak army into my castle."

Faelyn wiped blood from her nose. Behind her, a mage approached slowly, gathering his magic. Lord Jamison thought he was distracting her. Pushing aside the fear and bloodlust roiling through the room, she felt his confidence of a sure victory.

Faelyn grunted to her feet. "I'll give you one more chance to surrender, but it's more than you deserve."

His face finally lost its impassivity. He broke into a wry smile as if he found her antics amusing.

The mage behind her lunged. She ducked as the staff attempted to brain her. It grazed her hair as it passed. With all her might, she hefted her sword, slicing up. The blade stuck in the hard wood. Faelyn wrenched the staff out of the mage's hand, and it clattered to the ground.

Faelyn kicked it away and spun, facing her attacker. The woman snarled her fury and drew a sword. She thrust, but lacked any kind of form. Faelyn pivoted and struck deep into her side. The mage died quickly.

The release in the room was an audible whoosh as the shield around Lord Jamison disintegrated. Standing water cascaded into his elegant space.

Faelyn slowly turned, wiping the rain off her face. Staring Lord Jamison down, she cleaned the blood off her blade on the fallen mage's cloak, then pointed her sword straight at his heart.

"You wasted your last chance." Faelyn stepped forward to end this once and for all. For Alysies.

A surge of power shot from behind her. Her air cut off. She couldn't breathe. Twenty soldiers charged into the room. Faelyn turned to see Fenedict directing his glowing crystal at her. He shook his head with contempt. She collapsed to her knees, trying to counteract the spell. Air came rushing back. She took a deep breath, then it was gone again.

Faelyn looked to her friends.

Amerae had collapsed in a bloody puddle, eyes closed. A mage towered over her, panting.

Mason lay motionless on the ground, discarded. Avier bled heavily from a gash on his head, and was guarded by several soldiers.

Two soldiers forced Nolan to his knees, wrenching his arms behind him.

Kian. She watched in horror as soldiers swarmed Kian. He blew them back with wind, face contorted in agony and struggling to reach her, but more raced in. He was overtaken. They beat him, taking his staff and sword. They held him captive with his own blade.

Black spots bloomed in Faelyn's vision. She fell forward on her hands. Concentrating hard, she got another mouth full of air. Dizziness hit her in waves. Light mixed with darkness around the room—the glow of mage crystals, the glint off of swords. Someone rekindled the torches, casting shadows over the bloodbath that blurred in her vision.

Lord Jamison approached, leaning over her, carelessly close. "You made an impressive go of it, Faelyn. Or is it Ali?" His smug tone of triumph washed over her. "You've even made a believer out of us. How ironic it is that you should return now, only to have things end the same way they did before."

He knelt beside her, staring. Faelyn didn't meet his eyes. She looked at Kian, mind racing for a way to save him. He stared back, lips parted, brow creased in sadness. He struggled uselessly against his captors.

Faelyn's anger ratcheted her magic, allowing air to come in sips.

"King Samual had a sister, you know. I'm a descendant of her. Our king searched long and hard, never truly believing you were dead. You know what he wrote in his journals? What he swore to his dying day? That you'd come back, and we'd have to defeat you or perish." He chuckled. "I believe he was right. But before I end you, you get to watch your friends die."

Lord Jamison nodded, and the soldiers stabbed Avier through the chest. He collapsed, dead.

Anger and despair washed over her. Fury pushed her magic enough to take a full breath. Her cry of agony split the air. "No!"

Lord Jamison turned to Kian. Faelyn's mouth dropped open in horror. His nod would end the person she cared most about in this world. She was watching Mary die at the hands of the Daltieri all over again. Once more powerless to stop it. All the rage and pain in the world couldn't save him, just as it couldn't save Mary.

She took several deep breaths.

Lord Jamison paced in front of her. "My family studied you and the events of that day, even as we banned all knowledge from our people. King Samual did you a favor, really, when he murdered your father. You were finally able to leave the man who never loved you. Hated you, even, to have never named you heir, even to the detriment of his own kingdom. King Samual did New Daltieri a favor as well. Isaac turned his kingdom to ruin. And now look at how well we're doing." He raised his arms in the air.

Faelyn sagged to the floor, more black than color in her vision.

"Give her a breath, Fenedict. I'm not done yet."

The magical hold lifted slightly, and air came rushing into Faelyn's lungs. She coughed, taking in as many breaths as possible, and then the air was gone.

"Before I kill your next friend, I want you to know something, Faelyn. King Samual did have feelings for you. It was his only source of shame. That, and letting you get away."

Faelyn snarled, seeing red.

He gave the signal, and a soldier approached Kian, sword raised to end him.

She'd failed. Failed at everything, and those she loved would die once more, because of her. At least this time she'd die with them.

Kian stopped struggling, locking eyes with her. He gave a small smile, sending feelings of love as the sword swung fast at his neck.

With the last of her breath, she screamed. All the heartbreak she'd ever suffered and all the love she'd ever been given coalesced to a single point within her soul. It hurt like a wild, feral thing, begging for release. Time slowed down.

Yes, she'd suffered, but there had also been love. There was love, and she was deserving of it, no matter her mistakes in life. She was enough, and it was okay to admit that, and it was okay to forgive herself.

The pain eased to pressure—an untapped reserve of magic. The point within her soul strained and burst apart. Strength and magic unlike any she'd ever felt poured through her veins.

She was master of the elements—earth, wind, water, fire, and aether—and she was enough.

She thrust out her power and tore through Fenedict's restraints. Breath and life rushed back into her, and she pushed to her feet. "You will not take from me again!"

The wildness of the spell overtook her, and she gave into her instincts, not knowing what would happen. A fatal ring of all the elements she'd ever learned to wield, of all the strength ever hers to command, shot outward through the room. She poured the pain of all the love denied her, and the beauty of the love she'd been graced with into one final effort.

Tears stained her cheeks as constant waves of light filled the room in a blinding pool.

The soldiers rushed her, and the mages attempted to protect Jamison. Faelyn pushed and pushed until there was no more of herself to give. The magic granted to her by love, desperation, or Fate's design, depleted.

CHAPTER FORTY-EIGHT

Ardenis opened his eyes. Water dripped on his face in a continuous stream. *Drip, drip, drip.* He blinked and wiped his face. When he sat up, he groaned involuntarily. Pain racked his body, and his head throbbed. His robes were soaked through where he lay in the grass, shivering.

He and Rhea had crashed into a ravine. Someone must have pulled them out.

He raised his arm, and the patter of cold rain hit the back of his hand. *Rain!* It was raining in Acantha. He'd wished for this time and again, but never imagined it would actually happen.

Night washed over the courtyard. The only light came from the lanterns sheltered by buildings, and the lightning above. Acanthians surrounded him, staring into the sky. Where was Rhea?

"Rhea!" Ardenis got to his feet, head pounding with each movement. Mud was smeared over his blue robes.

"Ardenis." Rhea lifted her head from where she lay nearby in the wet grass.

Ardenis rushed to her side. He didn't see any visible injuries, but he knew from watching Thera that some injuries were on the inside and could kill you.

"Stop this, Ardenis." Rhea clutched his hand in both of hers. "We're counting on you." She brought his hands closer, then shoved them away. The motion forced him to stand to avoid sprawling backward. Her enforcers crouched beside her. "Go!"

Ardenis turned around and ran from the hordes of people surrounding the accident. Acanthians were ill-prepared to treat injuries or deal with the shock of the weather. He'd told his watchers, the only ones who might have thought to bring him and Rhea out of the rain, to go to the dining hall.

So much time had passed since the crash. Chasms had opened in the ground all over. Lampposts lay toppled. Too many buildings had cracks running through them or had collapsed completely. Things were much worse, and he had no idea how to stop it.

"What must I do?" The storm whipped his voice away.

Please, let me stop this. He shut his eyes while his feet carried him down the familiar path. Wind came in blasting bursts threatening to topple him. The Fates had to listen. *Help me know what to do to save us, and to save Faelyn. And Amerae. And everyone I hold dear. I'm here for a reason. I learned to love and sacrificed that eternal love for a purpose.*

He opened his eyes. *Love.*

Love was the key. It's what Ardenis knew that no other Acanthian did, save one. A burning in his veins carried him forward. His instincts roared to life.

The monotonous white houses of the residential section blurred past him. The homes had been abandoned, people seeking answers and refuge from the storm. All the houses remained dark. All except one at the end of the lane. The one he sought.

He knew who that house belonged to.

Hector.

The pain in Ardenis's body subsided. He dashed to Hector's house, dodging cracks and ravines that grew in size the further he went. He jumped over a sinkhole, barely clearing the edge. The ground on the other side of him split open, raising up and crashing down in a thunderous quake.

Ardenis stumbled to the house and threw open the door.

On the floor, atop a carefully laid blanket, Hector lay tangled with Cadence.

CHAPTER FORTY-NINE

Faelyn fell to her hands and knees in the water-logged room. Rain no longer pelted her.

Silence penetrated her mind as white light gave way to black night.

"My Queen!" Amerae, covered in blood, rushed to her side. Her face held a healthy glow, and she didn't wince when she moved. She'd been healed.

Faelyn blinked at her surroundings. Mages and soldiers dead all around her.

"Where's Kian?" The words came out half a whisper, burning as her throat tried to work around the roughness, as if she'd swallowed sand. Had she been too late?

Nolan fell to his knees beside her, water splashing. "You saved us, Queen Faelyn. You saved us." She saw him through her fae senses, and he was unscathed.

"Your magic destroyed them," Amerae said. "We've been healed."

Nausea spun the room. "Kian?" Her gaze shot from body to body. She silently begged them to end her torment.

A dark form stirred in the corner. A mage light came to life, bringing the room into clear focus. Bodies and weapons were piled around the edges, the walls and floor now bare of anything but bloody water.

"Faelyn." Kian's clear voice eased the tightness in her chest. He stumbled to his feet and rushed over to her. "You're hurt. You didn't heal yourself."

Faelyn sagged to the floor. Her friends were alive. "I'll be okay." Magic trickled in, healing what it could. She'd spent every last drop, and then some, to save them.

The door opened, spilling lamplight into the room. Three soldiers in Alysian armor stopped just inside.

"Oh, thank Acantha," one of them said. "We feared the worse."

"What's happening out there?" Kian straightened his shoulders.

Faelyn sat up. Exhaustion left her breathless, but it was still the sweet fatigue of relief.

The soldier bowed to her. "Your Majesty. It's not over outside. They fight on. We are sustaining heavy losses."

Faelyn gasped and pushed to her feet. The room spun, making her stomach roil.

Amerae, Nolan, and Kian put their hands out to steady her. "You must rest, Your Majesty," Amerae said.

They had to end this battle.

"Get Jamison's body," she said to the soldiers. "Follow me." Faelyn pushed passed the dizziness, feeling stronger with each step.

In the main room of the bunker, dead bodies and blood littered the ground. The main door was open, but the secret passage door more closely resembled a pile of rubble.

Stepping over bodies, her companions and the soldiers carrying Jamison's body traveled through the maze of tunnels. Faelyn averted her eyes when they reached Michael. Amerae's hitched breathing sounded behind her.

They'd honor him properly when it was all over.

The shouting and clanging of swords grew as they drew closer to the courtyard. The storm raged even stronger now, lightning and thunder punctuating the screams of agony and death. Faelyn stepped out into the dark of night, lit only by torchlight and random fires that had ignited around the courtyard.

Dead bodies made a sick puzzle of black and silver, pieced together and laying wall to wall in the wake of so much killing. Rainwater washed over the courtyard, taking their blood with it. Those still fighting did so as if through sand, with slow reflexes and heavy movements.

Kian and Nolan rushed into the fray to defend their people, battling fierce and strong. Faelyn smiled, breathing a sigh of relief. They fought with renewed strength, taking on more enemies than she would have thought possible.

But the Alysian numbers wore thin. They were horribly outnumbered.

Faelyn hurried, keeping close to the castle wall. Amerae shadowed her steps, a fierce sense of protectiveness emanating from her. Amerae knew how vulnerable Faelyn really was.

Rain battered their faces, and wind howled, threatening to carry them away. The storm grew more powerful, and the earth rumbled beneath their feet. What kind of weather was this? There was no sense of the time of day—no sun, nor moon, nor stars.

She crossed under the portico, her entourage following, then rounded a corner for the stairs leading to the upper level of the courtyard. There were few to kill on the way up. Both sides were fighting to the death.

Finally, they reached the top.

"Bring him to the railing." Faelyn motioned to the three soldiers carrying Jamison. "Hold him upright." They brought him forward, a display for all to see, unmistakable with his gray beard and regal clothes.

Faelyn stepped up to the banister. Reaching inside herself, she conjured a great, white light. It bathed the courtyard, illuminating it like day and chasing away the shadows. The fighting halted as men and women squinted, shielding their eyes. The number of soldiers in black absorbing each pinpoint of silver was alarming.

Kian grinned up at her through the rain. Enemy soldiers stilled by his side at the sight of their dead leader. They glanced at each other uncertainly.

Lord Calem, remarkably alive, came scrambling up the stairs. Helmet misplaced, he was red-faced and bleeding from his scalp. He moved to stand beside Faelyn, but Amerae stopped him, placing herself in the way and pushing him back gently by the shoulders.

"Lay down your arms, Daltieri." Faelyn's voice boomed out with the power of the wind, carrying to the furthest reaches of the castle, even over the storm. The authority in it was unmistakable. "Behold, I have slain your lord, as I will do to the rest of you. The castle is mine. Surrender or perish."

Would they listen? Faelyn watched them in the courtyard below, waiting. Even the storm seemed to hold its breath.

A single enemy soldier among the many dropped his sword. It clanged to the ground in the ominous silence.

Nolan.

He looked pointedly at the other Daltieri, then bowed to his knees. Faelyn hid her admiration. Armored in the black and gold of the enemy, the genius had placed himself right in the middle of the battle.

Several others spaced around the fray sent their swords clanging to the ground as well. Loyalists? They mirrored Nolan, taking to their knees.

With several Daltieri leading the way, the rest of them followed. In a reluctant and weary wave of black, they sank down, leaving only her soldiers standing.

"It is done, Alysies!" Faelyn raised her sword in the air. Rain plinked against the metal, and thunder accentuated her words.

The resounding roar of her army shook the foundation of the castle. The battle was won. Alysies would be free.

Kian bowed to his knees first, followed by Amerae and the rest of their army. Pride and love and the exhilaration of a promise kept filled her soul until it sang.

And still, the storm raged on.

CHAPTER FIFTY

Hector and Cadence moved together on the blanket. Ardenis's gut clenched as fear chased his shock away. How could they? This kind of love was for Thera. It didn't exist in Acantha.

They kissed, and lightning crashed with a deafening roar nearby.

Neither of them noticed the sound, just as neither of them noticed Ardenis. A sickness beyond anything he'd ever felt dropped from his heart into his stomach. His knees shook, and he nearly stumbled.

Their breathing hitched, increasing to what Ardenis knew would be the end of Acantha.

Without another moment's hesitation, Ardenis ran toward them. Using strength he never knew he had, he grabbed Hector by the shoulders and hurled him backward. Hector crashed into the table, snapping it beneath him. His wide-eyed shock turned into snarling fury. Cadence screamed and fumbled for the blanket to cover her nakedness.

Ardenis didn't give Hector time to get up. He clenched his fists, strode two paces, and began punching with all his might. Fear gave way to fury. Punch after punch, he laid into Hector's face. Hector fell unconscious after the second hit. Blood poured from his nose and face and mouth.

Cadence grabbed Ardenis by the shoulders. He paused only long enough to shove her across the room. Thunder shook the house.

Ardenis couldn't stop. He didn't want to. He wanted to kill Hector. For Laida and Faelyn. For Amalia. For Rhea. For himself. For every foul thing Hector had ever done. For Acantha, and Thera. For every soul Hector would have destroyed with his selfish, hatred-driven desires.

"Ardenis, stop!" Rhea's voice cut through the room like a knife, severing Ardenis's rage. With clenched teeth, he snapped back to reality.

His hands throbbed. He flexed his fingers and felt bone popping, sending agonizing pain up his arm. Hector's face was a bloody, swollen mess. Cadence wept under the cover of the blanket.

Ardenis panted hard. He grabbed Hector's arm and hauled him over his shoulders like a sack of grain.

He faced Rhea and her enforcers. "There's no time for a trial, Rhea. These two need to be born. Immediately. It's the only way to right what's been done here this day. It's the only way to stop the storm." Hector couldn't be exiled to the Dark Unknown without a unanimous trial, but they didn't have time to wait.

Rhea dropped her hand from her mouth. "That is not our way, Ardenis." She shook her head in horror, surveying Hector and Cadence as if she couldn't believe what she was seeing.

That same disbelief still raged through Ardenis. "Did you even know this was possible? They were performing the act of creating life. How can that even happen *here*?" They'd all but destroyed the balance between worlds.

Lightning flashed outside, and her expression transitioned to resignation. "No. We have no laws. There is no precedence for it." She stared wide-eyed, kneading her hands together. "You're right. My enforcers will take Cadence to the northwest transfer hall immediately. Hector will be born here."

So they wouldn't be born in the same region of Thera. Maybe that was punishment enough for their crimes, even if it wasn't exile.

Rhea turned to give them instructions. "Wait there until the transfers are working again, no matter how long it takes. Do not let her go until she is in the gateway." Rhea faced Cadence, who was now weeping in earnest. "You've nearly ruined us all with your selfishness. I pray your influence is not far-reaching."

Cadence said nothing in her defense. She wouldn't take her eyes off Hector's limp form. Ardenis sneered in disgust, then left her behind. He'd take Hector to their transfer hall, separating them forever. Rhea followed behind. Silent.

The rain had stopped, though the sky remained dark. All wasn't right yet, but it was about to be.

The transfer hall was mostly empty. Idonea met them just outside the main entrance.

"Ardenis Watcher Fater. Head High Councilwoman Rhea." Idonea nodded her respect, but the edge in her voice gave away her anxiety. Anxiety that hadn't been there before. "The water that came from the sky, it leaked into the transfer hall through the new crack." She took a deep breath. "But, they are working again."

Relief flooded through Ardenis.

"I need priority placement, Idonea," Rhea said. "Hector is to be born this moment by order of the council."

Idonea raised an eyebrow. "Hardly anyone is here. Please, I'll mark him in the record book myself. Follow me."

Idonea led them into the transfer hall. It was eerie seeing it so empty. Normally people bustled about, forming lines out the door waiting to be born. What would this mean for Thera, with no souls to supply them? Only a few workers remained, wiping up water where it had leaked into the building. There was never a need for buildings to withstand any kind of weather other than the gentle sun.

Ardenis marched right up to an empty gateway and threw Hector in. He landed hard on his side. His eyes fluttered beneath the swelling. He groaned in pain, then looked around. His eyes darted up to where Ardenis and Rhea stood above him.

"Where is she? What have you done?" His voice was pure panic. He struggled to his feet.

Ardenis tensed to prevent Hector's retreat.

"Hector, for the unprecedented crime of attempting to create life in the premortal realm, nearly causing the destruction of Acantha, you are sentenced to be born immediately," Rhea said. "Cadence will be born as well. In a separate region."

"What?" Hector screamed. His fists clenched so tight the tendons in his arms bulged. "Don't you understand? This world is a prison, trapping us here, denying us the very pleasures we can only have a short while once we're mortal." He stepped toward Rhea.

Ardenis put himself in front of her, making Hector hesitate.

What was taking so long? The transfer should have happened by now.

"I see, Ardenis. You can't have your love, and now you've prevented mine." Hector, mouth twisted with fury, pointed. "I swear to you here and now, I will make you suffer for this." His biting voice raked chills over Ardenis.

Hector gasped, staring at nothing. Thera had removed the veil. The fury of a thousand fires ignited in Hector's penetrating gaze, which slowly locked straight onto Ardenis. "I will strike where it hurts. One love for another."

Then he was gone, transferred to Thera, leaving fear in his place.

Ardenis's vision snapped, and he cried out. A Fating came upon him in a flash of light that gave way to an image. *Faelyn.*

She wore silver battle armor outside the castle in Pavora, a circlet on her brow. Amerae was next to her, older, outfitted in similar armor and wielding a sword confidently.

They fought side by side, nearly the last ones standing in a sea of black and gold that flooded a field of dead and dying.

The Daltieri soldiers converged on them in waves. Amerae was swallowed, killed by the enemy's blade. The pain hit Ardenis like a physical blow to his chest. Faelyn fought on alone.

A young man wearing Daltieri black with double gold spaulders and a gold cape strode through the ranks right toward Faelyn. Ardenis yelled out a warning. The man waited until her back was turned, fighting off another opponent, then he struck. Faelyn reacted, countering his strike, but it deflected into her arm.

"Kill the fae!" the man screamed. Faelyn was buried under a mountain of bodies.

Ardenis knew the moment she died. A part of him died with her. Agony ripped him apart, and he felt himself falling. When the vision ended, he was on the ground, weeping and shaking, Rhea kneeling by his side.

"She died, Rhea. She died." The words brought fresh pain and wracking tremors.

"Be still, Ardenis. What did you fate?" Her voice was so calm. She'd had centuries to perfect hiding her emotions, but she knew.

"Faelyn." He struggled to take in enough air. "I had a Fating of my Faelyn dying."

No. It couldn't be. He would not allow it. Something had to be done. He shot to his feet.

He would do the only thing in his power.

He ran one lane over and stepped into the gateway.

"What are you doing?" Rhea's voice rose, her cool composure slipping. "It's not your time yet. You can't help her."

"I'm going to try. It's all I have left in me. Acantha will be better without my influence." He watched Rhea step forward, Idonea behind her, and waited for the transfer to take place.

How could the Fates expect him to wait for his fated born when Faelyn was in danger?

Rhea's hands clenched and unclenched. She took a deep breath. "Journey well, Ardenis," she said with a forced smile and a resigned nod.

"Travel well, my friend." Idonea's eyebrows were drawn, but she smiled.

He hoped they'd be okay. He hoped Acantha could recover from the fear, doubt, and destruction Hector's actions had brought.

He took a shaking breath.

Like a gentle breeze, the last of his emotional veil lifted away. The love for Faelyn multiplied, the expanse of it lifting his soul to a fullness he didn't realize existed. A tear rolled down his cheek. He held tight to the promise he'd made her.

On hands and knees to the Hereafter, I will find you.

Then there was nothing but white light.

EPILOGUE

The next months were a chaotic whirlwind of activity. Faelyn sent a missive to the king of Daltieri, along with Lord Jamison's signet ring, promising to bring her army upon Daltieri's kingdom if they decided to attack. She didn't doubt for a second they would come to claim the territory back, but King Jeffe of Creadel had a surprise for her.

Soon after the fighting ended, King Jeffe sent an army to assist Faelyn in guarding the reclaimed northern border. A host of them fought, then promised to reside at the major crossing points until peace was restored. Faelyn was in his debt.

Droves of civilians arrived in Pavora over the following weeks after the battle. They came with crude swords and pitchforks, all ready to fight against the Daltieri. When they arrived to discover the battle had been won in a day, mayors and lords fell to their knees to swear fealty to the new queen.

They held a week-long vigil to honor the fallen heroes, Michael included. It didn't ease the sting of loss, but it was a place to begin healing from.

Couriers and word of mouth brought news that the cities

harboring Daltieri command posts had dissolved into skirmishes. Some of the citizens weren't ready to give up their Daltieri loyalty, mostly the rich who'd benefited from the enemy's greedy tactics. Some of her own troops, still battle-weary, were sent to restore order.

Faelyn allowed the citizens that chose to leave Alysies to do so in peace. Most laid down their arms and remained where their families had lived for generations.

With Nolan's help, Faelyn assembled a team of advisors to tackle the enormous task of unraveling the kingdom's financial situation. Eventually, she was able to decrease the amount of taxes due from each family. The money came to her instead of Daltieri.

Much work had been done, and much more work was yet to be done, but Faelyn had time. At her invitation, Kian and his soldiers stayed on at the castle. He became her head advisor. Trey and Marus returned to Seaside to take care of the people at home. Lord Calem and Amerae were placed in command of the army, which needed to be built up again after their devastating losses. With the fame of their great success, and the funds coming in to support them, the army swiftly grew.

Faelyn formed a trade alliance between Creadel and Alysies, making good on Kian's assurances to his king, and boosting their economy. King Jeffe would be in attendance for the coronation that would take place that day, on the six-month anniversary of their victory.

Faelyn and Amerae left Faelyn's new suite, her mother's old room, and walked down the castle halls. Kian fell into step behind her, followed by an array of newly acquired handmaidens and an equal number of guards. Nolan had done a thorough job extirpating those not loyal in the castle, but caution was wise.

Faelyn wore a pale blue gown of silvery silk. Kian had said it complimented her smooth hair and highlighted her bright blue-green eyes and the flush of excitement on her cheeks. She'd shoved him out of her room, his laughter lingering even after the door was shut.

She'd actually chosen the dress to compliment the turquoise stone hanging from her neck—a piece of her mother she'd always cherish. It'd been with her from the start, just like her mother's love.

Amerae, in her gleaming silver armor, cleared her throat. "Would you mind if I ask a question that's been weighing on me, Majesty?"

Faelyn raised an eyebrow as they continued toward the courtyard. "Of course. You are always free to ask what is on your mind."

"Who is Arden, Your Majesty?"

Faelyn felt the burning curiosity in the words, even as Amerae seemed hesitant to ask, like she might be afraid of the answer.

"Arden?" As Faelyn spoke the name, she felt a stirring inside, deep as if within her very soul. "I..." She was at a loss for words, suddenly remembering a different place.

White marble. Blue robes. A warm hand she ached to touch. A promise yet to be kept.

Faelyn blinked, and the memories were gone. "I've never heard that name before." It felt like a lie. "Why do you ask?"

Amerae's shoulders sagged. Her eyes fell downcast in true disappointment. "Because you asked for him after the battle, in your sleep. The name sounds... familiar to me, is all."

They crossed between stone columns and entered the back of the courtyard. The sun shone brightly on the cool day, and the gathered crowd instantly silenced.

Arden. Something drew Faelyn's eyes upward. "Must have been a dream." The words filled her with an inexplicable sadness.

In the courtyard, all signs of the battle had been eradicated. Spring had come full force. Fragrant roses edged the castle, and flowery vines climbed the walls, which had been repaired of all traces of war. The stones had been scrubbed clean, green moss giving way to the white-gray Faelyn remembered from her childhood.

Before thousands, Faelyn stood at the fated banister, heart near to bursting with pride and joy. The chaplain placed her new crown of silver and sapphire upon her head. The weight settled like it'd always been a part of her. When she straightened, there was no doubt the thunderous roar could be heard by their enemies all the way across the border.

Kian was the first to bow, grinning wide with pride beside King Jeffe of Creadel. Villagers, soldiers, lords, and ladies all followed suit.

Faelyn had fulfilled a promise and freed her kingdom. She couldn't deny that a part of herself felt free as well. She raised her chin high, looking outward toward her people. This was the role she was meant to bear. She would not fail her people ever again.

Love came in many forms and from many places, and it surrounded her.

"All hail Queen Faelyn!" The chants echoed into the night, and in the years that followed as they rebuilt their kingdom to greatness once again.

Did you like this book? Please consider leaving a review!

The adventure continues with the series finale, Fated Sworn, book 3!

Free Bonus Scene!

Scan the QR code for a free Fated Born bonus scene and to access Kristin's fun links!

ACKNOWLEDGMENTS

It's hard to believe Fated Reign is out in the world. There are so many people to thank. I'm going to break from convention here and start by thanking myself. Thank you, past self, for doing the hard work, for learning and growing and knowing when to lean on others so that present self can now publish this book.

Thank you to my husband, Jonathan, for supporting my decision to become an author in every way. To my daughters for reminding me to keep one foot in the real world and step away every now and then.

To Rachel, for always being willing to drop everything and give her honest opinions freely.

To my parents for their loving support.

To my beloved ARC readers. You guys have shown me and this series all the love, and I appreciate it every day.

And most importantly, thank *you*, my lovely reader. None of this would be possible or worth it without you.

About the Author

Kristin L Hamblin was born and raised in Tulsa, Oklahoma. She loves to read and write stories where fantastical things are possible, especially if they contain magic, adventure, and romance. Kristin lives in Oklahoma with her husband, raising their four daughters and a menagerie of pets, including two wiener dogs, Ruby and Sunny.

If you have any questions or comments about her books, or just want to say hello, she would love to hear from you on social media or at kristinlhamblin.com

www.ingramcontent.com/pod-product-compliance
Lightning Source LLC
Chambersburg PA
CBHW010141030826
48979CB00024B/1089

* 9 7 8 1 9 5 9 2 3 0 0 4 5 *